Shadow Sun

Consolidation

Shadow Sun Book 6

By Dave Willmarth

Chapter One

Assassins, Snorgs, And Lizards, Oh My.

Allistor stood on the roof of Invictus tower, pacing back and forth near the bar. Seated in the lounge area were Helen, Longbeard, Droban, Selby, L'olwyn, Harmon, and Master Daigath. The suns were approaching their apex in the sky above, and the group had been meeting since just after sunrise. It was the day after Allistor had killed Loki, and by extension Hel, and there were a lot of issues they needed to cover.

Harmon responded to Allistor's most recent inquiry. "The orbital defense system is installed and active. However, as I believe I mentioned before, it is designed to repel a small force. A concerted effort by a large fleet from a powerful faction would simply absorb the minor losses inflicted by the satellites, then proceed to attack the planet."

"And the space station?"

"Cogwalker and his clan are upgrading the station's systems, both offensive and defensive. Free of charge, I might add, as an apology for the attack on the station. He's downstairs now and would like to meet with you, in fact. But again, a large fleet…" The orcanin shrugged as he let his words trail off.

"Right." Allistor was getting annoyed, not so much at his large friend, who was an Emperor himself, but at the situation he found himself in. A dangerous situation that he had largely brought upon himself, and his people. "So if one of the factions I've angered this week decides to come and destroy me, or destroy Earth altogether, we're just lambs awaiting the slaughter."

"Not precisely." Master Daigath took over for the orcanin. "You have allies on this world. Emperor Harmon and the Or'dralon, along with the Stardrifter and Lighthammer Clans, have declared your Empire to be under their joint protection. And I believe were you to grant the Azure Order lands on Earth similar to those they've received on Orion, they too would come to your defense. Though, they are a neutral organization that will make no formal declaration of protection."

Selby the gnome fidgeted in her oversized chair a moment before adding, "The more of the powerful friendly factions you invite to establish a presence here, and on your other planets, the less likely you are to be attacked. On a large scale, at least. You still have to worry about assassinations, of course." She gave him a wide grin, as if the idea of assassination attempts pleased her.

Allistor stared at her for a moment, and was considering questioning her sanity, when Harmon spoke. "On the subject of assassins, I think you should call Cogwalker up here now. He's got information you should hear as soon as possible."

Allistor nodded, trusting his friend not to derail the meeting without cause. "Nigel, please bring Cogwalker up here."

He moved to the bar and grabbed a cold bottle of water, asking the others if they wanted one while they waited. Tossing bottles to Droban, Longbeard, and Helen, he grabbed one more for Cogwalker and offered it to the dwarf as he stepped off the elevator and approached the group. "Please have a seat, Master Cogwalker." He indicated a free spot on the sofa next to L'olwyn.

"Thank ye, Emperor Allistor." The dwarf looked uncomfortable as he hopped up onto the seat, his legs no longer reaching the ground.

"Please, call me Allistor. We're all friends, here." Allistor sat in a chair so that the dwarf wasn't looking up at him. "Harmon tells me you have news that can't wait?"

"Aye, and I wish I weren't bringin' it to ye." Cogwalker lowered his eyes and shook his head. In a sorrowful tone, he added. "I think ye be in danger. Immediate danger. The attack on yer station was carried out by a changeling assassin." He paused for a moment as Harmon and the other aliens all leaned forward, Selby gasping in horror, clearly no longer as enthused about the idea of assassins. Cogwalker continued on before they could ask questions. "Worse, we be nearly sure that it boarded yer ship after the attack, and came down to the planet with ye."

Allistor growled, his anger over the loss of Amanda still fresh in his heart and mind. "Nearly sure?"

Daigath answered for the now nervous dwarf. "Changelings are used as assassins because they are almost impossible to identify, or track. The fact that Cogwalker here is implying a changeling's involvement would suggest that they've brought in snorgs and confirmed the presence

5

of a changeling. Something his clan is uniquely qualified to discover." The ancient elf looked toward the dwarf.

Taking a deep breath, Cogwalker nodded in thanks to the elf. "Master Daigath be correct. We used snorgs to track a changeling across the station. Found more bombs set to explode. It killed one o' me clansmen during the trip to deliver the station to yer world, assumed his identity long enough to place bombs around the station, and in the gear o' several unsuspecting griblins." He paused, wiping his face with one hand, clearly upset. "The snorg teams tracked it to the landing bay where yer ship berthed. We figure it boarded *Phoenix* after the attacks on you n yours, and rode back here with ye."

Harmon swore quietly in his own language, words that didn't translate for Allistor. Daigath was already scanning the rooftop, a grim look on his normally placid face. It took Allistor a little longer to catch on, not having dealt with changelings before. But in short order it dawned on him. "So we've got a shapeshifting assassin running around loose that could be wearing anyone's face, and we'd have no way to tell?" He saw fear on the faces of his advisors, and his mind took the next leap. "It might not even be here anymore. It could have taken a portal to any place here on Earth, or Orion, and could be wearing any one of tens of thousands of friendly faces."

"Aye, now ye see why I, and me clan, be so concerned." Cogwalker leaned back in his seat while gazing longingly at the bar. He could use a stout ale right about then. Or something stronger.

Daigath, still shifting his gaze from one roof occupant to the next, added, "Changelings are adaptive by nature. They improvise, blend in to accomplish their objectives, and disappear. The Stardrifter clan and their purpose-bred snorgs are by far the best and likeliest way to track one down."

"With yer permission, we'll be bringin' the teams that already have its scent down here, startin' at yer ship. We'll do it quietly, just in case the beastie is still hereabouts. Our best hope o' catchin' it be surprise."

"And if the scent leads you to one of the teleport pads?" Allistor knew the answer, but hoped he was wrong.

"Then the odds o' findin' the changeling drop to nearly zero. We'd have to travel to each o' your pads and hope to pick up the scent. How many would that be?"

Allistor found he didn't really know. Some quick calculation in his head, and he guessed, "About three dozen?"

Cogwalker exhaled, seemingly relieved. "That be a smaller number than we feared."

Harmon chuckled. "Allistor has grown his empire quickly, and has had little time for infrastructure improvements." He turned to the dwarf. "Can I assume one of the teams will be assigned to Allistor on a permanent basis?"

"Aye, it be our gift to ye, Emperor Allistor." Cogwalker hopped down off the sofa, took a knee and bowed his head. "We'll not be stoppin' till we find this murderer for ye. But where there be one, should it fail, likely there will be more to come."

Daigath cleared his throat, motioning for the dwarf to rise. "When you find it, try to capture it. We'll want to ask it some questions."

Cogwalker nodded. "Aye, that be our plan. It killed some o' ours as well, and we'll be wantin' to know who sent it. The Stardrifter clan will soon be goin to war." He looked back to Allistor. "By yer leave, I'll be goin to organize the hunt. I'll have one o' the teams report to ye here in the tower within the hour. It might be best if ye stayed here, where yer protected, until they arrive."

Allistor, distracted with trying to remember who accompanied them to the station, and who had returned, didn't notice right away that the dwarf was awaiting permission to leave. When Selby cleared her throat, he caught on. "Of course. Do what you need to do, Master Cogwalker. Thank you." He gave the dwarf a brief nod, and Cogwalker all but sprinted toward the elevator.

"I don't remember any strange faces on the *Phoenix* when we boarded after the explosions. But then, I was distracted."

"Likely they boarded the ship before you did, hid in crew quarters or some out of the way place." Harmon suggested. "They wouldn't necessarily have to have been wearing the identity of one of your people if that was the case."

"Nigel are you detecting any non-citizens, other than our recognized guests, within the city at the moment?"

"*I am not, sire.*" The AI responded instantly, having already checked as it listened to the conversation. An assassin presented a clear threat to his master, and Nigel was hard-coded to react to threats. "*Nor have I detected any unauthorized entities since the undead attacked the city.*"

Allistor felt a moment of hope. "Maybe that means it didn't come here? Didn't board the *Phoenix*?"

"Unlikely." L'olwyn shook his head. "If it was tracked to the landing bay, it would have boarded the ship to make its escape. You must remember two things. First, as a changeling it could have become a bird and flown free of the ship without ever touching ground inside the city. Second, if it assumed the identity of a citizen, or an authorized guest, Nigel would have no ability to tell the difference, even with the upgrades and improved sensors you gave him during the battle with the undead. Changelings copy their victims right down to the DNA."

There was a long silence, until Helen asked, "What's a snorg?"

Daigath answered. "They are a distant cousin of the canids that spawned here during stabilization. But they evolved in a subsurface environment where light was poor or nonexistent, thus learning to depend heavily on scent and hearing during their hunts. They are the only creatures I am aware of that can detect the particular scent of a changeling."

9

Helen looked at Allistor. "Fuzzy is just going to love having a canid around all the time."

"He'll have to accept it." Allistor mumbled. "Though I'm thinking the snorg will spend most of its time protecting the kids." He looked up at Daigath. "Master, you told me not so long ago that if you wanted to make me suffer, you'd target the people I care about." He paused, getting to his feet and pacing again. "Nigel, send the kids up here, right now." He looked at Daigath. "There were multiple explosions on the station. The one that killed Amanda was first, and it may well have been aimed at me directly, but then why set off the others? Unless someone was aware they'd missed me, and wanted to make me suffer the loss of friends and family."

"The others may have just been a diversion." Harmon offered. "Triggered to allow the assassin room and time to escape. Or they may have been timed to take out the whole station, in an effort to make sure you died, one way or the other."

Droban the minotaur shook his head. "It seems unlikely that, if that were the case, so many of the bombs would have failed to detonate. Changeling assassins are no amateurs, and are not known for suicide attacks."

Helen, ignoring the discussion, had been watching Allistor. "What are you thinking, Allistor?"

"I'm thinking of the Matron." His statement made the others go quiet. The Matron of the fomorian clan that they had destroyed at the power plant had never been found. While he preferred to think that she'd been

10

vaporized in the bombing, he'd followed Daigath's advice in quickly getting rid of the clan's orb, hoping that if she lived, she would track it off-world instead of killing his people to get to it. "If she's alive, would she hire a changeling assassin to get revenge for us killing her mate and her scion, and taking her orb?"

"Little is known of fomorians, Allistor." Daigath shook his head. "But I have never heard of them doing such. Fomorians take their battles personally, and have been known to fling themselves into fights against insurmountable odds. I suspect if the Matron lived, she would come for you personally."

"There were factions, like the goblins, that disliked you well before you killed Loki and Hel." Selby reminded Allistor. "Shit, the changeling could have been contracted by either one of them before they died."

Longbeard added, "Changeling assassins do not come cheap. I doubt the goblins hired 'em. It would have been a powerful House, or a jealous Emperor, someone on that level. I'd guess someone who wants yer shiny new planet with an eternity gate. And while ye weren't yet Emperor o' Earth at that time, yer holdings as Planetary Prince were nothin' to sneeze at."

L'olwyn interjected a new idea. "On the topic of you becoming Emperor of Earth, it occurs to me that you may have already solved your problem." He looked around the group, looking almost as if he might smile. "If Selby is correct that the changeling might have been bonded to either Loki or Hel, it may be that it perished when they did.

Or was simply released from its contract. Droban is correct that they are not careless with their lives. Why make another dangerous attempt without the promise of payment or the looming penalties of a failed contract? The same might apply if it was contracted by one of the many bound subordinates of the ancient ones, who also perished with them." He paused to breathe. "There is also the possibility that, were the assassin hired by a powerful independent House or Faction, it might be recalled. The deaths of Loki and Hel opened up a literal galaxy of opportunities for those bold and powerful enough to act quickly. The assassin might have been recalled to take on a more urgent, strategic, or valuable target. No offense, sire."

"Ha!" Allistor couldn't help but laugh. "Having an assassin ignore me for being a small fish in a suddenly turbulent big pond is not the least bit offensive to me, my friend."

"Especially since you're the one who dropped the big-ass rock in the pond and caused the ripples." Helen winked at him.

Allistor's face fell. He still hadn't come to terms with the idea that he might have been the one responsible for the deaths of a million or more beings. Good intentions and righteous vengeance weighed against the loss of so many lives left him conflicted, to say the least.

"Sorry." Helen read him easily enough, and regretted her words.

Allistor sighed. "So there may or may not be an assassin among us, who may or may not still be trying to kill me, or some of you." He turned at the sound of the elevator doors opening, and waved the kids over. "Let's table this for now. I don't think we're getting anywhere anyway."

*****

Allistor, Helen, William, Sydney and Addy walked together out the gate of the Wilderness Stronghold. Just a few steps behind them walked two fully armored dwarves that fairly bristled with weapons. One of them held a leash, at the end of which walked a snorg. The canid-like creature constantly sniffed the air, or lowered its snout to the ground, searching for the scent of changeling.

It had initially been difficult to keep the kids from petting and cuddling the snorg when it appeared on the tower roof. But the dwarves had kindly yet quite firmly made it clear that she was a working animal, not a pet to be coddled. The kids had backed off without their feelings being overly hurt, but William's repeated furtive glances at the animal had prompted Allistor to declare it time to visit Fuzzy and Fiona.

The good news was that when they reached the tower teleport pad, the snorg detected no trace of the changeling's scent. Allistor fervently hoped that meant it hadn't left the *Phoenix* and made its way to one of his other properties.

As they began to follow the path that would lead them to their bears, Allistor turned and walked backward as he addressed the dwarves. "Are you sure your buddy there won't have a problem with the bears?"

"Aye, we're sure." The dwarf handling the snorg nodded. "She be trained not to react to other beasties. Though if attacked, she'll defend herself."

"I'll make sure Fuzzy doesn't attack, and ask him to do the same with Fiona. Fiona just recently lost her bond, so she's a little... off."

The dwarf looked sympathetic. "It be a hard thing, that. We'll give the lass the space she needs, do no' worry." He reached down and patted his snorg's back.

Allistor faced forward again, walking in silence with his family for a while, just enjoying the peace of the forest. Peace was something he hadn't had much of lately, and he didn't expect that would change soon. He found himself surprised, as he took in the sounds and smells of the forest, that the heavily armed dwarves behind him didn't make a sound as they moved. He could hear the snorg's snuffling, but not a breaking twig, crackling leaf, or squeak of armor from the dwarves.

He made quite a racket himself as he moved through the woods. Despite his efforts to learn how to move quietly, Daigath described his progress as "the stomping of a wounded ragosaur". Allistor hadn't had the courage to ask what a ragosaur was, simply assuming it was large, heavy, and clumsy. He felt especially clumsy next to Helen. Having been a park ranger before the world ended, she already knew how to move quietly in nature. Her chosen class, the skills that came with it, and her boosted attributes combined to make her just as silent as the dwarves. At least he wasn't walking with Daigath. That elf glided through the woods so smoothly and silently that Allistor suspected he wasn't actually touching the ground.

When they left the path, Helen took the lead, quickly guiding them to the clearing where the bears had been resting and munching on berries. Fuzzy let out a curious growl as they approached, then a series of happy chuffs when Helen quietly called out to him. He was on his feet and bounding toward the kids to greet them when he caught the scent of the snorg.

Freezing where he was, his hackles raised and his head lowered, and he let out a low warning growl.

"It's okay buddy, she's with us. She's a friend. As are the dwarves. It's a long story, I'll explain later." Allistor stepped between his gigantic bear cub and the suddenly worried dwarves. Allistor had told them he was on his way to see his bear cub, and they had expected a cute fuzzy critter, rather than the monster of a bear whose shoulders were on a level with Allistor's.

Trusting his human, Fuzzy gave another, more friendly chuff, then sat down and headbutted William gently. Which still nearly knocked the squire off his feet. The kids all piled on affectionate scratches as Helen quietly made her way over to Fiona. The despondent bear was laying on her belly, chin atop her crossed front paws. She perked up a bit as Helen approached, and was happy enough to lean into the ear scratchings that Helen offered as she sat down.

Allistor caught Fuzzy watching the interaction, and stepped closer to lay his hand on his bear's head. Almost instantly Fuzzy flashed him the familiar image of Helen and Fiona walking together.

"I know, fuzzball. I think it's a good idea too. Helen is willing, so I think we just need to wait for Fiona to be ready." He patted Fuzzy's head as his bear snorted in agreement.

Fuzzy played with the kids for a few minutes, then led them over to the berry bushes for a snack while Helen spent some quality time with Fiona, and the dwarves patrolled the perimeter of the clearing.

"Why don't you go see Daigath. I'll stay here with her for a while." Helen spoke just loudly enough for Allistor to hear. He nodded once, about to suggest that the kids stay with her, before he remembered that they needed to stay with the snorg, who had strict orders to remain near him at all times.

"Come on guys, let's go visit Master Daigath." He waved at the kids and the dwarves in one wide motion, then turned to head back to the path. William paused for a moment near Fuzzy's head, making a face that Allistor initially mistook for displeasure at having to leave the bear so soon. A moment later the young squire let out a fart so loud it scared the nearby birds.

"HA! Gotcha!" He shouted at Fuzzy before dashing away. "Sweet revenge!" He called over his shoulder at the clearly offended bear. Allistor couldn't help but laugh, having been the frequent recipient of similar chemical attacks from the cub. When he got close to Allistor, William grinned. "Been saving that one for like an hour!"

Proud of his squire's forethought and merciless execution, Allistor returned the grin and gave him a pat on the back. "Well played."

Behind them, Fuzzy let out a plaintive growl and shifted to face into the wind, rubbing his snout with one massive paw as if to wipe away the smell.

It didn't take long to reach Daigath's clearing, and the ancient elf welcomed them warmly. He offered each of them a bit of fresh honeycomb from a nearby hive he was cultivating, and all three kids, along with the dwarves, quickly became sticky with honey. Daigath's giant tiger companion, smelling the honey-covered small two-legged creatures in her territory, leapt out from the brush to investigate. The kids and dwarves froze in terror, one of the dwarves actually dropping his chunk of honeycomb to reach for his weapon as the tiger stalked toward them.

"Sher'gal, play nice." Daigath chastised the oversized predator, who ceased her stalking gait and simply trotted closer, her nose in the air as she made chuffing sounds. "Don't worry, children, she is my companion and will not hurt you. I'm afraid she's quite fond of honey."

The tiger demonstrated this by casually licking one of the dwarves' faces, her sandpapery tongue covering it completely as she cleaned the honey from it. Before the dwarf could recover, she lowered her head and gently scooped up the fallen honeycomb, swallowing it whole. When it was gone, she turned to William, who bravely stood his ground, though he closed his eyes and scrunched up his face in anticipation. Her tongue pushing against his face actually knocked him back to fall on his butt. Sher'gal shamelessly took the opportunity to steal his honeycomb, licking his hands clean as well.

Chuckling at the poor squire, Daigath asked, "How is Fiona?" before smiling at the snorg who took her cue from the tiger and was busily trying to lick honey from her distracted handler's beard.

"Helen is with her now. She seems… a little better, maybe? Fuzzy is determined to have her bond with Helen."

"I think that would be good for both of them." Daigath nodded slightly.

"Sorry for the unannounced intrusion, but we thought we'd give them some quiet time together." Allistor gazed in the general direction of the bears' clearing as he spoke.

"It amuses me that you believe yourselves to be unannounced. The forest told me of your presence long before you and your companions reached the bears." Daigath chuckled as Allistor shook his head.

"I guess I should have figured that." He looked up at Daigath's new home tree. "You've made some more improvements. It really is quite beautiful."

"Another decade or so, and it will rival my home on my own world." Daigath agreed.

"I think I'd like to visit there someday." Allistor was still staring up at the tree that was willingly altering its form to fit the ancient elf's desires.

"You would be most welcome there anytime." Daigath patted Allistor on the shoulder, the first time Allistor could ever recall the elf touching him. "And speaking of visiting other worlds, you should visit those you've just been awarded. Sooner rather than later."

"To claim the loot?" Allistor's lips pressed together in distaste.

"In a manner of speaking, yes. You need to make an appearance and stake your claim before others decide to try and take it from you."

"I'm not so sure that would be a bad thing." Allistor mumbled.

"Do not be foolish, boy." Daigath's tone grew serious. "Your current feelings are understandable, and I share them, to some extent. But you are an Emperor, responsible for the lives of millions, if not billions by now. You can not afford to let your personal doubts negatively affect your performance of your duties. Would you leave the inhabitants of those worlds to suffer at the hands of whichever tyrant or uncaring dictator felt strong enough to step in and take control?" The elf's eyebrows pinched together. "And even if the planets were uninhabited, could you not use those resources to help your own people thrive?"

Feeling ashamed of himself, Allistor shook his head. "I'll make arrangements for a visit as soon as we get back. Though Odin did tell me one of the worlds was much closer to the core of the galaxy, so it may be a long trip." Allistor had already told Daigath of his dream visit from the Allfather.

"Ah, but you are the proud owner of an eternity gate. I can say with reasonable assurance that a world owned by Loki that close to the core will have a gate of its own, or nearby at the least. So a short flight to Orion, a hop through the gates, and you'll be there in less than two days." Daigath paused. "The second world is not so far from the first."

Allistor had all but forgotten about the newly installed gate in orbit around Orion. Daigath's mention of it, and the convenience of fast travel through it, had him considering the risk versus reward calculation for installing his second gate near Earth. He was standing there next to the ancient elf, silently pondering this dilemma, when the forest around them went silent.

A second later the earth shook with a massive sonic boom, and all eyes went to the sky. Above them, a long vapor trail was forming behind what Allistor initially assumed was a falling comet. But when the fiery object slowed down as it passed overhead, he began to think space vessel. That thought was confirmed a moment later when Daigath spoke.

"That is a talon ship." The ancient elf's eyesight was far superior to Allistor's, who just saw a fiery glow ahead of the vapor trail. "I would guess it was damaged by the defense satellites, and pushed through."

"Talon ship?" Allistor was already reaching for his communicator. He had purchased a powerful coms system from Harmon and installed bases in every Stronghold, so that he was never out of touch with his people. It spanned the globe using the same satellites that had apparently just shot down the ship streaking across the sky above.

"A combat ship, most often containing a xylon attack force. A reptilian race, extremely hostile."

The device in his hand beeped at him just as Daigath finished speaking. Allistor answered it immediately. "Redd, are you calling to tell me about the big ship full of hostile lizards falling through our sky?"

Redd's confused voice answered immediately. "Hostile lizards, boss? Um, sure, I guess. I was calling to tell you that a ship that refused to identify itself pushed through the defense grid. They shot it up pretty good first, though." She paused for a heartbeat. "Lizards?"

"Master Daigath says they're called xylon, and they're unfriendly. I assume you guys are tracking them? Send *Phoenix* to Daigath's clearing to get us, have *Opportunity* and the other ships in the air ASAP, and on their way to wherever it comes down. Assume anyone who sticks their head out is hostile."

"Ships are already taking off, boss. We alerted them right before I called you."

"Good thinking, Redd. Keep in touch."

The kids and dwarves, followed closely by Sher'gal, had all gathered around Allistor and Daigath as they watched the falling ship disappear behind a nearby mountain. Sydney muttered "It's headed east, and a little south of us."

"Which would put it on track for Invictus City, or someplace in that general direction." Allistor finished for her.

Daigath, who had been speaking softly into his own communicator, confirmed it. "Harmon says the talon ship is seriously damaged, but still under control, and headed toward your capital. He has mobilized his troops, and is boarding his own ship. So far the talon ship has not responded to calls."

"Shit." Allistor began to pace. "It'll be on the ground long before *Phoenix* arrives, and our people might be fighting before I can get there."

Daigath agreed. "It would be faster to run back to Wilderness Stronghold and teleport to Invictus." He looked at the dwarves, who had no hope of keeping up. "Follow as best you can. I will protect Allistor until you catch up." His face turned to include the children as he added, "Keep them safe as you run."

Allistor gave all three kids a quick group hug. "Get to the tower and stay there. Stop and get Helen on the way back. Be safe." He wasn't truly worried about his kids, all of whom out-leveled anything they'd found in this forest so far. With the dwarves, snorg, and Sher'gal to guard them, they'd be safe enough. With a nod to Daigath, the two of them took off at a sprint down the path back to the Stronghold. Allistor was already calling Redd to order the *Phoenix* to turn around and await them at Invictus Tower.

Chapter Two

Leader of the Pack

By the time Daigath and Allistor had run back to Wilderness and teleported to Invictus, Kira had *Phoenix* hovering above the tower roof waiting for them. The tower was a hive of activity as raiders scrambled toward the elevators to join Allistor aboard the ship and help repel invaders. An alert had popped up as he was running through the forest, saying that Invictus City was under attack, with an accompanying defense quest. As soon as he arrived, Nigel's report told him why.

"*Sire, the unauthorized vessel crashed into the northern wall, then continued into the park. Repairs to the wall are already underway. Battle droids have been dispatched to gather intelligence, and Harmon's ship is hovering above the crash site.*" Nigel explained during the ride up to the roof.

Allistor spoke into his coms as he and the others leapt up into the loading bay. "Harmon, what do you see?"

"It is indeed a xylon talon. I see significant weapons damage on the hull, likely from the defense grid. The bow and one wing are badly damaged from the impact with the city wall. So far no one has emerged from the ship. Do you wish us to engage?" The orcanin's voice sounded eager.

"We're just boarding *Phoenix* now." He looked at Daigath, who gave his head a very subtle shake. "Please hold your position for now. Maybe they're not hostile?"

The tone of Harmon's voice made it clear he was skeptical. "I have never known xylon not to be hostile. But as there is currently no imminent threat, we will hold here. I suggest you let my troops secure a perimeter, at least."

"Great idea. Thank you, Harmon." Allistor waited for the last raider to hop up into the ship, then called out, "Kira, let's go!"

They all held on as the ship lifted and spun rapidly toward the north, then shot off over the city. It took less than a minute to reach the area of Central Park where the orcanin ship hovered.   Down below Allistor could see that Harmon's soldiers had already dropped to the ground and surrounded the ship, maintaining a distance of about a hundred yards from the wreck.

The ship was smaller than Allistor had expected after the big entrance it had made. About the size of the *Phoenix*, it was a bulky wedge shape with several guns mounted on the top side of the hull. As Harmon had described, its nose was partially crushed, and its left side lay half-buried in the soil of the park. A long trench stretched out behind it to its point of impact, small fires burning here and there.

Harmon himself waved from down on the ground, and Allistor ordered Kira to set down outside the orcanin perimeter. A minute later he, Daigath, and about a hundred raiders stood near Harmon, every eye on the downed ship.

"They still do not respond to attempts at communication" Harmon reported. "My scans show the weapons visible on the hull are still operational, though the batteries underneath have been disabled. It is unlike the xylon not to fire the moment we got in range."

"So maybe it's not the xylon inside?" Allistor looked hopefully toward the vessel. "Or maybe their coms and weapons systems are just down?"

"The latter is more likely." Harmon nodded. "If that is the case, we should breach the hull now before they have time to make repairs to weapons control."

Allistor looked at the obviously eager orcanin around the perimeter, and back at his equally anxious raiders. "I appreciate the help, but it feels like my people should take the risk. We can't always depend on you and your warriors."

Harmon nodded. "I will open a hole for your people to access the ship. And we will maintain the perimeter, in the unlikely event that the xylon attempt to flee." He motioned toward his second, who was standing nearby. A quick series of orders shouted in their own battle language, and three orcanin ran forward toward the ship. They attached something to the hull on the rearmost section, then retreated.

Allistor looked at his people. "Volunteers to take the ship!"

Immediately Kuhns stepped forward, his raid group right behind him. Bjurstrom's group was half a second slower, followed by the rest of the raiders. Every one of them was ready to go. These were among his elite fighters, and between the dungeons and raids they'd completed, the year of monster hunting, and the levels they'd just picked up at the Bastion when Allistor tricked Loki, most of them were over level fifty.

"Bjurstrom, Kuhns, your groups are first. Don't fire until fired upon, but if they attack, wipe them out. Try to leave one alive for questioning."

At a nod from Harmon, the explosives attached to the ship's hull activated, and a roughly ten foot wide section simply disappeared. The entire ship rocked from the explosion, then settled back on its side. Kuhns and his group dashed toward the opening, Bjurstrom's group slightly behind and to their left.

When they were about halfway there, four xylon stepped through the hole, weapons already raised, and fired. The tank to Kuhns' left took a hit on his shield and was knocked back, grunting in pain. His other tank managed to tilt his shield at about a forty five degree angle so that when a round hit it, it deflected upward, bleeding momentum off of the impact. Kuhns nodded at the man in approval. Instead of watching his people, he should have been minding his own business. One of the rounds struck him squarely in the throat, passing through his neck and severing his spine on its way out. His body took several more steps as his head flopped backward, nothing but skin and a little bit of muscle still keeping it attached to his body.

As his corpse finally fell, the others hit the dirt behind the tanks as orcanin fired weapons from the perimeter, and more raiders hit the lizardmen with spells and arrows. Bjurstrom cast *Vortex* into the opening, keeping any others from emerging while the initial four were cut down.

A hatch opened not far from the blasted opening, and a stream of the lizardmen charged out. Allistor focused on the one in the lead.

> **Xylon Pack Leader**
> **Level 57**
> **Health: 63,100/70,000**

The leader was already taking hits from every direction, but seemed to ignore the pain and the damage as it sprinted toward what was left of Kuhns group. Bipedal and standing maybe seven feet tall, it was humanoid, with a long torso and muscular limbs. It carried three-foot long curved blades in each clawed hand, and bared a mouthful of sharp teeth at the humans in front of it. Large eyes on either side of its elongated head featured bright red reptilian vertical slit pupils. Crimson scaled armor covered its torso and legs down to the ankles. Behind it, the other xylon wore similar armor, but in shades of green and blue.

Angry at the loss of their companion, the two human tanks got to their feet and charged toward the pack leader. The one who'd managed to deflect the initial volley got there first, and the impact stunned both lizard and human. When the second tank arrived two seconds later, the pack leader was thrown off its feet, its left arm clearly broken, and its long snout bloodied.

Bjurstrom's tanks were there a moment later, bashing into other lizardmen, stopping the momentum of their advance. And other tanks charged in from outside the perimeter along with more than a score of melee fighters with swords, axes, and hammers already in hand. Casters and ranged attackers focused fire first on the pack leader, then on two or three targets at a time, burning them down mercilessly.

Harmon's warriors managed to hold themselves at bay, but just barely. A melee fight out in the open was what every orcanin warrior lived for! They howled in encouragement even as they fired into the oncoming xylon. More were exiting the ship, and Allistor guessed there were fifty of them visible now. Already more than a dozen lay dead in the grass.

When Allistor noticed the pack leader, whom he'd thought dead, twitching on the ground as the battle raged around it, he made a quick decision. Running forward until he was in range, he cast *Levitate* on the badly wounded xylon, lifting it twenty feet into the air, then pulling it toward him. Seeing what he was up to, Harmon roared a command for his orcanin not to fire at it, while Daigath yelled similar instructions to the raiders.

Allistor brought the xylon close, its body dripping blood as it floated through the air, struggling weakly against the magic that held it. He set it down roughly on the grass, and Harmon placed a heavy foot on its back to hold it still. Allistor cast a heal on it, watching as the bleeding slowly trickled to a halt. Two orcanin warriors stepped from behind Harmon and grabbed hold of the pack leader, lifting it to its feet and roughly binding its hands behind its back with metal shackles. Another set went around its ankles before they knocked it face down on the ground. Both knelt on either side of its head, produced shields from their inventories, and slammed them into the earth, creating a barrier between the pack leader and its underlings.

"So that the xylon warriors cannot kill their pack leader to keep him from being interrogated." Daigath explained when Allistor raised an eyebrow.

Turning back to the battle, Allistor saw that several of his people were down, while only two of the lizardmen were still in the fight. Healers were already running forward, casting as they moved, while several of the wounded were producing potions from their inventory and gulping them down.

Allistor heard a roar from the orcanin on the opposite side of the ship, then the sound of steel clashing, as other lizardmen attempted to escape in that direction. Above the battle, Harmon's ship fired four rapid blasts down on the talon ship's visible weapons, which had begun to twitch to life, melting them into slag.

With all the visible xylon warriors down, the tanks from the two lead groups pushed through the two openings, melee fighters and additional tanks following close behind. A glance at Harmon showed the orcanin to be oddly relaxed.

"What are you smiling about?" Allistor asked.

"The pack leader is here. Your raiders should meet little resistance inside. The pack leader was the strongest xylon aboard the vessel, and he looks to have brought out his best fighters to be slaughtered alongside him."

"They would have demanded that honor." Daigath agreed.

Harmon's second grumbled something in their language, and Harmon chuckled. "My grandson expresses his hope that this is just the vanguard of an invasion force. xylon are strong warriors that fight with honor. A worthy opponent."

Allistor thought back as the occasional sounds of brief battles rang out from the ship. "I don't remember seeing any notifications about xylon when I killed Loki. Would they have been one of the factions that I offended?"

Harmon shook his head. "They are not political animals, at least not outside their own society. In fact, had they been watching, they probably would have been impressed by you." He looked down and nudged the prone pack leader with his boot. "When they are not making war against their own enemies, they sometimes hire themselves out as mercenaries."

Wounded raiders began to stream back out of the ship, staggering into the arms of waiting healers.

Bjurstrom was one of the first to appear, his left arm missing from just below the shoulder, his right hand cupping the stump as blood leaked between his fingers. Allistor ran forward, joining the healers in casting healing magic on his raid leader.

"What happened in there?" He asked when he was close enough to Bjurstrom, who was now laying prone on the grass.

"One of those damned things just hooked its claws into my arm and tore it off. It was already half dead, and it ripped me apart as it fell." Bjurstrom's voice was quiet, he was weak from blood loss. "I saw another one of them bite a guy's head, squeeze until his skull collapsed." He leaned to the side and vomited. A healer put a potion bottle to his lips, and he used the first sip to wash out his mouth before swallowing the rest.

McCoy was among the last to exit the ship, alongside others who were being supported or outright carried by their friends. He sported a nasty three-clawed slash to his face that barely missed taking his eye, and was already sealing itself as he walked. When he reached Allistor and the others, he plopped down on the ground next to Bjurstrom and waved a tired hand at Allistor. "All clear, boss. At least, I'm pretty sure. The last one tried to get to a console on the bridge, was reaching for what I assume is some kind of self-destruct button. Those bastards made us pay for every inch of that ship." He shook his head, looking around at all the wounded raiders. Off to one side, four of them lay under body bags, including Kuhns.

"A worthy foe." Harmon confirmed, a look of pride on his face. "Your warriors fought well. It was a good battle!" Behind him, his orcanin roared their approval.

Allistor didn't agree, but saw no point in contradicting the orcanin in front of everyone. Instead he distracted himself with casting heals on every wounded raider he could. The healers had things under control, but it made him feel better about foolishly rushing into the fight. He should have let Harmon's tougher and more experienced warriors handle it. They at least had known what to expect.

As the wounded began to get back to their feet, Allistor used *Levitate* to float Bjurstrom into the *Phoenix* cargo hold. He and half a dozen others who had lost limbs were being transported back to the tower infirmary, where their missing parts could be regenerated.

Harmon and Daigath approached, the pack leader being dragged by its feet behind them by Harmon's second. When they reached Allistor, Harmon offered, "Unless you object, we will question this one."

Still focused on the people he'd lost, and the many others he'd nearly lost, Allistor had no heart for what he assumed would be a tough interrogation. One that would probably include inflicting considerable pain on the lizardman. "He's all yours." He had faith that Harmon knew what information was needed, much better than Allistor did. There were probably questions that needed answering, that he didn't even know to ask. Instead, he added, "I'm going to arrange visits to my two new planets shortly. You're both welcome to accompany me if you like."

Both orcanin and elf nodded their agreement. Master Daigath hopped up into the cargo bay with Allistor, while the orcanin turned and headed for Harmon's ship. Allistor sat on a crate and watched as his people looted the enemy bodies. Gene passed by him, hopping down and headed toward the talon ship, presumably to explore the new technology inside.

"Hold on, Gene." Allistor called out, stopping the engineer, who turned around. "McCoy said one of them was trying to activate what he thought was a self-destruct. Let's leave that thing alone until some experts, maybe Cogwalker or someone more knowledgeable about alien tech, can clear it for us."

Gene looked insulted for a moment, then nodded once, returning to the *Phoenix* after a longing look toward the Talon. To make him feel better, Allistor added, "You could come with me to Loki's planets. I'm betting there's lots of cool new toys to play with."

Gene beamed at him. "Right! When are we going? I'll need to pack some stuff."

"Maybe as early as tomorrow. I have some things to work out here."

"I assume Kira is flying you?" Gene didn't wait for an answer. "We'd like the girls to come with us. They're well trained as bridge crew now."

"That's your call. Your girls, and Kira's bridge. I'm just a passenger with a fancy title." Allistor winked at him. He still hated the idea of kids being at risk, but was slowly convincing himself that they were always at risk in this new reality, and that making them stronger was the best way to protect them. "I'll issue a quest of some kind before we leave, so that the little ones can gain some xp even if there's no fighting."

With the trillions of experience points in his Emperor's pool from Loki and Hel's deaths, he could afford to splurge a bit on quests for the little ones and low-leveled among his people. He made a mental note to create a series of crafting quests and such to help out the ones who didn't run dungeons or hunt. And maybe some kind of standard initiation quest for new groups of survivors they encountered around the world.

He waited as the last of his raiders boarded the *Phoenix*, and Kira took them back to the Tower. He had her drop them off on the roof to save some of his recently healed wounded from having to walk back from the parking garage.

*****

Allistor spent the rest of the day checking with his advisors and ministers, the folks that were running the day to day operations of his empire. He started with Chris, to check on the state of his funds. Though the billions in gold reserves had initially seemed like a lifetime's worth of security, he'd been spending them faster than he ever imagined possible. Between the trainers, the defense grid, the money his advisors were spending on spies and spy hunters, Allistor needed to be a little more careful with his budgeting.

When he asked Chris about their funds, the man snorted. "Are you joking? Did you read your notifications? You picked up two new planets from Loki, as well as a space station owned by Hel. These weren't new planets or stations like the ones you already have, these are mature properties with bustling economies. My guess is that they have high tax rates and huge treasuries just waiting to be plundered."

"Oh, right. Maybe you should come with me to check those out." Allistor answered, chagrined. An idea struck him, and he asked, "What do you know about starting a bank?"

"You mean like a savings and loan type bank? I mean, we're basically already running one. If you're asking about regulatory requirements and paperwork shit, I don't know anything. The System might have some requirements, I guess. But dude, you literally own the planet. My guess is you can make any rules you want when it comes to that sort of thing."

"Would you look into that? Maybe ask Harmon?"

"Sure thing, boss. In my spare time." Allistor could hear the man rolling his eyes over the coms.

"Be ready to leave after breakfast tomorrow. We're gonna visit two new planets."

"Seek out new life…" Chris chuckled.

Allistor's next call was to Nancy, who was leading the effort of regenerating the limbs of the wounded. He was pleasantly surprised to hear that Sirina, the healer in training from the Factory stronghold, was there with Nancy, learning to use the alien tech. Both reported that they were making progress, and did not foresee any problems. The wounded would be back on their feet, so to speak, in a couple of days.

The kids and dwarves arrived, along with both Fuzzy and Fiona, shortly after he returned from the battle. Fuzzy immediately led Fiona out to the courtyard garden, where they plopped down in the warm sun. It didn't take long for word of their arrival to spread, and within minutes they were mobbed with children wanting to wrestle and play with the bears. Allistor was initially concerned about Fiona's state of mind, but Helen assured him she would be fine. His heart lightened a good bit when he saw her begin to swat playfully at the kids, patiently tolerating their battle roars as they flung themselves on her back.

"What are we going to do if they have cubs?" Helen smiled at him.

Allistor hadn't really considered that. "Bear cavalry?" He shrugged, smiling. "You think our people were excited about bonding with baby drakes? There would be a mob fighting each other to bond with mini-Fuzzy bears."

"Speaking of bonding, I think she's just about ready." Helen's voice was quiet, her tone hopeful. "I think

Fuzzy has been working to convince her. He's become incredibly smart."

"It's maybe a good thing he wasn't with us at the Bastion. If he had picked up as many levels as I did, he'd probably be the size of an elephant, and reciting poetry by now."

"Blueberries are tasty, fresh or in pies, don't be so hasty, come give them a try." Helen giggled at her own cheesy rhyme.

"Give me some space, or I'll eat your face." Allistor shot one back at her.

Daigath, who had been standing nearby and smiling at the frolicking bears, rolled his eyes. "You are both an insult to the word poetry, and merciless butchers of your own language." He teased before changing the subject. "Observing these little ones, I am reminded of another boon you received from Baldur. Where will you plant the seed he gave you?"

"The seed!" Allistor had forgotten about it. Baldur had included in his first reward for sparing Loki's life the seed of a tree that would shorten the gestation period of pregnant women and boost the growth rate of their children after birth. It would help the human race repopulate the earth at an impressive pace. Allistor hadn't yet figured out a safe place to plant it. "Are you familiar with that tree, Master Daigath? How fast will it grow?"

"On its own it will grow large enough to begin to bear fruit in two or three years. With druids like Lady

Nancy at hand, it would be safe to say the tree will mature in a year."

Allistor was slightly disappointed. He had envisioned a magical towering tree bearing thousands of fruit on day one. "So, after a year, maybe a hundred pieces of fruit? So a hundred women bearing children who will be born and grow faster."

Daigath shook his head. "The newly matured tree will indeed bear a hundred or so fruits, Allistor. But each fruit can be shared among half a dozen or more women. It does not require they consume an entire fruit for the changes to take effect."

"Alright, so maybe as many as a thousand women the first year. That's much better."

Helen cleared her throat. "Hold on there, buddy. We need to ask some serious questions before you start pushing women to eat this stuff."

Allistor turned toward her, seeing her standing with arms crossed, hip canted to one side, a scowl on her face. "I'm not looking to push anyone into being baby-making machines. I just assumed folks would want to start making families now that things are a little more safe and secure."

"They will, Allistor." Helen sighed, uncrossing her arms. "But you need to be very careful with your message regarding this. There will be a lot of women out there who'll jump into it just because their fearless leader thinks it's a good idea, or because they see it as an order from the

Emperor. You have a lot of influence among your people, my friend."

Allistor considered her words, horrified. After a few deep breaths, he said, "Then I won't make that announcement. Most of our people saw the seed at the Bastian, and know what it is. I'll plant it, and let you and Nancy and Meg start quietly spreading the word. Let folks discuss it quietly in their homes for the year that it takes the tree to grow. Is that better?"

Both Helen and Daigath nodded. Helen even smiled slightly. "We can add a little mystery to it, to make the rumors spread faster. 'Where did he plant it?' should work just fine."

"On that topic, might I suggest my clearing as a potential home for the tree? It is remote, yet still quickly accessible. And I could watch over it, protect it from poachers."

"If you would be willing to do that, it would be amazing!" Allistor couldn't think of anyone better suited for the job. Daigath was one of the most powerful beings Allistor had met, exceeded only by Baldur and his family, maybe a few others like the Arkhons or the head of the Azure Order.

"Since I shall be accompanying you on your upcoming trip, we'll wait and plant the seed when we've returned." Daigath decided, and Allistor agreed.

McCoy stopped by then, a grave look on his fully healed face. "We lost a total of six people, four outside, two in the ship. Another twenty were wounded, but it looks like everyone will recover."

"We'll hold a memorial for them tonight." Allistor was getting used to losing people, and he didn't like it.

"Also, I ran into Cogwalker, told him about the ship. He's going to take a crew out there and check for traps and such. He seemed especially interested."

Allistor simply nodded and thanked McCoy, distracted by something that was tickling at his consciousness, but that he couldn't quite grasp. His hand fell to the hilt of the sword he'd named *Unification*, the one he used to take Loki's head.

Seeing this action, Daigath asked, "You see something? Sense something?"

Allistor shook his head. "Nothing I can put my finger on." The two of them stood quietly alongside Helen, watching the kids and bears at play. At a discrete distance, two dwarves and their snorg surveyed the tower lobby with careful eyes.

*****

Morning came early for Allistor. He'd slept on the sofa again, still not comfortable in the bed he'd shared with Amanda. He had tossed and turned most of the night, not sleeping more than a couple of hours. The list of things that needed his attention was daunting, and he was feeling too tired or lazy to get up and grab paper to write them down. He worried about the kids, dealing with the loss of Amanda, and whether he could raise them properly without help. His gut twisted at the thought of an assassin targeting them, or them just being collateral damage when it came for him. That knot in his stomach twisted even tighter when he thought of all the unknown and possibly powerful entities out there that now considered him an enemy. Then there was the recent disappearance of something like a million undead who'd been attacking his city. Where did they go, and when would they return?

He was considering finding a new home for the kids, one that kept them at a safe distance from the dangers he felt pressing in, when he finally drifted off to sleep.

Now the first sun would be clearing the horizon in an hour or so, and he was wide awake. Allistor considered having breakfast sent up, but decided it would be a good idea to eat with his people down in the cafeteria. It was good for morale, and he could do some last minute checking on the preparations for their trip. Between himself and his family, the raiders he was bringing along, Daigath, Harmon and his orcanin, Gene and his family, Chris, and a few others he'd invited, there would be more than a hundred souls aboard the *Phoenix* when it departed later that morning. A hundred souls he was taking to an alien planet with unknown and likely hostile occupants.

He instructed Nigel to wake the kids as he stepped into the shower and got himself ready. When he emerged into the sitting area, they were all waiting for him. Allistor gave each of them a hug, and they all went down to breakfast together.

The cafeteria was already busy, a palpable excitement in the air. It wasn't every day that you got to explore a brand new planet. The raiders who were going along were anxious, and those who were staying were envious.

Meg emerged to hug the kids and pass them some pastries to take along in their storage. For Allistor, she had a stern look and a poke in the gut. "You take care of these babies out there, keep them safe!" she grumped at him before handing him some pastries as well. "If they come back with even a scratch, I'll poison your food and take over this empire myself!" There was a twinkle in her eye. "Empress Meg sounds much better than Lady Meg."

Allistor gathered her into a hug. "You'd have every other emperor and faction leader running scared inside a month."

"Unhand my woman, you cad!" Sam growled from behind Allistor, who gave Meg a final squeeze before complying. When he turned to face the old Texan, he found Sam in his full armor. When he raised a questioning eyebrow, Sam grinned. "Yep. I'm coming with you. Gonna help you kick some alien ass if necessary. Get me some sweet, sweet xp."

Allistor didn't argue, partly because it wouldn't make any difference, and partly because he'd be glad to have Sam with him. The man was like a surrogate father, and a combat veteran as well. Sam and George had used their experience and wisdom to save his butt more than once over the past year.

"You planning on bringing one of the Howitzers along, Sam?" he teased the old Marine.

Not missing a beat, Sam shook his head. "Nah, your ship has better guns on her already. I'm gonna spend a little time at the weapons station, practice shootin 'em. For... research" He grinned.

Chapter Three

It's Raining Elves

Sam wasn't joking. As *Phoenix* approached Orion, he took over the weapons station on the bridge and blasted several asteroids, shouting "Pew! Pew!" and giggling like a madman. When he was done, he got up and gave the station back to the crewman assigned to it. Passing by Allistor, who was standing next to Kira and the captain's chair, he was beaming. "It's just like Asteroids!" He gave them a little wave and left the bridge. As the door was closing behind him, Allistor heard a final "Pew! Pew!"

"What's Asteroids?" Kira asked.

Allistor shrugged. "Dunno. I vaguely remember someone talking about a late twentieth century game with that name…"

They both stopped talking as their attention was drawn to the fast-approaching Orion, and more importantly, the eternity gate in orbit around it. The thing was huge. A series of curved metal pieces connected by what looked from here to be metal wires, forming a giant ring. But Allistor knew that to be able to see them from so far away, those wires had to be as thick as a train tunnel, maybe bigger. At the top of the loop was a structure that was covered in some kind of glowing script that Allistor was inclined to call runes, though some of them seemed more like mathematical formulas than words. Each of the curved metal sections around the loop featured huge panels that

Allistor recognized as solar panels, collecting power from the suns to run the gate.

As they neared the planet, Kira asked, "Do you want to stop on the planet for any reason? Or do we head straight for the gate?"

Harmon cleared his throat. "There are several representatives from various factions on the station, awaiting a chance to meet with you. They wish to purchase property on Orion, and discuss access to the gate."

Allistor grimaced. He'd brought along Selby, Droban, L'olwyn and Longbeard to handle issues like this. He wouldn't have the first idea what to charge for gate access, what property was available, or what prices would be fair. "Do we need to meet them right now?"

"They have been waiting for a week or more already, a few more days won't do any harm." Daigath spoke up. "Besides, the longer they wait, the more money they spend on Harmon's space station." the old elf grinned at his friend.

Harmon returned the grin, adding, "And the more desperate they will be to throw money at you, Allistor. Right now they're sizing up their competition, worrying about how many others will arrive before they can reach an agreement with you. And you hold the upper hand in any negotiations. Not only are you the owner of the property they want, controller of the gate access, and Emperor of four planets now, but you're the bold slayer of two powerful ancient ones. Where many of them might have tried to intimidate you for a good deal a few weeks ago, now they are wondering how much of a premium they'll need to pay to avoid offending you."

Somewhere behind him, Helen snorted and mumbled something like "Emperor fancy pants." under her breath.

"Let's just head through the gate." Allistor decided to avoid the other topic altogether until they returned. "How does that work? Do we need to make a reservation? What's the fee?"

"It's your gate, Allistor. You don't pay to use it. And while yes, most reserve a transit time a day or more ahead of when they would like to travel through the gate, you take priority." Harmon leaned toward Kira and whispered, "Move us toward the gate, hold position to one side, about ten miles out."

Allistor nodded, still not used to the whole emperor throwing his weight around thing. "I don't want to displace anyone. I've made enough enemies already. Let's just squeeze into the next available opening. There can't be that much traffic already, can there?"

"Not yet, no." Harmon agreed. He checked something on his wrist unit. "Currently the gate is operating about thrice an hour. At peak capacity, ships would transition in or out every three minutes. It takes that long for the gate to power down, a new address to be programmed in, and to be powered back up."

"What if multiple ships want to pass through?" Kira asked.

"Once opened, the gate can remain so for up to six minutes. Longer than that puts a strain on the connection, and risks a malfunction." He looked at Kira. "But a large fleet, if well-organized, could pass through in six minutes. A hundred ships or more."

They were getting closer, and Allistor was feeling intimidated by the size of the structure. It was more than large enough for one of Queen Xeria's large harvester ships to pass. Allistor thought it might be large enough for a small moon to fit through. He'd been wrong about the wires. They weren't as wide as train tunnels. If he had to guess, he'd say the wires were about a quarter mile in circumference. One could probably drive four or five freight trains through it side by side, with room in between.

"Why is it so large? Are there ships out there that big?"

Harmon shook his head. "The gate can expand and collapse to accommodate larger ships. Obviously, the smaller the aperture, the less power it takes to open. You can see the solar panels on the solid sections? Well there are also immense diaphanous sails that can be unfurled to collect solar wind. It is a much more efficient collection method, as the surface area is several times larger than the panels. When traffic is light, or during a scheduled weekly shutdown, they extend the sails to boost power generation. They really are quite beautiful."

"And the sails aren't out now because… they knew we were coming and wanted to use the gate?" Helen guessed.

"Correct. We could instruct them to unfurl the sails for your viewing pleasure, but it would delay our transition by six hours."

Allistor shook his head. "I look forward to seeing them, but not today. Let's head through as soon as we can."

Kira listened closely as Harmon spoke to the gates controllers, and smiled a moment later. The ship began to move again, directed toward the gate. "They said we can go right now."

Ahead of them the glow from the control structure runes brightened, then began to spread. In ten seconds the entire gate structure was glowing blue. The solid sections seemed to retract some of the wire, and the gate shrank to about a quarter of the size it had been. A moment later a swirling purple event horizon appeared inside the circle, looking much like a dungeon entrance from the old VR games. The colorful swirl expanded to fill their vision as they drew closer.

"Slowly now, we enter the gate as slowly as possible. Never forget that. There you go... perfect." Harmon coached Kira, who was sweating profusely as she adjusted the ship's speed downward. Harmon counted down, "Three... two... one..."

Allistor's eyes rolled up in their sockets and his body suddenly felt so heavy his legs strained to keep him upright. A moment later he felt light as a feather floating on a warm breeze. The bridge around him seemed to stretch outward and shrink in toward him at the same time, as if the ship around him were elastic, and the word *solid* now had no meaning.

He did his best not to panic, telling himself that he was passing through a fold in space and time, and that any funkiness he was experiencing was temporary. It occurred to him that he should have warned the rest of the ship before they transitioned, and he wondered how the folks outside the bridge were taking it.

A moment later, he had time to wonder again. Then decided he was suffering from some form of déjà vu. At least until he came around to wondering again how the rest of his people were handling the transition.

Am I stuck in a time loop? And if so, would I remember having these thoughts before? I guess they weren't kidding when they named these things eternity gates. I feel like we've been in here for a good minute, at least. How long is this going to last? What if we're stuck in here for years? What will happen to Invictus and Earth? Can I move around while we're in here? Allistor tried to move. *Apparently not. Great, now I think I have to pee, and I can't move. Please don't let me wet myself on the bridge in front of everyone. Especially Helen. She'd never let me hear the end of it. How much wood would a woodchuck chuck if a woodchuck could chuck wood? That thing Ramon told me about Nancy being creeped out by his animated paper dolls was pretty funny. I wonder if I could get him to make a giant paper doll and have it stomp through Invictus City like Godzilla? Seriously, though, how long is this friggin transition going to take? Maybe if I sing a little song to myself, it'll pass faster?   But what song should I-*

His mental ramblings were cut off as the ship transitioned back into normal space. There was no physical sensation, the *Phoenix* just continued the slow forward progress from before it entered the other gate. Allistor's mind, however, felt like it reached the end of a bungee cord and snapped back.

"Shit, that was…" Kira muttered, rubbing her face as she checked her console. Allistor grabbed hold of the back of her chair to steady himself.

"Yeah, creepy." He agreed. A quick look around showed everyone but Harmon and Daigath were taking a moment to adjust. "How long were we in there?"

"Less than a second." Harmon replied, his face as sympathetic as Allistor figured an orcanin face could get. "It takes some getting used to."

"You guys warned me about the time dilation inside, but I guess I didn't really buy into it. I figured maybe a few seconds, not… that felt like several minutes."

"It is different every time." Daigath offered. "Speed of entry into the gate is certainly a factor, but it is not uncommon for crew members on the same ship to experience the same transition differently. For me, this jump lasted a half dozen heartbeats. That is how I measure them. The Arkhon are still studying this phenomenon, but none are sure what causes the differential. Most of us just assume it is a difference in brain chemistry, and accept the reality."

"Like I said, creepy. I'm not sure I'm ever going to get used to that." Allistor shook it off, looking up at the bridge's main viewscreen. "So, are we there yet?" He grinned at Kira, who stuck her tongue out at him.

"We're through the other gate, if that's what you mean. The planet is…" She paused to pull up the holographic navigational display. A blue map of the system in a three-dimensional globe appeared in front of her. There was a glowing golden triangle that indicated the *Phoenix*, and not far away a green sphere indicated their target planet. The gate wasn't in orbit of the planet, but it wasn't far away. "Ten minutes if we take our time."

"I'm not in a big rush." Allistor stared at the map as the ship indicator turned to point at the planet and began to move forward slowly. "Let's look around. Coms, let me know if you hear anything from the planet. We don't know if whomever is down there will be friendly. Tactical, be on alert. Shield up and weapons ready, just in case."

"You want my chair?" Kira snarked at him. "That's my job."

His cheeks reddened slightly at the jab. "Sorry, Kira. I'm trying to find the balance here, going from boss of everything emperor guy to just a passenger on a pretty spaceship. Please, do your stuff." He took a step back from the captain's chair and smiled at her.

"Incoming ship, fast-moving, headed on an intercept with us." Kira's daughter Brooke reported from the sensors station. A quick motion of her hand, and the ship appeared on the viewscreen. Before Allistor could ask, the ship was magnified.

"Too small to be a cargo or transport ship." Harmon commented. "Combat configuration. A single main cannon on the front, looks like missile launchers under the wings. Give me a moment." He tapped on his wrist unit.

"How long before contact?" Kira asked.

"Intercept in one minute." Brooke answered.

"Vessel in weapons range in ten seconds. Assume the same for their weapons." The young man at the weapons station reported.

"It's a Stryker fighter drone. Elven manufacture. Mid-grade attack ship." Harmon concluded, pushing a tiny hologram up from his wrist. "Standard weapons configuration is no real danger to this ship. Plasma cannon on the front, and four missiles under each wing. Even if they all hit, it is unlikely they could bring down our shield."

"How bout we don't test that?" Kira grumbled. "Preparing evasive maneuvers. Weapons, if that ship fires on us, blast it out of the sky."

Harmon looked at Brooke. "Scan carefully for more of them. They are usually deployed in groups of a dozen or more. There isn't much point in sending a single drone against this ship, unless…" his voice faded and his

53

eyes widened. "Kira, kill it now. It may have high yield missiles aboard!"

"Weapons, you heard him, take it down!"

The *Phoenix* shuddered slightly as all of her plasma cannons and her railgun fired. A moment later another small tremor indicated at least one missile was away. The bridge crew watched in silence as their projectiles screamed toward the still oncoming drone. A second later it loosed several missiles before spiraling sharply in an attempt to dodge incoming fire.

It was not successful.

The drone lurched as the railgun round slammed into one wing. A moment later two of the plasma bolts impacted it, burning holes through the fuselage. Lastly the missile, which had been moving slower than the kinetic rounds, homed in and impacted the engines at the rear of the drone. There was a flash of light, then nothing.

"Incoming!" Brooke shouted, her adrenaline getting the better of her. "Four missiles coming right at us!"

The kid at the weapons station didn't wait to be told. He activated the point defense turrets, which began spitting out hundreds of tiny rounds each, every tenth one a tracer. He also launched four missiles that, when they approached the incoming missiles, would explode and release a blast of magnetic chaff to both distract and destroy the enemy missiles.

One of the kinetic rounds took out a first missile, then a second almost at the same time. The remaining two continued on toward the *Phoenix*, their paths erratic as they attempted to evade the defensive fire. Ten seconds later the two chaff missiles exploded, taking both of the enemy projectiles with them as they flew into a cloud of sharp metal shards.

Brooke let out a relieved sigh. "It's okay mom. I mean, captain! All incoming missiles destroyed. No remaining bogies within sensor range."

Kira gave her daughter a proud smile even as Harmon leaned in close to her. "Captain, if you don't mind, may I?"

Kira moved her arm out of his way, and he punched several keys on the panel. "I'm tracking the flight path of that Stryker. We'll know where it came from in just… a… there!" The navigational hologram turned into a rendering of the planet, a dotted line tracing back from the *Phoenix*'s position to a location marked with a glowing red X on the planet. "The drone launched from there. I say we go pay them a visit." Harmon growled.

"What if they have more drones?" Allistor pictured them flying right into an ambush.

"I think if they had more, they'd have sent them with the first one. With high yield missiles, three or four of them might have overwhelmed us."

Trusting his friend's judgement, Allistor nodded at Kira. She gave him a wicked grin. "Right! Tactical, stay on alert. We're going in guns blazing!" She winked at Harmon, who chuckled. "I always wanted to say that!"

"Coms, have you heard anything?" She asked a moment later, looking at her other daughter, Hillary.

"Not a sound from anywhere on the planet."

"Try hailing them. Keep transmitting every ten seconds. Let us know if anyone answers."

Allistor heard her speak quietly into her mic, "This is *Phoenix*, flagship of Emperor Allistor, calling anyone planetside. Please respond."

While she was talking, Harmon had been speaking into his own coms. "Two of my ships from the space station will be coming through the gate behind us. I had them on standby. We'll have reinforcements in two minutes."

Phoenix was entering the planet's atmosphere when Hillary called out. "I've got something. Coming from the planet. It's just repeating over and over." She pressed a key on her console and a voice echoed across the bridge.

"Please don't attack! It wasn't us. That drone was automated! We had no control of it!"

Allistor tilted his head to one side as the message repeated. After another listen, he asked, "Does that... does that voice sound like Loki to you?"

"It does." Daigath confirmed as Harmon nodded his head.

"So it's a trap. A recording pretending to be innocent survivors."

"And anyone who'd never heard Loki's voice would fall for it." Harmon agreed.

Allistor looked at Hillary. "No other response at all?" The girl just shook her head. He looked at Kira "Do we still have any bombs on board?"

Kira grinned at him. "Gene left me four of them. One gut-buster, and the rest standard explosives."

"Let's use one of the standard bombs. I want to make sure nothing else flies out of that location to come at us. Call down to the cargo bay and tell them to get it ready. We'll drop it right through the roof." He turned to look at the target location, rapidly growing larger on the viewscreen.

The planet itself was varying shades of green and brown. It appeared from orbit to have large swathes of forest broken up by mountains and desert, with the occasional lake or ocean scattered here and there. Much less water than Earth, for sure. The location the drone was sent from was not far from the largest mountain range, built about a mile back from the shore of a lake. It was a large square-shaped building, but that was all Allistor could tell from their perspective high above.

He scanned the surrounding area, but the nearest structure was a tall tower built right on the shore of the lake, well out of range of any collateral damage. Beyond the lake there was what appeared to be a small city filled with towering spires of various heights, but the city was dark. Only the lone tower on the lakeshore showed any signs of life in the form of lights in the windows.

Kira drastically slowed their descent, expecting a trap. When she was just a mile above the square structure, she stopped completely. Without being asked, Brooke reported, "No motion of any kind below us." The viewscreen was now being fed from one of the cameras on *Phoenix*'s underside, pointing directly below at the building. Allistor saw no vehicles outside, no roads or even foot trails around it. Either the structure was only accessed by air, or there was a tunnel network somewhere below.

He looked up from the view screen to see a thumbs-up from Kira, indicating that the bombers in the cargo bay were ready to do their thing. When Allistor looked to Harmon and Daigath, both nodded their agreement, and Allistor gave the order. "Bomb away."

A few seconds later an image of the falling bomb came into view, and they all watched in silence as it impacted the roof of the structure and disappeared. A moment later the building and the ground around it erupted, debris and dust flung high into the air, blocking the camera's view. Just to be safe, Kira gained some altitude as they waited for the dust to clear.

It was now silent on the bridge, the recording no longer playing from the coms station. Their bomb must have destroyed the transmitter. From the sheer scope of the explosion, Allistor estimated it destroyed pretty much everything down there. He was sure their standard bomb wouldn't do that much damage, so they must have hit some stored munitions, fuel tanks, or something else that had increased the power of the blast.

When the smoke finally cleared, the camera zoomed in to show them a deep crater under where the building had stood. At least a hundred feet deep, and two hundred feet in diameter, it looked like a giant, jagged bowl made of stone and steel. Fires burned here and there, and broken pieces of infrastructure dangled over the hole.

"Land and check it out?" Kira asked.

Allistor, having flashbacks of the power plant and the fight with the fomorians in a setting that looked much like this, shook his head. "It looks dead down there. I don't even see any bodies. Let it burn itself out, and we'll explore it later. Let's check out that tower."

Kira gave a quick nod and maneuvered the ship toward the tower. There was a wide landing pad near its base, and she expertly glided them in for a landing. Allistor was already headed for the cargo bay by the time she set down, Helen, Harmon and Daigath right behind him. By the time they reached the bay and the ramp leading down, the orcanin and raiders had already offloaded and formed a semicircle of shields and bristling weapons between the ramp and the tower.

"Any sign of movement?" Allistor asked McCoy, who was leading the raiders while Bjurstrom was having his arm regrown.

"Nothing. No sounds, either. This place is dead, boss."

Allistor was conflicted. On the one hand, there should be life here, and if it was gone, that likely meant he had been responsible for the deaths. On the other hand, no life meant no resistance to him taking over, no fights that might get his people killed.

"See if you can find us an entrance. I don't see one, but it makes sense there should be one here at the landing pad. Keep your eyes wide open, and call out if you see any movement at all."

McCoy saluted, and his team of ten jogged across the wide landing pad toward the tower structure. The tanks took the lead, their shields up and ready, the rest of the team divided into two short lines running right behind the tanks. In the air above, two orcanin ships came screaming in. One hovered near the top of the tower, the other landed next to the *Phoenix* and began disgorging orcanin warriors by the dozen.

McCoy and his team didn't have to search long. As soon as the tanks approached the building, a wide doorway slid open, revealing a well-lit loading dock. The raiders passed through the door and took several steps inside, then the tanks took up station and the group assumed a standard combat formation. Behind them, orcanin streamed through to the left and right.

"All clear, boss." McCoy reported. Allistor moved forward across the landing pad with Harmon, Helen, and Daigath at his side. He left one team of ten raiders in the *Phoenix* cargo bay to protect the ship and the kids on the bridge crew, along with his own children. The others all moved forward, so that by the time he reached the tower doorway there were nearly two hundred raiders and orcanin warriors securing the loading dock. He paused before entering. There were likely deadly traps in this building, set for anyone attempting to take the tower. He took a moment to open his interface and create a quest. If his people were going to face danger, they deserved a reward. He shared the quest with Harmon and Daigath, as well as all his people. Then he spoke his concerns aloud.

"If this is a trap, we've got all our fighters clustered in this one room."

Harmon grunted, then spoke into his coms. Immediately ten orcanin charged across the loading dock and bashed into a doorway on the opposite side, while another group moved to the obvious set of elevator doors to the right. While they moved, Harmon tossed a handful of tiny drones into the air, which flew off to circle the room, scanning the walls and ceiling with beams of red light. As his warriors disappeared onto the elevator and through the now broken exit door, he reported, "No signs of weapons in this room." He paused, looking around. "But this is Loki's territory, and I would expect any traps to be well hidden."

There was an explosion somewhere higher up the tower, and a moment later a report that sounded like just a series of grunts to Allistor came across Harmon's coms.

"My warriors have encountered some resistance. Drones and weapons emplacements, no living foe has yet been detected." More orcanin dashed toward the exit door, presumably to replace wounded or dead warriors upstairs.

Swallowing the lump in his throat that threatened to make him vomit, not wanting to speak the words, Allistor said them anyway. "You're losing warriors, Harmon. You should let my people clear part of the tower."

"Harmon shook his head. "My orcanin are better suited for this work. Your people are good fighters, and brave, but inexperienced. Their armor is still substandard, and they are not familiar with the dangers my warriors are encountering. It would be suicide for your raiders, Allistor."

"But your warriors shouldn't have to die to conquer my property."

"Ha! They are having the time of their lives! This is what they live for. And when it is over, they will tell their children about how they conquered Loki's tower, defeated the forces of an ancient one!"

Allistor shook his head as Daigath placed a hand on his shoulder. "Harmon speaks the truth. His people thrive on conflict, and consider a good death in battle to be their ultimate achievement."

Harmon added with a wistful tone, "Were I not Emperor, I would be leading them myself."

"Thank you, Harmon. We owe you yet another debt."

"You owe me nothing, Allistor. You are giving my warriors the type of opportunity they crave. One they do not see often enough these days. If you had asked, they likely would have paid you for the privilege." He grinned down at his fellow emperor.

Above them they heard a scream, one that quickly grew louder. Looking up, Allistor saw a falling body rushing toward them. He and the others stepped inside the loading dock just as the scream ended abruptly upon impact. There was the sound of shattering bone and splashing blood as the corpse landed headfirst and splattered.

"What… was it?" Allistor asked. Both Daigath and Harmon shrugged. The corpse was too badly damaged by the impact to identify a species. Daigath offered, "Possibly an elf, but I can not be sure."

Another scream began up above, and this time Daigath stuck his head out to watch it fall. "This one is an elf." He confirmed before pulling his head in and taking a few steps back. The others followed his lead, not wanting to be splashed. Allistor thought it fell for a long time before hitting the ground outside with similar results. Harmon looked worried. If his warriors were tossing elves out of windows, it would mean war for his people. He barked an urgent command into his coms.

"How tall is this tower?" Helen was obviously thinking the same thing as Allistor.

Allistor was sticking his head out to look for himself when he spotted a blurred figure falling much more slowly than the first two. Pointing at it, he asked, "What is that?"

Helen raised the bow she instantly pulled from her inventory and sent an arrow streaking toward the still falling blur. When the arrow impacted, there was a short scream, and the image of an elf appeared, clutching an arrow in his gut. Whatever magic or device was slowing his descent failed, and he dropped the last thirty feet or so to the ground. Helen was about to put a second arrow into the elf when Daigath raised a hand. She held her fire, and the ancient elf strode out, glancing briefly upward to make sure there were no more falling bodies. When he reached the wounded elf laying on its side on the ground, he spoke softly.

After a brief exchange, he reached down and yanked the arrow free of the wounded elf's gut, then cast a healing spell. He helped the elf to his feet, then produced a beautifully crafted wooden sword and motioned for the prisoner to move.

When they entered the loading dock, Daigath made a show of bowing slightly to Allistor. "Emperor Allistor, I present Supervisor Dre'nir of the planet Skapa Far. It seems that upon Loki's death, the top several ranks of his staff here perished as well. Dre'nir is the most senior of those that remain."

"Meaning that he was ranked too low to have been life bonded." Harmon looked with contempt at the elf. "When we arrived, you sent the drone in hopes of… what? Eliminating Emperor Allistor and taking the planet for yourself?" He spat on the floor at the elf's feet. "And when that didn't work, when my warriors bested your defenses here, you cloaked yourself and attempted to sneak away like a coward."

The prisoner just glared at Harmon, one hand over the healed wound in his gut as if he could still feel the pain.

"What of these others?" Daigath asked, pointing toward the two scattered corpses on the ground. The elf's glare of hatred faded to discomfort as he turned toward Daigath. It was ingrained within elves to respect their elders from birth, and Daigath was possibly the most ancient of elders. "Answer me, child." Daigath growled.

"We all leapt from the roof. Those two had cast several spells as we retreated, and their mana was insufficient to keep the levitation spell active. When their magic failed, they fell."

"Why not just surrender?" Helen asked.

"To orcanin filth? It is better to perish." Dre'nir cast another hateful look at Harmon.

Harmon shook his head. "My warriors did not attack you, nor any of your kind. They know better."

"They were pushing through the defenses, and would have slaughtered and eaten us if we remained." The elf seemed so sure of himself that Allistor actually looked to Harmon for his response.

"Foolish little elf." The orcanin chuckled. "Your pathetic existence is not worthy of breaking our accord with the elves over. Your companions killed themselves for nothing, and you nearly died yourself because of ignorance and fear." He turned so that he could wink at Daigath without the other elf seeing. "Besides, elves don't even taste good. Unless you have time and spices on hand to prepare an appropriate sauce to baste them in."

"Can you deactivate the defenses?" Allistor cut in, his mind on the casualties happening above.

The elf growled, but did not answer, until Daigath poked him with the tip of the wooden sword. "I can not. I do not have the codes."

After a moment, Daigath nodded. "He speaks the truth."

Encouraged, Dre'nir added, "For the record, I did not send the drone. It was automated, and the last of its kind. There was a fleet of thirty drones, programmed to defend the planet in the event of our master's demise. Three other ships have approached since that sad day, and were destroyed. But they in turn destroyed all but one drone."

Again, Daigath nodded to indicate that the elf was telling the truth. Harmon, who had been suspicious of the single drone, grunted. "That makes sense."

Daigath spoke quietly but with a commanding tone. "Emperor Allistor is the rightful ruler here, having been granted this planet by the System when he took Loki's head." He paused when the prisoner glared at Allistor and actually took a step in his direction. The sword point to his chest halted him. "Do you recognize Allistor's right to rule?"

"I recognize no authority but my master's!" Dre'nir growled.

Allistor drew his sword and pressed the tip to the elf's chest, Daigath lowering his own blade as Allistor responded. "Your master is dead! I took his head with this sword." He pressed it a bit harder against the elf's chest until he flinched from discomfort. "I enchanted it myself. Do you know what it does? It causes its victims great pain, then steals a part of their soul." He smiled as the elf blanched. "That's right. Part of your master is trapped in here. Do you wish to join him?"

Dre'nir looked like he actually considered it for a moment before he shook his head no. Allistor lowered the blade, which seemed to hesitate to fall when he relaxed. Putting it back in its scabbard, he ordered, "Then tell Harmon here everything you know about this tower's defenses."

Chapter Four

Millions Upon Millions

Dre'nir turned out to be no help at all with the tower security systems, but he was a font of information about the nearby city and the planet in general.

The city was mostly full of crafters, and the slaves that served them. An entire army of enslaved creatures of many species. The majority worked gathering resources. Quarry workers and miners for stone and ores, beast handlers raising herds of creatures for both meat and useable body parts. Farmers growing food crops, herbs, and alchemical ingredients. Then there were the servitors who cleaned homes, cooked and served meals at inns and restaurants, swept the streets, transported goods, all the jobs the crafters and their families would normally have had to pay wages for. And lastly, there were the merchants. Those who took the goods from the crafters and sold them for a significant markup, a part of which was paid to Loki.

There had also been a large population of operatives working for Loki, or his underlings. Thousands of agents who lived in the city, but spent most of their time on other worlds gathering information.

"By necessity, because of the nature of their work, they were required to be life bonded to the Master, or to one of his trusted inner circle. When he perished," the elf gave Allistor another hateful glare, "they all perished. I witnessed many of them fall right here in the tower. One second they were walking or talking, the next they simply went limp as the light went out of their eyes."

"Good insurance against betrayal, I suppose." Helen mused. "They aren't going to challenge and kill you if it also means their own death."

"What purpose did you serve here?" Allistor asked the elf.

"I was the regional supervisor. There are ten of us on this planet, each of us overseeing one or two cities. We ensure that things run smoothly, that taxes are promptly paid, and that a steady supply of resources and slaves are available."

"What tax was Loki charging?"

"Thirty percent of every transaction."

"So he collected thirty percent of whatever the merchants paid the crafters, and another thirty percent when the merchants sold the goods to customers?" Allistor shook his head.

"And one hundred percent of what the crafters paid for their materials. Minus the costs of purchasing and maintaining the slave labor, of course."

Allistor could feel the anger burning in Harmon somewhere behind him, though the orcanin didn't make a single sound. Daigath stood to Allistor's right, a sad look on his face.

"Can I assume that the other supervisors have access to transportation? Either teleport pads or flying vehicles? And you have a way to contact them?"

"There are several teleport pads in each city, with a hub at each operations tower like this one." the elf confirmed. "And yes, we are all connected to a secure coms channel at all times, should the Master have need of us."

"Call them all here, right now. Tell them anyone who isn't here in ten minutes will be hunted down and executed by the end of the day."

The elf's eyes widened, but he didn't respond. He simply jogged over to a nearby panel, accompanied by an orcanin guard, and began punching keys on the holographic display. He returned less than a minute later. "Seven are coming, two have not responded."

Harmon spoke into his coms and a moment later both orcanin ships soared upward, heading into orbit to monitor traffic. Anyone trying to leave the planet would be captured, or destroyed.

Allistor waited patiently, making small talk with Helen as the clock ticked away the designated ten minutes. A flash on the pad outside the loading dock told them that the teleport pad was out there as well. Allistor hadn't noticed it on the way in, but he'd been focused on getting in the door.

Several orcanin warriors ran out to guard the pad as one after another the supervisors appeared. Each of them were elves, some of them looking middle-aged, which might make them quite old in human terms. When all seven newcomers had been herded inside to stand with Dre'nir, Allistor addressed them.

"I am Emperor Allistor, new owner of this world. I'm not going to bother learning your names, because I doubt most of you will live out the day. From what I gather, you're all slave traders at the very least, possibly worse. I detest slavery, and those who promote it." He held up a hand when one of them opened his mouth to speak. "You're about to say that it was Loki's system, his orders. I already killed Loki, and as much as I'd like to, I can't do it again. The fact that he was a tyrant, and that you all know the inner workings of your cities, are the reasons I'm going to give each of you one chance to save your lives. You will stand here, denounce any loyalty to Loki or your recently deceased superiors, then swear an oath to me and to Invictus. Do that, and serve me faithfully going forward, you may live. Should you refuse, I'll give you to Emperor Harmon here, who I'm sure can find ways to dispose of you that do not violate his accord with the elves."

Allistor stood still, one hand on his sword hilt, and waited. A few of the elves shifted their feet or twitched uncomfortably as he gazed upon them, but none spoke for half a minute. Finally Dre'nir stepped forward. "I will serve."

After he broke the ice, the others stepped forward in ones and twos. Before he had Helen administer the oath, he asked, "Who are the two that did not answer my summons? And what cities do they supervise?"

The elf at the far right of the line cleared her throat. "Your pardon, Emperor Allistor, but I suspect they did not attend because they are dead."

"Explain." was all Allistor said.

"They were the most senior among us, having served the Master, er... served Loki the longest. One was a former trainer of his spies, retired to a supervisor position. It may be that both had accepted bonds long ago, and perished with the others."

Dre'nir nodded. "They have not answered my calls since that day." Several others in the line murmured agreements. Daigath winked at Allistor to say that they were being truthful.

Allistor decided to table the topic of the missing supervisors. He walked along the line of elves as he spoke to them. "Before you take the oath, I'm going to tell you how things will be on this world going forward. First, slavery is abolished. All the current slaves are now free. You will each make your best efforts to arrange for them to be paid a fair wage, and I do mean fair, if they wish to remain in their current positions. For those who wish to return to their homes, or just to leave here and never look back, we'll find a way to make that happen. It may take some time, but we'll find a way." He paused, thinking on the fly.

"The miners, farmers, and other resource gatherers will be able to sell their goods to crafters, merchants, or directly in the market squares if they choose. Crafters will have the option to sell their goods themselves, or to the merchants. The tax rate for all transactions will now be ten percent, not thirty. Can I assume that Loki maintained a treasury where all the tax proceeds have been deposited?"

Dre'nir shook his head. "None of us had access to his treasury, which I assume was somewhere off-world. But each city does have a branch of the world bank, into which we deposit tax proceeds, and withdraw the funds needed for city expenditures. The m-… Loki would periodically withdraw any surplus for his own uses. But he rarely visited this world in the last several centuries. His last visit was… eighty years ago?" He looked down the line at the others, who nodded in confirmation.

"So you have nearly a century of this world's tax income, at a rate of thirty percent of all transactions, stored in the banks?"

"More than a century, Emperor Allistor." Another elf spoke up. "In my city, at least. He did not withdraw funds on his last visit."

Allistor looked confused for a moment, but Daigath whispered to him. "Loki held hundreds, if not thousands of planets, moons, and space stations. And he had a significant presence on many more worlds that he didn't own outright. I suspect he had more currency than he had use for."

Harmon agreed. "He was far more interested in power and intrigue, in manipulating people, factions, and entire systems, than the accumulation of something as mundane as wealth. It would have been nothing more than a tool for him."

Allistor accepted their explanation as logical, and in line with what he himself knew of Loki. Turning back to the elves, he said, "Then you'll have plenty of resources to pay the former slaves their wages. To get them started, let's say they will each receive the equivalent of six month's back wages immediately. That should allow them to purchase food and necessities while you all work out whether they're staying or going, and figure out their employment, housing, etc. You're going to be extremely busy for the next few months."

He stopped pacing and took a few steps back from the line. "Now is when you decide. Do you swear the oath, use your talents to better the lives of your fellow citizens, or do you refuse?"

The elfess on the far right end who'd spoken before was the first to respond. "Emperor Allistor, I was born on this world. My father was a supervisor, and I inherited his position when he was killed for suspected theft. From my birth I have served under a cruel and absent master, always watched by rivals and spies who stood to benefit from my demise if I made a wrong step. For two hundred years I have battled in secret to hold my place, avoid assassination, and protect my own children." She sighed, then straightened her back and looked him directly in the eye. "What you offer sounds too good to be true. I think you're soft, naïve, and likely doomed to a brief life cut short by a painful death." Allistor found her honesty refreshing, and couldn't say that he disagreed with her.

"But I would like to try living on the world you describe. So for as long as you survive, I will serve. I will take your oath." She took one step forward, holding his gaze. He gave her a brief nod, then looked to the others.

One by one they stepped forward, some speaking a few words, others remaining silent. When Allistor motioned for Helen to step forward, Daigath stepped into her place. "If you do not mind, Emperor Allistor?" He raised an eyebrow, and Allistor motioned for him to continue. The elves each stood a little straighter when facing their ancient elder. Daigath recited a modified oath to them, adding a few extra protections and penalties that the standard oath didn't contain, binding these supervisors much more tightly than their fellow citizens. Allistor supposed it was a good idea, as by their own admission these elves were schemers, assassins, slavers, and possibly worse.

When they were done, he added his own warning. "Know that from now on, scheming, murdering your rivals, or plotting their downfall will not advance your position in the least. You rise or fall in my esteem purely by what you do to protect, and improve the lives of, the citizens under your care. If one of you assassinates another, if the System doesn't destroy you for it, I will. That goes double for your charges. And let me be clear, you are not just responsible for those in your sector. Every citizen under my care on this world is under yours as well."

He turned his back on them, asking Harmon, "What do I need to do to make this official?"

The orcanin smiled. "You should find some waiting notifications in your Empire tab. You need to formally claim the planet, now that you're here, and then adjust the settings the way you want them."

Allistor stood still, eyes unfocused as he pulled up his interface, located the Empire tab, and opened it. As his friend had said, there were several notifications highlighted. He selected the one for Skapa Far and opened it.

> *For killing Loki, its former owner and Emperor, you have been awarded potential ownership of the planet Skapa Far. Do you wish to claim the planet? Yes/No*

Allistor selected *Yes*, and a new set of notifications flooded his view. The first was the kind of notice that kept getting him into trouble, causing people and factions to resent him.

> *System Alert!*
>
> *Emperor Allistor of Invictus, after taking the life of Loki the Ancient One,*
> *has claimed the title of Emperor of Skapa Far!*
> *May he rule long and wisely.*

> *Level Up! You are now Level Ninety Eight! You have earned two Attribute points.*

Allistor noted that he'd only received a single level for taking a planet this time, figuring it was a consequence of being a much higher level now. Each level required significantly more experience points than the last.

He worked through the other notifications, mostly demanding that he do things like decide whether to claim all the land for himself – which he did, temporarily – as well as set monetary and experience tax rates. He lowered the experience tax rate, which had been at thirty percent like the sales tax, to five percent, and the sales tax to ten percent. He waved aside the others, then took a moment to install a copy of Nigel from *Phoenix* into the tower where he stood.

"Nigel, please take control of the AI's in all the facilities on the planet of Stronghold size or larger."

There was a short pause before Nigel answered. *"That is a total of one thousand six hundred and ninety facilities, not including this tower."*

"Shit." Helen whispered as Allistor whistled.

"Do you have the capacity for that?" Allistor asked his AI.

"With the upgrades you granted me during the last attack on Invictus City, and the infrastructure available on this world, I can easily operate these facilities, and several thousand more."

"That makes sense." Helen looked up at the tower above them. "It figures Loki would have state of the art tech. At least, for whatever year he built this place. You basically just gave Nigel a hardware upgrade."

"Indeed, Lady Helen. I have not overwritten the AI that previously operated this tower and the other facilities. I have simply assumed control over it."

Allistor nodded, pleased. "Good. Then make sure no more automated drones or security systems attack us, Nigel."

"Of course, Sire."

"Alright, time to let the citizens of this world know about their new situation. Nigel, loudspeaker please, everywhere on the planet that you can." He waited a moment, then began to speak.

"People of Skapa Far, I am Allistor of Invictus, the new Emperor of your planet. I have come here today to introduce myself, and to make a few changes. First, there are no more slaves on this world. Everyone is, as of right now, a free individual. You will each be given the opportunity to swear a simple oath to me, and to Invictus, that will make you equal citizens. Any who do not wish to swear the oath are welcome to leave. And for those who choose to become citizens, you may also leave as you desire. I have a few other planets, or space stations, that you might enjoy better than this one." He paused to study the reactions of the elves who were still standing in line in front of him. Most looked pleased, a couple looked less enthused.

"All former slave owners who wish to retain their staff may offer them compensation in the form of fair wages, housing, and so forth. All former slaves are free to accept those offers, pending approval of the terms by your local supervisors to ensure their fairness, or decline the offers and choose to do something different. Over the next weeks and months, housing and food will be provided for all former slaves as you transition into your new situations. Those who wish to return to your home worlds, we will work to get you transportation there, free of charge. Please be patient as we work out the logistics of that endeavor. For all of you who gather, craft, or sell goods, the tax has been lowered from thirty percent to ten. That reduction in taxes should allow you to pay fair wages to any former slaves you hope to retain. I have also lowered the experience tax to five percent, in order to help all of you grow faster. In addition, for those who wish to hunt or fight to level up, we will provide assistance in the form of trainers and raid groups in the very near future. Any qualified trainers on this planet, please report to your regional supervisors as soon as possible to discuss contracts for your services." He took a deep breath, thinking quickly before he continued, not wanting to miss anything important.

"I am not Loki. I did not plan to own this planet, nor did I kill Loki with the intent to take it. I killed him for justice, and for vengeance, because he killed billions on my own home world. But I have accepted this world in hopes of making it a better place for all of you. You do not exist to serve me. In fact, it is just the opposite. I will do my best to make life better for all of you. I doubt that many of you will accept that as fact right now, but in time you'll see that it's the truth." He turned to Helen.

"Now, for those of you who wish to take the oath and become citizens today, Helen will recite the oath for you to repeat. If you can hear my voice, then you need only recite the words she gives you, and you will become citizens. Let me say it again. This applies to all of you, former slaves included."

Helen stepped forward and began to recite the simple oath they had created what seemed like an eternity ago, but was actually just a little more than a year past. As she spoke, Allistor stepped a few paces away and whispered, "Nigel, what is the current population of this planet?"

"The population within range of my sensors is one hundred twelve million, seven hundred forty thousand, six hundred fifty three."

Allistor wondered if this planet had been populated like Earth before Loki took it, and whether he'd committed a similar genocide here. A hundred million people seemed light for an entire civilized planet. He waited for Helen to finish reciting the oath, motioned for Nigel to turn off loudspeaker, then waited a bit for the oath to take effect on anyone who chose to take it. "Nigel, how many new citizens do we have now?"

"Twenty seven million, three hundred five thousand, two hundred ten, Sire."

"Holy crap!" Helen gasped, covering her mouth with one hand.

"That's... more than I expected." Allistor was a little stunned himself. "I'm guessing most of them are former slaves. Not a bad start. Nigel, loudspeaker again please."

"Well! It seems that about one in four of you have chosen to become citizens of Invictus! I officially welcome you, and thank you for placing your trust in me. In a moment you new citizens will all receive a quest that will grant you some experience, and assist you in beginning your new lives. For the other three quarters of you, I hope you will choose to join us in the coming days. You will be given the opportunity to take the oath each day for the next three days, or you can simply recite it within hearing of Nigel, the new planetary AI, at any time. Anyone caught harming another occupant of this world, stealing, or otherwise acting against the interests of my people will be dealt with in the harshest possible manner. That is all."

He made the cutting motion for Nigel to turn off loudspeaker, then said, "Nigel, please engrave the oath in prominent public locations at each property. Along with the poem."

"It will be done momentarily, Sire. Might I add that an additional three million citizens have been added in the last minute or so."

Daigath smiled. "Many would have wanted to hear the complete oath before swearing, and I do not blame

81

them. I believe you'll find that number increases greatly in a short time."

"I certainly hope so. These supervisors will have enough to do without having to worry about evicting a large percent of the populace for refusing citizenship."

One of the elves, a seemingly middle-aged male that had not spoken before, cleared his throat. "Sire?"

"Yes? You have something to add?"

"There are millions more who would not have heard your announcement, being out of range of significant structures. Mainly farmers, gatherers, and the like."

"Then please, all of you, return to your respective territories. Send out runners with a written copy of my announcement, which you can get from Nigel. If there are those who cannot read, have it read to them. Send along a copy of the oath, as well. And post a copy of both at every city gate, market square, and teleport pad. If you can think of better ways to get the word out, do that as well."

The elf smiled at a surprised Allistor before turning toward the teleport pad with the others. They had their marching orders, and with the stricter oaths Daigath had given them, they'd carry them out to the best of their ability, or forfeit their lives.

Dre'nir, not having gone anywhere, looked uncomfortable.

"What is it?" Allistor asked.

"Sire most, if not all, of my senior staff have perished here today." He waved at the splattered corpses on the ground at the base of the tower. "Either here, or in the corridors above. It may take me a few days to recruit and train replacements."

"Citizens only." Allistor nodded once. "Either those that have already sworn, or those willing to swear the oath before taking the position. Get the best people you can, Dre'nir, and do it quickly. In the meantime, I'll leave some of my people here to help. They can at least walk through the nearby city to spread the word, answer questions, administer the oath."

Harmon offered, "I can leave a squad of orcanin to guard the tower in each city temporarily."

"Guards. Shit." Allistor thumped his forehead. "Nigel, please have Prime order up a thousand battle droids for each city, and another… twenty for each Stronghold on this world."

"There are already twenty five thousand battle droids on this world, Sire. All are stored in warehouses near four of the cities. They are older models, approximately two hundred years older than those you have purchased, but will perform admirably as a guard and defense force."

"Even better! Please deploy them in the numbers I gave you, and keep the rest in storage. We may need them on the next planet, or to deal with any sort of uprising that happens here."

Allistor focused on his interface again, this time creating a quest. He set it for newly sworn citizens only, and it was simple. Report to their area supervisor and be recorded as a new citizen. Receive housing if it was needed, as well as back pay for former slaves. Completion of the quest would earn low level citizens enough xp to reach level ten. For others it would grant them enough for one level. Before finalizing the quest, he closed that tab for a moment to check something. His own experience bank held trillions of available points, but did Loki use the ones from this planet's experience tax, or...

There it was! He obviously hadn't been using it for his own growth, as there was a ridiculous amount saved up. Allistor supposed it made sense. At some point, a creature as ancient and high-leveled as Loki wouldn't need to concern themselves with personal levels anymore. It made more sense to use it as quest rewards. But since Loki hadn't visited the planet in nearly a century, it had just been building up.

That made Allistor wonder just how many planets Loki held, if he was ignoring one like this for such a long stretch. And what happened to the others? Were the various Houses, Factions, and Empires out there waging war over all of them? How many would perish in that fighting? Is that what Odin meant when he spoke about consequences?

Or maybe this planet was a relatively small fry like Orion, unimportant compared to others, awarded to him by the System because it decided he was an equally small fry in the grand scheme of things, and inexperienced. The planetary emperor's version of a noob zone.

He went back to the quest and finalized it, smiling to himself. Despite his misgivings around the ripples he'd created in the pond, as Helen had put it, it felt good to use Loki's resources to help people he had oppressed.

Allistor and company spent a little more time on Skapa Far, starting with a tour of the tower. He had Nigel give him an hourly update on new citizens, and by the time they finished the tour and Allistor had claimed a residential suite near the top floor for himself and his kids, all but a couple million had sworn the oath. "If only I had this much success on Earth." he muttered to himself. There was a distinct advantage here, inheriting all the land, all the structures, and being able to reach nearly everyone at once. On Earth he was having to send teams all across the globe, meeting with individual strongholds and groups of survivors. Unless…

"Nigel, as Emperor of Earth, can I make global announcements like the one I did here? And if so, will everyone hear it?"

"*You have the authority to make global announcements specific to a chosen planet, and every being on the planet that has a connection to the System will receive a notification. You also have the ability to make multi-planet or even empire-wide announcements, Sire.*"

Allistor sighed. He really, really needed to spend some time going through his tabs and reading the directions. Huge mistakes were being made, great quantities of time and resources wasted, because he wasn't aware of his own capabilities.

He immediately sat down and took out his pad and pencil to make notes for an announcement on Earth. It would need to be much different than the one he'd just made here. Longer, more detailed, more emotional. He needed to consolidate what remained of the human race, get them all moving forward together.

With only four percent of the human population having survived the first year after the apocalypse, according to the System announcement at the end of Stabilization, the human race was down to less than three hundred million souls. That was less than the population of the United States at the time the world ended. Allistor had no way to know how many more had died since then

Having created his Empire, he knew exactly how many citizens he had. But when Baldur granted him the remainder of the unclaimed property on Earth, it didn't give him any way to know who was living on the already claimed property. He made a note on the margin of his pad to ask Harmon about that. The orcanin inherited his empire already intact by killing the previous emperor, but he'd had many years of practice at running things since then.

While he had a few moments of peace, Allistor decided to assign his attribute points. It had been a hectic several days, and the last time he'd assigned points was at level fifty five. He'd had two huge jumps in levels since then, both centered around Baldur and Loki, and now had a total of eighty free attribute points to assign.

Right off the bat, with an assassin possibly creeping around, he assigned ten points to *Constitution* in hopes of having enough health to survive a backstab or poisoning long enough to heal himself. He was happy to see that the increase, along with his bonuses, brought his health up over one hundred thousand points.

Next he assigned ten points each to *Intelligence* and *Will Power* to increase his mana pool, spell effectiveness, and hopefully casting speed. The nearly fifty percent increases should also help him to process information more quickly, keep track of the myriad responsibilities he had, and make better decisions on behalf of his people.

He put an additional ten points into *Adaptability*, something he'd been considering since William made a comment about how it had helped him survive the early days. Ten points also went into *Charisma*, because he was living in a political arena now, and was about to try to convince most of the human race to join him. Another ten went into *Luck* – he was going to need all he could get. His remaining points went into what he considered less important stats. He put five points into *Strength*, and another five into *Agility*, for those times when he found himself in melee combat. Stabbing Loki through the neck and having the already weakened ancient being just shrug it off had him a little intimidated. But in his position, if he was fighting at all, it would probably be with magic, from behind a whole host of people.

Next he put seven points into *Stamina*, because he needed more hours in the day, and fewer dedicated to sleep.

And he assigned his last nine points to *Dexterity* in hopes of improving his crafting abilities.

Designation: Emperor Allistor, Giant Killer	Level: 98	Experience: 6,710,000/910,000,000
Planet of Origin: UCP 382 (Earth)	Health: 109,000/109,000	Class: Battlemage
Attribute Pts Available: 0	Mana: 29,000/29,000	
Intelligence: 35 (39)	Strength: 15 (23)	Charisma: 22 (26)
Adaptability: 18 (20)	Stamina: 20 (27)	Luck: 18 (24)
Constitution: 32 (37)	Agility: 20 (26)	Health Regen: 3,300/m
Will Power: 35(43)	Dexterity: 16 (20)	Mana Regen: 2,100/m

Chapter Five

No Groping Zone

Allistor and company boarded the *Phoenix* and departed the planet, leaving behind the two orcanin ships and the guards Harmon had offered. Allistor had purchased replacement drones from Harmon, with the high yield missiles. They would be delivered in a couple of days. With those drones, the orcanin ships could engage and distract any intruders, and the drones could sneak in and deliver damaging missile attacks.

This proved to be a valid precaution, when on their way back to the gate, just as they were coming out of orbit, an unknown ship appeared not far away, dropping out of faster-than-light into normal space. Kira immediately ordered the shields raised, and weapons readied. The two orcanin ships, holding orbit below the *Phoenix*, broke off and formed up behind them as the newcomer slowed to a halt.

Harmon pressed a few buttons on Kira's controls, then nodded at Allistor.

"Unidentified ship, this is Emperor Allistor of Invictus. What business do you have on my planet?"

Harmon had told Allistor when he first delivered the *Phoenix* that while she wasn't a warship, she was well equipped with both weapons and shields. The intruders must have noticed the same thing. Without answering, the ship turned around the way it had come, and disappeared into FTL again. Harmon grunted. "It was a transport ship, likely carrying a vanguard or scouting force for a potential invader. Having found us waiting for them here, they likely won't return soon. But others may come. I recommend you station significant forces here, in orbit and on the ground."

Allistor nodded as Kira resumed her course toward the gate. The two orcanin ships returned to their orbit, stationing themselves on opposite sides of the planet.

"Nigel, how many combat capable ships do we have now? Have they all been delivered?" After the auction for the orb was decided by the Arkhon bid of two eternity gates, Allistor had traded with several of the factions who'd been attracted by the presence of a gate on Orion. He provided them land on the planet and access to the gate in return for a great many things, including a fleet of ships, and a space station for Earth.

"There are ten colony ships with significant cargo capacity but limited combat capabilities. Twenty cargo transport ships with moderate weapons, heavy armor, and shields. Ten battle cruisers with heavy armor, shields, and significant firepower. Two combat carriers with heavy armor and shields, moderate weapons, and full compliments of twenty manned fighter craft and ten drones on each. Lastly eight destroyer class ships with heavy armor and shields, and what Master Longbeard calls 'irresistible force'. "

"That sounds like it should be enough to protect a planet." Allistor looked at Harmon, who was shaking his head in a negative manner.

"Combined, they might be enough to slow a determined attack. And they would be even more effective in conjunction with a defense grid like the one you have installed around Earth. But were I to attack your planet, for example, I would send a fleet ten times the size of your own. Your defenses might last five minutes."

Exasperated, Allistor thumped the arm of Kira's chair. "So no matter what, I'm still going to be unable to fight off any larger group that wants what I have. What's the point of all this?" His shoulders slumped, dejected.

Daigath put a hand on one of those shoulders. "You are correct that you will likely never match the sheer firepower of older, more developed Empires and Houses. But sheer power is not the only determining factor in protecting your empire. You have made strong allies, and have wisely encouraged many influential factions to become invested in your worlds. Even stronger enemies will think twice before attacking."

Harmon chuckled. "Not to mention your well-known penchant for vengeance. You decided and loudly declared in the first days of Earth's stabilization that you would seek revenge on those responsible for the genocide of your species. You never stopped striving toward that goal, never stopped promising revenge to your people. And the Collective watched, as in little more than a year you went from a homeless weakling with nothing but the clothes on your back to an Emperor with four planets who had killed not just one, but *two* ancient ones in your quest for retribution. You don't behave as an emperor should, doing things like crafting your own weapons, fighting your battles from the front, sacrificing your own safety and resources to strengthen those who serve you, yet still advancing at an incredible pace. The Collective at large has been paying attention, and are trying to figure out just how formidable you and your people might be. If one determined human can accomplish such feats, what could millions of them together do?"

"Harmon is correct. And as with everything else you do, this garners you friends who are interested in your development, or profiting from association with you. It also brings you potential enemies who may wish to eliminate a future power that could threaten their status."

"So everything I do to get stronger and secure my people's safety also makes me more enemies." Allistor's frustration was clearly written on his face.

"That is the way of the Collective." Daigath agreed. "The sooner you accept this, the better you will sleep. In the entire known history of this galaxy, no empire has lasted forever. That is the nature of life."

Allistor was silent as the *Phoenix* approached the gate for the return trip. He was still contemplating the futility of all his actions when they crossed the event horizon.

What's the point of all this? I could level every human up to one hundred, and we could still be wiped out by a bombardment from space, with no way to defend ourselves. Someone like Loki or Odin could destroy our world on a whim if I offend them. I'm in no way qualified – oh, we've transitioned. Shit. I really do not like this. Why does it seem to take so long to transit from one gate to the other? It happens instantly in real time. Time must operate differently in this... void? Alternate dimension? Hey, maybe if I level up my Dimensional Manipulation *skill enough, I could learn to make gates? No, that's ridiculous. Others have had millennia to try and figure it out, and only the Arkhons can do it. Maybe they haven't even figured it out, they just learned to copy someone else's work? Still, I should level up that skill, even if it's just to make better storage devices for my people. What would happen if I tried to cast that spell while I'm here inside the gates' dimension? Would it cause everything to explode? Best not to-*

Allistor's inner ramblings were cut off as the *Phoenix* reentered normal space. He gripped the chair next to him, the sudden transition throwing him off balance for a moment. He remembered the story of the first Arkhon who went into the gate and never returned, experiencing a surge of heartfelt sympathy for that poor soul. A notification popped up in his interface.

Spell Level Up! Your Dimensional Manipulation spell has increased by +1!
Sometimes having the wisdom to know when not *to use a spell is as valuable as practice.*

"Well, I guess that answers that question." Allistor mumbled to himself.

"What question?" Daigath's elven hearing had picked up the quiet comment.

"When we were in the void, or whatever it is, I was thinking about dimensional magic, and considering casting the *Dimensional Manipulation* spell to see what would happen. I decided not to, and when we came out, I picked up a spell level."

Harmon and Daigath both looked horrified. Before either could speak, he held up his hands. "Don't worry, I've learned that lesson on my own. No using dimensional magic inside weird dimensions."

"Not just that." Harmon let out a long exhale. "I keep forgetting how little you and your people know. We should have warned you, but this is one of those basic laws of the universe that everyone learns as a child. Never use magic of any kind while transitioning between gates. It will almost certainly destroy you and the ship around you, possibly the gates themselves."

"Well, shit." Allistor's palms became clammy as he considered how many of his people had just come with him through the gates. Twice. If he had considered casting a spell, how many others had as well? "Nigel, new rule. On every ship that is about to go through a gate, make an announcement reminding people not to use magic during the transition, and why. Every trip. No exceptions." He gave his two alien allies a look that clearly said that would have been good information to have earlier. Harmon looked slightly embarrassed, while Daigath just shrugged.

Kira, slightly shaken by what she'd just heard, cleared her throat. "Since you didn't kill us all on the way here, where to next, boss?"

Allistor had planned to visit the other planet he'd just inherited from Loki. But with all the issues that had arisen during the last several hours, he considered returning to Earth first. As he thought it through, he realized he couldn't accomplish anything more by being physically on Earth than he could from where he was. "How long is the flight to the other new planet?"

Kira punched a few buttons on her holo display, which she had called up immediately upon returning to normal space. A representation of their new home solar system showed the dual suns with the planets orbiting around them. There was a green globe indicating Earth, a blue globe for Orion right next to the golden indicator that denoted *Phoenix*'s position. Both planets were near the inner boundary of what Earth scientists referred to as the Goldilocks zone, the area of space that wasn't too close, nor too far from the suns to support life. The new planet was marked in red, and was placed nearer the outside of the habitable zone.

"A few hours at top speed." Kira reported. "Much faster if we go FTL."

"Let's take the slow route." Allistor decided. "I need some time to think, and to send some messages, before we take on whatever problems that planet will represent."

"You got it boss. The scenic route it is. This is so cool! Just casually cruising through a new solar system, no big deal." Kira grinned at him.

He returned the smile, happy to see her so happy. Her first year after the apocalypse had been pretty hard on her and her family. Now she and her kids were living a life of comfort and adventure, and Kira was living a pilot's dream, driving a spaceship.

"I'll be in my quarters if you need me. Give me a heads up maybe... fifteen minutes before we arrive." Allistor patted Kira on the shoulder as he turned to leave the bridge.

*****

The first thing Allistor did when he reached the owner's suite on the *Phoenix* was pull an emerald from his inventory as he sat in one of the ridiculously comfortable chairs. He wanted to test out his improved *Dimensional Manipulation* spell before he forgot. He spent a little time pondering the dimension within the gates and how time seemed to drag. Then he thought about how time must be completely inert within the storage devices, making it possible for items to be perfectly preserved. He wondered if it was even possible to completely stop time. He whispered to himself, "Maybe I'm not actually stopping time within that void, maybe I'm just slowing it? Like a hot cheeseburger stored in there might actually cool off if I left it there for a thousand years?" he took a deep breath and stared at the emerald as he followed that train of thought. "Or maybe the void is somehow just outside the flow of time? Like an air bubble in an ocean, time just flowing around the outside of it like water? That makes more sense than a weak mortal like me having the power to somehow stop a force as powerful and inevitable as time."

He focused his will on the emerald and cast the spell. A moment later he was pleased to see that he was now able to match the number of slots to the emerald's max capacity, which was fifty! A far cry from his first attempt, which had netted him a single storage slot in a similar stone. Practicing the spell on his own, combined with coaching from Master Daigath, had significantly improved his results.

Putting away the gem, he pulled out his pad and pencil and began to make a list of things he had to address. The first that sprang to mind was that he needed to publish a set of laws, a sort of Constitution like the former United States had had, for the citizens of all of his worlds. Several disturbing thoughts had come to him regarding Skapa Far's citizens. For example, he suspected that some of the former slaves, those who were not bound by the oath, might decide to exact retribution against their owners in violent ways. Or that angry former owners might do the same. He hadn't specifically stated that murder was illegal, and those who hadn't been bound by the oath might take advantage of an open loophole. So for that reason and many others, laying down the law, so to speak, was going to need to be a priority. He'd ask his alien advisors to help, as there had to be situations outside of human experience that would require specific solutions.

Next on his list was his space fleet. He had what he considered a large number of ships now. The problem was, he didn't have the crews to man them. Many of his citizens had volunteered as crew, human and non-human alike. The beastkin and dwarves especially had significantly more experience than the humans, most of whom had never been to space. With that many ships, he needed to train, or hire, several thousand crewmembers. Prime had told him that his battle droids were capable of operating ships, so he could technically field the fleet with them at the helm, but he wasn't comfortable with that. The same with having the ship's AIs at the controls. He wanted live crew with the instincts and intuition of living souls. As intelligent as Nigel was, he still felt that the human or alien brain were better. Again, this was a high priority, as he now had four planets to defend, two of which had no allied presence on them as yet. He felt relatively confident that Earth and Orion were safe, for now, due to the mutual defense agreements that were in place. But the other two were still ripe for the picking, so to speak.

Though they were already somewhere on an older list, which he had misplaced, he added his dungeon cores next. With millions of new citizens, and hopefully millions more humans becoming citizens shortly, he needed ways to help them level up as quickly as possible. There was a limit to how many fetch or harvesting quests he could give people before he drained his available experience pools. It was best to use those points to bring low level citizens up to at least level ten so that they could select a class and use it to develop more effectively. Those first few levels were cheap experience point-wise. He mentally chastised himself for not inquiring as to whether Skapa Far had any dungeons. Hopefully some naturally occurring dungeons would be discovered on Earth and the other planets as well. He'd need to act quickly to seize control of them and manage access.

The seed, which Allistor still couldn't successfully *Examine*, so he was calling the turbobaby seed in his mind, was next. He'd already made arrangements with Daigath to work on planting the seed, but it didn't hurt to include it on the list. Restoring the human population had been high among his priorities from day one. Right now his non-human citizens outnumbered his humans by something like three hundred to one. If you added in the non-citizen alien residents of his worlds, including aliens that had colonized Earth before he took control, that ratio only worsened.

Though it was a much lower priority, he wrote a note about improving his personal crafting, combat, and spell skills. He was nearing level one hundred, but his abilities were lagging back at where they'd been when he was level fortyish, in most cases. This wasn't his fault, it was simply due to the massive jumps in level he'd received recently. Even the extended fight with the undead hadn't yielded many increases, as his targets were mainly lower levels than he was.

The next item was a simple note to follow up with Cogwalker on their progress regarding the changeling assassin. Last he'd spoken with the dwarf, they had confirmed the scent of the changeling on board the *Phoenix*, though only in the cargo bay. And they had not been able to track it anywhere in either the parking garage, the tower roof, or the tower teleport pad. The snorg crews were going to expand their search, and Allistor hadn't checked in with them since. He assumed that the dwarves would reach out if they found anything, but it couldn't hurt to inquire. He had added the words *recruit the rest of humanity* on his list, then sidetracked himself by flipping to another page and beginning to compose his worldwide announcement, when the ship shuddered and an alarm started blaring.

"Nigel! What's happening?" he called out, already on his feet and headed toward the door.

"*The ship has been attacked, Sire. Sensors are reporting two enemy ships, the same configuration as the one that crashed into Invictus City's wall.*"

"The lizardmen?" Allistor was now dashing into the elevator that would take him down to the main deck and the bridge. The ship rocked again, more violently this time, sending him careening into the elevator to slam his forehead into the back wall. The doors closed behind him as Nigel sent the car down. Allistor shook his head and touched his fingers to his forehead to check for blood, finding none. He was a lot harder to damage these days. The doors opened and he sprinted the short distance down the corridor to the bridge. He arrived just as tactical was reporting, "Shields are holding!"

Kira shouted, "Weapons! Knock them down already!"

The young man at the weapons station was hunched forward over his controls, shaking his head as his fingers flew over the hologram keys. "I've already scored several direct hits, but their shields are holding too!"

Harmon, standing right behind Kira, spoke calmly to her. "Come about so you can use the main railgun. It will likely penetrate weakened shields. Focus all weapons fire on a single spot on one ship, then follow up with the railgun."

Kira began to bring the ship around. "You heard him! Focus fire!"

A moment later Allistor saw one of the triangular-shaped ships come into view on the main screen as *Phoenix* came about. Both enemy ships had approached from behind, and one of them had adjusted to remain aft of *Phoenix*. Every weapon on her hull targeted the more damaged ship in front of them, and the entire bridge crew cheered as the talon ship's shield turned red, then collapsed. A moment later *Phoenix* shuddered slightly as her main railgun sent a meter-long projectile forward at blinding speed to slam into the enemy ship's hull. The heavy round's momentum took it deep into the talon ship where it caused something to explode. Several interior sections of the ship were suddenly exposed to the vacuum of space before the explosion ripped the ship in half.

Already forgetting the crippled ship, Kira began maneuvering the *Phoenix* to get a better shot at the remaining talon ship. The pilot of that ship was not cooperating, keeping the talon at their rear, firing into her as quickly as they could. Allistor watched as all the weapons emplacements that could rotate backward began firing on the pursuing talon, tracking it even as the two ships spun and rolled in space. The enemy shield flared repeatedly, but held.

Kira was cursing under her breath as she did her best to outwit the other pilot. Harmon was speaking into his communicator, probably summoning more ships from his Orion station. If they used FTL, they might be able to join the fight quickly enough to make a difference. Assuming the *Phoenix* shields held up long enough. Allistor watched the display for ten seconds or so, noting how the enemy ship mimicked each move Kira made, a fraction of a second after she made it, in order to remain behind them. A flashback to his high school days hit him, and he had an idea. "Kira! Pick and roll!"

"What?!" She glanced at him briefly before returning her focus to the controls. "What the hell is that?"

"They copy every move you make, right? Head toward the dead ship! Pass right next to it, and the second you're past it, turn hard right behind it. If they follow your move like they have been-"

"They slam right into it!" Kira finished for him, a wicked grin appearing on her face. "And if they don't, they shoot on past, and I can get behind them. Right on!" She adjusted course even as their shields took another hit.

The tactical officer called out "Shields at seventy percent!"

Allistor gripped the back of Kira's chair so hard the material squeaked a bit as he watched the wounded ship come into view dead ahead. Kira increased their speed, flying directly toward it. The explosion had truly ripped the larger ship apart, its front third barely attached to the rest by one corner. The flames from the explosion had died in the vacuum of space, the area around the ship littered with floating debris and bodies that left a trail behind it. Instead of passing to one side of the ship, at the last moment Kira nudged the *Phoenix* downward, passing below the ruined hull. Then she jerked it upward, gritting her teeth as the ship bashed its way through debris to pass between the two sections of the broken ship. Cursing as she bumped slightly against the rear section, she continued the loop, pushing the *Phoenix* up and over backward until it came around to their previous position facing the dead Talon.

The pursuing ship hadn't been able to follow, and had instead passed underneath its companion ship, then began a turn. As it came around, it was face to face with an already firing *Phoenix*. Every weapon blasted at the nose of the talon, even as it fired back. This time the weapons officer didn't wait for the shield to collapse before firing the main railgun. The moment the shield turned red, he loosed the kinetic projectile. It covered the distance between the closing ships faster than the eye could register, and burst what little remained of the weakened shield on its way through. This time it hit the nose of the talon, taking out half of its bridge on its way through. The crew that weren't killed by the impact were sucked out into space. Kira spun to one side as, lacking any commands otherwise, the talon ship continued to race toward them. Kira moved out of its way, allowing it to crash into the other talon. Both ships spun away, broken, crumpled, and dead.

"Whew." The tactical officer reported in a shaky voice. "Our shield was down to five percent. A couple more hits from them, and..."

"Don't say it." Kira warned. "How long until the shield is back up to full?"

A quick check of the tactical console, and the answer came. "Two minutes. Damn, that's fast." the crewman whistled.

Harmon chuckled. "Without the drain of incoming fire, the shield can restore itself quickly. The ship will prioritize repairs to any damaged shield generation components."

Kira called out to her daughter. "Sensors, any sign of more of them?"

Brooke answered, "None. But then, I wasn't able to detect those two until they were right on us."

"If there were more, we'd already know." Harmon reassured them. "They would have attacked as soon as the first talon was disabled. And they certainly would not allow us time to recharge our shield."

Taking a couple deep breaths, Allistor tried to calm himself. His pulse was racing, adrenaline rushing through his bloodstream, making his pulse pound in his ears. While Kira called for a damage report, he focused on the viewscreen and the two ships floating in space. "Why are the lizardmen attacking us? And how would they know to find us here?"

Neither Daigath nor Harmon offered any explanations.

"Could it be coincidence? I mean, the attack on Earth was obviously intentional, but maybe these two were just out here for unrelated reasons and we stumbled into them?"

Master Daigath shook his head. "The odds of that are... unlikely in the extreme."

Harmon shrugged. "I have only suspicions. It seems likely that the lizardmen, or their employer if they are acting as mercenaries here, are interested in your new planet. The attack on your city could have been an attempt to distract you while their main force conquers this planet." He waved at a secondary viewscreen that showed the planet they were approaching. "Or it may have been an attempt to eliminate you directly, thus voiding your claim over this planet."

As they approached the planet's orbit, Allistor could make out a large space station. It appeared to be several times the size of the one he'd just installed above Earth. "Is this one of the stations I got from Loki?"

Harmon nodded, punching up some information on his wrist unit. "It is. The station is actually the main habitation center for this world. The planet's surface is sparsely populated, being a mostly agricultural world. The station serves as marketplace and shipping hub for the crops grown down below, and is run by a consortium of Tinkers."

"Tinkers?" Helen asked. "Are they what they sound like? They fix broken stuff and invent crazy gizmos?"

Harmon chuckled. "That is as good a description as any. Tinker is a class, as well as a calling, and a species. Most are born with an affinity for mechanical skills. There are, of course, exceptions. There are mages, administrators, and others who fill the necessary support positions. But the vast majority spend their time crafting… what did you call them? Gizmos?"

"I'm guessing that's why the station looks like it does? They've been adding on to it?" Instead of the smooth, sleek lines and curves of his own station, this one was boxy, the exterior hull a patchwork of different colors and shapes that looked to have been welded together one section at a time."

Daigath smiled at the object on the viewscreen. "I once visited the Tinker homeworld. There were four such stations in orbit around it, and they had grown so large as to seem like moons rather than stations. One could walk for days within the corridors of a single station and never set foot in the same hall twice."

Allistor noticed the smile. "You like them."

"They are… an acquired taste, but yes. I have grown fond of them. Several have come to visit me over the centuries, wishing to learn to shape wood properly.

They are inquisitive and enthusiastic, and for the most part harmless. They would much rather craft and learn than conquer." He paused, coughing slightly as he grinned to himself. "And the weapons they create often backfire or explode, making them more dangerous to themselves than to their foes. One of those I agreed to teach nearly burned down my home tree testing out a new rocket boots design. It took a week to regrow his feet and repair his cracked skull."

In short order the *Phoenix* had docked in what the station controllers referred to as their VIP bay, and Allistor led his company down the ramp from her cargo bay. They were greeted by a crowd of small humanoids that Allistor assumed were the tinkers. Taller than gnomes, but shorter than dwarves, they had short arms and legs attached to bodies that were longer than normal human proportions. Each wore a variety of tool belts and bandoliers, some decorated with shiny badges that Allistor guessed were marks of rank. The one that stepped forward and bowed to him had silver epaulettes on his shoulders and bright white hair.

"Greetings, Emperor Allistor! Welcome to Rumikol Station! It is an honor to meet the hero who slew Loki and freed us from his rule!" The crowd of tinkers that had now surrounded Allistor's group cheered and raised fists into the air. Allistor was reminded of a scene from an old holovid of The Wizard of Oz. He had a fleeting thought about asking to meet the head of the Lollipop Guild, but dismissed it with a private smile. The leader of the tinkers took the smile as a good sign. "I am Master

Tinker Megaspindle." He bowed again. "Come, we have prepared a feast in your honor." He waved a hand and the crowd parted, creating a path toward the exit door.

As Allistor walked next to Megaspindle, there was a high-pitched scream behind them. As Allistor spun, already drawing his sword, the crowd around them gasped or mumbled. Allistor scanned the area, quickly finding a single tinker writhing on the ground, curled up in a fetal position at Helen's feet. Helen looked down at the little fellow, her eyes blazing. "What happened?" Allistor scanned the crowd, but none of them seemed hostile. In fact several seemed quite amused.

"This tinker snuck up behind me and grabbed my ass. So I kicked him in his little tinkerballs."

Chapter Six

What's In the Box...?

As Helen passed Allistor on her way to the exit, he watched several of the tinkers help their comrade to his feet. One cast a heal on him, while some pointed and laughed, and a few quietly asked him what Helen's rear end felt like, casting admiring glances at her as she walked away. Trying not to smile at their antics, he turned and followed Helen and Megaspindle to a large meeting hall. Down the center was a long table piled high with food and drink, low benches along each side. Luckily for Allistor and company, a second table had been set perpendicular to the first at one end, forming a sort of T shape. At this table the tinkers had placed chairs of a more appropriate size for their guests. All but Harmon, anyway. But the orcanin casually removed a comfortable looking stool from his inventory that was both wide and strong enough to support him, and low enough that his legs fit under the table without banging his knees. His feet stuck out beyond the table's other edge, but everyone pretended not to notice.

The room was abuzz with conversation as they were served a delicious meal of meat that tasted like pork, a variety of colorful and tasty vegetables, warm bread, and a light, sweet fruit juice. Daigath carefully scanned Allistor's meal before nodding to him that it was safe to consume. Allistor left his gloves on as he ate, keeping in mind L'olwyn's warnings about leaving DNA where strangers could get to it. Megaspindle proudly informed them that everything on the table was a product from the planet below, including the ceramic plates and lightweight metal utensils that were basically sporks.

"So there are mines on the planet as well as farms?" Allistor spoke around a mouthful of meat.

"Mines, farms, ranches that raise livestock, forests from which we harvest wood and herbs, several small cities and towns, even a couple of dungeons. Though we rarely make use of those. Mostly we collect the fees that Loki charges... charged others for entry into the dungeon. And provided burial for those who requested it, also at a hefty fee."

"Burial?" Helen asked in a polite tone. A full belly had improved her disposition toward tinkers in general.

"It doesn't happen often, but occasionally a party will emerge from one of the dungeons carrying their dead. Rather than transport them home in dimensional storage devices, or pay to ship them as cargo, they arrange with us to have them buried in the nearby cemetery. Their families, should they wish to, can then come and claim the remains at their leisure."

"What can you tell us about the dungeons?" Allistor was tempted to rush to the surface and try one himself.

"I have never entered them myself. One is an aquatic dungeon, meaning it is filled with aquatic species, and several of the levels are actually underwater. The other is an elemental dungeon with just three floors – water, earth, and fire. I'm told that one's core is nearly ready to expand and add another element, but I do not know how accurate that information is."

"Only three floors, that would make it a relatively new dungeon?" Harmon asked.

"Possibly. It was discovered a few years ago by our miners as they extended a side shaft. It may be that the dungeon is old, but has been isolated, and therefore had no visitors to kill and absorb." Megaspindle shrugged, clearly not caring either way. "Even after it was discovered and made available to dungeon delvers, it has not exactly been popular. And it has only killed a few entrants that I'm aware of. It is currently rated for levels ten to twenty."

"So a starter dungeon. Nice." Allistor was pleased. "We can bring low level citizens here and run them through for experience."

"And what fee will you be charging?" Megaspindle tried to act casual, but Allistor saw his lips press together and his hands press harder on the table.

"Well, for citizens of Invictus, there will be no charge. For outsiders, I don't know. I have no experience with renting out dungeon time. And from the sounds of it, not a lot of folks are scrambling to get into them anyway."

The tinker's leader paused for a moment, looking down at his hands, carefully placing them in his lap. "And what will you be charging for citizenship?"

Allistor paused, his forkful of meat halfway to his mouth. Setting it down gently on the plate, he shook his head. "I guess I should have covered that right away." He looked down the length of the long table, where every tinker had stopped talking and was now listening intently.

Rather than get up and tower over his hosts, he remained in his seat and spoke loud enough for those at the opposite end of the room to hear. "All I require from you in order to become citizens of Invictus is to swear an oath, and support your fellow citizens. It's a simple oath, one I don't think you'll find offensive. You agree not to harm each other, or me, and to contribute in some way to the greater good. In return you receive all the benefits of citizenship." He spent another couple minutes outlining all the amenities, responsibilities, and rewards of being citizens. Then a bit longer to explain that should they choose not to become citizens they could leave in peace with their belongings.

When he was done speaking, the buzz resumed as all those at the table began to discuss their options. Allistor looked to Harmon, who was sitting on the other side of Daigath to his right, and asked, "Can I claim the planet from here, or do we need to travel down to its surface?"

"Since the planet has been administered from here, you should be able to assert your claim from here as well."

While his diminutive hosts discussed their options, Allistor opened up his interface and Empire tab. He located the blinking notification about the space station and planet below, and confirmed that he wished to claim both.

System Alert!

Emperor Allistor of Invictus, after taking the life of Loki the Ancient One,
has claimed the title of Emperor of Aegrin! May he rule long and wisely.

The moment the alert appeared, the room went silent. All eyes went to Allistor, but he didn't find the hostility he had half expected. Some looked curious, others simply looked resigned, as if thinking *meet the new boss, same as the old boss.* Or maybe *same shit, different day.*

Megaspindle stood and bowed again, more deeply this time, until his head was lower than his toolbelt. "We thank you for the generous offer you have made us, Emperor Allistor. If you would extend a further kindness, we would request a little time to discuss this amongst our brethren. Decisions such as this should be voted on by the entire clan."

Allistor responded to the bow with a slight nod. "Would a day be sufficient?"

"More than sufficient." The tinker looked slightly uncomfortable, as if concerned about offending Allistor, but after a moment he added, "Might we know the wording of this oath?"

Allistor motioned toward Helen, who stood up to recite the oath. The moment she did, applause broke out, along with some whistles and other appreciative sounds. After a brief scowl at the lecherous tinkers, she spoke the words of the oath, then sat down.

Megaspindle blinked a few times, staring at Helen, then at Allistor. "That is all?"

"That is all. I suppose we could add more if you feel it necessary…"

The tinker clan leader held up both hands and patted the air in Allistor's direction. "No, no. I am just surprised. That is… never mind. We must still put it to a vote, but I believe I can assure you that we will want to become… Invictusans? Invictusites?"

"Citizens of Invictus." Allistor chuckled. "Are there inhabitants here in the station or on the surface that are not of your clan?"

"There are." Megaspindle looked uncomfortable. "There were many more before Loki's demise. Those that were in charge here simply perished, along with some of their servants. Others quickly fled, taking all the ships docked here at the station, regardless of who owned them. About a third of those who are not clan to us are slaves, owned by miners, ranchers, and merchants, mostly." Seeing the dark look that appeared on Allistor's face, he quickly added, "None of the clan own slaves. It is against our laws. And under Loki, though we were technically contracted employees, we ourselves were little better than slaves."

Allistor quickly installed Nigel, then spoke to the tinkers. "I'm going to make an announcement to everyone within range of Nigel, the new station and planet AI. I will depend on you to get the word out to everyone else on the surface as quickly as possible. Can you do that?"

114

"It would be our pleasure, Emperor Allistor." This time every tinker in the room stood and bowed to him.

He had Nigel activate loudspeaker, and gave a speech nearly identical to the one he'd given on Skapa Far earlier. He informed the slaves that they were free, explained to them the benefits of citizenship, reassured them about housing and food for the near future, and potential employment, all of it. When he made the cutting motion to Nigel to indicate that he was through, the tinkers were silent.

Allistor broke the silence by addressing Megaspindle. "Discuss what you need to among your people, and get the word out to the others as quickly as you can. I'll return tomorrow or the next day to hear what you've decided. If you choose to leave rather than take the oath, we will arrange some type of transportation. Though that may take a little while." He paused, looking down at his plate. "Thank you for the delicious meal, and for your hospitality."

When he got to his feet, so did everyone else in the room. His entourage followed him as he exited the room and retraced their steps back to the *Phoenix*.

*****

Allistor instructed Kira to take the slow way home, in case there were more talon ships lurking in the area. He'd rather have them attack his ship than the station and its inhabitants. He mentally berated himself for not asking if the tinkers knew anything about the talon ships.

Since he had a few hours, and his mind was much too occupied to sleep, he decided to craft something. The ship's engineering deck had a well-appointed crafting section, and he had decided to make an enchanted weapon for William. A quick check of his inventory showed that he wasn't carrying any metal, but he remembered that there was some in *Phoenix*'s massive dimensional storage down in the cargo bay. He took his time walking down there, greeting crewmembers and raiders that he encountered along the way, even stopping a few times to chat with folks he recognized, and be introduced to a few he didn't.

When he reached the cargo bay there were just a few raiders scattered here and there who had hung hammocks to rest in. A couple waved silently to acknowledge him, while others were already snoring. It initially struck Allistor as strange that the hammocks didn't sway, until he realized that *Phoenix* was in space, not on the ocean.

Stepping over to the corner where he thought the storage compartment containing the metal was located, he looked around, confused. He knew there were dimensional storage compartments, but had no idea what they looked like. After a moment, he shrugged. "Uh, Kira?"

"Yeah, boss. What's up? No, we're not there yet." He rolled his eyes, picturing the grin on her face.

"I'm trying to find the storage thingies in the cargo bay. Do you know where they are?"

"You mean the dimensional storage? Sure. We did a complete inventory check a few weeks back. Uhm, hold on, I'll send Hillary down to show you."

"Thanks." Allistor sat on a crate, feeling silly. He should know his own ship better. And it hadn't even occurred to him to check and see what goodies might have been in the storage when Harmon first delivered the ship. The only reason he knew there were metal ingots in there was because he'd asked Michael to have his people put some in. For that matter, he wasn't even sure his instructions had been carried out, because he'd never checked. His smithy atop the tower had been stocked with all the metal he'd needed up to that point.

Hillary appeared a minute or so later, having probably run the entire way. She flashed Allistor a bright smile, which he returned. "The storage cabinets are right over here." She moved to an interior wall of the cargo bay, not far from where Allistor had thought they'd be, and touched a section of the wall with a finger. Now that they'd been pointed out, he could see what looked like a set of cabinet doors on each of the three sections. "Here, here, and here." She pointed out the others as well. Then she unfocused her eyes and concentrated for a moment. "Mom said you'd want a copy of the full inventory, including what's in the crates here in the cargo bay, so here you go!"

A notification told him that she'd shared the inventory of all three storage devices with him, and he opened it just long enough to see that it was a very, very long list. Waving it away, he smiled at her again. "Thank you, and thank your mom for me. I can take it from here.

Better get back to your coms station in case we get any important phone calls."

Her eyes widened briefly before she realized he was teasing her. With a snort and a look that reminded Allistor of his little sister when she was younger and tugged at his heart, she bolted away.

Allistor retrieved the ingots he wanted and returned to the crafting section. It was a wide open space with several work benches, racks and cabinets of tools, and in one corner a futuristic looking forge. He didn't know what the heat source was – there was no visible fuel or flame – but it got hot quickly, and he was soon pulling glowing steel from it to begin hammering out a short sword for William. Though with his attribute increases the boy was now stronger than nearly any human had been before their world ended, he was still short of stature. Allistor wanted him to have a weapon designed and balanced for his current build. As he grew bigger, the squire could convert the short sword to an off-hand weapon and wield a longer, adult proportioned weapon in his main hand.

He had finished shaping the sword, and sharpened it, and was contemplating what enchantment would be best to add to the blade when Kira announced that they would be arriving at Invictus City soon. Allistor placed the blade in his storage and took a few moments to clean up the work area before heading down to the cargo bay. Most of the others had gathered there by the time he arrived, ready to depart the ship.

Still thinking about the enchantment of William's weapon, Allistor wandered back over to the storage cabinets. His personal supply of gems was dwindling quickly, so he decided to see what the ship's stores held. He placed his hand on the leftmost cabinet, a different one than he'd pulled the steel from earlier, and mentally pulled up the cabinet's inventory to search for diamonds or other gems that held enchantments well. He was trying to figure out if there was some kind of keyword search function that would allow him to avoid scrolling through the slots, when the description entry for the most recent item deposited caught his attention. Curious, he read it, then read it again, blinking a few times. "It can't be... can it?"

Suddenly cautious, he called out, "Nigel, please have Cogwalker meet me here the moment we land. Tell him to bring his people. All of his people."

Having heard the tone of his voice, several of his raiders hurried over, hands on their weapon hilts or spells at the ready. McCoy asked, "Problem, boss?"

"I'm... not sure." Allistor had taken a couple steps back from the storage cabinet, staring at it like it might bite him. From where he stood, it looked like a standard eight foot by three foot wall section. Which is probably what it had been before someone modified it to become dimensional storage. The others, not aware of what the cabinet actually was, were wondering what could possibly be there that would make their level ninety eight boss nervous.

"Is it... a bomb, or something?" McCoy asked, leaning in toward the wall slightly, and sniffing the air as if he could detect something with his weak human olfactory abilities. "Is that why you called for the dogs?"

"Something like that." Allistor didn't want to voice his suspicion in case he was wrong.

The ship touched down a moment later, Kira having rerouted them to the tower roof at Nigel's direction, to meet with Cogwalker more quickly. The dwarf and two of his snorg crews rushed into the cargo bay as soon as the ramp was lowered.

"Emperor Allistor! Ye called fer us?" Cogwalker pushed through the gathered raiders, who made way for him and his canines.

"Thanks for coming so quickly." Allistor nodded his head toward the wall. "That's a dimensional storage device. Nigel, authorize Cogwalker to access that storage. Cogwalker, take a look at the most recent item deposited. Is that what I think it might be?"

Confused, the dwarf stepped forward to touch the indicated cabinet. A moment later his look of confusion turned to one of surprise. He backed away from the cabinet and turned toward his crews. "Weapons ready." He looked up at the raiders. "All of ye. Form a perimeter." He turned back to Allistor. "Aye, I think ye may be right. It would explain a lot."

McCoy cleared his throat, standing next to Allistor with his sword now drawn. "Boss, what's goin on? Is something about to jump out of there at us?"

"Not jump out, but about to be pulled out. And more like a some*one*." He took a breath, drawing his own sword and preparing to cast *Mind Spike*. "I think the changeling that killed Amanda is in there. The last item deposited is listed as *unknown biological*."

A ruckus broke out behind him as the raiders and dwarves reacted to his statement. The raiders pressed forward, forming a tighter ring around him, eager for some payback.

Cogwalker raised his hands to get their attention. "Easy now. I believe that be the changeling in there, sure enough. But all of ye know that nothin' livin' survives in the void. We're takin precautions in case changelings somehow be an exception to this, but I'm thinkin if it were alive, it woulda emerged and escaped by now."

The dwarf turned to Allistor, raising one eyebrow. "Do ye want to pull it out, or shall I?"

By this time Helen, Harmon, and Daigath had joined them in the cargo bay. The giant orcanin volunteered, "I'd be happy to remove it for you, my friend."

Allistor shook his head. "No. If that thing is in there, and still alive, I'm going to kill it. All of you back up. Nobody interferes unless it's about to kill me." He took a ragged breath, his emotions running high. Exhaling, he added, "This is for Amanda."

He stepped forward, placing his hand on the surface of the wall. He took another deep breath, then willed the unknown biological item to be withdrawn. Instantly he felt a great weight in his hand, which was tugged downward. He lowered the item in his hand to the floor and let go, stepping back and raising his sword. A moment later, he lowered it again.

Laying on the floor in front of him was what appeared to be a life-sized statue of a dwarf. It was extremely lifelike, down to individual whiskers of its beard, eyes open wide and a mouth that appeared to be screaming. It held a dagger in one hand, and its other was clenched into a fist. Around its waist was a toolbelt much like the one Cogwalker habitually wore.

Cogwalker was first to speak. "That be him. It. Whatever. It still be in the form o' me clansman that it killed and replaced." He stepped forward and nudged the hardened form with a steel-toed boot, not gently. "It be dead, sure enough. Guess that answers the question about whether changelings can live in the void." He chuckled to himself, kicking the petrified changeling a bit harder, impact making a satisfying thunk. "This be what happens to 'em when they die. I've seen it meself once before."

Allistor felt a huge weight lift from his shoulders, while at the same time he felt disappointment at not being able to take retribution on the creature that had killed Amanda. His shoulders slumped as he sheathed his sword.

Daigath stepped forward and placed a hand on the statue's chest. His hand glowed green briefly before he pulled it away and stood. "It is indeed deceased."

Cogwalker bent and lifted the statue by the shoulders, standing it upright on its feet. The legs were bent and the feet turned, so it couldn't stand on its own. Holding it steady, he pointed toward the lounge area on the roof outside the cargo bay. "This'd make ye an impressive trophy, Emperor Allistor. We could build a proper base for ye, have it set up in an hour, if I could borrow yer forge for a bit."

Allistor was disgusted by the thought of keeping the creature around, especially atop the home he'd shared with Amanda. He was about to tell them to take the *Phoenix* up a few miles and toss it out, when Harmon spoke again.

"My friend, I see your feelings written plainly upon your face. But do not be so quick to destroy this thing. Master Cogwalker is correct in that it would make a good trophy, though he used the wrong word. Items such as this can be totems. As an emperor, displaying artifacts and totems, symbols of your victories or achievements, can have a palpable impact. Though you did not slay it yourself, displaying the petrified form of a changeling that took a loved one from you would make for a powerful display."

Allistor stared at Harmon for a moment, then at Daigath, who nodded once in agreement. The dwarves were all nodding along as well, a few of them quite enthusiastically, while the two snorgs sniffed curiously at the statue.

Daigath, seeing that Allistor was still unconvinced, offered more. "This is one action that you may take that will gain you respect and reputation with most factions, and cost you very little. Not to mention the morale boost among your own people, and the potential benefit to the city."

Allistor was still battling his emotions when Helen decided to give him some time. "I don't understand what happened. If everyone knows that nothing living can survive inside our storage devices…?"

Cogwalker waved at the cabinet. "That looks like just a standard cabinet. Me guess is that the changeling, after setting off the explosions on the station, snuck onto this ship hopin' to ride it down to the planet and escape. This would have looked like an easy place to hide. And it was likely already inside the cabinet, and therefore placed into dimensional storage, before it realized the danger."

"Really? This badass assassin that everyone has been so nervous about just… hopped into a box and killed itself? That seems… stupid." She crossed her arms in disgust and scowled at the statue.

Cogwalker and most of the others chuckled at her statement. The laughter died down when Daigath mused aloud, "I'm afraid you may be wrong about one thing, Master Cogwalker." He waited until the dwarf turned to him, eyebrows raised in question. "We do not in fact know that being placed into the void storage is what killed this

124

creature. It is possible that it survived in there, unaware of the passage of time, until Loki and Hell perished. If it was bound to one of them, or their minions, that might have caused its demise."

The dwarf considered it for a moment, then shook his head. "Aye, that be possible, fer certain." His face broke into a wide grin. "We'll just have to test it next time we kill one o' these beasties!" The dwarves behind him became enthused at the idea as well. "They're not easy to kill, these changelings. Ye gotta chop 'em into wee bits, burn, or otherwise destroy 'em. If we can just drop 'em whole into void storage and pull out a lovely statue like this one here, that'd be right handy! And we could charge our clients extra for the..." he paused and smiled sheepishly at Harmon, "totem."

Allistor, having had a few moments to gather himself, nodded at the dwarf. "Alright, do what you need to. You're welcome to use my forge, or the one here on the ship. But I don't want it up here. We'll find someplace else to put it."

Cogwalker bowed before barking a command. Three of the dwarves grabbed hold of the statue and whisked it off the ship, moving to the forge in one corner of the roof. The others all departed down the ramp and headed for the elevators as Kira lifted the *Phoenix* away from the roof and flew toward the parking garage.

As Allistor watched the ship move away, he remembered something and muttered to himself. "Shit. I forgot to look for more diamonds. Nigel, please ask Kira to grab some diamonds from the ship storage on her way back here. Thanks."

Not wanting to hang around and observe the dwarves at work on the statue, he decided William's weapon could wait. He followed the others toward the elevators and made for his analyst's floor in the tower. He had a lot of new items to cover with them.

Chapter Seven

A Bear's Gotta Bear

Allistor rounded up Helen, Fuzzy, and Fiona, as well as his kids, and led them all to Master Daigath's clearing the next morning. It was time to plant the seed that Baldur had given him for delaying his revenge against Loki. He also invited Nancy, Ramon, and Chloe, Sirina from the Factory stronghold, all of his advisors and Stronghold leaders, Harmon, the Or'Dralon elves, and former Secretary of State Marschner, who now ran what remained of the U.S. government.

The ancient elf greeted them all with warm smiles as he was introduced to those he had not met, obviously looking forward to planting a new tree. Though he had lived longer than most beings, he had never encountered this particular tree. In fact, he shared a suspicion with Allistor.

"I have never heard of such a tree, and due to its described properties, I do not believe it is natural. In my opinion, this is a unique creation of either Baldur's or Odin's magic, designed specifically to aid in your species' recovery."

Allistor shook his head. "I don't even know what it's called. When I try to *Examine* it, I just get question marks."

Daigath held out his hand, and Allistor obligingly placed the seed in his palm. The elf stared at the seed for a moment, then read the description.

> **Seed of Revivification**
> **Item Quality: Unique, Legendary**
> *The Revivification Tree grown from this seed will bear fruit of great benefit to humanity. Women who ingest the fruit shall become more fertile, and their gestation period will be accelerated to three months. Children born of the fruit will develop at twice the standard human rate from birth to physical maturity, at which point their growth and aging will slow to human norms. This tree will produce one seed every one thousand years.*

Allistor had briefly tried to do the math when he'd first received the seed, and found he wasn't up to it. Women could give birth three times as fast, that math was easy. But with their children maturing in half the time, and those children presumably being able to give birth just as quickly as their mothers… Allistor decided to just be happy with the potential population explosion. With four worlds under his control, and the potential for people to migrate out into the galaxy, there was plenty of room for humanity to expand.   And with the growth magic Nancy and the druids had available, for both crops and livestock, there would be no shortage of food.

"Thank you for reading that, Master Daigath. Shall we plant it? Is there something special we need to do?"

Daigath waved a hand to indicate the center of the clearing. "Simply make a small hole, place the seed in it, and cover it. The earth here is fertile, the mana dense, and we shall give the seed some of our magic to help it along."

Allistor did as he was told, walking to the center of the clearing. Fuzzy walked with him, obligingly using one massive paw to dig a hole for the seed. When Allistor had placed it very gently into the soil and covered it over, they walked together to join the gathered crowd.

Daigath then smiled at Nancy, one eyebrow raised. She beamed back at him and stepped forward, as did he, along with Sirina, Chloe, all the Or'Dralon elves and several of Invictus' druids. Together they each cast whatever form of growth magic they possessed onto the newly planted seed. The earth glowed briefly in shades of green, yellow, brown, and gold before the spells were absorbed and their light faded.

Allistor held his breath, waiting to see a seedling sprout from the loose soil. A moment later he let it out, only to gasp in surprise and wonder.

A seedling did appear after a moment, but didn't remain a seedling. With its inherent magic, combined with the nature magic imbued into it by a few dozen druids and elves, the Revivification Tree grew at an astounding pace. The crowd watched, murmuring, and in some cases crying, as the seed grew to a beautiful twelve foot tall tree. It's trunk was thick, easily two feet in diameter, with a smooth amber surface. It sprouted a wide canopy of branches that hung low to the ground as well as reaching upward toward the suns, all of them sprouting beautiful golden-hued leaves. The entire tree glowed faintly in the light of the twin suns.

Nancy got down on her knees and hugged Chloe tightly, both of them with tears in their eyes, Sirina standing next to them with one hand over her mouth. Lady Melise cried openly as she stood with several of her clan. All of the druids and nature mages who participated received a notification.

> **You have received: Blessing of Revivification!**
> *For bestowing life and growth upon the Revivification Tree, it has in turn bestowed its blessing upon you. +3 Will Power; +10% to growth spells.*

Fuzzy ambled over to sniff at the new tree, and being Fuzzy, promptly lifted a leg and watered the trunk. Chloe made a disgusted face as most of the adults laughed. "Ew, Fuzzy! Gross!"

Daigath gave Fuzzy's head a good scratching as the bear returned to the crowd. "Now that the tree has been properly blessed, let us leave it to grow on its own for a bit." This got a few more chuckles from the crowd as Fuzzy raised his head and grunted with pride.

Chloe looked up at the elf. "How long before the fruit grows?"

Daigath looked at the tree again for a long moment before reconsidering his previous estimate, and answering. "I would think a month, no more."

"Thank you, Master Daigath, for agreeing to watch over the tree. It couldn't have a better guardian." Allistor bowed his head to his mentor.

"Speaking of guardians, Allistor, I would like to propose something."

Allistor waved at the departing crowd, all but Helen, Fuzzy, and Fiona heading back toward Wilderness Stronghold and the teleport pad. "What is it?"

"I have ranged widely through this forest, as well as the forest near your Factory Stronghold, and the one inhabited by the Or'Dralon. Nowhere have I seen any sign of woodkin, nor have the trees I spoke to had any memory of them."

"Woodkin?" Helen asked, intrigued. Her background as a ranger had involved extensive study of trees, which she quite enjoyed.

"Woodkin are beings evolved from the most ancient of the tree species. They are sentient, and they wander the forests fostering growth while protecting the forests from hostile intruders. They come in different forms. Some resemble giant trees with trunks for legs and branches for arms. Others are more humanoid, such as dryads, who bind their souls to a single tree and protect the area around it."

Helen nodded. "We have similar creatures in our myths and stories. One of our greatest storytellers called the big ones Ents. And dryads appear in some of our earliest legends, along with nyads, selkies, sirens, satyrs, and such. But I don't think there's ever been any evidence found of real ones."

"While I do not recognize all of those names, the woodkin are certainly real. As are satyrs, assuming you refer to the horned creatures with hooves for feet and humanoid torsos, arms, and heads." He waited for a moment as Helen and Allistor both nodded, then continued. "Woodkin in particular are vital to the health of a forest. I am sad to say that the forests on your world have been badly neglected, if not outright abused or destroyed. Your people have not treated them well. Which I'm sure contributed to the System's judgement of you as a contaminant."

Allistor bristled slightly, having to remind himself that Daigath was in no way responsible for the near genocide of the humans on Earth.

"With your permission, I would like to travel to my world, and a few others, to attempt to recruit some woodkin and other guardians to serve here on Earth."

Allistor didn't need to think it over. For one thing, he trusted the old elf completely. And the idea of having storybook creatures like these wandering his forests appealed to him. "Absolutely, Master Daigath. Do you need anything from me to assist in the effort?"

"A ship, the largest you have, and permission to use the Orion gate."

"Of course you have permission to use the gate, anytime you want." Allistor paused as a slight tingle told him he'd just made a System-recognized agreement. "But what's the ship for?"

"Many woodkin dislike traveling by teleport. They will be more willing to follow if we can accommodate them on a ship. And as some of the larger ones are quite tall…"

"You need a large ship. Of course. It may take a few days to arrange a crew. I'm afraid I don't know which of my ships would best suit your needs, or whether it has a crew yet."

"There is no rush, Allistor. A few days, a week, will make no difference. When your ship is ready, I will go." He looked over his shoulder at the new golden tree. "I believe that just the chance to meet this one will entice many of them to make the trip. That, and the idea of an entire world with no woodkin guardians."

Allistor produced his note pad and scribbled a reminder for himself to arrange a ship and crew for Daigath and the woodkin. When he was done, he asked, "Master, I'm nearly level one hundred now. I'd like to learn some more powerful *Battlemage* spells, if you have time?"

"Certainly! We have been lagging behind in your training, as you have been understandably preoccupied. Let us address that right now."

Helen and the bears went to more closely examine the new tree while Daigath and Allistor worked to catch his class abilities up with his new levels. The old elf took it slow, not wanting to overload Allistor's primitive human brain.

First, he imbued the knowledge of a spell called *Battle Dome*, a shield spell that was a much-improved version of *Barrier*, which Allistor had leveled quite a bit during battles. The spell allowed Allistor to create a strong barrier in the shape of a dome with a radius of ten feet from his location. At higher levels the dome would get both larger and sturdier, providing more protection. At very high levels, the dome could act as camouflage, or even a curtain of invisibility.

Next came a much more powerful variation of his *Storm* spell. Instead of lightning and wind, *Meteor Storm* dropped balls of molten stone in a one hundred foot wide area. Unlike *Storm*, this channeled spell would do damage to friend and foe alike. The longer Allistor pumped mana into the spell, the more meteors would fall. Higher levels would bring larger more deadly meteorites, and widen the area of effect.

Allistor received a spell called *Transport*, a close cousin to *Dimensional Step*. This one allowed him to teleport everything within ten feet of him that wasn't tied down in some way, like trees or buildings. People, supplies, anything moveable within the effective radius would be transferred. The range was limited at level one, maxed out at half a mile. As he leveled the spell that would increase, as would the area of effect.

After imparting the knowledge of those spells, Daigath took a step back. "Rest a moment, young man.

Those three were the easy ones, as they were all similar to spells you already possess. This next one will be more challenging."

Already feeling a slight headache, Allistor happily obliged. Crossing his legs, he sat in the grass and produced a pair of water bottles, offering one to Daigath. The two of them sat in silence as they drank. After several minutes, the elf leaned forward. "Remain seated for this one, I think." was all he said before placing his hand on Allistor's head again.

The pressure in his brain increased quickly as Allistor learned a skill rather than a spell. *Kinetic Thrust* was a melee skill that allowed a *Battlemage* to jab a sword, spear, or blunt one-handed weapon at a target with extreme velocity. Smaller weapons such as daggers or even stones could be launched through the air. The skill provided sufficient force to drive a dagger blade hilt-deep into stone. It drained both mana and *Stamina*, and was meant to be a one-shot kill against a single normal foe, or a finishing move against a stronger opponent. Using the skill would leave Allistor feeling drained and unsteady afterward, making it unwise to use it in the middle of larger fights.

"This skill may save your life in the event of an assassination attempt. Assuming you survive an initial stealth attack." Daigath explained. "It would be a good idea if you practiced keeping your *Barrier* spell active at your back at all times."

Allistor was about to say something about the changeling being dead, when he realized that as an

Emperor, he was likely to be the target of more attacks. "Thank you, Master Daigath, that is good advice."

"One more spell. This one is tied to dimensional, light, and elemental magic. It is normally taught at around level fifty, and your actual skill levels are slightly below that at the moment. But I believe you'll be able to comprehend it." Daigath waited for Allistor to nod his agreement before once again placing a hand on his head.

Allistor began to sweat after ten seconds. At twenty seconds he was gritting his teeth to keep from screaming. When it was over, he lay back in the grass, panting.

Banish was a complex spell that first incapacitated an enemy, then sent them off to the void. The spell's actual form varied depending on its target. An undead, for example, would be encased in a bubble of painful light magic before being banished to the void. A being that favored the fire element would be encased in ice. The spell would determine what magic or element the target was most susceptible to, and use that to incapacitate it. Then the dimensional aspect of the spell would remove the target from Allistor's presence. It was an expensive spell, costing roughly a third of his total mana pool at ten thousand mana, and taking three seconds to cast.

Daigath warned, "Do not cast this spell if you are under attack and at risk of being interrupted. The backlash from having this spell interrupted during casting might hurl you into the void instead of the target. Or best case, incapacitate you for as long as a minute."

"Got it. Thank you, Master Daigath, for all of the training." Allistor bowed at the waist, wanting to show his heartfelt respect.

"You are most welcome, Allistor. Practice these spells, as well as your others, and when your skill levels have increased significantly, I will provide more."

*****

Back at the tower, Allistor sat in his customary spot in the lobby lounge area. His people were taking the opportunity to stop by to ask him questions, request favors, or simply congratulate him on recent accomplishments. Though he still had a long list of important items to handle, it felt good to relax and spend time with the very people he had been fighting so hard for.

He was smiling to himself as he watched through the lobby windows while Fuzzy romped around the courtyard. Ramon had created a two-foot tall paper golem, and was using it to play tag with the bear, much to the delight of a dozen children. The golem was surprisingly agile, able to dodge and leap over swipes of the massive bear paws Fuzzy aimed at it. Not that he was trying very hard to kill it. His bear cub made exaggerated leaps and mighty growls as he pounced and rolled, pretending to be afraid when the golem leapt on his belly and attacked. Allistor laughed aloud at his half-ton monster of a yearling that behaved like a puppy.

Ramon had just sent the kids into the fray, though it wasn't clear whose side they were on, when Allistor heard L'olwyn clear his throat nearby. He turned to face his elven advisor, still smiling.

"My apologies, Allistor." The elf bowed his head. "It is time for you to return to Aegrin and speak with the tinkers."

"Right." Allistor got to his feet. He was pretty sure the tinkers were going to join him, but he didn't want to negatively impact their opinion of him by not showing up when he told them he would. "How are we doing on a ship for Master Daigath?"

"One of your carriers will be ready tomorrow. Its hangar bays should be large enough to accommodate the woodkin comfortably. Gralen is arranging a full crew of experienced beastkin and dwarves, with some human trainees to fill out the roster. Prime is sending along a hundred battle droids to protect the crew in case there is trouble."

Allistor began walking out of the lobby and down the street toward the parking garage where the *Phoenix* waited. "Great! I'm excited to meet these woodkin." He paused for a moment as L'olwyn called out, jogging up behind them. When they started walking again, he asked, "Anything urgent we need to cover?"

"We have hired an additional six analysts, and plan to continue interviews until we find about the same number again. Most of these will be dedicated to analyzing and monitoring the various factions that have shown up in recent reputation change notifications. We have also employed and deployed nearly a hundred intelligence operatives. So far, there have been no imminent threats detected. Though a significant number of factions and more than one Emperor now view you with extreme disfavor, they appear to be occupied with scheming and fighting over the crumbs left behind by Loki and Hel."

"Have you been able to determine why the lizardmen are attacking us?"

"Not yet, Allistor. The xylon are a secretive and xenophobic species, not trusting of anyone who isn't one of them. We have been unable to infiltrate their ranks, and none of the factions we *have* infiltrated so far have given any indication of having hired them."

"Any chance we could get a meeting with… do they have an emperor? A king? Whatever they call their big boss, can we meet with them and try to work out whatever their issue is?"

L'olwyn grimaced for a moment. "That is… unlikely. But we shall make an attempt to reach out. I recommend doing so via a hired third party. There is a good chance any emissary who approaches them will be killed."

"I don't want to purposely send an innocent to their death." Allistor began to cancel that plan.

"There are those willing to risk their lives for a significant reward, Sire. Any emissary we send will be aware of the risks, and will assume them without hesitation."

"Alright, let's try it." Allistor couldn't be responsible for the lives of every being everywhere. And if they were successful, it might solve one of his most urgent issues. "Will we have an escort today?"

"The *Opportunity* and one of your new battle cruisers are already in orbit waiting to escort you to Aegrin. Which brings up an inquiry I must pass along to you. The battle cruiser is manned mainly by Stardrifter clan members. They have asked if they might be allowed to become citizens of Invictus…"

Allistor opened his mouth to say that of course they were welcome, but the elf held up a hand to stop him. "But they also wish to remain members of the Stardrifter clan at the same time."

Allistor closed his mouth and considered the request as they covered the last block to the parking garage. As they approached the elevator, he asked, "I assume they all took some sort of oath to the clan. Is there any danger to them in swearing our oath as well?"

"Only should the interests of the Stardrifter clan and Invictus contradict each other in a significant manner."

"I can't imagine we'd find ourselves at war with Stardrifter anytime soon, but I suppose anything is possible. In which case, I might have an entire crew, and the space cruiser they control, switch sides to fight against me."

"That is unlikely, Allistor." L'olwyn shook his head. "They might refuse to participate on your behalf, and remove themselves from the conflict. But taking an active role against you in violation of their oath would likely result in the System ending their lives."

"Then it's alright with me. But before we accept, let me speak to Cogwalker. I don't want him to think that we're attempting to steal his people."

"Cogwalker is the leader of those who wish to join you." L'olwyn actually smiled at Allistor.

"Ha! Okay, well then I suppose the answer is yes. We'll allow dual citizenship for any Stardrifters who want it. How many are there?"

"Approximately two hundred. The majority of those who remained on the station. Including many of the griblins. I believe they wish to prove that they were not involved in the attacks against you."

"Please let them know that I don't hold that against them. They were as much victims as we were. The same for the dwarves, and any other races among the Stardrifters that were involved."

They boarded the *Phoenix* and made their way toward the bridge as L'olwyn suggested, "It might be better if they heard that from you directly."

Reaching the bridge, the first thing Allistor noticed was that neither Harmon nor Daigath were there. Feeling slightly insecure without his two most experienced advisors, Allistor felt a small knot form in his gut. Doing his best to ignore it, he asked, "Kira can the *Phoenix* dock with the cruiser that's going to escort us?"

Looking up from her captain's chair, her eyes widened. "I… don't know? I would assume so, but it's not something I've tried." She looked around at her human crew. They were her most experienced, but they were all still relative noobs.

Nigel's voice echoed through the bridge. *"There are three standard docking bays with which Phoenix could safely connect to the cruiser, which currently has no name. I am thoroughly familiar with the protocols, and can guide you through the maneuver, Captain Kira."*

"Thank you, Nigel." Kira grinned up at the ceiling, then at Allistor. "Yep, we can dock."

Doing his best not to roll his eyes, Allistor said, "Alright, please contact the cruiser's captain and let them know we want to dock when we reach orbit. Have them gather the crew someplace big enough to fit everyone, so that I can speak to them."

Kira simply nodded, then gave her daughter a significant look. Hillary was already turning toward her coms station to relay the message.

It only took a few minutes for *Phoenix* to leave Earth's atmosphere and rendezvous with the other two ships. Nigel coached Kira as she positioned the ship above the hull of the cruiser, using the docking ring underneath *Phoenix*'s cargo bay to secure the two ships. Allistor, Helen, and L'olwyn made their way down, and found an open hatch with a platform in its center. Rather than a ladder, the platform served as a lift that lowered the trio down through the short corridor that extended between ships.

When it stopped moving, they were standing in a wide corridor inside the cruiser. Cogwalker bowed in greeting as they stepped off. "Welcome to your new cruiser, Emperor Allistor. The crew is gathered in the main mess, which is right this way." He motioned down the corridor behind him.

"Thank you, Master Cogwalker." Allistor began to walk, and motioned for the dwarf to walk beside him. "L'olwyn has informed me that you and some of your clan wish to join Invictus. While I'd be happy to have you, are you sure that it won't cause an issue with the clan?"

"Aye, I'm sure. Already cleared it with the clan elders before we submitted our request. We won't be abandonin' the clan, after all. They see it as I do, a way to strengthen our bond with an ally."

"In that case, you're more than welcome to join us." Allistor started to reach out for a handshake, only to retract his hand as L'olwyn cleared his throat behind them. The dwarf just grinned in understanding.

After a short walk through the surprisingly large ship, they reached the mess hall. Inside was a series of tables with benches laid out cafeteria style, with a buffet line at one end, behind which was a serving window that led into the galley. Most of the tables were filled with Stardrifter clan, with a few humans scattered here and there. All of them rose to their feet the moment Allistor stepped through the door, and bowed their heads.

"Please, take your seats." Allistor asked them, still uncomfortable with the protocols that came with his titles. "I won't keep you long." He waited for them to settle. "First, I want to thank all of you for the excellent work you've done in delivering and setting up our orbital station. It's beautiful, and I was quite impressed." He watched as many of them smiled or nodded.

"Next, I want to assure you that you bear no responsibility for the attack that killed both my people and yours aboard the station. We know the explosions were planned and executed by a changeling, and we have recovered its body. I have no doubt as to the integrity and loyalty of any Stardrifter clan member here." There were many more smiles now, and some muted cheers among the crew.

"In fact, I am extremely pleased to grant your request, and welcome those of you who wish to become citizens of Invictus!" He opened his arms wide to encompass the entire crew, though he wasn't sure all of them wanted to join. The cheering was louder now, and crewmen patted each other on the back.

"Those who wish to join us, please stand. Helen will administer the oath, and we'll get underway."

All but the humans in the room, who were already citizens, stood and repeated the oath as Helen recited it. The familiar glow engulfed them all. As soon as it was over, Cogwalker began barking orders, and the crew scrambled out of the mess to their stations.

*****

The trip to Aegrin was uneventful this time, no talon ships waiting for them. When *Phoenix* set down in the landing bay, Megaspindle and what must have been every tinker on the station were waiting for them.

"Welcome back, Emperor Allistor!" the lead tinker and all of his people bowed deeply as Allistor stepped off the cargo ramp. "I am pleased to announce that we have decided to become citizens of Invictus, if you will still have us."

Allistor noticed that the tinker seemed slightly nervous as he spoke. Immediately a twinge of suspicion struck him. A quick glance at Helen showed that she had detected it as well.

"Has something changed since I was here last?"

"We… tried to stop them." Megaspindle let out a ragged breath. "We warned them that you would not stand for it! But they would not listen, and we… we are not warriors, your Emperorness." The tinker's shoulders slumped and his lowered his head, gazing down at his navel. "There was nothing we could do."

"Do about what? Or whom?" Helen prompted the tinker to elaborate.

"Hours after you departed, three xylon colony ships arrived. They descended to the planet on the far side, out of range of our limited weapons systems here on the station. Their pack leader sent a message informing us that Aegrin was now under their protection, as ordered by you. We did not believe them, as we are aware you destroyed a pair of their vessels yesterday. But there was nothing we could do. We are no match for a xylon pack."

"Why did I not get a notification from the System if my planet has been invaded?" Allistor asked nobody in particular, fervently wishing that Harmon or Daigath were with him. They'd know the answer. Instead, Megaspindle offered a suggestion.

"Possibly because they claimed to be 'protectors' acting in your name?"

"I made no protection agreement with any xylon pack, or anyone else, for that matter." The moment Allistor said the words, a notification popped up on his interface.

Planetary Alert! Aegrin has been attacked!
Defend your territory!
Reward: Variable

Allistor sighed as the tinkers looked on. He and Helen, as well as all the crew aboard *Phoenix*, had received the notification. But the tinkers, not being citizens yet, had seen nothing.

"There it is." Allistor looked up at the ceiling. "Nigel, message Invictus. Tell them I need every available raider on a ship and on the way here ASAP to repel a xylon invasion."

"*Immediately, Sire. Shall I message your allies, as well?*"

Allistor thought about it for a moment. "Sure. Invite anyone who feels like earning some experience. The ones we fought on Earth were decently high leveled." While he was thinking about it, he looked at the tinkers. "If you still want to swear your oaths, do so now."

Megaspindle bobbed his head, and Helen proceeded to administer the oath to all those present. The moment the expected glow had suffused all of the tinkers, Allistor opened his interface and shared the quest with them. He watched as their eyes unfocused briefly, then they began to smile. Immediately there was a wave of excitement.

"Arm the weapons systems!" Megaspindle shouted. Turning to Allistor, he was fairly vibrating with excitement. "We have never been in a battle before! None would dare attack a world controlled by Lord Loki. If you can scare the xylon off the surface, we will clobber any ship that comes within range!" He pumped a tiny fist into the air with enthusiasm. "We will not let you down!"

Allistor smiled down at him. "I believe you will. But be careful. I have at least one more ship coming, and I wouldn't want you to shoot them down by accident. Only fire on xylon talon ships. Or whatever those colony ships were."

"Death to the evil xylon invaders!" Megaspindle shouted. The cry was taken up by the few dozen tinkers that hadn't yet departed. "Death to the xylon!"

Chapter Eight

Here Leezard Leezard...

It took a couple of hours to assemble the various forces and get them to Aegrin, even with the ships using their FTL drives. When they arrived, Allistor's defense force consisted of two more of Allistor's ships filled with nearly five hundred human, gnome, minotaur, beastkin, and dwarven raiders, Harmon's flagship with two hundred orcanin, two Or'Dralon ships with an unknown number of elves led by Lady Melise, and the cruiser filled with the newly recruited Stardrifter clan members. In addition to the station full of tinkers, and the twenty raiders that Allistor had with him aboard *Phoenix*.

All of the ships docked at the station, and the various leaders met Allistor in the mess hall. Harmon was the first to arrive, a wide grin showing off his massive, sharpened tusks. "Another opportunity to battle the xylon so soon? You do keep life interesting, Allistor."

Allistor was not nearly as enthused. He'd lost some good people in his last land battle with the lizardmen. "Thank you for coming. I don't know how many of them there are, but one ship was almost too much for us last time, and now there are three."

"I have already sent reconnaissance drones to help answer that question." Harmon tapped his wrist device. "We should have reports in a few minutes."

"Speaking of drones, I guess we'll need another planetary defense system here. Can you arrange for that?"

"I can." Harmon nodded, smiling. "It will take fewer satellites, as this world is only about two thirds the size of Earth, so the cost will be lower. We can have it installed within the week." He paused, looking at Megaspindle and Cogwalker. "I would recommend upgrading both the weapons and shields on this station, as well." Both the engineer and the tinker seemed excited by that prospect.

"Let's do that." Allistor agreed. He was going to ask about the cost, something he rarely did with Harmon, when the orcanin's wrist unit chimed. A moment later he had it projecting a holo-display of the surface below them.

"The drones have located the xylon's landing site." Harmon made a motion with two fingers, and the display zoomed in on a location at the base of a mountain, part of a larger range that ran along the shore of an ocean. Parked among the jagged rocks at the foot of the mountain were three large ships. They were larger than the talon ships Allistor had already faced, at least twice their size. "Colony ships." Harmon grunted. "Looks like they're planning to stay."

"Is this why they attacked us?" Allistor stared at the hologram. In the area near the ships he could see a significant number of lizardmen moving around. Some were unloading supplies, others appeared to be digging holes with heavy equipment. "They planned to eliminate me and take the planet for themselves? Is there even anything down there worth taking?" He looked to Megaspindle for an answer.

The tinker shook his head. "As I said before, there are some mines, farms, forests, a few cities, the usual resources found on any planet. There are the two dungeons as well, but they are nothing outstanding."

Harmon scratched the back of his head with one claw, thinking. "It may be the planet in its entirety that they're after, rather than one aspect, like the dungeons. Their leader likely has ambitions, but would never have attacked a planet that Loki controlled. It would be a death sentence for them, and potentially their entire species if Loki was feeling punitive."

Allistor caught on, and finished the thought for him. "But a weak new Emperor of a nearly extinct species that no one has heard of, might be easy pickings."

"If they moved fast enough, and didn't have good intelligence on you, they might have hoped for an easy gain." Harmon confirmed.

"And if ye don't mind me pointin' out the obvious, Emperor Allistor, they won't be the last to try."

Allistor considered his position for a long moment. "It's a small planet, compared to Earth, but there's still plenty of room down there. Are they likely to listen if I ask for a truce and try to talk to them?"

Cogwalker was already shaking his head in the negative as Harmon answered. "That would depend on who is leading them. The xylon are an aggressive species,

151

and they've already attacked you more than once, meaning you've killed a few hundred of their people, even if it was in self-defense. But I suppose anything is possible."

"So my choices are to try and make peace with them, which may not work..."

Cogwalker interrupted him, saying, "If ye reach out and they reject ye, it'll make ye look weak. Also, if ye simply forgive their attacks against ye and make peace, it'll make ye look weak to certain factions."

Frowning, Allistor repeated himself. "So I can try to make peace and possibly look weaker to my potential enemies out there, or I can... wipe them out? A brutal response to their attacks to make myself look like a harder target?"

"Aye, that pretty much sums it up." Cogwalker nodded, along with Megaspindle. Harmon just watched Allistor with a neutral expression.

Helen spoke up from behind him. "As the tinker said, no one would have dared to attack this place when Loki was in charge. His reputation let them live in peace in safety, without any kind of defense satellites, fleet of ships, or large army in place. You have already started to earn a reputation as the scrappy little human who killed both Loki and Hel. Maybe that's your most effective tool, for now."

"Become the tyrant I killed to defend what I hold?" Allistor growled, not liking the idea at all.

This time Harmon did speak up. "You don't have to be a tyrant to defend what's yours. You treat your people better than most leaders, my friend. You have given much of yourself to protect those under your care, and they love you for it. You've also earned a reputation as one who does not hesitate to fight, and to kill ruthlessly, when it was called for. I believe it would be a mistake to step away from that image now that your responsibilities have grown. As Master Cogwalker has said, you might be painting a larger target on your back."

Allistor's gut knotted up again, and his last meal threatened to expel itself. Not over the idea of killing a group of xylon who attacked him. It wasn't his first choice, but he could do what was needed. What was bothering him was the question of how many more times he'd have to make decisions like this. Was his life from now on going to be a never-ending series of choices between distasteful options? How many of his people would he sacrifice in the name of defending the others?

Taking a deep breath, Allistor pointed at the middle of the three ships. "This one is larger than the other two. Would this be their flagship?" When Cogwalker nodded, he continued. "Here's what we are going to do. We'll leave two ships here to defend the station. The rest will come with me to this location. Cogwalker, you'll use our new cruiser to destroy that center ship. No warning, just kill it from orbit if you can. Or from as far away as possible." He paused to look at Helen and Harmon.

"Then we'll give them a chance to talk. If they surrender, I'll consider granting them some space on the planet. If they're good fighters, they might make good allies." His face turned grim. "But if they continue to fight, we wipe them out. No mercy."

*****

Allistor watched from the bridge of the Phoenix as Cogwalker's cruiser fired several of its weapons all at once. His gaze switched from the side monitor that showed the cruiser in orbit next to them, to the main viewscreen that was focused on the xylon ships down on the surface. They had detected Allistor's fleet as it moved into position above them, and the lizardmen crews had scrambled to board their ships. All three of them had just begun to lift off when Cogwalker fired. A few seconds later the center ship, which he hoped was the xylon flagship, practically disintegrated. Fiery bits of it rained down upon the landing site, killing more than a few of the xylon still on the ground. The two remaining ships continued to gain altitude as Allistor nodded to coms, who began to transmit.

"This is Emperor Allistor. Your people have attacked me, repeatedly, and attempted to colonize this planet without invitation or permission. Stand down, and we can discuss your reasons for such actions. Stand down, or we will destroy your remaining ships, and all those you left on the surface. You have two minutes to comply."

He watched the viewscreen, his teeth clenched and his grip tight on the back of Kira's chair, as the two xylon ships continued to rise. They were well within his own ships' weapons range, so he assumed they could have been firing themselves if that was their intent. Each second seemed to drag as they all watched, fingers on the triggers, so to speak.

After more than a minute, Hillary reported, "We have an incoming message."

Kira nodded for her to put it up on the screen. The face of a xylon appeared, with several more standing behind it. This one looked different than the pack leader Allistor had seen on Earth. It had reddish scales and a bright red plume running from its forehead back along its skull like a mohawk.

"I am Brood Daughter Grinzla. I will speak with you." The half dozen lizardmen behind her bared their teeth and growled while raising weapons, but went silent when she turned and hissed at them.

"Have your other ship land, and your ship can follow us to the space station." Allistor instructed. "We can speak face to face. Do I have your word you will not attack?"

"I said I will speak. My word is given." The brood daughter's reptilian features managed to look offended before the transmission cut off. Almost immediately the second xylon ship began to descent back to the surface.

"Cogwalker, you come with us. The rest of you remain here and guard the xylon. Watch for more incoming ships, in case this isn't all of them." Allistor motioned for Kira to follow the xylon ship back to the space station, which she did, while Cogwalker's cruiser took up position slightly behind and to the other side of the alien ship. As they traveled back around to the space station, Harmon gave him some background. "A brood daughter is a respected member of xylon society, high in their societal ranking. They are a matriarchal society, with their queen ruling over the entire species. Below the queen is their horde leader, a male who functions as warlord or general, and is the queen's mate. Below him are the brood mothers, or what you might think of as princesses. They command anywhere from a single pack to several hundred. Next come the brood daughters, who will mature to become brood mothers in their own right, should they survive the infighting long enough. And then there are the pack leaders, males who lead units of their fighting forces. You've already met one of those."

Once the xylon ship and Phoenix were docked in the landing bay, Allistor and company departed and joined the crowd of tinkers and battle droids waiting outside the alien ship. Almost immediately after he arrived, the ramp at the rear of the ship lowered, and Grinzla strode down, three lizardmen striding behind her as an honor guard. When she was within three paces of Allistor, she stopped, and the plume atop her head went flat against her skull.

"I have come as instructed, Emperor Allistor. We will talk."

Allistor considered inviting her to a conference room where they could sit. He was slightly uncomfortable, staring up at this alien who was a good two feet taller than him. But he decided the landing bay was good enough. Motioning to the Megaspindle, he whispered quick instructions. The tinker waved several others over, and they pushed three cargo crates over. They stacked one atop another, and left the third in front of that pair. Allistor turned his back to the lizard people and used the first crate as a step, hopping up to sit atop the other two. Now he was slightly taller than Grinzla, and seated while she stood. Harmon grunted his approval.

"Grinzla, the pack that attacked my capital city, and the two talon ships that attacked me near this planet, were they yours?"

"Not mine. My Brood Mother's packs. She was on the ship you just destroyed."

"Why did she attack us?"

"You are responsible for the deaths of many of our people." The xylon was extremely succinct and direct. Allistor found he sort of liked it. He had a sneaking suspicion he knew how he was responsible for the deaths she described, but had to ask anyway.

"In what way am I responsible. Until your pack attacked me, I had never even heard of your species."

She tilted her head to one side, much like a dog who'd just heard an interesting sound. "Are you not the slayer of the Ancient One, Loki?"

"I am." Allistor sighed.

"Our home was a small moon in this system, awarded to Thrinza, my Brood Mother, as payment for mercenary services. Our packs squashed a rebellious faction on the world that moon orbits, fighting on Loki's behalf. We continued to provide soldiers to maintain his control on the planet." Her voice turned into a low growl. "When you slew Loki, what remained of that faction, along with its allies on the planet, attacked our moon. Nearly half of my people were killed before we managed to evacuate."

"And you thought this world would make a good replacement for your lost home." Allistor shook his head.

"It is not ideal for us. But Thrinza noted that this world had been awarded to you, the one who brought this fate upon us. She thought it fitting that we take our new home from you."

"There's a weird sort of logic to that, if you look at it a certain way." Helen mumbled unhelpfully beside him. He glared down at her, but she simply rolled her eyes.

Allistor addressed Grinzla again. "I killed Loki because he caused the deaths of billions of my people."

The brood daughter nodded respectfully. "We watched you take his head. It was an honorable killing, and justified. We raised a toast in your honor, and praised you for achieving vengeance. You were admired among our people, until your actions resulted in our own losses."

Now Allistor had a problem. He'd basically done to them exactly what Loki had done to humans, even if it had been unintentional. This was the type of consequence Daigath had attempted to warn him about. And now he couldn't bring himself to punish these xylon for doing exactly what he'd fought so hard to do to Loki. He had a brief urge to argue that mercenaries risked retaliation for their actions as a consequence of their own choices, but decided there was no point.

"I did not wish any harm upon your people. And though your attack killed some of my citizens, I do not wish you harm now. If I allow you to settle in the place you have chosen on this world, will you swear an oath and live in peace with us?"

"We are warriors. We do not live in peace." Grinzla's plume popped back up and seemed to throb in anger, or maybe pride.

"You could serve as my warriors. Fight my enemies. Or continue to serve as mercenaries when I don't need you. The oath does not require you to stop fighting, it simply prevents you from fighting *my* people. Here, listen." He motioned to Helen, who recited the oath.

Grinzla seemed surprised by its simplicity, as had most of the others who'd sworn it already. "If we fight for you, we would be paid?"

"You keep the loot from your kills, and I will provide quests with rewards." Allistor confirmed.

"And when we are not fighting?"

"What were you planning to do when you landed here?"

"We brought equipment for mining. There is good ore under the mountain there. We can refine it and use it to make weapons."

"Then that's what you'll do when you're not fighting. Or you can farm, or trade, or whatever you like. You can even sell the ore, or the weapons you craft, to the tinkers and merchants on the space station."

"Farming is for the weak or cowardly!" Grinzla growled. Allistor, having spent a summer working on a farm as a kid, disagreed. But he kept it to himself. "But trade is... acceptable." she finished.

"Then your people will take the oath and become citizens?"

Grinzla shook her head. "I must first confront my younger Brood Sister, who is on the other ship. If she accepts me as Brood Mother, or I kill her in combat, we will agree. If she is victorious, then you must speak with her."

Without waiting for a response, Grinzla turned and strode back toward her ship. Her escort parted to let her pass, then followed behind. In moments the ship was closed up and lifting off to exit the landing bay.

"Well, I guess that's settled." Helen chortled. "I like her. She's got style."

Allistor, hopping down from the makeshift crate throne, looked around at the others. "How long do you suppose we'll have to wait?"

Harmon snorted as they walked back toward the *Phoenix*. "xylon. They are often crude, but they are honest. Sometimes brutally so."

When they'd boarded the *Phoenix* again, Harmon asked to speak with Allistor in private. The two of them retired to his quarters to talk while they awaited the xylon decision. When they were both seated comfortably, Harmon began.

"I wanted to tell you that was well done." He gave Allistor a tusk-filled grin. "You asked intelligent questions when presented with the xylon problem, then acted quickly and decisively. You killed the entity directly responsible for the attacks on your citizens, and the invasion of your planet, using overwhelming force. And rather than simply eliminate the whole colony, you offered mercy, and may have converted a powerful enemy into an asset who can assist with your defense. Not to mention a potential trade partner."

Allistor gave a small shrug. "I got lucky, taking out the brood mother in that ship. I didn't even know there *was* such a thing as a brood mother until you told me after it was over."

Harmon held up a finger. "Ah, but you instinctively went for the flagship, assuming that whomever was in charge would be on it."

"I guess." Allistor wasn't convinced, but he'd take the win. "So you think all of this will be good for my reputation." It wasn't a question. Allistor was already very tired of everything he did having some larger impact on his relations with people he'd never met or might never meet.

"Like everything else, it will help you with some factions, and hurt you with others. Though there is little to find fault with in this instance. Only the most bloodthirsty, or those who have reason to hate the xylon, would have wanted to see you wipe them out completely. And, of course, there will always be those who want you to fail just because they've decided they don't like you. You'll continue to lose reputation with them anytime you are successful. Or anytime you're not. I believe Lady Meg called them... trolls?"

Allistor snorted. "Yeah, trolls. Wait, is that an actual species out here in the universe?" When Harmon looked confused, he added, "Big, hairy, nearly indestructible because they regenerate so quickly that even missing limbs regrow in a few hours."

The orcanin nodded. "Ugly, stupid, foul-smelling species, eats almost anything, afraid of fire? They are called skrex. Generally despised by every other species. They are often used as frontline fighters because of the damage they can absorb." Harmon made a disgusted face. "I fought one once as a youngling, some of its blood splashed on my armor. It smelled so bad I had to burn it, and it took a week of bathing before others would stand near me."

"That sounds about right." Allistor grinned, picturing a stinky young orcanin being shunned by his comrades.

Harmon got up and retrieved a bottle from the bar, along with a couple of glasses. Sitting back down and pouring, he said, "Now, let us discuss some business. I would like to purchase some space on each of your two new planets, as well as this space station, and the ones you have not yet visited..."

Allistor relaxed slightly and leaned back, sipping his drink and listening to his friend's words, a smile on his face. This was one battle where no innocents were likely to be hurt.

*****

As it turned out, it only took a few hours for Grinzla to return to the station. Once again as she stepped off of her ship, she was all business. "I am now Brood Mother Grinzla. I speak for all twenty packs and the thousand non-warriors of my brood." Allistor tried to remember how many lizardmen had been in the pack that attacked Invictus. He thought it might have been around a hundred, though he never saw how many perished inside the talon ship, or tried to retreat into the orcanin perimeter on the other side of the ship from him.

"And you wish to become citizens of Invictus?" Allistor smiled at her, being careful not to show any teeth. He'd read somewhere that flashing teeth at predators was considered a challenge.

"We will become citizens, and serve you, Emperor Allistor. Until we grow strong enough to challenge you." Grinzla flashed her teeth in what Allistor hoped was a smile. He couldn't tell if she was joking.

"Oh, I do like her!" Helen grinned at the reptilian as she stepped forward. "Let's go back to your people, and we'll administer the oath to everyone at once."

Grinzla bowed her head, then turned and walked back onto her ship. To Allistor's surprise, Helen followed along with her, disappearing from view as the much larger honor guard took up their positions behind the two females.

"She'll be fine." Harmon reassured Allistor.

This time there was no escort as the Phoenix followed the xylon ship back to the surface. The two ships assigned to monitor their landing site were still in orbit, and reported no issues. Kira took the ship down, landed not far from Grinzla's ship, and they all gathered in a clearing at the base of the mountain. Already the holes that were being dug before Allistor attacked were much deeper, and a few basic shelters were being constructed. At the center of the clearing a long spear with wicked barbs on both sides had been stuck into the ground. On the shaft just below the barbs sat the impaled head of a xylon.

Grinzla, noticing Allistor's inspection of the display, grunted. "My younger sister chose to challenge me for the right to rule the Brood." She grabbed the weapon, held up her arms and let out an impressive roar, spinning in a circle as her gaze took in all of the gathered xylon. An answering roar and stomping of feet from her people shook the ground. Allistor couldn't help but be impressed.

"Now you will talk to my children. Then they will take the oath." Grinzla's straightforward tone sounded more like an order than a request. He stood next to the newly crowned brood mother and spoke loudly to the few thousand gathered xylon. He told them of the benefits of citizenry, reassured them that they would be allowed to fight on a regular basis. When he mentioned that as citizens they would be allowed to run the dungeons free of charge, the roar of the crowd was nearly as enthusiastic as when they'd cheered for Grinzla.

When he was done talking, Grinzla turned and grabbed Helen by the shoulders, lifting her off her feet, stepping forward and placing her in front of Allistor. "Friend Helen will speak the oath. You will all repeat."

Keeping her demeanor calm, Helen recited the oath. A moment later the binding glow surrounded every member of Grinzla's brood. Allistor, who had been observing their camp while Helen was talking, turned to Grinzla.

"I would like to present you with a gift, in honor of your new position. A leader of warriors such as yourself should have a Stronghold. I can construct one for you, if you will accept it?"

Grinzla's eyes widened in obvious shock, and several of the males within earshot bared their teeth and growled. Confused, Allistor took a step back and put his hand on the hilt of his sword.

Behind him, Harmon spoke very quietly. "Among the xylon, a male who wishes to mate with a female presents her with gifts. A gift as large as a Stronghold suggests that you wish to become Grinzla's permanent mate."

Allistor coughed once as his cheeks reddened in embarrassment. "To be clear," he announced loudly, "this is a gift to you *and your people* from your Emperor."

The males calmed down as Grinzla's eyes narrowed slightly for a moment. Then she appeared to calm down, nodding once. "We accept your gift, as it was intended."

Allistor quickly pulled up his interface. Staring at the shelters they had begun to construct, he made the appropriate selections to turn them into a proper Stronghold. Based on the size and number of xylon present, and the possibility that more might be flying around in ships, he decided to go big. He selected half a dozen long buildings that could be used as barracks or warehouses for the mining operation, along with an inn with a tavern for when they had visitors. He created a huge common building with two large kitchens, meeting spaces, and large offices. The xylon were nearly as tall as orcanin, though not as bulky, and he figured they needed some space to stretch their legs.

"What type of housing do you prefer?" He asked Grinzla. When she gave him a questioning look, he added, "Do you prefer your homes above ground, or below? Smaller individual homes, or more like apartment buildings?" He placed a few blueprint mockups atop the grid that was laid out in front of them, pointing to each type as he listed them. She chose one large house for herself, apartments for the rest. Allistor obligingly set up enough buildings to house all the xylon he saw, plus half that number again. When he was done with that, he left some empty space for additional buildings, then put a wall around the whole thing, with a single gate facing toward the mountain, where he assumed any mining operation would take place.

After confirming that this was what Grinzla would like, he pressed the button to execute the construction. Allistor was a little disappointed that the lizard people weren't amazed by the Stronghold springing up from the ground, but he supposed that unlike humans, they'd seen it before. The last thing he did was include Grinzla and his inner circle in the permissions to make alterations to the Stronghold, and install Nigel as its AI.

"Thank you for this gift, Emperor Allistor." Grinzla bowed her head and held it there as every other xylon took a knee and bowed their own heads.

Allistor replied quickly. "You are most welcome. Congratulations on becoming Brood Mother, and welcome to Invictus!" He called out the last bit more loudly, so that all could hear him. Grinzla raised her head, and the others stood, then simply went about their business.

Obviously no longer needed, or probably wanted, Allistor boarded *Phoenix* with his people and quietly departed. The xylon could reach him through Nigel if he was needed, and vice versa. Though Allistor hadn't specified it, Nigel knew to install a communication array that would allow nearly instantaneous contact even from opposite sides of the solar system. But that thought led to a question.

"Nigel, can we communicate with Skapa Far from here? I mean, do we have to open the gate to send a signal?"

"Yes, and no, Sire. We could send standard burst signals directly at any time, and they would take several days to reach Skapa Far. Or we can use the gate network as relays. Being the owner of the nearest gate, you may send signals via micro-gates established for that purpose. They require much less power and can be left open at all times. Each gate mechanism features a thousand micro-gates, which you may choose to lease to others who wish to maintain communications with their own worlds. You might also trade access to micro-gates with the owners of other gates, like the one nearest Skapa Far"

"And if we use FTL on both sides of the gate, how quickly could *Phoenix* get from Earth to Skapa Far?"

Nigel took a whole two seconds to calculate. *"With Earth, Orion's gate, and Skapa Far in their current positions, it would take approximately forty minutes, assuming no delay at the gate, Sire."*

"And a big chunk of that is slowing to a crawl to transition through the gate. Thank you, Nigel." Allistor was impressed. Humanity had dreamed of faster than light travel, but had not come close to achieving it. The fact that he could now travel nearly halfway across the galaxy in less than an hour was hard to wrap his mind around.

The *Phoenix* made a quick stop at the tinker's station, where they left two cruiser class and two transport ships, and twenty raiders who wanted to check out the dungeons on the planet. Then Kira took them home, the rest of the fleet following behind.

Chapter Nine

Zombie Magnetism

Deep below Invictus City, a lone being walked through an old, abandoned subway tunnel, leaning heavily on a staff that oozed an oily black light so thick that it almost seemed liquid. Behind the staff-wielder shuffled thousands of undead in various stages of decomposition. Some were fresh bodies of humans who had survived the apocalypse, only to be brought down by an undead horde. Others had risen from graves dating back hundreds of years, called to service by the minions of a necromancer that had himself perished recently.

As the lone adept remaining after her master's demise, the staff-wielder had slowly gathered her master's wandering former minions together. Nowhere near the original size of the horde that had attacked the city above, her own gathered force was sufficient for her purposes. She would continue her master's work, achieve the goal that he set aside.

And her reward would be power.

She had absorbed the essence of the first several hundred undead she had encountered, including many of her former fellow adepts, using the staff their master had left behind. It acted as a battery of sorts, though she did not make that connection, having lost her first life long before batteries were invented. All she knew was that the staff would store great amounts of power, which she could use to grow stronger, to control more minions.

The undead moved slowly, and she had no trouble locating hundreds, then thousands, then tens of thousands of her master's minions, a small fraction of the million or more that were released to wander aimlessly around the former New York City. They seemed almost eager to answer her call, giving some purpose to their tortured existence. Though she did not have the power to directly command more than a few hundred at a time, the power she carried was a sort of beacon to the others, a reminder of the power of the adepts that had raised them from their graves and commanded them so recently.

And so, like an undead pied piper, she led them through the depths of the ruined city. Through steam tunnels and old rail tunnels she shuffled, and now found herself in the abandoned 66th street subway tunnel that ran under the lower end of what had been Central Park. More importantly, it ran under a section of the park that was now within the walls of Invictus City.

The moment she crossed under the walls above, she felt a pulse from her staff. An awareness had taken note of her presence. Though she didn't understand that the awareness was an artificial intelligence named Nigel, she instinctively knew that her discovery meant her time was short. Defenders would be coming. The same defenders that had slaughtered hundreds of thousands of her master's minions on the surface outside the city's walls.

Beckoning her few hundred controlled minions to follow as quickly as she could, she hustled forward down the tunnel, deeper into the city. She projected a longing, a need as deep as the soul she had surrendered to her master, toward the thousands of following minions that packed the tunnel, urging them to move with her. It was the best she could do. She had a job to complete, and time was growing short.

Stopping at a spot where the tunnel curved, she slammed the butt of the staff into the stone, pushing some of the stored power into the tunnel floor. She thought she could hear the stone itself wail in despair as it dissolved under her feet, and smiled at the sound as her body lowered itself into the widening pit.

Above her, the minions pushed inward, falling over the edge of the gaping hole, their bodies raining down around her. More and more pushed in from behind, increasing the rate of falling corpses. Their bodies were consumed as they hit bottom, their essence absorbed into the staff as the spell dissolved stone and flesh alike. As her power increased, the pull was felt more strongly by the shuffling minions in the tunnel, and they pushed harder to reach her. Across the surface of the ruined city, wandering undead minions she had not taken the time to gather up also felt the pull from as far away as several miles, and turned in her direction.

When she felt she was deep enough, she caused the burrowing spell to cease. Her senses registered a small natural cavern in the surrounding bedrock. Stepping toward one wall, she ignored the continuing rain of corpses, shrugging off a few impacts that struck her. The corpses that fell now remained intact, though bones shattered and flesh ruptured as they hit the cavern floor, or impacted their predecessors, creating a growing pile of undead.

The adept reached the side wall and put her back to it, taking a seat with the staff across her lap, watching in the faint purplish glow of the gem at its tip as the mound of corpses grew in front of her. A few near the edges managed to crawl away into the open spaces of the chamber, but it didn't matter. They wouldn't get far.

The adept began to chant, pulling the knowledge of the spell she wanted, the spell she had existed to bring to fruition, from the staff itself. As she spoke the wholly alien words, the staff brightened, pulling more power from the still-growing pile of undead minions. It was begun. She was near to fulfilling her destiny. Now there was only one question.

Could she complete the ritual before the living arrived to destroy her?

*****

Allistor was in the main cafeteria, sharing lunch with Helen, the kids, Sam, and Meg, when Nigel called out.

"Sire, the city is under attack! A large force of undead have passed under the walls near the north end of the city, underneath the park. More continue to enter. I count nearly ten thousand so far."

Allistor and every other citizen in the city received a notification offering them a quest to defend the city.

"Shit! I knew they'd be back." Meg grumbled, stuffing the last bite of a brownie in her mouth as she got to her feet. "Kitchen staff! With me!" she yelled across the large room. Looking at Allistor, she added, "We'll get to making sandwiches and portable food for the folks doing the fighting. We'll be ready to feed… what? Ten thousand fighters? By suppertime."

"Thank you Meg, you're the best!" Allistor raised his arms as he got to his feet, threatening to hug the old woman, a wide grin on his face.

She stuck her tongue out at him as she retreated, mumbling to Sam as she went. "You see that? Youngster always getting all fresh. I tell you, he's trying to steal me away from you, old man." Sam tossed Allistor a wink over his shoulder as he followed his wife into the kitchen.

"Nigel, please send a message to Lady Melise of the Or'Dralon, let her know that the undead have returned, and that we invite her and her light mages to join in the battle. Send the same message to the dwarves at Lightholm. And give me loudspeaker please, everywhere on Earth." He waited until Nigel had time to activate the coms, then spoke as he left the cafeteria and entered the lobby.

"Hello everyone, Allistor here. The undead that previously attacked Invictus City have just returned. They're underground this time, and we don't yet know how many we'll be facing. I need all available raiders, and anyone who wants to gain some experience fighting the

174

zombies, to report here as soon as you can. There's an active defense quest, which you'll receive when you arrive, and a ton of kill experience available, along with whatever loot drops." He paused for a second, recalling the previous battle, which had happened several weeks earlier. "Those with light magic, or resistances to dark magic, or with AoE damage spells, will be particularly useful. No one under level twenty. I'll see you soon."

He stood in the lobby as he waited for his raid commanders to find him. They all knew this was where he'd be, at least until they departed for the tunnels.

Reflecting on the last few weeks since he'd claimed his additional planets and space stations, he shook his head. Things had been quiet, peaceful even. Though he'd been as busy as ever. There were two additional space stations to claim, previously owned by Loki. Both had orbited planets owned by other factions, whom he had met with and reassured that he had no designs on conquering their worlds. They were established trade stations, and he was happy to leave them that way. L'olwyn had accompanied him, and been instrumental in establishing new trade and tax agreements with the locals in both cases.

Allistor had also spent several days traveling across Earth with a group of his people, both raiders and trainers, making contact with groups of survivors. At each stop he'd offered food and supplies, given his pitch, and done his best to recruit. His job was made easier by the planetwide announcement he'd made about a week after returning from his encounter with the xylon. It had taken him that long to compose the statement, with the help of Helen and Selby, finding a balance of authority and kindness, motivation and hope, in his words.

After the announcement he had his communications people reaching out with wideband broadcasts, and a dozen ships with similar groups of raiders and trainers, healers and crafters, packed with resources for those in need, spread out around the globe. Those groups hit mostly smaller settlements that had been identified by their satellite teams, while Allistor reserved the larger and potentially more dangerous groups for his team.

He'd found and recruited new citizens from Norway to South Africa, Australia, Japan, Alaska, even a huge group of more than twenty thousand who'd established a Citadel of their own in Moscow. The Russians had been the most difficult to convince, and Allistor had eventually given up, wished them luck, and flown away without recruiting them. It was only two days later that they had reached out via radio and asked him to return.

After a solid two weeks of nonstop recruiting missions, along with those who had been desperate and simply sworn the oath that had been included in his worldwide message, Invictus now boasted more than ten million human citizens. There were nearly twenty teleportation hubs placed at larger settlements, and more than two hundred teleportation pads at mid-size settlements scattered across every continent.

The human race was slowly but surely coming together again.

Allistor had been ecstatic over their accomplishments. Each ship captain, raid leader, and advisor had been authorized to create quests sufficient to bring new recruits up to level ten so that they could choose a Class. Trainers were cycled around to the various new settlements, and lists of available class training were handed out everywhere Allistor's people went. Resources were delivered where needed, which was the one low point of this period for Allistor.

He'd almost forgotten how rough it had been for him and his friends early on. And many of the groups they encountered were barely hanging on, surviving at a subsistence level. When reports of these groups started coming in, Allistor had prioritized them over the larger groups, increasing their allotment of resources, having his people improve their living conditions with larger or stronger Strongholds. He himself visited several of these groups, offering them fetch or crafting quests to bump them up beyond level ten in many cases.

And he had the ten most experienced, or most willing to fight, from each of these groups brought back to Invictus, leaving a raid group and some trainers at their settlements to protect them. He gathered those new recruits into mixed groups of twenty and sent them through the dungeons on Aegrin to gain experience and loot some better gear. The mixed groups fostered cooperation between the various settlements, allowing their leaders to form bonds that Allistor hoped would last, and help bring them all together.

At the same time, Selby and Droban had brought him several applications from non-human entities and factions asking to purchase some land and the rights to establish colonies on Earth or Orion. They had already investigated the applicants, rejected a few who were from suspicious or outright hostile factions, according to Allistor's long list of notifications. Those they submitted to him were approved, pending agreement on location and price.

And much to Allistor's surprise, some of the non-humans who had already claimed property on Earth before Allistor became Emperor had requested the opportunity to become citizens of Invictus as well! Not in large numbers, but there were several dozen new alien settlements whose owners and residents were now a part of Invictus.

Now several of those new leaders, human and otherwise, were appearing in his lobby to help fight off the undead invasion. He smiled, welcoming each of them as they appeared. When the lobby was full, they moved out into the street as his commanders took roll call and began to form fighting groups.

Bjurstrom grabbed a bullhorn and quieted the group, then proceeded to give them tips on how best to combat the undead. He warned them of the necrotic spells, the need for light magic healers in each group, and the absolute necessity of protecting those healers.

As this went on, Allistor received periodic updates from Nigel. He heard about it when the adept began to form the pit, when she stopped in the cavern. He got updates on the enemy numbers as new undead crossed under his walls, and as the adept ended the existence of thousands down in the pit. With each update, he itched to get moving. But sending his people in unprepared wasn't something he was willing to risk.

Lady Melise arrived with a couple hundred light mages, all eager to resume the fight with the undead. They had all leveled up several times during the last fight, and were looking for more of the same. Harmon and a thousand orcanin joined them in the streets, even as Longbeard's dwarves from Lightholm mixed with beastkin, gnomes, minotaurs, and other races.

Finally, Allistor raised his hands, casting *Levitate* on himself and rising up above his citizens until all could see him. When the group got quiet, he called out, "Nigel, show us where they are."

A holo projection of the city shone out from a tower window, filling the air above his head, large enough for all to see. It zoomed into the northernmost area of the city, which was the southern half of Central Park. It zoomed further to the 66th Street area, then blue lines appeared to delineate the tunnels underneath. An orange section of the old subway tunnel that ran under the park indicated where the undead were coming into the city under the wall. A bright red star showed the location of the pit the adept had created.

"It seems they haven't spread out since entering the city." Allistor called out. "That should make it easy to pin then down. They've dug a deep hole where you see the star. We don't know yet what that's about, whether they're looking for something, or someone, or trying to create some sort of trap, or defensive position." He looked across the crowd of ten thousand or so. "There isn't room down there for all of us. And I'll need most of you to man the walls, in case this is just some sort of diversion. Last time they attacked underground after the surface battle had already begun. I expect more of the same today."

When he saw disappointed looks on many faces, he grinned. "Don't worry. This might be a long battle, again just like last time. If nothing's happening on the surface, we'll cycle teams down to the underground battle. And regardless of whether you see action underground, you'll receive rewards for the defense quest." He waited as a semi-enthusiastic cheer rose from the crowd.

"Thank you all for coming, for being willing to fight for Invictus. Together we can overcome any challenge!" He pumped a fist in the air, and the crowd roared with approval, especially the orcanin warriors, who startled some of the newcomers with the volume of their approval. Orcanin despised necromancy and the undead, and these warriors were anxious to wipe this enemy from existence.

Allistor took a moment to share the defense quest with everyone present, including the non-citizens like the orcanin, who hadn't already received it just by showing up. The rewards hadn't been established yet, as the size of the enemy force was still unknown and growing. But based on the previous battle, each participant, regardless of whether they got any personal kills, should receive decent experience from a successful defense.

Though Allistor didn't know it, inside the tower Kira was gathering a few thousand children from the various Strongholds, especially the newer, recently recruited settlements. In some cases nervous parents accompanied them, so that the crowd spilled out of the cafeteria into the lobby and the courtyard outside. The lower-leveled children and parents all received the defense quest as well, and would gain experience just from being in the city. Children were unfortunately rare on Earth these days, as very few of them survived the apocalypse, so it was important to take advantage of every opportunity to help them safely earn experience and levels. It was a sort of loophole that Allistor was fond of exploiting, but that he'd been too distracted to arrange himself this time.

Another important fact that Allistor wasn't aware of was that the lich who had attacked him twice before was now dead, along with almost all of his adepts. Bjurstrom planned the battle as if they'd be facing those adepts, along with their deadly necrotic spells, with even the orcanin taking the upcoming battle seriously. A few of them had been lost atop the city wall to those necrotic attacks before the light healers had been properly organized.

So when Allistor and a thousand or so raiders, healers, and warriors set off at a jog toward the north end of the city, his gut fluttered with nerves. He'd lost Goodrich and his entire experienced raid group in an underground battle against these undead, and since there were no survivors, he didn't know the details of how or why they'd been defeated. The groups sent to rescue Goodrich and company reported some nasty opposition when they arrived. Allistor now expected more of the same.

"What are they after?" He asked himself aloud as he jogged. With his superhuman attributes, he could sprint for an hour before tiring. This easy ground-eating lope barely had his heart beating faster than normal. "Is there some kind of artifact down there, or something? And if so, how would they know it was there?"

"Dinosaurs!" McCoy happily offered from just behind him. Allistor turned his head as he continued on, seeing the wide smile on his friend's face.

"What?"

"Dinosaurs! That's what I think they're after down there. The necromancer wants to revive some old T-Rex bones or something, get himself a dinosaur army strong enough to take us down."

"Yessss!" Bjurstrom leapt up and kicked his heels together in the air. "We get to fight a T-Rex!!"

"Goofballs!" Helen snarked at them from Allistor's side.

Nigel interrupted any further jibes as he spoke to them through the surrounding buildings. *"Sire, I have detected more undead approaching on the surface. Only several hundred so far, but the number is steadily increasing."*

"Thank you Nigel, please inform those who are heading to the walls to move as quickly as possible. Use the ships to shuttle folks up there. The battle droids can handle things until our people arrive."

"Of course, Sire."

"Another battle on two fronts." Allistor sighed. "Maybe more, if they have penetrated other underground areas. At least with Nigel's upgrades he can detect them now."

Bjurstrom cleared his throat. "Uh, boss? I've got a quest here, don't think you're gonna like it."

"Tell me." Allistor raised one eyebrow, curious as to why one of his knights would receive a quest not issued by him.

"It says to protect my Emperor, which I obviously would do anyway, but it offers me a huge xp bonus if I keep you out of the fight altogether." The man paused, jogging along silently next to Allistor for a moment. "It's really a LOT of xp. Like more than a level's worth. So I was wondering… are you going to voluntarily hang back? Or am I gonna need to hogtie you, or something?" He grinned at Allistor, who snorted.

Behind them, McCoy and a few others who'd chosen to receive the rank of Knight and follow the path of that Class called out that they'd received the quest as well. The pouting look on William's face made it clear he was extremely jealous.

Seeing that Allistor had zero intention of hanging back, Helen nudged him. "They're right. The System has given them the quest because squishy baby Emperors shouldn't be on the front lines if they don't need to be. And this is going to be a tunnel fight. Close and dirty for the group up front, but mostly standing around and waiting their turn for everyone behind them. Your big spells, like *Storm*, are better suited for open areas where you can hit big numbers at once. And most of the spells you have that would be useful down there, like *Vortex* and *Mind Spike*, and the rest, you've made sure that we all have too. Let the raiders do their thing, and the knights complete their quests. Sounds like it would be way more xp than they'll earn from the fight itself."

It went against everything Allistor felt inside to let others take on a fight he wasn't ready to jump into himself. From nearly the first day after the world ended, he had led his friends, his adopted family, and then his raiders, into nearly every battle they'd faced. He'd been injured alongside them, nearly died beside them more times than he wanted to remember. Despite knowing in his mind that Helen was right, his heart wasn't ready to let him hang back.

Harmon cleared his throat from Allistor's other side, getting his attention. He waved for Allistor to accompany him into a side street, then motioned for Helen and the others to keep going. When the two of them were out of earshot of the small army jogging by, the orcanin stopped. "I know you wish to fight. You have proven yourself to be a fierce warrior in battle after battle, though I know you are not a warrior at heart. You fight when you must, to defend those in your care. When you are forced into it, you have demonstrated the ability to be cunning and ruthless, both good qualities in an Emperor." Allistor grimaced at the compliments, expecting the 'but' that he was sure was about to follow.

"You must learn that you can not be everything to everyone. That you must forego your own wishes for the greater good more often than you can indulge in them." Harmon paused, seeing that his line of reasoning wasn't working. "If I were to be killed today, there are half a dozen of my children and grandchildren whom I would trust to take my throne and lead my people well. Who would replace you if you die in a tunnel today?"

Allistor opened his mouth, about to say "Amanda," then shut it again. Before he could respond, Harmon continued.

"You are no longer the scrappy human boy who overcame the odds to protect a few dozen, or even a few thousand, of your followers. You now rule a true empire of several planets and many millions of citizens who depend on promises that you made to them."

Allistor's shoulders slumped a bit as he considered his fellow emperor's words.

"I can think of few among your people who could effectively take your place. The best possible candidates would be Lady Meg and Sam, the old warrior. But if you die, and force that jewel of a woman to run your empire instead of cooking me delicious meals, I will curse your

185

soul for all eternity." He grinned at Allistor, giving him a hardy thump on the back. Then his face grew serious again.

"Do not risk abandoning your people to ease the guilt you feel from letting others fight this battle. You will learn that this will be among the easier decisions to face. Compared to the guilt of losses from an all-out war between empires, or the helpless feelings when thousands or millions fall to a disease or natural catastrophe that you couldn't have prevented anyway, this day, this decision, will seem easy. Let this be a small step in your journey toward becoming a true Emperor."

Allistor nodded once, overwhelmed by the pressure from Helen, Bjurstrom, Harmon, and apparently the System itself, which offered a ton of experience to his people to keep him out of the fight. "Alright, I'll stay out of this one." He sighed, then held up a single finger. "But that doesn't mean I'm willing to sit out every fight from now on!"

"Nor should you!" Harmon happily agreed. "There will be fights that demand your participation, or that favor your particular skillsets. There will be fights that require you to be seen leading your people, for the sake of their morale, if nothing else. This will not be one of those fights."

Allistor wondered what Harmon knew that he didn't, but he accepted his much more experienced friend's advice. The two of them turned and resumed their run, chasing the now retreating column of raiders that were several blocks ahead of them. He began planning how to monitor the battle on multiple fronts from a safe location.

*****

They ultimately decided to split into three groups and descend at three subway stations. One group at 57th & 7th, one at 5th & 59th, and the last group at 63rd & Lexington. The groups would then locate the undead and engage them. According to Nigel, the horde was moving in from the east along what had been the Q line tunnel, so the group dropping down at 63rd were most likely to encounter them. For that reason, this was the largest group. They would cut into the horde at that station, then part of the group would hold there, blocking any additional infiltration through that tunnel, when the rest pushed toward the pit from the east. The others would clean up any stragglers who had wandered past the pit, and push in from the south to deal with whatever was going on there.

A much conflicted Allistor agreed to remain at the Lex & 63rd station, where he was closest to both battlefronts. The walls where they were repelling the surface invaders were a short run from there, or he could descend into the tunnels if needed. Harmon chose to remain with him, as did Helen and the kids. Addy and Sydney, seeing the obvious stress Allistor was feeling, hummed a calming duet that actually did relax him a bit.

Bjurstrom reported in from directly below Allistor. "We've spotted the zombies. They're moving west through the tunnel, just as Nigel said. I'm seeing mostly lower

187

levels, between ten and twenty. There's an occasional higher level wearing post-apocalypse gear, but not many. Recommend letting a lower level raid group take the lead here. At least they can get some xp from the kills."

Allistor gritted his teeth as he spoke the words. "You're the boss down there, do what you think is right."

"Roger that, Emperor Allistor." The snark in Bjurstrom's voice made Allistor's lips twitch into a brief grin. He probably understood how hard it was for Allistor to remove himself, and was trying to lighten his burden as well.

McCoy reported in a few minutes later. "We've joined up with the third group, no baddies so far. Proceeding north toward the curve where the pit is located."

A voice Allistor barely recognized reported next. "Things are slow up here on the northeast wall. They're filtering in, but not in big groups. And so far none of those necro attacks from the adepts, boss." She was a mid-level raid leader named Hope. Allistor recognized her as a druid who had taken a beastmaster specialty and volunteered to give up raiding to help Schinhofen handle the drakelings after bonding with one. Allistor couldn't remember which color. She'd been at the Silo the last few times he'd visited, and had recommended they relocate the baby drakes up to the surface where they could get some sunlight and fresh air, as well as do a little hunting on their own.

"Thank you, Hope. Let us know if you see any adepts, or the numbers increase significantly. If you don't need everyone up there, start rotating them in thirds so that everyone gets some rest."

"Just like last time, got it boss." The tone of her voice made it clear she'd already known to do that, but was humoring him. Allistor rolled his eyes, feeling silly and nearly useless. He itched to get into the fight somewhere.

He was pacing back and forth with his hands clasped behind his back when McCoy's urgent call came through coms. "Boss, we're here, and something's happening in the pit! The dead are just throwing themselves into it, not even slowing down. But now there's this dark purple light pushing up out of the hole, and all the undead have stopped moving. Their eyes are glowing and-" There was a scream in the background that had Allistor running toward the stairway leading down into the station, but he paused when McCoy continued. "Back! Everybody back! Retreat! Get the hell out of here!"

Allistor could hear the man breathing hard as he ran and yelled at his people to do the same. "Boss! The hole started sucking everything into it. One of my people was too close and got pulled in! The zombies still aren't moving, just sort of swaying back and forth, until the magic sort of... dissolves them! I think we're at a safe distance now..."

"Pull back farther. As far as you can while keeping the pit in view. Toss some flares if you need to. Tell me what's going on." Allistor growled, holding his position. Whatever was happening would likely be over before he could get there.

Bjurstrom's voice cut in. "The zombies here have all stopped moving as well, same purple glow in their eyes. My baby raiders were just cutting them down like wheat until we heard McCoy's report. I'm pulling everyone back."

Harmon cleared his throat to get Allistor's attention. "I believe I know what is occurring, Allistor. Best to vacate the area around the pit. Get your people safely back to the surface."

Allistor gave the command, staring at the orcanin as he did so. "Okay, what's going on?"

Chapter Ten

To the Core

In the cavern at the bottom of the pit, the adept's mouth was held open in a silent scream as every muscle remaining in her rotted corpse contracted beyond normal limits. For the first time in over a century, she felt pain. A pain unlike any human had ever experienced. Her body was literally tearing itself apart, fiber by fiber, in slow motion.

The agony only increased along with the glow from the staff as it consumed more and more essences from the oncoming undead. Even if she could manage a coherent thought, there would have been no way for her to keep track of how many had been sacrificed.

She was momentarily distracted by a scream, one that grew louder as it grew closer. Somehow a living human had been pulled into the pit, screaming on their way down, until the sound ended abruptly when they hit bottom. The variance from the silent expiration of the thousands of minion registered briefly before her consciousness was once again overwhelmed by pain.

It came in pulses now, which was even worse than constant agony, as the brief reprieves only made the returning agony worse by comparison. Her deteriorated bones cracked, overwhelmed by the contracting muscles they supported. She felt ribs snap, their jagged edges pushing deep into her torso. Her spine creaked, discs grinding, then shattering. She was vaguely aware that her desiccated skin had begun to melt away, sucked into the gem at the end of the necromancer's staff.

Though she couldn't form a clear thought, her last emotion, beyond the pain, was one of regret. But that didn't last long, as her consciousness fled along with her very essence.

The process that seemed to last an eternity for the adept actually took just a few minutes. The staff, once the ritual had been activated, took over and did its job quite efficiently. It used the adepts emotion, her suffering, to set the tone for its creation, as the necromancer who created the ritual had intended.

The dark purplish glow increased as it sucked in the essence of the last few undead within its range, until it filled the cavern and shone up through the pit above. It pulsed, slowly at first, then more rapidly as it began to expend the energy it had collected. Eventually the pulses came so quickly as to seem to be a constant glow that brightened by the second. The very walls of the cavern began to warp, the stone wailing its objection to the unnatural process.

The gem then ate the staff that held it, absorbing every iota of power imbued into the bone. Once free of its physical confines, it floated into the air, positioning itself in the center of the cavern, directly below the pit. With one final, cataclysmic expulsion of power, it altered the fabric of space and time around itself, establishing a new domain. Now only faintly glowing, the gem fell to the stone floor, which melted beneath it. The liquid stone embraced the gem, pulling it down into the bedrock a good ten feet before solidifying.

Within the stone, the adept's consciousness awakened. Confused by a total lack of input, of sensation of any kind, it panicked.

*****

Harmon wasn't sure if he was about to impart good news, or bad. He would view the coming event as a blessing. But Allistor often did not share his point of view.

"I believe we are witnessing the birth of a naturally forming dungeon." He stated, watching Allistor's face closely. "Or, rather, an unnaturally forming dungeon, as it is being purposely created by the undead, I suppose. What I mean is, instead of planting an existing core to create a dungeon, someone down there is using the essence of many thousands of undead to create a core, which will then create its dungeon."

"That damned lich!" Allistor guessed, then proceeded to curse long and loudly. When he was done, Harmon agreed.

"Very likely, yes. That may have been his intent all along, and you and your city simply got in his way. Remember, he was raising and gathering the dead here well before you claimed this territory. His first attack on your city was likely done out of frustration after he failed to eliminate you out west."

"So there's about to be an undead dungeon right under my city? Can we stop it?"

"Probably not." Harmon shook his head. "But take a moment to think about whether you actually *want* to stop it."

"I can't have a dungeon full of zombies sitting under my capital city, just waiting to break loose and eat everyone's face."

"That scenario is unlikely in the extreme." Harmon took a seat on the hood of a nearby car, its suspension squealing under the weight. "To begin with, the newly formed dungeon will be weak. Probably somewhere between level ten and twenty, though possibly a bit higher based on the number of undead essences it likely absorbed. So let's say worst case, level thirty. It might make for an excellent training ground for your lower level raiders, and especially for light mages like those the Or'Dralon have sent you." He paused, gauging Allistor's response and his willingness to listen.

"You have several options here, Allistor. And time to consider them." He held up one finger. "First, you could send in a higher-leveled team to clear the dungeon and capture or destroy the core. That would eliminate any possible danger to your city, and give you a core you could plant someplace less valuable to you, or even sell for a significant sum to some other faction."

He raised a second finger. "Second, you could leave it where it is, and use it as I described, to train your people. It would have a limited but useful purpose, granting your low level fighters some experience and loot. Allies might pay well to buy access for their own people to do the same. A regularly culled dungeon will almost never grow strong enough to break free of its natural bonds and pour its minions into your city."

Another finger went up. "Third, you could feed it. Dungeons grow stronger by killing and absorbing the essence of beings that enter its confines. Feed it, let it grow stronger, then use it to train your higher level fighters as it grows more powerful."

Allistor grimaced. "Feed it what? I'm not sacrificing my people to grow a dungeon as an asset."

Harmon shrugged. "Feed it your enemies, your captured prisoners of war. Murderers, rapists, goblins, those you would normally put to death anyway. Toss them inside with a basic weapon and some water to give them a fighting chance if your conscience requires it." Harmon grinned.

When Allistor blanched at the idea, Harmon offered an alternative. "There are still many, many thousands of undead roaming the area. Seal off the side tunnels, post guards at the junctures, and allow the undead to wander in. We've already seen that despite not being alive, their essence will feed the dungeon. If necessary, send out teams to herd the surface undead toward the correct tunnel, or round them up and deliver them."

Allistor's face brightened a bit, liking that idea much better. It was just his kind of 'two birds, one stone' solution. He could rid the area of wandering zombies and build a more powerful dungeon to train his people. He was already considering the logistics of what Harmon had described when he felt a pulse of filthy, oily power pass through him, and a notification flashed up on his interface.

Empire First!

A new dungeon core has been created within Invictus City's boundaries!
Dungeon Core Type: Undead
Dungeon Level: 3, Instanced; Difficulty Level: Moderate
Recommended level of delvers: 30 to 40
Significantly increased rewards awarded to the first delvers to conquer the dungeon!

Allistor received an additional notification that the others didn't, offering him the option to name the dungeon. He waved it away as the others around him cheered. They clearly considered the new dungeon a good thing.

Harmon chuckled. "An instanced dungeon, and higher level than I expected. This could be quite a boon, Allistor."

"Does instanced mean what I think it means? More than one group can run the dungeon at the same time?"

"Correct. Usually the number of groups is limited by the dungeon level. So in this case, three groups at once, each group experiencing the dungeon separately. You will have to explore it and have your groups compare notes as soon as possible. For some instanced dungeon, each group's experience is nearly identical. While in others, they face completely different challenges simultaneously. This is quite exciting!" the huge orcanin grinned at Allistor, who knew what was coming next.

"I take it you just happen to have some orcanin between levels thirty and forty who would be willing to help us explore this dungeon?"

"Now that you ask, I believe I do!" Harmon's attempt at an innocent grin was pathetic, and unabashed.

Allistor chuckled despite himself, his stress level lowering steadily. He'd been planning to seed some of his dungeon cores anyway, and though the idea of an undead dungeon under their feet still didn't sit well with him, he told himself this one was no different than the insectoid dungeon he was going to create.

"Alright, since it was you that convinced me to leave this dungeon in place, one of the first three teams will be orcanin." He had a sudden thought. "Unless you'd like to mix your warriors into other teams?"

"That is an intriguing idea. I shall choose a team, then offer them the choice."

Allistor nodded, then called out to Nigel for loudspeaker, everywhere he could reach.

"Attention citizens! As some of you have already heard, a new dungeon full of undead has been created under Invictus City. This was not our doing, but we are going to take advantage of it. The dungeon is recommended for raiders between level thirty and forty. We will be sending three teams, or fifteen raiders, in the

197

next few days. And the first team that completes the dungeon will receive what sounds like a *First Kill* bonus! So if you meet the level criteria and want to challenge the dungeon, let Nigel know. We'll hold a lottery tomorrow and pick the teams. Meanwhile, those of you on the city walls, please stop killing the undead. We have a new use for them. Monitor them closely, and if they begin to pile up near the top of the wall, take them down. Thanks, and have a great day."

Harmon asked, "Why only five per team? Most dungeons will allow up to ten members in each group."

Allistor shook his head. "I'm not sure I want to risk that many on the first run. At least until we know more about what's in there. Besides, smaller groups means better experience per raider."

"And if a team of five cannot defeat the dungeon?"

"Then they'll retreat, and we'll send in larger teams." Allistor shrugged. "I'll give them strict instructions to back off if a fight looks too difficult, or they begin to lose people."

As he finished his statement, Lady Melise appeared beside him, making him flinch in surprise, as she seemed to enjoy doing. She bowed her head as Allistor gathered his wits. "Emperor Allistor. Congratulations on the formation of a new and exciting dungeon!" She waited for him to nod in return. "I would like to inquire… might a few of our light mages be allowed the chance to participate in the first attempts at clearing the dungeon?" She smiled so sweetly that Allistor's mouth went slightly dry.

He instantly felt bad for not offering. Though her people were not citizens, they were certainly allies, and had saved hundreds of his citizens' lives with their healing during the first undead attack.

"Of course, Lady Melise. My apologies for not offering as much myself. Would three positions be acceptable? One per team, or all on one team, as you decide? And you are certainly welcome to send through subsequent teams in the future, at no charge, of course."

"That is most generous of you, Emperor Allistor." Her smile grew even brighter, which Allistor would not have guessed would be possible. "We accept, of course." Her face turned to a slight pout, which tugged at Allistor's heart. "Unfortunately, the last time we fought together, I achieved level forty one, excluding me from this particular adventure. But I will choose three of my best to accompany your teams."

"I have a feeling your light magic healers will contribute greatly to the teams' success." He smiled back at her. She bowed gracefully before practically skipping off to find her people, her ever-present bodyguard jogging after her.

"Between my people and hers, that is more than half of the available positions for the first run, Allistor. I urge you again to send three teams of ten. I will limit mine to five warriors, leaving you with twenty two of your people, instead of just seven. My fighters will join your teams."

Allistor nodded. "Alright, we'll make it teams of ten. I'll surprise everyone with that news tomorrow when we choose the lottery winners. The teams can spend the rest of the day getting to know each other and figuring out how best to fight together, and take their shots at the dungeon the following day."

"Excellent! Now, do you have engineers and earth mages among your people? If not, I can loan you some of mine to help seal off tunnels and direct the undead to the dungeon…"

*****

Baldur watched as Allistor discovered the dungeon, and accepted Harmon's counsel on how best to deal with it. He was proud of the young man for the decisions he'd made. Odin had not informed Allistor of the lich's demise caused by the destruction of its phylactery on Hel's moon. The lich had already withdrawn its forces and ceased attacking the city by the time Allistor took Loki's head, indirectly causing its destruction. Baldur knew that Allistor fully expected his raiders to have to face the lich as the dungeon boss, and was worried that they might not be able to defeat it. That was, Baldur suspected, the reason the boy had wanted to send fewer people into the dungeon. A being powerful enough to raise hundreds of thousands of minions would seem like an extremely difficult challenge. He was surprised and proud that Allistor hadn't tried to go in and face the danger himself.

Using the sensors aboard his ship, which was currently cloaked and in orbit around Earth, Baldur scanned the newly formed dungeon. The mists that filled his chamber vibrated and swirled as he spoke to himself. "Level three, with five floors. The final boss is... one of the lich's former adepts? A level forty undead elite. Not easy to kill, but if each team has a light mage of sufficient level, and good healers, they will have a fighting chance." He nodded with approval.

Baldur and Odin had both been monitoring Allistor more closely since Loki's death. They had watched him travel to his new planets and incorporate them into his Empire. Odin had actually smiled when Allistor had efficiently eliminated the xylon brood mother that had attacked him, then recruited her daughter. Everywhere he went, the young human's sincerity and kindness, combined with iron will and willingness to fight for his people, inspired affection and loyalty. His determination to treat his people equally and fairly induced strangers, even former enemies, to join his Empire as vassals.

In fact, in Baldur's most recent conversation with Harmon, the orcanin had laughingly disclosed that, were he not needed to serve his own people, he would be tempted to join Allistor's. Master Daigath, an elf so ancient and powerful as to be universally respected even among Baldur's race, had chosen to stay with the boy and mentor him, something he rarely did. Even Baldur, and Odin himself, were fond of the tenacious human.

Baldur had mourned the terrible loss of humanity that Loki had triggered. He felt a deep shame, that Odin shared, for not seeing and preventing those actions in time. Now he was able to find a bright side in the actions of Allistor and those like him, who faced an apocalypse and stood fast, overcoming terrible adversity to survive and thrive in the new world that had been thrust upon them. Allistor was the most outstanding example, but human leaders across the globe had stepped up and saved groups of various sizes, protecting and guiding them through the Stabilization period. And now Allistor was working to gather together as many of those leaders as he could.

For beings who were physically weak and woefully underdeveloped for membership in the Collective, the humans were quite impressive.

*****

The following morning during breakfast, Allistor had Nigel randomly pick twenty one of the several thousand lottery entrants. He'd decided to have six orcanin, just so that there could be two per team. That left twenty one slots for his citizens. He made a brief announcement that he was doubling the teams to ten participants each, which caused a rousing cheer.

When all the names were announced, there were thirteen humans, three dwarves, two gnomes, two beastkin, and a minotaur to go with the orcanin and elven team members. Allistor gathered them together in the courtyard outside the tower lobby. Gazing over the crowd, he only saw a few familiar faces. But they were all well geared, and of appropriate level, none of them under thirty five.

"Congratulations on being chosen. As I'm sure you are aware, the first team to complete the dungeon will receive superior rewards. I know that your competitive spirits and simple desire for epic loot will entice you to push yourselves. But let me be clear. I want all of you to come out of that hole alive. Don't push too hard and get someone killed just for the sake of loot. Experience and better gear can be earned elsewhere. Lives cannot be replaced." He stared at each of them as he spoke, getting head nods and smiles of agreement.

"Now, for the rest of today, you're going to be fighting each other. Bjurstrom and McCoy will be working with you, breaking you into groups for mock battles, then breaking those groups up and reassigning you, until we have three teams that work well together. They'll be asking you about your classes and skills. Please be as forthright as possible with them, so they can place you where you'll be most useful. Once the groups are established, we'll conduct a few more team fights so that you can learn how best to coordinate skills and abilities within your group." He paused for a moment, looking for any sign that one or more of them weren't up to the task.

"Good luck to you all. Be safe down there." He turned and stepped into the lobby, not wanting to taint the proceedings by participating. He'd spent a good part of the evening with his best raiders, coming up with ideal team criteria and ways to structure the practice battles to best challenge his groups. A few had wanted to send them into the dungeons on Aegrin for practice runs, but in the end it was determined that supervised mock battles were more effective. The experienced raiders could observe, offer notes, and make adjustments to team rosters as necessary that way.

Allistor had asked Lilly to provide any gear upgrades that she could for all the team members before their dungeon run. She and half a dozen of her crafters would be examining and interviewing the team members to see what they could improve from their current stock. He also asked her to have an upgrade of some kind crafted for each of them, to be presented later.

He planned to distract himself during those runs by crafting a few enchanted weapons to be awarded to each team's MVP, to be voted on by the team members themselves. While the weapons he could create weren't very high quality, Droban had assured him that being awarded a weapon hand-crafted by an emperor would be a high honor, and greatly appreciated. "Should Argrol, the minotaur who won a position on the teams, be awarded such a weapon, it would be passed down to future generations of his family, and occupy a position of honor in his home."

Allistor hadn't been hard to convince. He was often able to lose himself in the process of crafting weapons, and it would keep him from anxiously pacing, or driving his staff crazy, while they awaited the emergence of the teams. He was already planning what type of weapons to craft. Having no way to know ahead of time who would win the gifts, he decided to go with swords, which nearly everyone could use. He'd make them larger than normal, in case an orcanin or the minotaur won, but lightweight enough that humans or gnomes, even casters without much investment in *Strength*, could wield them. And he'd save the enchanting until he knew who the winners were, to make them more appropriate. That part only took an hour per weapon, at most.

*****

Hope ducked a sword that flashed toward her head, dropped to one knee and thrust forward with her spear, its dulled point bouncing off the ribs of the orcanin in front of her. The sword, swung at half speed by her pretend foe, had still barely missed her. The orcanin were accomplished and powerful warriors, and she was glad they'd be on her side tomorrow.

The orcanin grunted, raising a hand to acknowledge her hit, then gave her a nod of respect. As it would not have been a mortal wound for the immense warrior, the observers whistled a single note, indicating he should continue the fight. With a happy grin that Hope thought made him look hungry, the warrior stepped back into melee range and thrust his wooden blade at her. Hope scrambled to move aside, using both hands to push her spear shaft outward to one side, deflecting the blade, using the momentum of the heavy weapon to push herself into a backward roll that took her out of danger for a brief moment.

Over on the sidelines, her drakeling screeched in anger upon seeing her in danger. Hope spared a moment to call out as she leapt to her feet. "It's okay, Ruby, momma is just playing with the big scary orcanin!" Her foe chuckled, sparing a glance at the drakeling himself as two druids tried to wrangle the feisty little red drake. Upon hearing from her bonded, Ruby settled down and allowed herself to be petted as she watched the warrior try again to remove Hope's head from her shoulders. This time only a low rumble echoed from deep in the drakeling's belly as her tail twitched back and forth.

"Cute companion." The orcanin rumbled, allowing Hope a moment to catch her breath. Around them, the members of both their teams battled each other with blunted weapons and fake spells that the casters called out as they thrust a hand forward, rather than risk damaging an ally with an actual spell. "Does she breathe fire?"

"Not yet, but soon, I'm told." Hope smiled up at the warrior who stood a good two or three feet taller than her. She lunged forward, aiming her spear's tip at the orcanin's groin, causing him to parry with his oversized sword.

"Will she fight with you in the dungeon?" The warrior took no offense at her attempt to poke him in the nobblies.

"Not this time. We've been training together, and as you can see, she loves to fight. But she's not quite ready yet."

The orcanin nodded, turning his back to her as he pivoted to bring his weapon around in a backhanded swing. Hope used the butt of her spear to push herself off from the ground and leap back out of range. The tip of the blunt weapon still scraped across her chest armor. Had the orcanin been moving at full speed, she'd now be cut in half. Taking that into consideration, the observer blew two whistle blasts, indicating a mortal blow.

Thankful for the reprieve, Hope bowed her head to her opponent, who mimicked her action. "Thanks for the fight."

"You are skilled, for a puny human." the giant smiled as he offered the compliment. "I would be proud to fight alongside you."

"And I with you." She replied with a wink as she stepped off the battlefield to comfort her distressed drakeling. "You move quite gracefully for a giant slab of muscle."

Hope had been thrilled to have won a spot in the lottery. She was now a much lower level than McCoy and the others she'd raided with for the better part of six months. She'd been at the Silo working with the drakelings when Allistor had won some of his biggest battles, and lost out on a great deal of experience because of it. This dungeon was a great opportunity to regain some of what she'd missed out on.

When they had initially gathered, she (and everyone else) had expected the orcanin to demand to be tanks, their enthusiasm for battle being well known. She had pictured them charging forward, pounding zombies into paste before any of the rest of the team could land a blow or cast a spell. So she'd been surprised when the huge warriors obligingly deferred to the senior raiders' opinions on their proper places within each team. Two of the three teams would indeed have an orcanin tank, but one of the human warriors who'd won a position was a better tank, and a higher level, than the other four orcanin. Those had agreed to accept melee positions, and to act as off-tanks should they need to defend their group's rear, or create a shield wall at the front. They considered their inclusion a great honor, and were happy to be killing undead. The potential to achieve a dungeon's first kill didn't hurt, either.

She petted a now purring Ruby as the relieved druids stepped away. The little drake was only about five feet long from nose to tail, but she was strong. Holding her back from charging in to defend Hope had been no easy task.

They watched together as the remainder of both teams whittled each other down. When the battle was over, Bjurstrom called all three teams together. It had been a long day of battle after battle, during which they'd been assessed and eventually assigned to the teams they'd be going into the dungeon with. Her team was one of those with an orcanin tank, along with an elven healer with light magic, a gnome rogue, another human druid as healer and ranged damage, two more melee dps, one human, one orcanin, two human dps casters, and herself. She could cast damaging spells as a druid if necessary, but favored melee combat using her spear.

All of those who were citizens could cast the standard spells. The basic *Restoration* at least, *Light Globe*, *Mind Spike*, and *Fireball*. Both of the dps casters, Hope herself and Dan the other druid, could cast *Vortex* as well. The elf had some damaging light magic that would be her main function in this run, as well as dispelling any necrotic magic cast on the group so that Dan the druid healer could heal everyone. All in all, she thought they had a very effective team. They'd spent the last four hours being attacked by the other two teams, and attacking in return, to hone their teamwork. It had initially been awkward, and more than a little embarrassing. But now she felt they were comfortable enough with each other to go into battle.

"Alright, that's it for today. All of you get a good night's sleep. Breakfast at sunrise, then report back here for some last minute planning. We'll escort you to the dungeon entrance, and keep it clear for when you come back out." Bjurstrom waved a dismissal at them, sending them to supper, and their beds.

Chapter Eleven

First In, Last Out

The entrance to the dungeon turned out to be a swirling purple and black disc with an occasional streak of sickly green flashing through it like a static charge. The disc lay flat, horizontally across the hole in the subway floor.

As they approached, one of the gnomes asked, "Are we supposed to just jump into that thing? What if we fall a hundred feet and die?"

The orcanin nearest him shook his head. "Dungeons always allow safe entry. You will arrive in a small room or cavern that is a safe zone, where the dungeon's minions will not attack."

They all watched as a dozen or so undead shuffled the last few feet toward the side of the pit opposite their group, and simply fell through the opening. Other groups of raiders had sealed off the side tunnels and funneled the shambling undead toward the pit, where they were unflinchingly offering their essence to feed the dungeon. So far there had been no notification that it had leveled up from the near constant feeding, but the groups were anxious to get inside before it happened. If it leveled up again, it might be too difficult for them.

Hope ventured a question as another zombie took a nose-dive through the swirling entrance. "Anybody know if they're getting absorbed by the dungeon when they fall?

Or are they like, becoming minions that we'll have to fight through?" She started wondering how many more had jumped into the hole in the last thirty six hours or so.

When nobody spoke up, Bjurstrom shrugged. "Guess you'll find out when you get in there." He paused, looking at Hope. She had been assigned as raid leader for her group. "Team one, you won the roll. You're first. Team two will be one minute behind you." He motioned toward the opening. "Step on in, and good luck to you."

Taking a deep breath, trying not to show just how much she was creeped out by the oily-looking swirling entrance, she nodded to her team and stepped forward. Her heart thumped loudly in her chest, and her stomach lurched as she took that first step out into space. She closed her eyes and committed, leaning onto her forward foot.

There was a brief cold sensation, then her foot landed just as it normally would, and she opened her eyes to find a small cavern about twenty feet across, lit by a half dozen torches in sconces bolted to the walls. She took a few more steps forward even as others appeared behind her, still a little off after not experiencing the expected fall down into the pit.

When they were all in the room and had their wits about them, Hope got to work. "Alright folks. You know the formation. Weapons ready, check your potions one more time, we move out in thirty seconds."

She took several slow, calming breaths as she produced her trusty spear from inventory. It was an uncommon quality weapon she'd received as loot when she helped Allistor conquer the goblins and seize Orion. Sized to fit her body, it was sturdy but lightweight, and had a Sharpness enchantment on it courtesy of Michael and his enchanters. Her hope was that a better weapon would drop in this dungeon.

Looking around the room, she saw only one exit, besides the swirling wall behind them. A wide stone archway led to a dimly lit stone corridor that stretched off into the distance. A torch was placed every thirty paces or so as far as she could see.

"Tank to the front, let's move." She ordered. "Keep calm, call out any mobs you see, and be careful of your line of sight. We will not have any injuries from friendly fire." She waited as the orcanin tank took up position in the doorway, and the others moved into their assigned pattern. She was behind Sean the rogue, and other melee dps, in front of the healers and casters. Their second orcanin brought up the rear holding a massive metal crossbow, a six foot tower shield slung across his back.

They moved forward as a unit, letting the tank set the pace. He walked with his shield held ready, a thick spear with a head the size of a bowling ball in his right hand. Sean the rogue faded almost completely from sight as he followed, ready to sneak behind enemies and deliver critical backstabs and crippling slashes. Though, with the undead, only kill shots had any effect. The zombies didn't care about sliced tendons or punctured kidneys.

The group traveled in silence down the first hundred feet of corridor before they reached a door that Hope hadn't been able to see from the safe zone. Without a word the tank stepped past the door and set himself facing further down the hall, while the second orcanin moved up and traded his crossbow for sword and shield. Hope took hold of the door handle as the backup tank positioned himself in front of the door, two steps back. When he nodded, she pushed down on the door's handle and yanked it open. The orcanin pushed through, shield high, scanning the room. With a snort, he lashed forward and bashed an undead with his oversized shield, knocking it back into three others that had started forward. The melee fighters moved into the room behind him, and the fight was on!

The tank and melee teammates quickly killed three of the zombies, two of them losing their heads while the other had its skull crushed. The orcanin was about to take down the last one, when Hope hissed out a command. "Wait! Let our light mage have this one. I want to confirm that they're still susceptible to her magic."

The tank obligingly stepped back, allowing the zombie to recover its balance and shuffle forward. The elf stuck her head in the doorway, made a slight hand motion toward the mob, and a beam of pure white light shot forward to pierce its face. The light bored a hole completely through its skull, leaving the surrounding skin and bone smoldering.

"Good deal. We'll save that for when we really need it, so we're sure you have plenty of mana." Hope smiled at the elf. She was carrying a half dozen mana potions herself, and knew that each of the team carried the same. But better to be safe than sorry.

"Check the room quickly for loot, and we'll move on. We've got a first kill to win!"

*****

Hope was tired by the time they reached the final boss chamber. Her team had fought well against so many undead that she'd lost count. Each room, each corridor they entered had been a battle. Most of the undead had been simple zombies that were easy enough to kill on their own. But they didn't attack alone. They always attacked all at once, whether there were just two or three, or fifty of them. Their orcanin tank had performed miracles, keeping their attention focused on him with growls, shouted insults, hammering of weapon on shield, or simply hitting every monster in sight to get their attention. He had taken a lot of damage, required a lot of healing, and even with his huge stamina and health pool, he was starting to slow from loss of blood.

The dps members of the group had quickly learned to coordinate their attacks, targeting different undead instead of wasting damage by overlapping. The second orcanin blasted away at walking corpses with devastating headshots from his crossbow, or spear thrusts to the face. The two casters, Cary and Doug, sent lightning bolts that stunned and crisped skulls, and small, concentrated fireballs that immolated corpses in seconds. They channeled *Vortex* to use as crowd control when the group faced larger packs of shuffling zombies.

Even the little gnome rogue Sean had found a way to be useful, leaping atop the backs of undead near the rear of the pack and inserting a dagger at the base of the skull with surgical precision, snuffing the un-life in an instant before hopping to the next victim. In one instance, when the crowd control wasn't working on a group of nearly one hundred zombies in a wide cavern, the speedy little Sean pulled off a few dozen of them and kited them around the outside walls until his comrades had time to get the rest burned down. Then he led them within range of the casters, the zombies accommodatingly following him to their doom.

Their druid, Dan, had been able to handle the majority of the heals, only having to use two mana potions through the entire five floors of the dungeon. The elf had contributed occasionally, when Dan was falling behind or running low on mana. But mostly she had been using her bow to contribute to the zombie death toll, saving her mana for emergencies. Twice she had needed to cast light magic at a floor's mini-boss, sending beams of pure light into their faces to interrupt a spell or distract the higher level elites so that their tank could get them back under control. The mini-bosses had obviously been higher level post-apoc humans who had gained some skills and abilities before being killed by the lich's horde. One had been an armored warrior with an oversized axe that, when he triggered a skill that sent him into a spinning attack, was able to knock the orcanin tank back off his feet. The pain from a beam of light to the face distracted him enough to interrupt that skill.

Hope herself had spent most of the fights using her spear. She stabbed and smashed from behind the tank, or next to him during larger fights, using her magic for an occasional heal, or to interrupt a zombie caster with *Mind Spike*. During one exceptionally long fight on the lowest floor, watching with more than a little jealousy as Cary and Doug burned zombies two and three at a time, she'd sort of stumbled upon the ability to modify *Spark* to imbue her spear's blade with fire, doing nearly fifty percent more damage to the undead as she sliced and stabbed at them.

Now, nearly six hours after they'd dropped through the dungeon entrance, they stood at the entrance to a mid-sized cavern. At the center of which stood the dungeon boss. It wasn't the lich they had expected, though. When Hope and the others used *Examine* on the boss, they were surprised.

Necromancer's Adept
Undead Elite
Level 50
Health: 0/0

Like all the undead in the dungeon, this one had no visible health pool that they could monitor. It was annoying, and made it difficult to plan a fight. The mini-bosses had skills and abilities that Hope and the others *thought* might be triggered when the zombies reached fifty percent or twenty five percent health levels, but there was simply no way to tell, or predict when that would be.

Hope took a moment to look over her group. They were tired, battered, but clearly anxious to keep going. Their tank was actually leaning forward slightly toward the boss, as if about to tip over and rush forward.

"I'm proud of you guys. You've done an amazing job so far. Now, just one more smelly old zombie to kill, and we can collect our sweet, sweet loot!" The others chuckled or grinned at her, the gnome giving her a double thumbs-up, an expression he had learned from one of the casters. In an effort to speed up their progress, they had foregone in-depth looting after the first few rooms, pressing on to the next fight as soon as they finished clearing each room. They still looted the fallen corpses, as all it required was a quick kick or touch as they passed. But there were scores of rooms and caverns they hadn't bothered to search thoroughly.

"Alright, you guys know the drill. Keep in formation until the boss gives us a reason not to. Be prepared to scatter, or bunch up, on my call. If you see something strange, call it out. No detail is too small." She watched as they all nodded, familiar with the speech by now. She gave it anyway, having made it part of her pre-fight ritual. "Make sure you've got potions ready. Let's go kill this thing!" She nodded at the tank, who grunted with approval, then turned and began to stalk toward the boss. The others followed in formation, weapons and spells at the ready, looks of grim determination or excitement on all of their faces.

The boss didn't appear intimidating, except for her nasty looking staff that gave all of the raiders the creeps when they gazed upon it. She was standard size for a human, with the pale, rotting flesh they'd come to expect from undead. Her head sported only a few ragged wisps of long white hair, and half of the skin had rotted away from her face. She had no nose, just the boney gaps of her skull's sinus cavities, and her lips had retreated so far as to be non-existent. She did have one ear, but it looked as if it had been gnawed by rats at some point. She wore a surprisingly clean black robe with silver stitching, and matching black gloves covered her bony fingers.

"So, the very first visitors to my new home." She rasped at them, thumping the stone floor with the base of her staff. "And not all human? What a strange place our world has become." She took in the non-humans with a tilted head, even managing a curious expression, no easy feat with so much of her flesh missing. "How do you like my creation?"

Hope paused, not having expected the boss to talk, let alone ask a question. She was immediately suspicious. Was the boss buying time for more minions to arrive? "It's mostly dark, moldy, and smelly. If you don't mind, we'd prefer to just kill you quickly and go grab a shower."

The adept took a moment to gaze around the cavern, as if taking it in through Hope's eyes. "I suppose you're right. One of the drawbacks of being undead, I'm afraid. Endless life, no need to eat or sleep, but I keep losing bits of myself." She carefully grasped one long wisp of hair and held it forward to examine it. "I was beautiful once…"

She let go of the lock of hair and glared at Hope. "Soon enough, you will look as I do! I will claim your souls, and make minions of what's left of your corpses!" Her eyes flashed a sickly green as she lowered the tip of her staff toward the group. "You will wail in agony as you die!"

A visible ray of oily dark magic sprang from the gem at the end of the staff, speeding toward the group almost faster than they could follow. The tank raised his shield in time to catch it, but the ray broke into a wave on impact, splashing over and around the shield to continue onward, forming an AoE effect that encompassed the entire group. Immediately Hope began to wretch, her muscles spasming as her stomach ejected its contents all over the poor unstealthed gnome in front of her. The agony the adept had promised washed through her, every muscle screaming in pain as they locked up and began to rot at the same time.

There was a high pitched scream of anger as the tank, being the least affected by the necrotic spell as it mostly washed past him, activated an ability and rushed forward to slam his shield into the adept. She was knocked from her feet, but the spell had been cast, the damage done.

Behind Hope, she heard the elf groan as she struggled to cast a spell. As a light mage, the dark magic was particularly damaging to her. But the elf's elevated *Will Power* prevailed, gasping with relief a moment later as she managed to dispel the necrotic damage over time spell on herself. She immediately began casting it on the group, one by one, starting with the tank. With him back on his feet and dealing with the boss, the elf started with Sean, the poor gnome had the lowest health pool and was thus closest to death. Next came the human casters Cary and Doug, then melee fighters, including Hope, and finally the second orcanin, who had been valiantly resisting the agonizing muscle seizures to fire a few crossbow bolts at the adept's head.

The moment Hope had regained her senses, she charged forward toward the boss, casting *Mind Spike* as she ran. The spell was only partially effective on the higher leveled boss, not stunning her, but causing her to shake her head briefly to clear it. That was long enough for the tank to slam her again with his shield, and the ranged party members to hit her with everything they had.

Hope swung the butt of her spear around and slammed it into the adept's shoulder, her aim slightly off. She'd been hoping to break the undead's neck. Still, the blow staggered the boss, causing her to step back a half step and turn her head toward Hope. The soulless eyes flashed green again, and a hand gesture by the adept sent a snakelike black stream of magic at Hope. It struck her weapon as she held it up in an attempt to block, and Hope's initial sense of relief was quickly dashed as it first wrapped around the shaft, then slithered lightning quick up her left arm, across her shoulder, to wrap itself around her neck. Her skin immediately began to blister and burn as it squeezed tighter, cutting off her airway.

Not willing to give up, Hope reversed her weapon, cast her new modified spell, and jabbed the now flaming point at the adept's face. The boss shifted to one side, but not quite fast enough, the spear's point etching a flaming line across her cheekbone, then further back above the ragged ear along her scalp. A few of the remaining hairs burst into flame as the rest of her skin crisped along the edges of the wound.

The adept screamed in pain even as Hope grew dizzy from lack of oxygen and stumbled backward, trying to use her spear to steady herself. She felt a heal wash over her as her vision began to black out, and she felt herself fall.

Another scream from the adept penetrated her barely conscious thoughts, then she felt the pressure on her neck lift. The burning pain eased, and she was able to breathe again. Tightening her grip on the spear, she tried to spring to her feet, but stumbled, still slightly dizzy from lack of oxygen. When she looked up, she saw the adept laying at the tank's feet, a clean hole burned completely through her head. When Hope looked for the light mage, she found her being supported by Dan the druid and one of the casters. The elf was uninjured, but looked exhausted.

The irrepressible Sean leapt high into the air and cheered. "Yessss! We did it!" He ran and leapt to stand atop the fallen boss, holding both daggers high above his head. "Gnomes Rule!"

The others chuckled at his antics, having heard this particular declaration before during their time together. But they all froze when his contact with the boss's corpse counted as looting, and their interfaces all filled with notifications.

Congratulations!

Achievement Earned: First Kill!
You are the first group to defeat the Master's
Legacy Dungeon!
For being the first, all loot received will be
upgraded by two quality levels.
Experience earned is doubled! Each group member
shall receive a single soul-bonded item appropriate
to your chosen class.

As each group member was surrounded by the glow
that indicated they had leveled up, the adept's corpse faded
away, revealing a glowing treasure chest. The moment
Sean finished with his notifications, he pounced on the
chest and opened it.

"Woooo!" He held up a pair of tiny daggers with
glossy black bone blades, then hugged them to his chest.
"These are epic!"

One by one the party members reached into the
chest to claim their prize. The tank pulled out a short
sword (sized to his giant body) with the same dark bone
blade as the gnome's daggers, that did a small amount of
necrotic damage with each hit. The second orcanin
received a pair of bone vambraces that he reported were
enchanted to allow him to shrug off grievous wounds and
keep fighting, much as the undead did. The elf received the
adept's robe, which she initially was reluctant about, until
she saw that it increased mana regeneration by twenty
percent. She stowed it in her inventory, wanting to wash it
several times before actually wearing it.

The others were all equally pleased with their loot items, with Hope going last as group leader. She withdrew a sturdy bone shaft, all one smooth piece about six feet in length, with a surprising feature. The tip was a gem, much like the adept's staff had held, with a silvery metal claw holding it in place. But the gem was shaped into an extremely sharp spear point. It was lighter weight than the spear she'd been using, and offered +5 to both *Will Power* and *Agility*, as well as the ability to store up to three instant-cast spells inside the gem.

"Alright team, great job! Now, let's search this cavern, see if there are any hidden treasures. Then we'll work our way back up and loot all the rooms we cleared. Everything we find should be upgraded from the first kill bonus, so search carefully!" The others cheered as they broke up into pairs and began searching the cavern for any hidden doors or secret stashes. The rooms above had held desks and cabinets, workbenches, and even an armory. Plenty of places for interesting items like scrolls or enchanted weapons to be stashed.

Hope was about to join in the search when she noticed that the reward chest hadn't disappeared. Peering into it, she saw that the bottom appeared to be covered in gold coins. When she reached in to touch one of them, the whole lot disappeared, and her inventory was suddenly a thousand gold coins heavier. She watched as the others froze, straightening up as they received similar amounts. "Yeah, there were ten thousand gold coins in the chest, too." She grinned at them. "We're rich!"

*****

Allistor paced back and forth, nervous about his team. He'd seen the notification over an hour earlier saying that Hope's team, the first to enter the dungeon, had earned the First Kill achievement. Since then, the two other teams had both emerged, one of them missing a single member, a human caster that was killed in the boss fight. They were disappointed about not winning the race to kill the boss, but overall pleased with the loot they had received.

The problem was that Hope's team hadn't come back out yet. People were beginning to mutter, wondering what had gone wrong. Questions were asked of the two other teams about what kind of fights they encountered, whether they saw any traps that might have taken out the team after the boss fight. Both teams reported only minor traps that they disarmed or tossed zombies into to set them off, none of them serious enough to take out a whole party.

But that was assuming that her whole party survived the boss fight.

With a whirlwind of dire possibilities spinning through his head, Allistor paced more quickly. He was helpless in this situation. Since the dungeon was instanced, he couldn't send in a rescue party. Communications didn't work inside the dungeon, outside the party coms, so he couldn't call them for a report. All he could do was wait, and imagine the worst.

Others around him were showing similar concerns, feeding off of his obvious worry. He forced himself to hold still, then to walk over and congratulate the raiders who had emerged. He plastered a fake smile onto his face and praised them for their bravery and adventurous spirit, making sure they knew to attend a celebration in their honor that evening.

He was running out of ways to project calm and confidence when Hope's team finally emerged. As the crowd in the tunnel roared their approval, Allistor held his breath, focused on counting bodies. When he saw that all ten of them had survived, he exhaled sharply and strode forward, relief flooding his body and relaxing his muscles.

"Team One! Congratulations! And what the hell took you so long!?" He shouted above the noise, causing the much-relieved crowd to laugh. Hope actually blushed as she bowed her head to Allistor, along with the rest of her team.

"Apologies, Emperor Allistor. We made an early decision to forego looting to get to the boss faster. After we killed her, we had to go back and search all the rooms."

Allistor chuckled, as did most of the crowd. He didn't blame them one bit. Loot was half the reason for going into a dungeon in the first place. "Ha! Good plan, and it obviously worked. I hope the dungeon rewarded you accordingly?" He'd already heard from the other groups, and knew the dungeon offered good drops.

"It sure did!" The gnome rogue piped up, emerging from behind Hope's legs. "We're rich! I won't have to work for a year!" Hope rolled her eyes, but nodded her agreement.

"Well, I'm proud of you." He turned to face all the raiders. "All of you! Well done!" He began to applaud the three groups, encouraging everyone else to join in. After a few moments, he held up his hands for silence. "Alright, let's get everyone back to the tower so you can share your stories, and earn lots of free drinks! There will be a celebration dinner later, so don't get too drunk to enjoy it!" He turned to Bjurstrom. "Get the undead traffic flowing again, funnel them into the entrance." He paused, then leaned in and added more quietly, "Also, get each group to vote on their MVP, and find out as discretely as possible what weapon enchantment might benefit them the most." Bjurstrom nodded and began speaking into his coms.

Allistor led the group down the southern tunnel to the 57th Street subway station, then up to the surface, where thousands more citizens were waiting. They cheered and stomped their feet as the raiders emerged, quieting briefly when they noted that one team had only nine members. Allistor gave them a minute to celebrate, then led the now much larger procession down the streets of Invictus City to the tower. There he left them to celebrate while he excused himself and rode the elevator up to his quarters. It had been a stressful day, and he needed to unwind in private for a little while.

Sitting on the sofa in the common area of his suite, he let his head fall back and rest on the cushions, closed his eyes, and just breathed slowly and deeply for a few minutes. His concern for his people, combined with the frustration of not being able to help them, and his need to try to put up a good front for everyone else, had put a strain on him.

Allistor smiled slightly as he remembered a conversation with Amanda on this very sofa, shortly after they'd claimed the city. His holdings were expanding rapidly, and the responsibility was weighing on him. She'd coached him on the breathing exercises he was now using, then kissed him gently and told him how proud she was of him. Just then he could almost feel the sensation of her lips on his, see the smile in her eyes as she patted his cheek.

A pang of sorrow caused him to open his eyes. He gazed at the ceiling for a moment, deciding now was not the time to reminisce. "Nigel, please ask my advisors to join me in their conference room in five minutes, if they're available."

"*Of course, Sire.*" The AI replied.

Allistor took a moment to pull out his notepad. He tore out a single sheet, then began listing the dungeon cores that he held. Next to each one he added either a potential location, or a question mark. It was time to place the cores and get the dungeons operating, and he needed some advice.

When the list was complete, he stepped into the elevator, then out again one floor down. He found all of his inner circle of advisors already awaiting his arrival in the conference room. Taking a moment to pour himself a glass of orange juice from a side table, he joined them.

"Thanks for coming on such short notice. I'm sure you've all heard that we successfully cleared the undead dungeon, losing one raider out of thirty. Initial reports are that the loot was significant in both quality and quantity. People are already clamoring for a chance to take their turn inside." He watched as the others all nodded. A few of them were of the appropriate level to run the dungeon themselves.

"So I want to discuss two things. First, we need to work out a system for approving and scheduling raiders for dungeon runs, in this one and all the others. Second, I want your input on where to place the remaining cores that we have, as well as what type of dungeon to make from the unaligned core."

Chapter Twelve

Getting to the Core of the Matter

For the next week Allistor traveled around, planting dungeon cores and visiting settlements. His first stop was his shortest trip, he simply stepped through the teleport to Ramon and Nancy's Citadel. Nancy was their best horticulturalist, and an accomplished alchemist as well, so when it came time to choose a place to create the plant-based dungeon, it seemed obvious. After checking with the both of them to make sure they were willing to have a dungeon within their Citadel, they took a short hike around the property formerly known as Governor's Island. The space was already pretty well spoken for, Nancy and Chloe having greatly expanded the beehives, gardens, orchards, and greenhouses on the island. Ramon had likewise extended the living and working structures. He now had more than five hundred citizens working as inscriptionists, calligraphers, and scroll-makers, with another five hundred in training, and the operation required a great deal of space. But the group found a spot near the opposite end of the island from the teleport pad and most of the inhabited buildings.

Allistor had been surprised by how simple it was to create a dungeon using one of the purpose-created cores. He simply had to set it down where he wanted it, place one hand on it, and choose the activation command. In this case, they chose an old stone tool shed that was no longer in use, since storage rings were a much more effective place to keep your tools. When Allistor set the core on the ground inside and activated it, they all took several steps back to watch what happened.

The result was a bit anticlimactic. The bright green orb pulsed several times, then sank through the floor of the shed. The ground under their feet trembled slightly several times, dust from crumbling mortar in the shed's walls obscuring their view until a breeze cleared it out. There was a shout of distress from the direction of the beehive, where the trembling had caused the bees to swarm. Nancy and Chloe were about to dash off to help corral the bees when a softly glowing green portal appeared in the center of the tool shed. It stretched from wall to wall, floor to ceiling, swirling slowly in an inviting manner.

Allistor immediately received a notification letting him know the dungeon was level two, not instanced, and awarding him a significant amount of experience for creating the dungeon. All of which went to his personal pool, as he hadn't thought to dedicate a portion to the general pool.

"Is that it? Is it done? Let's go in and look!" Chloe was already half a step into her charge toward the portal when Nancy grabbed her by the back of her shirt.

"Not so fast, little lady." Nancy hugged the little girl close to restrain her. "Maybe when you're older, and bigger. We don't know how dangerous this dungeon is."

Ramon agreed, giving Chloe a conspiratorial wink as he spoke. "Your mother is right. There could be giant Venus flytraps and other carnivorous plants in there, just waiting to snack on a little girl your size. Or vines that could grab you up and tickle you till you pee!"

Chloe's suspicious glare told him she wasn't buying it, but she let the matter drop with just a single foot-stomp, crossed arms, and a pouty face. She hadn't really expected them to let her into the dungeon, but it had been worth a shot. She imagined it was filled with all sorts of wondrous plants and crafting ingredients.

There was no shortage of volunteers to make the first run, and Allistor left his friends to organize things. He wanted to stay and make sure whatever group went in came back out safely, but he was training himself to accept that he couldn't protect everyone all the time. These were grown adults, aware of the risks, and willing to take them in pursuit of growth, loot, and wealth. He had to learn to trust in his people's judgement and abilities, or he'd make himself insane.

Before he left, he took a moment to ask two of his oldest friends their opinion on the unaligned core. His advisors had given him several recommendations, which he was still considering, but none of them really spoke to him.

Still maintaining a tight grip on a squirming Chloe, who was wistfully eyeing the dungeon entrance as Max gave it a good sniff, Nancy didn't hesitate with her recommendation. "Can you create a giant child-care dungeon? One we can send unruly children to for the day? Filled with nannies, puppies, crayons, and child development experts who will teach them to listen to their parents? Maybe some quests to do educational crafting and learn to read?"

"Ha! I'd be the most popular emperor anywhere in the galaxy." Allistor leaned in to give her a side hug. "I'll even ask if that's possible, just for you."

Ramon shook his head. "I can't come up with anything better than that." He kissed Nancy on the cheek. "Except maybe that cooking dungeon we talked about before. I'd give my left…" he paused and glanced down at Chloe. "umm, butt cheek to watch Meg take on that dungeon."

"You'd look silly with half a butt!" Chloe stuck her tongue out at him, then giggled.

"If we let Meg into a cooking dungeon, she'd stay and become the final boss." Allistor offered Ramon a fist to bump. "Alright, thanks for the input. I'm off to visit a new settlement, then plant another core. Have fun storming the dungeon!"

*****

Gene was flying the *Phoenix* as it landed in a wide open field near a Citadel in Norway. Kira had volunteered to fly a group of Lightholm dwarves that wanted to visit an active volcano somewhere out in the Pacific, using one of Allistor's captured goblin ships. After working to stabilize the Yellowstone supervolcano, the dwarves had taken it upon themselves to secure more of them. Allistor had given them the choice of payment for their services in the

232

form of currency or merchandise, or the rights to mine those volcanoes once they were made safe. The dwarves were much more interested in mining, and Allistor figured it cost him nothing, since few people wanted to live next to active volcanoes anyway. And his agreement seemed to make the Lightholm dwarves very happy.

As Allistor, Helen, McCoy and twenty raiders, half a dozen battle droids, and a score of trainers exited the Phoenix via the cargo ramp, a similar number of armed individuals exited the Citadel gate in front of them. They advanced maybe fifty yards out from the wall as the gate closed behind them, keeping their weapons in hand, but pointed at the ground.

Allistor raised both hands to show that they were empty, then lowered his left and used his right hand to wave as they approached at a sedate pace. Seeing the concerned looks the Norwegians were giving the battle droids and non-human trainers, Allistor asked them to hang back until introductions could be made. The folks in front of the gate looked relieved when they obeyed Allistor's request, and their leader nodded in thanks.

"Hello there!" Allistor waved one more time, now about twenty paces from the group. "I'm Allistor, and I thought I might come pay you a visit, see how you're all doing." He paused to look up at the wall, which was lined with defenders, most of who were holding rifles or longbows.

"Allistor, as in the man who calls himself Emperor of Earth?"

Allistor sighed. It was going to be one of *those* meetings. "Yes, that's me. Only it's not something I call myself. It's a title assigned by the System. I accepted it, because it gives humanity better control of our world." He paused, looking at the leader. "Can I assume this is your Citadel? I believe the System granted you a noble title when you upgraded it, right? Was that something you chose?"

The man grunted, nodding once to acknowledge the point. "Are you here to claim our land?"

"Absolutely not! What's yours is yours. I did come to talk to you about potentially joining us, but should you choose to do so, you still own whatever land you've claimed, or was granted to you after Stabilization. I literally have more land than I can ever make use of, or manage, and have zero interest in obtaining more. I'm here for you, my fellow humans, not for material things." He turned his gaze to the folks standing behind the big man in front, then those on the wall. "I'd just like to speak with you a while. If you don't like what I have to say, we'll leave you in peace."

"The people behind you, they look like fighters. Too many to allow inside our home."

Allistor didn't look back, but smiled slightly as he pictured McCoy and all the raiders behind him suddenly doing their best to look innocent and harmless.

"They are fighters. Some of the best on the planet. But they mean you no harm. They're actually here to speed things up, to answer questions for your people, should you choose to ask them. We've been through this process about a hundred times now, and have sort of streamlined things." Allistor held his hands out to either side, making sure everyone saw that they were empty. "As for your safety, let me tell you this. I'm nearly level one hundred. If I meant to harm you or your people, I could destroy you all by myself. I dislike doing this, but if you need proof, raise that rifle and try to kill me. I promise not to retaliate." He cast *Barrier* in front of himself as he spoke.

The people he faced made varying noises of surprise at his declaration. The average level of humans outside of his own citizens was still in the twenties. Few had advanced to fifty or higher. At most of the settlements he and his people had contacted, a significant percentage of the population, mostly the non-combatants, children, and support folks, had not reached level ten.

Next to him, Helen snorted. "At least you didn't cast your *Storm* spell this time." He shot her a dirty look, and she just blew him a sarcastic kiss.

The leader shook his head. "That will not be necessary. Regardless of your level, I know you could have destroyed our home with that ship from beyond our reach. I believe you have good intentions. My name is Andersson. Welcome to our home." He waved Allistor forward, and his people parted to allow Allistor and his twenty raiders to walk through. McCoy spoke into his coms, and the droids escorted the trainers back to the ship to await an eventual summons in comfort.

"Those were aliens you brought with you." Andersson observed quietly as Allistor drew close. He fell in beside him and escorted him through the gate. "I saw what I think are gnomes, elves, dwarves, and others I do not recognize."

"They are indeed from other worlds. We call them non-humans or off-worlders, rather than aliens, a more polite term. They are also class trainers, a small part of a large group I hired to help our people grow stronger. One of the benefits of being a citizen of Invictus."

The man paused for a moment, looking back over his shoulder at the retreating crowd. "And the robots?"

"Battle droids. I use them as guards, escorts, and a fighting force when necessary. They have saved my life more than once." Allistor explained, holding nothing back. "You can purchase them yourself, I believe, as the owner of a Citadel."

Andersson just nodded, continuing their walk. Behind them, Allistor could hear some of the locals begin speaking with his raiders. That was a good sign. His people knew to casually mix and mingle whenever possible. As he'd said, this wasn't their first rodeo. They tried to learn from the mistakes and challenges of previous first contact interactions.

The inside of the Citadel was sparse, the buildings clean and orderly, with a lot of straight lines, natural colors, and wood accents. It all had a distinctly northern European feel to it, and Allistor decided he quite liked it. Hundreds of people were standing in small groups in front of those buildings, all of them looking his way. He smiled widely and gave several friendly waves, especially to curious children. People always felt better about visitors who were nice to their kids.

"We can talk inside, if you wish some privacy." Andersson offered, motioning toward a building directly ahead that resembled a medieval keep.

"That's up to you. I have nothing to say that I'm not comfortable with everyone hearing, but if you'd like to have a private discussion instead, I'm all yours."

"I would ask you some questions regarding your intentions, just you and I." Andersson puffed out his chest slightly, looking down on Allistor despite his System-enhanced growth spurt. The man was over seven feet tall, with shoulders that could support an entire building, and Allistor suspected that he'd had his own growth due to attribute increases. He'd put about even odds on the man if he was to wrestle a grizzly. Not Fuzzy, of course, but a normal grizzly. Assuming there were any of those left.

"Then I'll follow you, and we can talk. Would you like my people to return to the ship? They can be quite chatty, and I don't want them divulging information you'd rather not get shared."

Andersson looked thoughtfully at the raiders, who were indeed doing their best to look harmless. McCoy had his hands clasped behind his back and was whistling a nursery rhyme about a weasel. Allistor rolled his eyes at the display. Andersson just snorted. "No, they may remain. I am sure my people wish to speak with them. I am no dictator, wishing to limit my people in some way to protect my authority. If they can learn valuable things from your people, that is a good thing."

Allistor nodded at McCoy, saying, "I'll be back... in a bit. Answer whatever questions these nice folks have." He turned and followed his host inside. Almost immediately after they crossed the front threshold, they took a right turn and stepped into a small meeting room with exposed stone walls, a round table and eight chairs. Andersson motioned for Allistor to sit, waiting until he did so before taking his own seat.

"I have wondered if you would come here." Andersson started without preamble. "Though I expected a less friendly encounter. Myself and my senior staff, we assumed you conquered many settlements like ours to rise in rank."

Allistor sighed. This was a common assumption around the globe. Human nature being what it was, he didn't blame them for thinking the worst of someone who appeared to rise so rapidly. Humans hadn't had the opportunity to observe each other the way alien factions watched them during Stabilization and beyond. For most of them, their only information on him were the worldwide notices when he accomplished certain goals and achieved new titles. And those were short on details, leaving folks to make their own assumptions as to how he achieved them.

"In the early days, I did have to fight for a few properties. But only against people who were victimizing other people." He took a few minutes to tell Andersson about his encounters at Luther's Landing, and the fight at the supply depot in Laramie. He also mentioned the need to clear some places of monsters before he claimed them, like the Stadium at Laramie, and Dover Castle. Since he'd told Andersson about Luther and George, he mentioned that they'd lost George taking Dover castle.

His host nodded thoughtfully, remaining silent for a long moment. Finally, he spoke. "I too have had to kill other men to keep my family safe. We were attacked more than once by those who wished to take what we built for themselves." He gave Allistor a significant look.

Allistor again held up empty hands, then placed them flat on the table. "I don't want to take anything from you, Andersson. I now own four planets, including Earth, and have tens of millions of citizens, human and otherwise. I have billions worth of gold, an entire fleet of spaceships, several space stations, and two eternity gates that let me travel across the galaxy nearly instantaneously." He waited a moment for all of that to sink in.

"From the first days after the world ended, I have fought for one thing. For people. Initially, my friends, then for the few dozen who joined me, then a few hundred, and so forth. I fought almost non-stop for that first year, doing everything I could to make us, humanity, stronger. Was I motivated in part by a need for revenge? Youbetcha. And as I'm sure you saw in the notifications, I eventually managed to claim the life of Loki, who was the being that initiated Earth's induction several centuries early, and purposely killed off most of the human race." He took a deep breath. "I'm not strong enough to pursue further vengeance right now, or even anytime soon. So now I'm focused on bringing together as much of humanity as I can, making us stronger, and ensuring that as many of us as possible survive."

"That sounds like a fairy tale. No offense." Andersson leaned back in his chair.

"Everything about our new world sounds like a fairy tale." Allistor smiled sadly. "And my story does sound more like one than most. I've risen quickly, in large part due to a few lucky breaks, and because I've been willing to risk everything to push harder. Now I can use the power that comes with my position to protect our world, our people."

"And what would you have of me?"

"Ideally, I'd like you and your people to become citizens of Invictus. To share in the work of making us all stronger, while reaping the benefits of citizenship." He took a few minutes to give his standard recruiting speech. When he was done offering the carrot, he finished with, "But if you don't wish to join me, then we might become allies, or trade partners. It would not be as beneficial to you, as you'd need to pay for things like class training and whatever supplies you might need from us, but it would probably still improve your situation greatly. Or… and this is my least favorite option, you can tell me to kiss off, and we'll leave you in peace today. You'll still fall under the general protection I'm providing for the entire planet, like defense against alien invasion on a large scale. But we'd have no other interaction."

"Why would you do this? Why put so much effort into strangers?"

Allistor considered the question for a moment. He'd been asked it before, but his reasons had evolved over time. "In the early days, it was pure survival. There is safety in numbers, yes?" He waited for the man to nod. "Then it was to protect people who had become like family to me. When I got a little stronger, and strangers began to follow me, I had visions of a vast human army of badass warriors and mages rising up to avenge our dead. But that was mostly a pipe dream. One I used to motivate myself to achieve the first part of that vision, which was to make humanity strong enough to defend itself when the evil alien colonists came. I suppose that was my main goal, my major motivation, until very recently. Over the time since Stabilization ended, I have come to realize that most evil aliens aren't evil at all, they're just like us. Many of them oppressed by those who are more powerful, just looking to earn a living, feed their families, and live in peace. Except for the orcanin... those guys seriously just love to fight." He grinned at the orcanin-sized man across the table.

"Now some of my closest friends and most loyal advisors are non-humans. They have helped me grow my empire, saved my life more than once, and I can't imagine how much worse things might have turned out without their support." Allistor blinked a couple times, realizing he'd gotten off track.

"But I guess the simplest answer to your question is... I do this because I can. Because it's what I've told myself I need to do for the last year and more, and it has become a sort of reflex. I have incredible resources in the form of property, wealth, and power. But the most important resource is the one I'm still trying to gather. That's you and your people." He leaned forward, pressing his chest against the table. "I know, it sounds cheesy. But I invite you and your people to take a tour, visit any of my properties, on any of the planets except maybe the one that you need to travel through the eternity gate to reach, and ask anyone you see whatever questions you like. Let them tell you their stories, and you can judge for yourself if my intentions are sincere."

Andersson was still looking thoughtful. "You make some convincing arguments. How many other settlements have joined you? And how many have refused?"

Allistor deflated slightly. "I know of twenty two who have refused, if you go back to the early days. Several of those are trading partners, or even allies. But nine have declined our offer since I became emperor and began reaching out like I am with you. As for how many settlements have joined, I'm ashamed to say I don't know the exact number. I have several teams roaming the planet and approaching settlements like yours. But hold on a second." He raised his wrist and spoke into his coms. "Nigel, how many settlements here on Earth have joined Invictus in total. Counting all those who joined up since I created the Bastion."

The reply took just a few seconds. *"Two thousand three hundred sixty one settlements of Stronghold level or higher, Sire. An additional hundred and thirty seven*

smaller communities have joined, all of which have been
upgraded to Stronghold status by yourself or your teams."

Both men's eyes bugged out for a moment, until a
realization hit Allistor. He looked at Andersson and
smiled. "We didn't visit all of those. A bunch of people
swore the oath and became citizens after my worldwide
message. It seems we picked up whole communities that
way. A bunch of them." He motioned toward his wrist
unit. "Meet Nigel, by the way. He's the AI that operates
all of my properties. He's full of useful information and
quite handy to have around. Say hello, Nigel."

"Hello, Nigel." The AI deadpanned, Allistor
snorted.

"He's apparently developing a sense of humor, as
well."

"Hello, Nigel." Andersson grinned as he replied,
enjoying the joke. Looking across the table at Allistor, he
crossed his arms. "I have spent a good deal of time
planning how to repel your eventual attempt to take my
Citadel. In my mind, you have been a threat to me and
mine. Now... now I find that you are maybe not so bad a
fella." He uncrossed his arms and reached one hand across
the table. "It is good to meet you, Emperor Allistor."

Allistor initially froze, having trained himself at
L'olwyn's insistence not to allow anyone to touch him.
But since the elf wasn't looking, he took the man's hand in
a firm grip and shook it. "The pleasure is mine, is it Baron
Andersson? Or Viscount? I forget which comes with the
Citadel."

"Ha! The System made me a Baron, but in the tradition of my homeland, my people call me Jarl. It is mostly a term of respect and endearment, less an actual title."

Allistor had a thought, and thumped the table. He instantly regretted it when Andersson jumped in surprise, becoming wary. "Sorry. Listen, any chance you're considering joining Invictus yourself? Just you, personally, not speaking for your people."

The man nodded slowly... still a little wary. "Ya, I am... considering."

"Good! Hold on a second." Allistor opened his interface and sought out the tab that let him grant titles. He hadn't used it since he'd had a little fun naming his friends ministers and knights. A moment later he smiled as he saw Andersson's eyes unfocus to read the notification he'd just received.

The man coughed into his hand. "You are offering me... to be a vassal?"

"More specifically, an Earl. Which is basically the same as a Jarl. If your people think you should be one, who am I to argue?"

"But... I must think." The man shook his head, focusing back on Allistor.

"No problem. I made the offer good for forty eight hours. If you're not ready by then, just refuse it, and we can revisit that later." Allistor had just thought the man would be amused by a stupid emperor trick, but was belatedly realizing it might look like he was trying to pressure him with a bribe. "Either way, your choice won't have any impact on whether you and your people are welcomed to join us as citizens. I just thought you'd all get a kick out of it."

"I understand, and appreciate the gesture." The man actually bowed his head. "There are other leaders like me here in Norway, and declaring myself a actual Jarl, or having you do so, without consulting them first might create hard feelings. The title implies sole sovereignty over this region, one step below a King."

"I have a way around that, as well. If you decide to join me, we'll upgrade your Citadel to a Bastion, and the System will make you an Earl. I think. Then you can just blame it on the system reacting to your success. Assuming that would interest you. But I completely understand if you'd rather wait and consult with each other. In fact, I'd be happy to fly around with you and visit the others, gather everyone up for a... council? What would you call such a meeting?"

"A meeting." Andersson laughed. "And all of this should be discussed after my people have had a chance to speak with you and decide for themselves." Allistor got a notice that the man had rejected the offer of promotion. He nodded.

"Fair enough. Do you have more questions for me? Or should we go speak with them. I'll follow your lead here. If you'd like us to give you some space and come back in a few days, we can do that. Having a ship that circles the globe in less than an hour comes in handy sometimes."

"Heh. I imagine so. I am a pilot myself, or I was before Ragnarok. I have not been able to obtain a plane to fly since then."

"I'll introduce you to Gene. He's piloting my ship today, and is an engineer. He and his wife are plane nuts. Er, plane enthusiasts. That sounds better. Anyway, they've been collecting and improving planes for months now. Everything from private prop planes to private jets and big old cargo transports. I'm sure they'd let you play with a few of them. They actually helped me earn the *Pilot* skill, and I can now fly a few of the planes."

"That sounds exciting." The big man's eyes actually seemed to sparkle at the idea. "I may take you up on that. Now, I think I have no more questions. At least, none that cannot be asked in front of everyone outside. Let us go and speak to them. Then I would like to see this ship of yours. It looked beautiful up in the sky."

"You've got a deal!" Allistor got to his feet, offering the man his hand to shake once again. It felt good, and Allistor hardly felt any guilt at all for sneaking a handshake or two past L'olwyn.

As the two men stepped outside, Allistor found McCoy and most of his raiders with mugs in hand, raising a toast to their hosts before drinking deeply. The locals were imbibing just as enthusiastically, cheering as McCoy tilted his head back and drained the full mug. When he finished, he wiped some foam from his upper lip and shouted, "Skol!"

Next to him, Andersson let out a deep belly laugh. "It seems our people have already decided to be friends."

By nightfall, Andersson and more than a thousand Norwegians became citizens of Invictus. The trainers were invited inside the walls, and the celebration that ensued lasted nearly until dawn. Allistor, true to his word, gave the big man a tour of the Phoenix, and introduced him to Gene. The two men promptly fell into an animated discussion of planes, leaving Allistor to his own devices.

Having had more than a few drinks himself, and feeling pleased with the day's progress, he took a few minutes to send messages out before turning in. First he messaged Kira to let her know that Gene and *Phoenix* were staying in Norway overnight, in case Gene was too distracted to handle that himself. He checked in with Nancy, who was ecstatic over the materials the first group had brought out of the plant dungeon. Her enthusiasm didn't even wane when she had to admit to Allistor that she'd allowed Chloe to name the dungeon, an option they were given because it was inside their Citadel, and that the little stinker had decided to call it the Daisy Dungeon. Allistor assured her that it was a wonderful name in his sweetest, most innocent tone, causing her to snort.

The final call was to his kids, who had already been tucked in by Meg. He told them where he was, updated them on the day's progress, and asked them how their day had been. Assured that everyone was safe and content, he slipped into his quarters aboard the ship and caught a few hours of sleep.

Chapter Thirteen

Dwarves Can Sing!

The next dungeon core Allistor placed was a no-brainer. He gathered up Harmon and his ten most senior raid leaders, along with his kids, Helen, and the bears, and the whole group took a stroll through the city, down to Battery Park.

Along the way, Allistor observed the changes to his city since he'd claimed it and raised the walls. The mostly broken and burned buildings along Broadway, the main north-south street in the currently occupied section of the city, had nearly all been restored or reshaped. Most were set up as housing, though Allistor was surprised to see several of the shattered storefronts had been turned into shops. There was a bakery, a daycare center with an indoor playground, a clothes store that sold citizen-crafted items as well as what appeared to be salvaged goods, a bookstore that looked like it had been a bookstore before the apocalypse as well, even a small store that sold musical instruments. One of the retail spaces had been turned into a massive gym for folks who wanted to raise their stats the old fashioned way, and it included a refreshment bar with a lounge area so folks could socialize between sets.

They were a good ten blocks south of Invictus Tower before the buildings on either side of the road reverted back to the unclaimed, damaged husks that filled most of his city. That amount of recovery and expansion was an encouraging sign for such a short period of time. Allistor was proud of his people.

Another big difference from the city's first days was that the road was clear. As were the first few blocks of all the side streets. Abandoned and destroyed vehicles had been hauled away to be used for salvage, while the smaller debris had been swept up and removed. The street was still pitted and scorched, but it was looking a hundred percent better than the last time Allistor had traveled this way.

He set a slow pace, and they covered the dozen or so blocks to Battery Park in just a few minutes. They could have taken the teleporter directly from the tower, but Allistor wanted to walk. He hadn't spent enough time getting to know his city and its citizens.

They walked across the park and into the gate of Castle Clinton, the old national park monument. Its round structure was the first Stronghold Allistor created in the city, and was the perfect place for a dungeon. Looking around, he noted the teleport pad off to one side of the fort's interior. Fuzzy and Fiona, bored with the non-bear activities going on, drifted back out the gate to go sniff around the park.

Moving to the opposite side from the teleport pad, Allistor chose a medium sized room within the interior of the fort. He retrieved the combat core from his inventory, and held it up. "I think this is a good spot for this, don't you?" He asked Harmon.

"This may be your most valuable dungeon, Allistor." Harmon reached out with a single finger to touch the glowing core. "The plant and mineral dungeons will produce worthy crafting items along with the experience they provide. But a combat core is a useful and vital tool for training whole military units, from squads to whole regiments."

"Which is why I wanted to place it here in the city, where we can protect it." Allistor agreed. "This park has room to land a large ship carrying troops, in case we allow visitors to use it. It's within sight of the city walls and their defensive turrets, as well as the Stronghold walls and their defenses. Not to mention the teleport pad being here, in case we need to send our own troops in quickly." He paused to look around, picturing a battle between his people and a force of misbehaving visitors. "We could trap any bad actors in here and cut them to pieces."

Helen, the Minister of Parks, added, "Plus, this was one of the original forts built to defend New York City against the British ships and troops. It's sort of fitting that it be used to train *our* troops."

"When we actually *have* troops." Allistor grinned. "Right now we have a few thousand raiders and citizens who can fight. But I suppose we should establish a standing army of professional soldiers, sooner rather than later."

"And this will help you." Harmon nodded. "Your soldiers will gain both experience and training inside. You can adjust the dungeon's settings with each session, changing the size and scope of the battles, the types and difficulty of the enemy your soldiers face, even the types of weapons used in the engagements." He looked into Allistor's eyes. "But be aware, this dungeon is no safer than any other. Arguably less so, in fact. Those who die inside are gone for good. The battle parameters may be controlled, but accidents happen, and weak or careless soldiers will still die."

Allistor grimaced, but nodded his head. "Unlike some of the other Emperors you've told me about, I'm going to make this particular type of training optional for my soldiers. They'll be warned of the dangers, and prepared as well as possible before entering. Their fellow soldiers will be looking out for them, not allowing them to become meat for the grinder. No one will be forced to face death inside the dungeon."

"Well said." Harmon gave him a respectful nod. "Now, place the orb, and let us see what you get!" the big orcanin's eyes shone with anticipation.

Allistor did just that, placing the core on the stone floor of the chosen room, then activating it. Like with the plant dungeon, the core glowed brightly, pulsing several times before sinking into the stone. This time it was several minutes before the dungeon had formed itself, a bright blue and red portal appeared inside the room, and Allistor received the notification.

"This one's a level five dungeon! But with only two instances." He reported. "It says it can be adjusted down to level two, for participants between level twenty and thirty, or set at level five for fighters between level fifty and sixty. That seems like a pretty good range." He didn't share the information about the experience he received for successfully creating the dungeon.

"A good range indeed!" Harmon agreed as the others clapped or quietly cheered behind him. "And as the dungeon grows, the range will increase. In a century or two, it might be an effective tool for warriors approaching level one hundred!"

Allistor looked away from his friend, not wanting to think about the dungeon leveling up by killing and eating his people. It was a fact of life in this new world, one which he accepted, but didn't feel like celebrating.

Seeing his reaction, Harmon placed a comforting hand on his shoulder. "You have already stated that you'll do your best to keep your own soldiers from perishing inside. But there is nothing stopping you from allowing less... conscientious leaders to send in their warriors. Ones who will be less supportive of their troops, and willing to sacrifice their weakest to improve their armies overall." He shook his head as Allistor opened his mouth. "They would make these sacrifices anyway, whether in your dungeon, or another. Better to strengthen your position by charging them exorbitant sums for the privilege, and allowing them to level up your dungeon for you at the same time."

Allistor liked that idea only slightly better. Weaklings being sacrificed to the dungeon made him sick. But he knew, even based on his limited experience with the powerful entities of this new world he found himself in, that the weak would be sacrificed with or without his participation. If it wasn't in his dungeon, their deaths would make someone else more powerful. Probably someone less interested in the well-being of their people.

"Bjurstrom, same setup as last time. Hold a lottery for… let's start with a group of fifty. Five groups of ten. You can train on how to coordinate groups into a single force." He looked at Harmon. "Do you want some spots?"

The orcanin shook his head. "The point of this dungeon is to teach your fighters to work as a unit. Adding in my warriors would just slow that process. But I thank you for the offer."

Allistor nodded, then added to his instructions for Bjurstrom. "No one under level forty. Experienced fighters only. Raiders, hunters, healers if they've been in some real fights. No one who just cashed in on defense quest experience, or a few of the other big level boosts. And if any of the trainers want to participate, let them."

Bjurstrom saluted with fist to chest, and began talking into his coms.

Harmon kept pace with Allistor as he strode away from the dungeon entrance. "Have you decided what to do with the unaligned core?"

"Not yet." Allistor shook his head slowly, thoughtful. "There are so many options, and I'm trying to figure out which type would most benefit my people."

"Now, or later?" Harmon looked down at Allistor.

"What do you mean?"

"Are you looking for the most benefit to your people as they are right now, or as they will be ten years, fifty years from now?"

"I'm not sure I get what you mean. They'll be higher level by then, or at least most of them will be. But the dungeons should level up with them."

"There are two wrong things in that statement, my friend. First, dungeons level slowly. Your people, all but the civilians who remain sheltered, will out-level them quickly enough in the short term. But in a very few years you will find that your people's growth will slow. In part because higher levels are harder to achieve, and in part because this world will stabilize. The high concentration of mana generated by the billions of deaths in a short period will be absorbed, and there will be fewer spawns. Fewer monsters to kill, and those few will be more powerful. Meaning your people will have to band together to kill them, and share the experience. The dungeons will help some, certainly. But not enough for you or your warriors to keep their current pace of growth."

"Do you have a recommendation?" Allistor was curious what his friend was leading up to.

"No, I do not. I don't know your people as well as you do. And while I have significant experience with a wide array of dungeons, I would not presume to instruct you in this matter. I am simply suggesting that you cannot continue to simply react to the challenges you currently face. As an Emperor, you need to do a great deal of long term planning. Set future goals, anticipate future challenges, and begin to prepare for them."

Allistor contemplated those words as they strolled back toward the tower. Helen had whistled for Fuzzy and Fiona to join them, but most of the others stayed behind in hopes of being able to get in on the first kill dungeon run. Allistor could have allowed two groups to run against each other, but he didn't want the raiders focusing on anything other than the dungeon objectives.

"You're saying... hold that core in reserve, until I have a better idea how best to use it."

Harmon smiled, but replied. "I have said no such thing. Though I commend you on reaching such a wise and well-considered conclusion completely on your own."

"Ha! Okay, I get it." Allistor shook his head, a rueful grin on his face. "It's not like we have a shortage of dungeons to run, now. And as you mentioned, there are still whole cities, forests, and even oceans full of monsters to hunt. Did I tell you about the gigantic sea monster we encountered out west?"

The two chatted amiably as they perambulated through the southern part of the city.

*****

Helen pointed to a point on a holographic map projected above the conference table. "There are large settlements here, and here. Like, Citadel sized, maybe larger. Thousands, maybe tens of thousands of people at each. They've not answered any radio calls, even when we found a few translators to try broadcasting in their language."

The locations she was indicating were in what had once been China. National boundaries had become a thing of the past in most areas, along with their governments. There wasn't a need to enforce borders anymore, even if there was enough manpower to do so. Which there wasn't, even in a heavily populated nation like China.

"We shouldn't need translators, the System should be handling that." Allistor observed, staring at the map.

"True. But when they didn't respond, we just thought we'd try that, in case they were being stubborn, or something."

"That's a good point. Alright, send a couple of ships, standard first contact crews, but include a couple people on each ship that understand their culture. Maybe they're offended by the idea of having an Emperor again? Or they're still holding on to the tensions between east and west from before the world ended."

Helen raised an eyebrow. "You don't want to lead the missions yourself?"

Allistor shook his head. "From what I remember from school, they are very conscious of station and levels of respect. If they're being uncooperative, I'm not giving them what they would consider the honor of having the world's leader appear at their doorstep. They can deal with my representatives until we have a better idea what their mood is, or their issue."

"Alright, emperor fancypants, we'll do it your way." She elbowed him gently in the ribs as she teased him, then went back to the map. "We've made contact with large groups on every continent now. We're stabilizing those that need it, and encouraging them to reach out to the smaller settlements around them." She tapped the map in several dozen places, then waved her hand, and concentric rings began to spread out from those locations, looking like ripples from raindrops on the surface of a pond. Smaller dots appeared inside those rings to indicate other settlements that had been reached. "We've still only covered about a tenth of the planet, including all the locations here in the US. At this pace it'll take more than a year to reach everyone."

"A year isn't so bad. Imagine how much longer it might have taken without spaceships and all the other resources at our disposal."

"We've invested heavily in teleport hubs and pads, but I think we're going to have to start limiting where we put them. Or requiring them to pay for their own."

Allistor shook his head. "No, we'll pay for them. Assuming they become citizens. If they remain independent, then yes, have them buy their own if they can. We'll work out authorization to connect with our pads on a case by case basis. If they can't afford a hub and pads, and they want to be trade partners, we can assign a few of the goblin ships, or even some of our modified planes with the hydrogen engines, to start traveling trade routes. I'm sure we have people who've chosen merchant classes of some kind. And with storage devices, cargo space isn't an issue anymore." He briefly considered getting a fleet of oceangoing ships active as well, but thoughts of the sea monster had him setting that aside.

"Speaking of trade." L'olwyn spoke up. "We've received a shipment of trees from Queen Xeria, and I had a thought that I wanted to share."

"Sure, what's up?" Allistor took a seat at the table.

"I would like to plant a grove of them around the edge of the clearing where you planted the Revivification Tree." The elf held out a hand and adjusted the holographic map to zoom in on the Wilderness Stronghold, then the clearing on the other side of the lake. "They would act as guardians, protecting the tree from any serious storms that pass overhead."

Allistor had a brief vision of the legendary tree and its priceless fruit being struck by lightning. "Seems like a good idea to me. Have you asked Master Daigath? That's his home, after all."

"I wished to get your approval before speaking with the Master." The elf's voice held a tone of respect when he mentioned that elf that he never showed Allistor. Sometimes Allistor forgot just how ancient and revered his mentor was. High level dignitaries and faction heads that visited Invictus for the auction had bowed to Daigath first, and most deeply. "I believe in addition to protecting the

259

tree, the guardians might provide it with extra energy from any lightning they harvest."

"If that turns out to be true, then we should start planting one near each of our orchards. Maybe one or two per Stronghold." Allistor couldn't think of a single instance where lightning had damaged one of his properties, but he liked the idea of harvesting lightning to juice up their crops. "Maybe we'll get some kind of mutated fruit buff, or something."

L'olwyn smiled, bowing his head slightly. "We shall look into that." His smile faded quickly as he changed topics. "There have been more than a hundred additional requests to purchase land on Orion and Earth. All from friendly factions, so far. How would you like to proceed?"

"As long as they're friendly, I suppose we sell them some land. Find out what locations they want, have a team inspect that land to make sure there aren't any wild dungeons or valuable resources we don't know about. Charge whatever you think is fair. Or... whatever you think they'll pay, without it costing us reputation points?"

The elf nodded. "Very good, Allistor. I shall endeavor to find that balance."

Helen tapped the table when she saw that L'olwyn was finished. "If you're not going to supervise recruitment visits today, what have you got planned?"

"I was thinking we'd take a little trip to Lightholm and set up the mineral dungeon core there. Who better to make sure it gets mined regularly?" He looked sideways at Longbeard, who thumped the table.

"Ye'll not be sorry! Me clan will protect the dungeon, and mine it, and give ye... twenty percent o' the ore that drops as loot, and thirty percent o' the ore mined after the dungeon be cleared."

"How about forty percent of the ore that gets mined, and you keep the loot drops? And that will go for anyone using the dungeon. They keep all loot drops, and either pay forty percent of the mined ore and gems, or simply allow your people to go in and mine it after the dungeon is cleared. They do that, they don't have to pay to use the dungeon."

The dwarf's grin grew wider as Allistor spoke, and his beard bobbed as he nodded his agreement. "Ye know as Emperor, and owner o' the dungeon, ye could demand more."

"And I could raise everyone's taxes, and draft firstborn children into my army, and make everyone take a knee when I enter a room." He rolled his eyes. "Not my style. Just make sure the Invictus share of mined ore and gems gets to Michael and his guys. They can distribute it for crafting and enchanting."

Allistor looked around the table. "Any other matters, urgent or otherwise, we need to discuss?"

Chris raised his hand. "We're draining your gold reserves pretty quickly. We're nowhere near empty yet, but there are a few things I recommend we cut back on."

"Like what?" Allistor drummed his fingers on the table in front of him, a sign he was slightly nervous.

"Well, for one thing, the loans for building Strongholds. It was manageable when you had a few thousand citizens. But now…"

Allistor raised a hand. "Nuff said. Everyone who was a citizen… let's say before Loki died is still eligible. Anyone newer than that is out of luck. I'll make sure that option's not included in the recruiting pitch from now on."

"Membership has its privileges." Helen mumbled.

Chris made a note, adding, "And actually, about half of those we originally gave loans to have paid them back, or will have it paid back soon. They've been making money selling loot or scavenged or crafted items, and some have been receiving salaries for working in your Strongholds. The loans didn't have to be all that large to create a Stronghold, and people are proud to be able to repay them. It has turned out to be a great program."

"In that case, maybe establish a waiting list or something, and we revisit this later. Use the funds that are being repaid to establish a new loan as each one is paid off."

"Or use the funds to pay for the bajillion teleport pads you're buying." Helen snarked.

Ignoring her, Allistor added, "I'd like to give special attention to former slaves on Skapa Far who want loans to build or buy homes of their own. Inside the cities they wouldn't need Strongholds, so hopefully the costs would be lower." He looked sideways at Helen, but she didn't have any snark for that idea.

"You could always claim sections of the city for the Empire, then sell the individual buildings at a discounted rate." Droban suggested.

Allistor shook his head for a moment, thinking. "I don't want to seize property from people I just took in as citizens. But that does give me an idea. For any of the former slave owners, crafters, or merchants who chose not to become citizens and are leaving, we will offer to purchase their properties at a steep discount. Likewise for any who did choose to be citizens, but cannot continue to operate their properties without slave labor. Then we'll sell whatever we buy with zero markup. Former slaves will be given priority to purchase those properties. I'm not going to enable a merchant to become a land baron on discount property."

"We can make that happen." Selby vigorously nodded her head, liking the idea. "You'll need to authorize the… what were they called? Supervisors? You'll need to authorize them to construct new buildings within their cities. Assuming they don't already have that authority."

"Now that you mention it, I don't like that term, supervisors. Let's make them ministers, like Helen here. Or better yet, administrators. And go ahead and authorize them to do what's needed. Though I don't trust them yet, their oaths will keep them in line. And Nigel is monitoring them, just in case there's any abuse of their power."

He looked around the table at some of his closest advisors. "If there's nothing else, we're off to Lightholm." When nobody spoke up, he got to his feet and headed out, Longbeard right behind him. "Anybody who wants to come along and watch is welcome. Though, I gotta say, the process is not very impressive. I drop the core, it pulses, the ground shakes a bit, and it's done. I thought it would be more exciting."

*****

Longbeard had sent word ahead to Lightholm, the moment Allistor had suggested it as the home for the mineral dungeon core. By the time he and Allistor arrived through the teleport pad, there were hundreds of dwarves gathered around. They cheered as soon as the pair materialized on the pad, surprising Allistor and making Longbeard laugh. A dwarf Allistor didn't know stepped forward and bowed deeply.

"Welcome to Lightholm, Emperor Allistor. We're pleased and grateful that ye chose our home to host a dungeon core." There was more cheering from the enthusiastic dwarves behind him.

"It was an easy choice." Allistor nodded to acknowledge the bow. "I have great faith that the dwarves of Lightholm will be excellent protectors and stewards of this mineral dungeon." He paused, a smile creeping across his face. "And I thought you might enjoy the loot!"

This time the cheers turned into a roar accompanied by stomping feet. The dwarf whispered something to Longbeard, who waved for Allistor to follow him. Apparently they'd already chosen a location for the dungeon. As they walked, the dwarves fell in behind, marching along with stomping feet that beat out a rhythm as they chanted a mining song. The voices were deep, and the song echoing off the walls as they walked vibrated within Allistor's bones. A moment later a notification appeared to tell him that he'd received an eight hour *Stamina* and *Constitution* buff.

Longbeard, noticing the look on Allistor's face, nodded. "Aye, it be a handy boost when yer headin into a mine for a long day's work." He winked and nodded his head as they came to a stop at the chosen location. "There be more to see in a moment."

Allistor looked around. They'd chosen a spot in the cliff face just outside of Lightholm's wall. Anyone trying to gain access would face blistering fire from both automated weapons emplacements and dwarves atop the wall. There was a slight indentation in the stone, not enough to call a cave, but maybe enough to provide shelter from the rain for a small group.

"We chose a spot outside the walls so that visitors we're not fond of can set up camp and use the dungeon without entering our home." explained the dwarf who had greeted them. Allistor was trying, but just couldn't remember his name.

"Looks like a fine spot." Allistor produced the core and held it up for all to see. "I'm placing the responsibility for this core in your capable hands!" He called out loud enough for the whole group, which was now more than a thousand dwarves, to hear.

Within seconds, the dwarves broke into another song. This one was more solemn, with a slower cadence, sounding sorrowful yet hopeful at the same time. As they sang, the core began to pulse along in rhythm, and glow more brightly. Allistor looked to Longbeard with a raised eyebrow, and the dwarf held up a finger for him to be patient.

When the song ended, he nodded at Allistor, then looked toward the alcove. Allistor took the hint and set the core down on the stone as far back as he could. When he stepped back, and the usual process began, the dwarves resumed their song.

Longbeard stepped closer to Allistor and motioned for him to lower his head before whispering. "We have a secret I'd share with ye, but I'll need ye to swear to keep it to yerself."

Allistor nodded, mumbling, "I will keep your secret."

As the core disappeared into the stone, and the ground began to rumble, Longbeard said, "When we mine ore and gems, we use this same song to infuse our picks with mana. It makes 'em stronger, and more effective at cuttin' into the stone." He gestured with one hand toward the alcove, still whispering. "When we're inside a dungeon, there be an added benefit. Dungeons consume mana to make them more powerful. When we mine with the infused picks in a dungeon, it absorbs a bit o' the mana with each strike. And since dungeons use their mana to create monsters, and in this case more minerals, we help ourselves by helpin' the dungeon. We have found that the loot, and the resources we mine afterward, are better when we've been offerin' mana to the dungeon."

"And you all just sang this song…?"

"To gift the core a blessing o' our mana. To maybe make it stronger, to ask it for better loot!" the dwarf grinned up at him.

Allistor chuckled. "I hope it works! Better loot is always a good thing." He looked around at the crowd. "I have to hold a lottery for the first raid group, as I've done with the other cores. But your people get first priority on the mining. I'll leave it up to you how you choose the ones who go in."

"Ah, that be easy. The highest level miners will be the first. It be their privilege." He paused for a moment. "When the raid group is ready to leave, if there be none in the group with the mining skill, the raid leader will need to remain inside until we can send in our miners. Otherwise the dungeon will reset."

"I'll make sure they know that. We should maybe post a sign here next to the entrance, as a reminder. Or send a miner in with each group? They can wait in the safe zone until the dungeon is cleared?"

Longbeard shook his head. "That would leave the raid group short one member. Miners can wait outside easily enough. We'll be settin' up a hospitality station out here, as well as a smaller defensive perimeter. Each group will have to check in, and will be told the rules. Includin' that, should they try n take the core, they'll die where they stand the moment they step out."

Allistor hadn't considered that non-citizen dungeon groups might try to take the orb. He made a mental note to address that possibility as the dwarves were doing here. It would mean assigning some high level guards, and possibly some battle droids, to each dungeon entrance.

He was broken out of his contemplation of security measure when the dungeon portal appeared and the notification popped up.

"Level six!" He shouted for all to hear. "Not instanced, though." He looked at Longbeard. "That's the highest so far. Maybe your song did add something."

"Aye, we'll take credit for that!" his advisor grinned at him as the nearby dwarves celebrated. "Level six be very good. It means we'll be minin' ore as high as mithril, and gems up to diamonds. There'll be great wealth harvested from this dungeon, Allistor."

"May your people put their share to good use." Allistor patted the dwarf on the shoulder, causing him to start slightly in surprise, then offer a wink to let Allistor know he wouldn't tell L'olwyn. "Nigel, please announce a lottery for the first run of the mineral dungeon.

Experienced raiders only, between level sixty and seventy, a group of ten."

"*Of course, Sire.*" the AI replied. "*That is a much smaller pool of candidates. Only a hundred and eight citizens with substantial raiding experience are above level sixty.*"

"Thank you, Nigel. And if any of them won a spot in the first combat dungeon run, disqualify them from this lottery. Can't have people doubling up and making others jealous."

Chapter Fourteen

The Price Of Victory

"Sire, an urgent message from Skapa Far." Nigel's voice rang out across the tower roof, loud enough so that Allistor could hear it over the banging of hammer on steel. It broke him out of the fugue he often entered while smithing.

"What is it, Nigel?"

A voice he didn't recognize emerged in place of Nigel's voice. "Emperor Allistor, this is Administrator Dre'nir. Skapa Far is under attack! Several warships dropped out of FTL and assumed orbit around the planet. They are bombarding our cities!"

"Nigel, is this live? Can they hear me?"

"Yes, Sire."

"Citizens of Skapa Far, this is Allistor. I've received your distress call, and we're on our way! Take shelter where you can!" Allistor made a cutting motion to let Nigel know to end the transmission, "Nigel, notify our allies. Get half our fleet ready to go in the next five minutes! Notify our top five hundred raiders to board the nearest ship and be ready to fight."

He was already stepping into the elevator. "Nigel, open the channel again to just Dre'nir." He waited a moment, then asked, "Administrator Dre'nir, is there any indication of who is attacking?"

It took a moment for the reply to come, the signal being sent across two solar systems and through a microgate each direction. "They are not ships we recognize, Sire. They have refused all attempts at communication, simply taking up position over six of our cities and commencing attacks. My own city is one of their targets. I'm afraid casualties are already... significant. We had almost no warning, no time to alert our people."

Growling to himself, Allistor rushed from the elevator and across the ground floor lobby, headed toward *Phoenix*. He saw Kira and several of her crew running half a block ahead of him. Staying close to buildings as he ran so that Nigel could hear him, he answered, "Help as many as you can get to shelter. It'll be the better part of an hour before we can be there. Have you launched the drones?"

"We have. Of the dozen ships that appeared above us, the drones destroyed three, and disabled three more. The orcanin ships have not fired on the invaders, but are maintaining a close orbit."

"The orcanin ships what?" Allistor's mouth dropped open as he ran. He was about to ask for clarification when an orcanin warrior sprinted up behind him. Catching up, he spoke quickly.

"Emperor Allistor. My Emperor wishes you to know that the force attacking Skapa Far is an elven faction. Our ships can not fire on theirs without-"

"Without starting a war with the entire elven race. I understand." Allistor wondered why Harmon hadn't just called him on coms, but he shrugged off the thought as unimportant. "Give him my best regards, and ask him to coordinate the defense of Earth should an attack come while we're gone. I'll leave enough of my ships that your people shouldn't have to fight."

The orcanin bowed briefly, then saluted with fist to chest, and reversed direction. He was already sprinting around a corner before it occurred to Allistor to ask which faction the ships belonged to. He was about to call Harmon and ask, when he remembered that his friend had sent a runner rather than discuss the attack on coms, so there must have been a good reason.

Allistor finished his run to *Phoenix*, running up the ramp and through the ship, reaching the bridge just as Kira and her crew were settling in. He'd noticed dozens of his raiders running behind him, and assumed they were boarding the ship.

"How soon can we lift off?" He asked Kira.

"Two minutes. Systems check has to be done, and we've still got folks running in from the tower."

Allistor gritted his teeth. He knew two minutes was fast when it came to mustering a fighting force, but every second seemed like an hour when his citizens were being slaughtered. "Nigel, please connect me with Commander Enalion of the Or'dralon."

Two seconds later he heard the elf's voice. "This is Enalion. What can I do for you, Emperor Allistor?"

"Commander, a dozen ships just attacked my planet Skapa Far. I'm told they belong to an elven faction. Any idea who that might be?"

There was a short silence before the elf answered. "I am just receiving a report myself, Emperor Allistor. I do not yet know who has attacked you. We are mobilizing ships to assist from every system under our control. The first will arrive in…" There was another pause as he received information from his staff. "Twenty five minutes."

"That means they'll get there before us. Thank you, Commander. That helps a great deal."

"We could do nothing less for a valued ally, Emperor." There was a sincere note of respect in the commander's voice, a far cry from their first meeting on Allistor's maiden voyage into space. "My ship will rendezvous with *Phoenix* at the Orion gate."

The transmission cut off, and was immediately replaced by another. "Emperor Allistor, this be Cogwalker. My ship and the rest o' yer fleet be in orbit, awaiting orders."

"Take half the ships and get to the Orion gate, now! Don't wait for me! The rest are to remain here to protect Earth, in case this is just a diversion. We'll be right behind you."

"Aye, we're on our way. I notified the Stardrifters, and they be sendin' ships as well." The dwarf reported before his transmission ended.

Allistor was kicking himself. He'd discussed placing a satellite defense grid around Skapa Far with Harmon, but the hardware wouldn't be delivered for another couple days. Did the enemy know that? Is that why they attacked now? And he should have stationed at least two of his own ships at the planet, in case this very scenario occurred, and the orcanin ships left to guard it couldn't engage. It simply hadn't occurred to him.

He paced back and forth behind Kira's chair as the crew flew through the process of getting the ship powered up and in the air. Realizing he was not needed on the bridge, he made his way back down to the cargo bay. There he found Bjurstrom and nearly a hundred raiders gathered.

"What's going on, boss?" Bjurstrom approached with several other raid leaders behind him as Allistor felt the ship lift off. Sam was there as well, along with Helen, William, Droban and Longbeard.

"A dozen ships have attacked Skapa Far, and are bombing cities from orbit. They are apparently an elven faction, so the orcanin ships we left there cannot engage. Our drones took out half of them. We're taking half our fleet, and both the Stardrifter clan and Or'Dralon have sent ships. They'll get there before we do."

"*Sire, a message from the Azure Order.*" Nigel reported.

"Put them through, Nigel. Everybody quiet!" Allistor raised his hands and the room went silent, all the raiders now watching and listening.

"Emperor Allistor, this is Omidia of the Azure Order. I have some information for you."

Allistor tried to control himself enough to observe required protocol. "Always a pleasure, Grandmaster. Thank you for reaching out. What information would that be?" He grimaced at how awkward he sounded to himself.

Getting straight to business, Omidia replied. "We had a ship on the way to your world, Skapa Far, to pick up a shipment of crafting ingredients. Our crew witnessed the initial attack, and is observing the ongoing battle." She took a breath, and her tone became apologetic. "Our ship has little in the way of offensive capabilities, and would likely be destroyed if it tried to interfere."

"I understand, Grandmaster. My cargo ships are not well armed, either."

"I thought you'd like to know that the ships attacking you belong to the House of Al'drong. A once powerful mid-level elven House that has fallen from favor in recent centuries. One of my staff is from that House, and she tells me they have been accepting mercenary contracts of late. She does not know why they are attacking Skapa Far, but I have instructed her to find out. I will update you as soon as I have further information."

The moment she spoke the name of the attacking House, Allistor received a notification.

Empire Alert!

The planet Skapa Far is under attack by the House of Al'drong!

275

Defend your world and its citizens!
Reward for successful defense: Variable
Penalty for failure to defend: Loss of ownership
of Skapa Far and its resources. Decreased
reputation with interested factions.

Allistor blinked away the notification, briefly wondering why it had only then appeared. "Thank you, Grandmaster. We'll be there shortly, and your ship is welcome to take position behind our fleet for protection, if they like."

"I'll let them know." She replied before going silent.

"Nigel, please get me Enalion again." Allistor called out as the people around him mumbled. He tried, but could not recall any reputation notices with the name Al'drong.

"Emperor Allistor?" Enalion's voice came through.

"Commander, the Azure Order informs me that the attacking ships belong to the House of Al'drong. Can you tell us anything about them?"

"A minor house, fallen from a higher position. They were once respected for their crafting and ship building skills. A thousand years ago, maybe a little longer, their patriarch died under suspicious circumstances. The heir decided to build an armada and attack a rival House, claiming they assassinated his father. He turned a peaceful and prosperous House into an aggressor, and triggered a short-lived war among a dozen allied mid-level

Houses. Al'drong lost, and was shunned after it was revealed that the heir had murdered his father as an excuse to start the war. They lost all but their homeworld, and many of their famous crafters were killed or captured." There was a moment of silence before he continued.

"I… am afraid I know little of their actions since then. They have kept to themselves, as far as I know. Quietly selling what little they still produce. I will make inquiries."

"Thank you, Commander." Allistor signed off. Looking at Droban and Longbeard, he said, "I suppose that makes sense? If they're crafters, Skapa Far has a lot of valuable materials."

"Aye, and skilled crafters to take hostage."

Droban shook his head. "But if that's what they're after, why the indiscriminate bombardment from orbit? They risk killing and destroying the resources they're after. Why not strike on the ground once the drones were defeated?"

Helen coughed gently to get Allistor's attention. "Maybe it's not about what they can gain? Maybe it's about what they're losing. The strike could just be an attempt to eliminate competition."

Allistor and the others nodded. "That makes more sense." He agreed. Then a chill went through him. "But if that's the case, they have no reason to hold back, to leave any survivors."

"Shit." Bjurstrom echoed Allistor's feeling of dread. "We need to get there ASAP."

*****

Captain Sh'erilan of the Or'Dralon warship *Daktar* held her breath as they transitioned out of FTL to normal space. Behind her, three more Or'Dralon ships emerged as she took in the planet before them.

Skapa Far was a small planet, mostly mountains and forest with three large oceans and a scattering of freshwater lakes. There were ten major cities scattered across the planet, and right now six of them were being blasted by orbiting ships.

Ships she and her small fleet had been sent to destroy.

Her orders had been simple. Stop the attacking Al'drong ships by any means possible. She'd been told that reinforcements were coming from Invictus, her own House, and the Stardrifter clan at least, but would not arrive for several more minutes. In the meantime, allied civilians on the surface were being murdered every second. She had received the same System-generated defense quest as Allistor and the rest of his allies the moment she'd received her orders, and was anxious to reap the potential rewards.

"Teams of two! Engage the two nearest ships and destroy them as quickly as possible!" She ordered. Her ship and one other moved toward the nearest Al'drong vessel. Elven protocol demanded that she try to contact them, so she did. "Al'drong vessels this is Captain Sh'erilan of the Or'dralon! You are attacking an allied world, and are ordered to cease all hostile actions immediately!"

She waited and watched, but the enemy ship neither replied, nor stopped its barrage. "Al'drong vessel, respond or be destroyed."

Again, there was no response. "Weapons, the moment we are in range…"

"Firing!" Her weapons officer responded before she even finished the thought. The ship shuddered slightly as four massive plasma cannons fired at once. Several smaller vibrations a moment later told her that they'd come within range of their railguns as well. This finally triggered a reaction from the enemy ship, which ceased firing at the city below and moved to evade her attack. It turned as it moved, bringing its main weapons to bear on *Daktar*.

Her sister ship had fired seconds after *Daktar*, and between the two salvos, half a dozen rounds struck the Al'drong warship. Shields flared, but there was no apparent damage visible. A fact confirmed by her sensor technician a moment later.

"Fire at will! Shields, alert me if we drop below fifty percent."

The Al'drong had been accomplished ship builders, and the warship she faced was formidable. Typical of elven construction, it was designed with sleek lines and gentle curves. The hull was practically bristling with weapons from oversized cannons to small point defense turrets. One on one, *Daktar* would have been outgunned, if only slightly. But with her sister ship, the Or'Dralon vessels had clear superiority. Still, the enemy seemed determined to go down fighting. It fired seven plasma cannons and six railguns at *Daktar* even as it continued its evasive maneuvers.

Sh'erilan didn't have to order her helmsman to take evasive action, the ship was already moving to avoid the incoming rounds. Or'Dralon ships were well shielded and nimble in space, and none of the enemy rounds even came close. Though, as the opposing ships drew closer, there would be less time to dodge, anDad more dependence on shields.

Another round of projectiles was unleashed from *Daktar*, her sister ship waiting a moment to see what direction the enemy would move before firing. This was standard practice when two or more ships were able to focus on the same target. Evasion did little good if you moved out of the path of one salvo directly into another. This time only two of *Daktar*'s projectiles struck the enemy ship's shields. But as it moved, all but one of the other Or'Dralon ship's shots struck home. The enemy shield flared, then failed.

"Firing for effect!" weapons called out, each of *Daktar*'s weapons firing the moment it was reloaded, rather than in a single burst. This kept a constant stream of rounds pounding at the enemy, preventing their shield from reforming, while doing mounting damage to the hull.

Already half the enemy's hull-mounted weapons were destroyed or disabled, and the hull had been breached in four places that she could see. She grimaced as the bodies of elves were ejected into space. She did not enjoy killing other elves. Her race was long-lived, but slow to bear young.

"Enemy vessel is calling! They surrender." Her coms officer reported.

"Cease fire. All of them are surrendering, or just this one?" She watched, relieved, as the target vessel powered down and ceased firing at her.

"Just this one. The others are still fighting."

"Helm, move to the next target. This one is out of the fight." She took a seat in her chair and looked toward the planet's horizon, where the next enemy ship wasn't quite visible yet. They were ten seconds into their adjustment when sensors called out. "The defeated ship just fired on the planet again!"

"Damn those lying, treacherous Al'drong vermin!" She growled. "Reverse course. Destroy that ship! No quarter! Weapons, if you see escape pods, remove them from the sky!"

The weapons officer visibly gulped, but nodded his head as he turned back to his console. The moment they were back within range, he went about dismantling the Al'drong ship. Their sister ship continued on toward the next target, needing to stop the bombardments as quickly as possible. It took only thirty seconds before *Daktar* had reduced the enemy ship to scattered debris. Not a single escape pod had been launched.

"On to the next one!" Sh'erilan ordered. "Top speed! We can't leave our sister ship outmatched."

*****

When *Phoenix* arrived at Skapa Far and dropped out of FTL, Allistor was nearly frantic with worry. It had been fifty minutes since he'd received the message about the attack, and he could only imagine the damage done to the cities in that amount of time.

Ten of his warships emerged from FTL behind *Phoenix*, along with six Or'Dralon ships, including Commander Enalion's, which had joined him at the Orion gate and transitioned through alongside his fleet.

The viewscreen showed Allistor very little at first. There was an obviously burning city visible directly below their position, and he could see the two orcanin ships that had remained behind, as they were moving rapidly toward his position. But he saw no attacking ships. Almost immediately an orcanin face appeared on one of the side screens. The ship captain bowed his head, a look of anguish on his face.

"Emperor Allistor, my deepest apologies. We have failed in our mission to protect this world."

"The failure is not yours, it is mine." Allistor didn't know the captain's name. "You had no choice but to stay out of this fight, captain, and have nothing to apologize for. What can you tell me about what's going on?"

The captain instantly brightened. "Your allies have been victorious so far, Emperor Allistor. The Or'Dralon ships have destroyed all but two of the attackers, which they are engaging now on the far side of the planet. We estimate that the battle will be over in less than-" The orcanin stopped, looking toward his left for a moment as his eyes widened. "More enemy ships! Another dozen ships have just dropped out of FTL behind you, Emperor! Beware!"

Allistor looked toward sensors, who was nodding, wide-eyed. "Confirmed! Twelve more ships arriving! They're firing!"

"It were a trap!" Longbeard grumbled as he gazed up at the main screen, which now showed a fleet of ships spreading out and firing at them.

"Shields up!" Kira called, "Weapons, return fire!" The enemy ships were closing rapidly even as Allistor's ships and their allies were turning to bring their main weapons to bear. Already the shields on Cogwalker's ship and a few others were flaring brightly with impacts.

Allistor's warships were no pushovers. Built by the dwarves, they were well armored, shielded, and carried significant firepower. The carrier that had accompanied the fleet was already launching a small swarm of drones and manned fighters, mostly piloted by experienced beastkin. Any one of his combat cruisers should have been a match for one of the Al'drong warships. But Allistor's ships had mostly inexperienced crews, and they'd been caught by surprise with their backs to the enemy.

Allistor watched the viewscreens as his ships took blow after blow, their shields holding, but just barely. The six Or'Dralon ships were more agile and experienced, and they were already pounding on the enemy, focusing their fire on three enemy vessels. They quickly disabled one that had been pounding on Cogwalker's cruiser, reducing the damage being done and allowing its shield to recover a bit.

One of the other cruisers was not so fortunate. Targeted by four of the enemy ships, its shield went down in less than half a minute. Rounds began slamming into the outer hull, opening the ship like a tin can, peeling back or simply puncturing the armor. Allistor's heart sank as the ship exploded, leaving little possibility for any survivors. He imagined the screams of the crew as they burned, or were jettisoned into space.

He was so focused on the loss, the next words he heard barely registered for a moment. He blinked as his mind replayed them for him. "The orcanin ships are moving in between us and the enemy!" It was Kira's daughter Brooke at the sensors station.

"They're what?" Allistor was horrified. If the orcanin ships attacked elves of any faction, they would plunge Harmon's people into a war with the entire elven race. He looked up at the main screen, where the two ships were indeed moving toward the enemy. "What are they thinking?!"

A few seconds later, Longbeard provided the answer. "Look at 'em! Those brave bastards!" He pointed at the screen. "They're sacrificin' themselves to protect ye!"

Allistor watched, shaking his head in denial as the two massive warships moved into the stream of fire coming from the enemy ships, blocking the projectiles from hitting two of the most damaged among Allistor's fleet. Their shields lit up immediately, but they didn't fire a single shot.

Longbeard sniffed, nodding his head with respect. "Nothin' says they'd can't let the elves shoot at 'em. As long as they don't fire, they won't be breakin' the covenant."

Allistor's captains quickly took advantage of the reprieve, the damaged ships moving back behind those in better condition, the entire fleet continuing to fire around their orcanin allies.

Allistor called out, "Nigel, open a channel to the orcanin captains! I've got to stop them!"

"*Go ahead, Sire.*" The AI responded as the same orcanin captain who had apologized just a few minutes earlier appeared on the screen.

"Captain! Move your ships! I appreciate your heroic effort to defend us, but please don't sacrifice your ships and crew. Save yourselves, and help us with the recovery efforts on the planet when this fight is over."

The captain shook his head. "We can not fight our former oppressors, but we can give our lives in defense of our allies. Emperor Harmon would have it no other way. We die with honor, so that you may prevail!" The crew behind the captain roared their approval, even as the bridge shook from an impact. A quick glance at the main screen showed that both orcanin shields had failed, and their ships were taking damage. Not nearly as quickly as Allistor's cruiser had, but the punishment was taking a toll.

Allistor was about to try again when the orcanin cut the signal. He watched in horror as a plasma cannon round tore into the side of one of the ships, and a compartment vented its atmosphere.

He was about to order his ships forward to make a similar blocking move, when Brooke called out, "Sensors show more ships coming out of FTL! Ten of them!"

Allistor's heart sank, until Hillary at coms shouted, "They're calling us! It's the Stardrifters!"

The ten ships streaked into existence, transitioning to normal space directly above the enemy fleet. Within two seconds a blistering salvo of plasma and kinetic rounds blasted down into the Al'drong ships, combining with the fire from Allistor's fleet. The enemy shields evaporated as Longbeard shouted "Get 'em, lads!"

The enemy fire continued long enough to take out one of the orcanin ships. It didn't explode, but went dead, floating in space with all signs of power or life extinguished. The other orcanin vessel, no longer being fired upon as the enemy shifted their fire to the newly arrived Stardrifter ships, limped over to dock with the first ship, hoping to find and retrieve survivors.

Allistor called out. "Carrier, send healers in a shuttle to those orcanin ships! Save everyone you can!"

Two of the enemy ships on the left flank exploded, taking out a third in the blast. Allistor clenched his teeth, surveying his fleet, taking in the visual damage to all the ships. Two of the enemy had briefly focused fire on the *Phoenix*, but her superior shielding had held up until the Stardrifter warships arrived and distracted the enemy. Another enemy ship broke in half, the front section's momentum pushing it into one of its allied ships. The collision didn't cause an explosion, but that ship's weapons did. The drifting forward half of the broken ship moved directly into the other ship's line of fire, getting ripped to shreds at point blank range, and exploding right next to the firing ship's hull. That ship took significant damage, half its weapons going offline and its hull caving in several sections.

Brooke called out again. "Or'Dralon ships coming around from behind the planet!"

Allistor looked at another side screen, seeing the four battered elven ships that had taken down the initial wave of attacks speeding around on the right flank. Within seconds they were adding their firepower to that of the combined Invictus, Or'Dralon, and Stardrifter fleet. Another enemy ship on that flank erupted, scattering debris and bodies into space.

Small explosions between the enemy ships caught Allistor's attention. When he focused on them, he realized he was seeing a dogfight between his fighters and drones, and those of the enemy. They danced around each other in incredibly fast zero-gravity maneuvers, firing from guns both fore and aft. He was amazed that the smaller ships could move anywhere without hitting the debris that was rapidly filling the space around both fleets.

"Recall the fighters!" He shouted. "They have no business being out there. Bring them back here where it's clearer, and let them play defense if the enemy fighters get close. Let the drones continue to engage."

He watched as Brooke relayed his command, and a moment later his manned fighters broke off and retreated, several of them taking fire as they ran. Allistor hadn't counted them when they launched, but it seemed as if there were a lot fewer of them now. Again his gut churned, feeling responsible for the losses.

Three of his ships were now incapacitated, floating without shields, few if any of their weapons still firing. One of the Or'Dralon ships that had come with him through the gate was dead as well, and two of the Stardrifter ships were badly damaged but still gamely firing.

Only four of the Al'drong ships remained in the fight, the others either destroyed or disabled. As if receiving some final command, all four of them directed their fire at *Phoenix*. Allistor's heart raced as the massive volley of plasma and magnetic rounds raced directly at them on the main viewscreen. Kira was screaming for more power to be directed to the shields. She had taken the helm herself and was violently maneuvering the ship out of the path of what looked like certain death. Being so close, though, there wasn't enough time. She managed to dodge more than half of the incoming fire, but a dozen or more rounds slammed into Phoenix's shields. The combined fire overpowered the shields, which flared briefly before winking out. Three kinetic rounds pounded her hull, rocking the ship violently to the port side. Allistor reached out to grab Kira's chair for balance, but was too slow, hitting the floor as she fought to right the ship.

Alarms began to blare, and Bjurstrom's voice filled the bridge a moment later, screams of pain echoing behind it. "Explosion in the main mess! Multiple casualties! We need healers!"

Allistor started to run for the elevator, but Droban grabbed his arm and held him back. When he growled at the minotaur, Longbeard took his other arm and spoke quietly. "Ye leave that to the healers, lad. Yer place be here."

Allistor strained against his two advisors in vain, both of them being stronger than him. As he came to his senses, he called out, "Nigel, damage report!"

"*A single hull breach in the crew galley, as reported. A kinetic round pierced the outer and inner hulls. Temporary force fields have activated, sealing the exposed compartments. There are eight fatalities, and twenty three wounded, six of them critical.*"

"Dammit!" Allistor growled. "Why the hell is this happening?" He shook off his advisors, who released his arms when they saw that he wasn't going to charge off the bridge. He looked up at the main screen expecting to see

289

more rounds coming their way, but instead witnessed the last of the enemy ships exploding as nearly every ship in his fleet fired into it.

Realizing the fight was over, he felt his legs go weak and grabbed the back of Kira's chair for support. Adrenaline rushed through his system still, and his heart pounded in his ears. Longbeard unobtrusively gripped his left bicep from behind, holding him upright. "Steady, lad. It's all done with. Now be the time yer people need ye to be strong." the dwarf whispered. On his right, Droban stepped closer as well, ready to support his emperor if needed.

"Coms, get me all the ships captains you can on the main screen, please." Allistor's voice was jittery from the ongoing adrenaline rush. It took a moment for the screen to fill, and even then there were only twenty five of the thirty two captains whose ships had shown up for this fight. It took him a moment to realize the others were either dead, or desperately dealing with damage on their ships. "I'll make this quick. Thank you, all of you, for what you've done here today. We have disabled ships that need our help! Please do whatever you can to assist them. When everyone up here is stabilized, we've got half a dozen cities full of wounded to tend to. Anything you or your people can contribute would be appreciated. Again, my most heartfelt thanks. We owe you a great debt."

Most of the captains simply nodded and disappeared. Commander Enalion remained, along with Cogwalker, who was bleeding and looked as if half of his face had been burned, and the surviving Orcanin captain.

The orcanin spoke first. "We have recovered survivors from our disabled ship. The healers you sent have arrived, and are greatly appreciated. I have already contacted Emperor Harmon, and thirty more ships are on the way." He saluted and disappeared before Allistor could reply.

Enalion spoke next. "My people are already gathering for an assault on the Al'drong homeworld, Emperor Allistor. By this time tomorrow there will not be a single living member of that House."

Allistor shook his head. "Please hold off on that attack. It's fine to prepare, but I want to find out what this was about. And I'm sure there are innocent people on that world, just like there are here on Skapa Far. I'm not interested in genocide as retribution. Can you set up some kind of blockade to keep those responsible from fleeing the planet?"

Enalion said nothing, just nodding in affirmation before signing off.

"Cogwalker, you need a healer." Allistor took a harder look at the dwarf. Half his hair and beard were burned away, and one eye was swollen shut."

"Bah, I can wait. There be those aboard that need healin' much more than I do." The dwarf coughed, then spat a bloody wad onto the floor. "Me ship be space-worthy still, but just barely. We'll be movin' at sub-light speed for the next while. There be a Stardrifter station on the far side o' this system. With yer permission, we'll make our way there fer repairs. Me clan's warships will be stayin' here, and a relief convoy will be comin' tomorrow early."

Allistor took in his badly damaged fleet on the main screen. "Permission granted. Take any damaged ship that can fly, or that you can tow, along with you. That includes any Or'Dralon, orcanin, or Stardrifter ships that want to tag along. I don't think any ships should be out there alone right now. I'll send an FTL capable ship full of healers from home to catch up to you." He nodded at Hillary, who immediately began calling in those orders.

Cogwalker saluted, the thump on his chest causing him to cough again before his transmission ended. Allistor immediately called out, "Bjurstrom, how are you doing down there?"

The tone of the reply frightened Allistor into motion more than his senior raider's words. "We lost nine people, boss. It's... pretty bad. The wounded are being seen to, and I don't think we'll lose any more. We've used up all the potions we had on us, and I sent McCoy down to the cargo bay to get more."

Allistor was already off the bridge, Longbeard and Droban right behind him as he dashed to the elevator. It only took seconds to reach the main galley level, and Allistor all but sprinted down the corridor until he reached the open door. The sight he found there nearly broke his heart.

Chapter Fifteen

Goodbye, Old Friend

The scene inside the mess hall area was horrific. A gaping hole in the outer wall was sealed with a faintly glowing force field that covered the gap between the edges of peeled-back metal. The opposite wall, the one to Allistor's right as he paused in the doorway, was splattered with blood and gore. Between the two was a trail of broken bodies and body parts, with wounded sitting or laying on the ground to either side. The bodies had not yet been covered, and as Allistor's gaze swept across him, he saw too many faces he knew.

"Boss." Bjurstrom held up a hand to get his attention. The raid leader was sitting on a table not far from the splattered wall, his feet up on the bench, his elbows on his knees. The look in his eyes, and the tears on his face, scared Allistor more than a little. He picked his way over to the table, doing his best not to step on any of the gore, then froze as he followed Bjurstrom's gaze to a body that had been hidden behind the table.

There lay Dawn, one of his oldest living friends. She had been with him and Helen through some of the worst early battles, and had been living in Cheyenne last he heard. She was one of the senior raid leaders, and a wonderful friend. Allistor had a flash memory of her riding with him in one of the juggernauts, defending her addiction to pink Sno Ball treats.

Now she lay on the cold floor in a pool of blood, her left shoulder and most of her chest missing. Sam was on one knee next to her, just starting to pull a blanket from his inventory to cover her up with. The old man was also injured, bloodstains covering a torn shirt over his left ribs. He held that arm close to his chest. Allistor immediately cast his best heal on his old friend, even as he stumbled forward and fell to his knees next to him.

He gently took the blanket from Sam. "Let me do that." Sam just nodded, letting go of the blanket and getting slowly to his feet. He joined Bjurstrom in sitting on the table, his eyes never leaving their friend as Allistor covered her.

The old man let out a shuddering breath as Allistor bowed his head, tears falling on the blanket. His voice was hoarse as he spoke. "She was right in line of the round when it punched through, and never saw it coming, didn't feel a thing, if that helps at all."

Allistor nodded in silence. It didn't help, not one little bit, but there was no need to voice that to an obviously hurting Sam. "I'm glad it was quick." Was all he could manage, his voice thick with grief. He hadn't even noticed that Dawn was on the ship. She would have been among the raid leaders that gathered around him in the cargo bay earlier. When had he gotten so callous that he didn't even acknowledge old friends when he saw them?

He placed his hand on the blanket over Dawn's forehead. "I'm sorry, my friend. I'm so terribly sorry."

Standing up, he sniffed once, then used his sleeve to wipe the snot and tears that dripped from his nose.

Sam was receiving more healing, and was moving his arm carefully, wincing at the lingering pain in his ribs. The healer tending to him scolded him. "Serves you right for making us fix the others first. Don't be such a baby." The old man grunted at the healer, not arguing her point at all.

A thorough look around the room told Allistor that all the injured were fully healed, or very nearly so, and being tended to. Helen took control and began to herd everyone out of the room. They didn't need to be there staring at the remains of their friends. She sent a few of the uninjured running down to the cargo hold to start arranging crates to sit on and hammocks to lay in for the recovering wounded.

Allistor sighed, staring down at his friend again. The blood soaking through the blanket reminded him there were likely tens of thousands of dead and wounded down on the planet.

"Nigel, get me administrator Dre'nir and the others." He sat next to Sam and Bjurstrom, who weren't moving to leave with the others, while he waited.

"Emperor Allistor?" Dre'nir spoke. "We monitored the battle from down here. Thank you for keeping your promise and coming to our aid. Condolences on your losses. They will be hailed as heroes across our world."

"Thank you, Dre'nir. How are things down there?"

"The six cities that were attacked have suffered heavy casualties. We are obviously still mobilizing, but our best estimate is just under two hundred thousand dead, maybe two million injured."

Allistor bowed his head, fresh tears forming and falling onto his knees. It took him a moment to be able to speak. "All you administrators, use every resource we have available. Stored potions, bandages, food, everything. Take it from the undamaged cities. Along with whatever manpower you need, at least until we can get more ships here with resources. Buy whatever you can from the crafters or merchants. If they won't sell, take it from them, and we'll deal with them later. The wounded and displaced are your number one priority."

"Efforts are already underway, Sire." the elf responded immediately. "We will do whatever is necessary, and let the people know that the aid they receive is at your insistence."

"No need for that. Just get them the help they need as fast as possible." Allistor sighed. This was not a time for politics. But he understood the former supervisor's inclination to help boost his reputation. Then it occurred to him that the people down there were likely scared, and he needed to reach out.

"Nigel, loudspeaker everywhere on the planet." He waited several seconds, then began to speak. "People of Skapa Far. Let me start by apologizing to you for failing to prevent today's attack. It is my responsibility to protect all of you, and I have utterly failed in that." He had to stop for a moment to draw a ragged breath and keep from sobbing. "The attackers have been destroyed, and help is on the way. I ask each of you to do whatever you can for the injured around you until help arrives. We are dedicating every possible resource toward getting to you as quickly as possible. This goes for all of you, citizens and non-citizens alike. No one in need will be turned away or ignored. Merchants, we will be coming to you to purchase any healing potions or other medical aids you have. Hold nothing back. You'll be paid a fair price. Crafters, we ask that you create as many healing supplies as you possibly can, as quickly as you can. We will also purchase those directly from you at a fair price. Any attempt to hold back, or to negotiate a better price, will be dealt with harshly. On the other hand, cooperation will be rewarded. There are millions of your friends, family, and neighbors who need immediate assistance. Let's all work together toward that end. Thank you."

Allistor put his head in his hands, overwhelmed by the scope of the damage done to his people, and the recovery effort ahead of them. And by more than a little anger toward those who'd executed the attack.

But vengeance would have to wait. The Or'Dralon, and presumably some other friendly factions, would ensure that the Al'drong were not going anywhere. He needed to focus on his own people first. Starting with those who'd lost their lives right there in that room.

"Bjurstrom, please have someone bring up body bags from the cargo hold."

*****

Down on the planet Allistor stepped off the *Phoenix* cargo ramp into a hellish scene of carnage and destruction. It had only been an hour since the battle ended, a few minutes longer since the cessation of the bombardment of the city. He'd spent most of that hour scraping up and cleaning away the remains of his raiders, placing what parts they could identify into body bags, disposing of the rest.

Now he stood amongst thousands more bodies, many of them half-buried under rubble, or burned beyond recognition. Shell-shocked citizens roamed the area, some helping the wounded, others attempting to dig out partially covered bodies. Behind him, his healthy raiders immediately fanned out to help, casting healing spells and grabbing potions from their inventory. Allistor had already had them clean out the ship's storage for distribution. Potions, food, water, anything that might help, including any low level gear that provided boosts to health or stamina. The few among the group with the alchemy skill had been sent to the crafting stations onboard ship with every available ingredient for making more. The cooks in the galley were creating whatever food with buffs they could manage.

Longbeard had been on the coms nonstop, and approached Allistor with an update. "I spoke to L'olwyn. Relief ships be on the way, and the others be organizing more. He says the ships we destroyed likely be most of the Al'drong fleet, with a few ships held back for planetary defense. There will be no attack on Earth or anywhere else. A few o' your ships will remain in orbit around Earth and Aegrin, just in case. Orion be protected by a whole fleet o' friendly ships and the space station already, and more be movin' here with resources. Some be arriving already." He pointed up at the sky, where Allistor saw half a dozen cargo ships approaching through the atmosphere. "There be ships goin' to every damaged city."

"Thank you, Master Longbeard. Please instruct L'olwyn to double the lands we've granted to the Or'Dralon, Stardrifters, Harmon, the Azure Order, and anyone else who assisted with the battle. And let him know we'll reward those who provide relief assistance and resources as well. We have valuable land to offer, we might as well use it to our advantage. Also, the aforementioned elves, dwarves, orcanin, and mages get free passage through my eternity gates from now on." The dwarf raised his eyebrows at the value of the rewards, but didn't argue.

"Also, arrange some form of substantial payment to the families of everyone who perished up there. From every faction. Especially the orcanin who so selflessly sacrificed themselves."

"Aye, I'll be seein' to that personally." Longbeard nodded. "Bravest damned thing I've seen in centuries."

Leaving the dwarf to his work, Allistor began to pick his way through the rubble. He lifted a stone here and there to help free a trapped body, most of which were corpses. He couldn't contain a sob of despair when he uncovered a beastkin woman who had tried to shield her two children with her body, all of them having the life crushed out of them. The sorrow building inside him threatened to cripple him, and it became difficult to breathe. He stepped back, dropping the stone in his hands, tripping over another. He barely felt the sharp hunk of metal that stabbed into his back as he landed, just laying there trying to breathe. A moment later Droban grabbed hold of him and lifted his body. Helen cast a heal on him as the minotaur set him back on his feet.

"I feel as you do, Sire." The minotaur growled softly so that no one other than Helen could hear. "But you must stand upright. You must continue the work here, not succumb to the despair. That is for later, when you are alone, or among only friends." He placed a hand on Allistor's shoulder. "We will stand with you, Sire."

Helen nodded her agreement, tears streaming down her dust-caked face as well. Dawn had been one of her closest friends. "Just focus on the next step, the next job. That's how we get through this. One step at a time. We're doing everything possible, Allistor." She stepped forward and hugged him, holding him for a good long time before letting go. He took a deep breath and smiled his thanks.

"Alright, we keep going." He looked over at a ship that was landing in an open square nearby. Before it even touched down, several hundred battle droids were leaping from the cargo bay and spreading out. They immediately began to dig through the rubble as General Prime trotted toward Allistor.

"Prime, thank you." Allistor spoke to the boss droid as he drew closer. "It never occurred to me to have your battle droids help out here."

"There are one thousand droids headed for each city to assist with recovery efforts. Each group has brought chargers and replacement parts sufficient for them to remain at peak functionality for as long as necessary, Sire." The droid offered a salute. "We can excavate in areas that would present significant danger to flesh and blood citizens."

"Preventing further injuries. Good thinking, Prime." Allistor's anxiety level lowered just a bit with the droid's presence and forethought. With a thousand droids to help, maybe some citizens would be saved that otherwise might have died before help could reach them.

With all the technology at his disposal, it frustrated him that there was no way to quickly free the injured from the rubble, or recover the corpses. He'd used *Levitate* to lift several stones that were too heavy for even his improved body to move, but had stopped after nearly straining himself like he'd done with the K rail in the battle against the goblins. Anything that he couldn't lift alone, Droban was by his side to help with. And now he had the artificial muscle of the battle droids.

Spotting a teleport pad covered in rubble, he moved his party over and began to clear it. The moment it was clear of anything larger than a pebble, he called out, "Nigel, this pad is clear, please start using it to transport goods and people from the undamaged cities."

"Of course, Sire. There are citizens who have been waiting." Almost immediately a group of twenty people appeared, along with a stack of crates. Allistor and company immediately began helping them move the supplies off the pad. Allistor introduced himself, the new arrivals blinking in surprise at seeing their Emperor dirty and disheveled, lifting crates alongside them. He thanked them for their willingness to help even as he cleared the last crate, and another group arrived.

"Nigel, I should have thought of this before. Tell the others to make it a priority to find and clear the pads."

"That effort is already underway, Sire." The AI reassured him.

Allistor surprised another dozen groups before moving on to help elsewhere. By the time the sun went down, Dre'nir and the other supervisors had better numbers for him. The elf met him in the lobby of an intact hotel building near where Allistor had been clearing another teleport pad, and had taken a seat before receiving the report. He was both physically and mentally exhausted.

"Within the six cities that have come under fire, there are just over three hundred thousand dead, another forty five thousand still missing. Recovery efforts are underway in each city, led by your extremely helpful droids, Sire. Thank you for that."

"Thank Prime, he thought of it." Allistor motioned toward the droid who was hovering just behind him. The elf gave the droid general a nod, then continued. "We estimate approximately one third of the missing may be recovered alive. Healers are working as quickly as they can, and more are arriving with each ship. We have distributed more than a million healing potions, and twenty thousand mana potions to those who can assist with their magic. Food and water are being provided to all those who ask, and we are working as quickly as possible to provide shelter for everyone whose homes were destroyed or damaged enough to make them unsafe."

He paused, his lips twitching with a slight smile. "Of the ships that have arrived, every single crew has offered their shipboard quarters to survivors. The crews are planning to sleep out in the open." He watched for a reaction from Allistor, but got only a tired half-smile and a nod. "The orcanin ships that have been arriving the last three hours have delivered tens of thousands of tents and temporary shelters, compliments of Emperor Harmon. They are being distributed to the hardest hit areas as we speak."

Allistor started to get to his feet. "I really need to call Harmon and thank him, for everything. His two ships, the way they sacrificed themselves..."

"Please rest, Sire. Emperor Harmon is on his way here, and should arrive momentarily. He came through the gate with several dozen cargo ships laden with troops, crafters, heavy machinery, and supplies. He wanted to arrange their distribution before coming to meet with you."

Allistor shook his head, then gave a ragged half-snort. "I wonder what all that's going to cost me?"

The elf looked up from the pad he had been referring to, and replied, "I did hear him mention something about placing a space station in orbit above this world, Sire."

Allistor was grateful, and not even a little bit surprised. The trade that could be conducted above a planet filled with crafters, and the taxes that would be generated by that trade, could make someone very rich. Though Allistor had learned by this point that his friend cared much less about the money than the excitement of creating new trade opportunities and haggling with worthy adversaries. He suspected that Harmon had volunteered, rather than being 'chosen' to deliver the *Phoenix* to him on that first day after Stabilization.

And if Harmon wanted to bring a space station to Skapa Far, he was absolutely welcome to do so. As far as Allistor was concerned, the orcanin merchant-slash-Emperor could take his pick of any high rise on the planet and establish another market like the one in the former Trump building. Some of the local merchants might be upset, but Allistor had a sick feeling that more than a few of them had perished, and there was room for his friend to help pick up the slack.

*****

Allistor stood on the bridge of the *Phoenix*, looking down at a planet via the main viewscreen. It was a mostly green planet, covered by seemingly endless forests broken occasionally by a mountain range or large body of water.

Exactly the kind of place he thought elves would like. He was aware that this was a stereotype based largely on fantasy literature he'd read, holovids he'd watched, with a little bit of input from the Or'Dralon and Master Daigath. In his mind, all elves loved trees.

"How many people live on the planet?"

L'olwyn made a quick check of his wristpad. "Less than five million. The ruling House never allowed any other Houses or Factions to settle there. Everyone living on the surface is either Al'drong, a slave, or a paid employee."

"Still no communication from their leaders?"

"None. Oddly, there has been no detectable transmission of any kind. Not between cities, not to the ships that retreated to the surface when our allies arrived, nothing at all."

"If they have an AI like Nigel, they could be communicating without us knowing, right?"

"*That is correct, Sire.*" Nigel answered before the elf could. "*And this house has certainly been in place long enough to have an AI at my level, or higher. They were once quite prosperous.*"

"Alright, so they could be down there planning something. It has been a week. Wouldn't they have made some kind of move by now if they were going to?"

"We still do not know their purpose for attacking Skapa Far." Droban pointed out from his position near the door. "It seems clear that their initial attack was a lure to bring you to the planet, where they sprung a trap. A trap that would have been successful had not our allies arrived in a timely manner. Bringing this fleet here may just be another level of that same trap."

"Possible, but unlikely." Selby piped up from where she was spinning around in a vacant station's chair. She stopped spinning long enough to add. "We have found no major ties to other factions, other than some limited trade. The Al'drong have alienated nearly every faction that they once called allies, and have cultivated few new ones. Certainly none with the resources to challenge this fleet, or our own alliance." She motioned to the side screen over her head, which showed a fleet of more than one hundred vessels arrayed around the planet. Allistor's allies had showed up in a big way. That was not even counting the hundreds more ships that were still assisting with the recovery on Skapa Far. Ships were bringing in supplies, ferrying out survivors that wished to leave the planet, some to other planets within Allistor's empire, others to neutral locations. There had been more than a million survivors of the attack that still did not wish to become citizens of Invictus. Their rapid relocation had helped to alleviate the housing crisis in the damaged cities.

Allistor drummed his fingers on the back of Kira's chair, thinking. "We can't stay up here forever. Do we risk going down to talk to them?"

Longbeard shook his head. "General consensus be that any ship attempting to land will be destroyed. In addition to the half dozen ships on the ground, there be significant hard defensive installations, with powerful shield domes."

"The most common advice from our allies is to simply bomb the House headquarters from orbit. They will either respond at that point, or perish."

"And how many innocent lives do we take if we follow that plan?" Allistor shook his head. "I'd rather just walk away and leave them to their fate than murder innocents."

"That would be unwise." L'olwyn began to explain, but Allistor held up a hand.

"I know, the factions. I'd look weak, and that would encourage other, larger factions to attack. I need to be merciless in my retribution for the sake of my empire."

"Not merciless, Sire." Droban shook his massive horned head. "But decisive, and firm. You could negotiate. Promise them the freedom to live in peace in return for the heads of their patriarch and his heir. Or offer those outside the bloodline the chance to become citizens if they rise up and destroy the House."

"Which would probably get just as many, if not more, innocents killed. And no, I don't mean total innocents. Just innocent of the attack on my people." He looked sideways at Helen, who was about to tell him for the third time that it was unlikely there were a lot of innocents down there. He sighed, tired of covering the same arguments for the umpteenth time. They had been having this discussion for several days. Allistor knew in his gut they would need to attack, but the notion made him sick. "How do I negotiate with someone who won't acknowledge us?"

"How precise can our weapons be from up here?" He asked Harmon, who was the most expert of those in the room when it came to weapons.

"We can accurately strike any target you choose the size of a land vehicle or larger, with a margin of error of no more than three paces in any direction."

Allistor was impressed. And a new option entered his mind. "So why don't we start with one of the ships on the ground. There likely aren't any innocents aboard a warship. We have multiple ships target one of theirs, and all fire at once. Obliterate it completely, leave nothing but a smoking crater. Then we give them another chance to talk. If they still refuse, we repeat the process."

Allistor watched as the others briefly considered his words and began to nod. "It is simple, decisive, potentially effective, and I see little downside for you." Droban approved.

"Kira, let's make that happen. Have… let's say twenty ships all fire at their largest ship down there on the surface in a combined attack. That should be enough to break its shield and incinerate it."

Kira nodded once and got to work as Allistor began to pace. There was still a chance for collateral damage, but he believed he'd minimized it enough that he could live with himself. After the traumatic losses he sustained a week ago, he was still a little numb.

"Ready to execute in one minute." Kira reported. Allistor stopped pacing and stared at the main screen. Twenty ships were moving into position on either side of Phoenix, which Kira had set to hover in orbit directly above the structures designated as the House headquarters. The ships that had retreated to the surface had all landed within a few miles of those structures. Allistor noted that there were elven, dwarven, and human ships among the twenty. No single faction would take the blame for the attack. "Weapons, fire in ten... nine..." Kira started the countdown, and when it reached zero, *Phoenix* fired along with the other ships. It took only a few seconds for the converging rounds to impact the surface, and a pinpoint explosion was visible from orbit as the target ship disappeared. The viewscreen zoomed in, magnified a hundred times as they waited for the smoke to clear.

As Allistor had demanded, there was nothing but a scorched crater and bits of burning debris where the largest Al'drong ship had been.

"Damn." Helen muttered from his left. "That was... wow."

Allistor looked at Kira. "Send the message again. Offer them the chance to talk. Let them know they have one hour to respond, or we fire again."

Kira nodded at her daughter, who began speaking into her coms unit.

Helen tugged on Allistor's sleeve. "Let's go get something to eat. Kira will call you if they agree. If they don't... well, we have an hour."

Allistor agreed, and everyone who wasn't bridge crew made their way to the owner's galley on the upper level. After what happened the week before, none of the crew were ready to eat in the main mess yet. It had been scoured clean, then cleaned again, but the memories weren't fading. On this trip the *Phoenix* held only its standard crew, plus Allistor and his advisors, Harmon, and Prime. There was no need to bring raiders for what everyone expected to be a space battle, where they might become helpless casualties. Allistor had learned that lesson the hard way.

They ate slowly and talked quietly amongst themselves for most of the hour, before returning to the bridge. Kira immediately shook her head, indicating there had been no word from the surface. When Allistor nodded, she began to coordinate the second attack. They would wait the full hour, plus one minute.

Just as the hour was about to expire, Hillary called out. "We're receiving a visual message from the Al'drong!"

"Put them on screen." Kira instructed quietly. "Alert the other ships to hold fire."

Allistor changed the order a bit. "And transmit this call to all the ships." Hillary nodded, and the face of a dark-haired elf appeared on the screen. Allistor had no way to judge whether the elf was twenty years or, two hundred, but had the impression he was young.

"Emperor Allistor, please do not fire again. My name is E'bron Al'drong, nephew of the Patriarch, who is now deceased, along with my father, his brother. I am heir to the House, and we wish to surrender."

The bridge was silent for a long moment as everyone absorbed that information. L'olwyn was the first to respond. "E'bron Al'drong, I am Minister L'olwyn of Invictus. Was your uncle the Patriarch aboard the ship we destroyed?"

The elf shook his head. "The ship was empty. We had no hope of victory against your fleet, and it was deemed that to fight in space was a waste of resources and lives. The crews of all the ships were recalled to help defend the family residence." He paused, looking down at his hands for a moment. "My father killed my uncle, sacrificing himself in the process." He shook his head, a look of sorrow on his face. "He did it to place me at the head of a defeated House with no future. Such a waste."

"Maybe not." Allistor offered. "If your first act as Patriarch was to surrender, saving the lives of those around you, then maybe your father's sacrifice had meaning."

The elf looked up. "I had not considered that. Thank you, Emperor Allistor. Do you wish to discuss the terms of our surrender at this time?"

Allistor growled at the implication that the elf had any leverage for negotiating terms. "There will be no terms. Your surrender is unconditional. Your House murdered hundreds of thousands of innocent civilians, and tried to murder millions more. I have a fleet in orbit above you that is capable of destroying every living thing on the surface without risk to my people. Your lives, your planet, your House are mine to dispose of as I see fit. The only question here is what punishment you deserve."

The elf, whose eyes had been narrowing as Allistor spoke, opened his mouth to argue. Instead, he let out a sigh, and nodded once. "As you say, Emperor. We place ourselves in your hands, and hope for mercy." As soon as the words left his mouth, Allistor received a couple notifications.

System Alert!
Emperor Allistor of Invictus has defeated House Al'drong and
seized ownership of planet Rivian! May he rule long and wisely!

Congratulations!
You have defeated House Al'drong after successfully defending against their attack on Skapa Far. Your alliance has seized their homeworld, planet Rivian, and unseated their Patriarch.
Rewards: 700,000,000 experience; Ownership of Rivian; Al'drong treasury.

Level Up! You are now Level Ninety Nine! You have earned two Attribute points!

Allistor waived away the reputation notifications as all around him his people were leveling up from the experience gained by defeating an Elven House and capturing a planet. While none of them earned nearly the amount of experience points that Allistor had as Emperor, all of them received at least a few levels. Kira and her crew nearly passed out from earning as many as ten levels at once.

The elf on the screen waited patiently, obviously aware of what was happening. He likely had received a few notices of his own regarding his surrender, and the reputation gains or losses that went with it.

Allistor took a moment to consider, then spoke to the Al'drong Patriarch. "I believe I would be within my rights to order the execution of your entire House. Your senseless attack has engendered a fury within me that I have never experienced before." He stopped there, waiting for a reaction from E'bron. When the elf just stared at him, a look of defeat and acceptance on his face, Allistor decided to cut him a break. "Before I decide on that course of action, I would like more information. Get in one of your ships, with just a skeleton crew, and join us in orbit. We will speak face to face."

Chapter Sixteen

Do The Crime, Do The Time

The former patriarch, whose rule over his House lasted less than an hour, stepped into the main mess hall escorted by Droban, the biggest most intimidating escort Allistor had available on the ship at that time. The minotaur growled and motioned toward the table where Allistor sat. "Bow to your Emperor."

The elf didn't hesitate, bowing deeply at the waist, not saying a word. Allistor, on the other hand, had some things to get off his chest. "Take a seat, Patriarch E'bron." He widened his arms to take in the sparklingly clean crew galley. "Do you know where we are?"

The elf sat, looking around the room, confused. He shook his head silently.

"This used to be where my crew and I shared meals. We talked, and laughed, enjoyed each other's company." He lowered his arms, placing his hands flat on table and fixing his gaze on the elf. "Now it's a tomb. Nine of my raiders, my friends, died here when your ships fired on mine. I found a very good friend of mine laying in a pool of her own blood on the floor just behind where you now sit." He pointed at the floor, and the elf paled visibly and gulped, turning to look.

"I am... sorry, Emperor Allistor. I know that means little to you. I was opposed to attacking your planet, as was most of my family. My uncle was... unbalanced.

Obsessed after centuries of mediocrity. After our house was disgraced by his father, he did his best to bring us back to our former glory, but encountered one setback after another. I believe the unending shame wore on his sanity." He took a deep breath before continuing.

"My uncle had been observing you, intrigued by an Emperor who crafted his own weapons. He began to call you the Crafter King, even arranged to purchase one of your weapons through an agent, which he mounted on the wall in his office. After Loki's death and your inheritance of Skapa Far, he insisted that if we struck quickly, we could eliminate a major competitor, seize resources, and possibly some talented crafters as a bonus. He imagined that one act would put us on the path toward restoring our House, and would not listen to our warnings."

"Did you participate in the attack?" Allistor had held the meeting in that room as a reminder of the losses caused by the Al'drong. He refused to feel anything but anger, and was looking for a reason to vent it.

"I did not. I am a crafter, not a fighter. My father planned the attack, the ambush." E'bron had the grace to look down at his hands, ashamed. "He objected to the plan, but my uncle left him no choice. It was either cooperate, or die. Six of my bloodline have lost their heads in the last year to my uncle's tantrums. When the attack failed, my uncle blamed my father. But rather than execute a valuable warrior, he planned to execute me as a rebuke for my father. To motivate him to do better. My father learned of this, and took the only action he could. He requested a meeting with his brother, poisoned a bottle of his favorite wine, and they drank to the warriors who died in the battle."

"And made you the new Patriarch." Allistor shook his head.

"Yes. The Patriarch of a defeated House, with no home, no future. Quite the prize." the elf's tone was bitter. "All I have left, the only action I can take to preserve my House, is to willingly offer you my head, and request that you spare the rest of my bloodline." E'bron's gaze met Allistor's and there was nothing but sincerity there. The elf was willing to die to save his family. As if one death would pay for the murders of so many.

Allistor got to his feet and began to pace angrily back and forth. He believed E'bron was telling the truth, but had no way to prove it one way or the other. His logical mind told him that the elf was probably not responsible for the attack, but his heart raged and demanded retribution.

A glance at Droban, who was filling the doorway with his bulk, reminded him of something the minotaur had said to him a short while ago about being decisive, but not merciless.

"This is what's going to happen. I've taken your planet, and all of your assets. You, and everyone that shares your bloodline, are going to Skapa Far. There you will serve the citizens your House tried to destroy, in whatever way you are best qualified. You will help to rebuild the damaged cities, to ease the pain of those who lost family and property. You will be provided with food, housing, and a meager salary in return for that work. You will all swear an oath that will prevent you from doing any further intentional harm, on pain of death."

Allistor placed both hands on the table and leaned forward, placing his face close to the elf's, and growled. "Any of your bloodline who refuse this offer will be summarily executed. I'll take their heads myself."

E'bron leaned back slightly, the aura of fury radiating from the human a palpable thing. When Allistor straightened back up, the elf nodded. "That is more than fair."

Allistor took a few deep breaths, then sat down across from E'bron. "Your employees and slaves will be given the option to choose for themselves. They can swear a different oath and become citizens of Invictus, after which they will be allowed to remain on Rivian, or move to one of our other worlds. Or they can refuse, and either join you in service on Skapa Far, or be relocated to another nearby world." Again, the elf nodded.

"That is… better than I anticipated, Emperor Allistor. I fully expected to die here today, a short while ahead of the rest of my family." He stood up, then took a knee, bowing his head almost to the floor. "I thank you for your mercy."

Despite his desire to hate the elf, and inflict pain, Allistor was moved by the gesture. He took a breath and held it for a moment, then let it out slowly. "Take your seat."

The elf got up and quickly resumed his place at the table. His eyes never left his hands, which were now folded in his lap.

"On the topic of your family... I have decided not to disband your House. If you and yours honor your oaths, work hard and honestly for a period of... ten years, I will give you the opportunity to redeem your house as a vassal to my own."

E'bron's eyes widened, and one hand twitched slightly in his lap. "Truly?"

"This is no gift, E'bron. You and your House have a tremendous debt to repay. The people of Skapa Far will not embrace you. They will be prevented from harming you, but you'll be reviled and despised. You'll work harder than you ever have before, every day. Should any one of you fail to fulfill your oath to the best of your ability, I'll take your heads. Assuming the System itself doesn't handle that for me."

"We will redeem ourselves, in your eyes, and theirs. I swear this on my own life." The elf surprised Allistor with the fervent promise, which was recognized by the System a moment later, as evidenced by the swirling blue light that surrounded them both.

"Then return to your home. You and your family gather some clothes and personal items, no valuables. This includes everyone with a hint of your bloodline in their veins. We will provide transportation to Skapa Far. To begin with, you'll likely be living in tents, as there is a sudden and severe housing shortage." E'bron grimaced, then nodded, getting to his feet. Droban stepped out of the doorway and motioned the elf through.

When they were gone, Allistor stared at the empty tabletop for a while. He was conflicted about his decision to show mercy. After some contemplation, he spoke aloud. "Nigel, please take charge of all the facilities on the planet. Let me know when you have control, so I can speak to the people down there. Also, please ask Longbeard, Selby, Droban, Harmon, Helen, and L'olwyn to join me here. We have some things to discuss."

He got back to his feet and paced for a bit, then went to check the galley for something to drink. He grabbed several water bottles and protein bars and carried them back to the table. His people were going to have to start using this room again, and they might as well start now.

The others began to arrive a minute later, Droban being the last after seeing E'bron off the ship. When they had all retrieved a drink and taken a seat, Allistor filled them in. When he was done, he looked at his advisors.

"Was I too lenient? Are the other factions going to see this as a weak response?"

Several of them exchanged glances before Selby took the initiative. "Obviously, those who already dislike you will view mercy as weakness. Nothing you can do about that. But I believe most will respect your choice."

"Aye, lad." Longbeard smiled at him. "Ye defended yer property, took the fight to the enemy, executed a smart and effective strategy, and won yerself another planet! The sentence ye gived the Al'drong be no light thing. They be pampered nobles, used to having servants to bring them tasty food and drink at their whim. The life ye sentenced them to will be hard, and humbling."

Droban and L'olwyn nodded their agreement, and Harmon grunted his approval.

Helen patted his back. "I think you made an excellent choice. Instead of a pile of corpses and more blood on your conscience, you have... what? A few hundred talented crafters and servants to help our people rebuild."

"More like a few thousand. It is an old House, and I expect you'll find E'bron has quite a large family." L'olwyn corrected.

"Even better!" Helen grinned at the elf.

"It was well done, Allistor." Harmon flashed his tusks in the orcanin version of a smile. "I am proud of you."

Curious, Allistor asked, "Would you have done anything different?"

Harmon looked at the ceiling as he considered his answer. "Assuming they were not elves, whom I am not permitted to harm, I might have taken E'bron's head as a symbol. And I would have imprisoned his family, possibly ransomed them to an ally willing to pay. It would not have occurred to me to put them to work as you did. Just one of the many ways you humans think differently than the rest

320

of us. Everything is new to you, and everything is possible, because you don't know any better."

"Thank you for that." Allistor smiled at his big friend. "Now, we've got a lot of work to do. I need someone to oversee the roundup of the family and transport to Skapa Far. L'olwyn, if you wouldn't mind composing an appropriate oath for them to take? Any who refuse, set aside and I'll deal with them. Maybe a public execution as the symbol you mentioned, Harmon." He glanced up at his friend. "I suppose I'm going to need another planetary defense grid." This time Harmon's smile was wide.

"I'm going to offer you, the Or'Dralon, and Stardrifters significant properties on Rivian, since you all helped me obtain it, and in defending Skapa Far. As well as a place for the Azure Order to establish a guild house if they so desire. And yes, before you ask, you're welcome to place a space station at each planet." He had to struggle not to smile when the orcanin gave him a double thumbs-up, a gesture Allistor himself had taught him.

While thinking about the space stations, specifically the one Harmon had above Orion, a thought occurred to him. "You know, I never asked, where in the galaxy is Rivian?" Allistor knew they had used the Orion gate to travel here, but didn't know if they exited through the same gate they used to reach Skapa Far, or a different one.

Harmon used his wrist unit to project a hologram of the galaxy. He punched a few buttons as he spoke, and green dots appeared one by one. "Here is the twin system where Earth, Orion, and Aegrin are located. You now own the majority of habitable planets in that system, by the way. Three of five." Another dot appeared much closer to the galaxy's core. "This is Skapa Far's system." Another dot, about halfway in between, appeared. "This is the station you inherited from Hel, which you have yet to visit." There was a mild rebuke in his tone. The last dot was roughly an equal distance from the core as Skapa Far, on one of the inner spiral curves, but on the opposite side. "And this is Rivian."

Allistor nodded. "How far is the nearest gate from here?"

Harmon touched his wrist unit again, and a red dot appeared. "The one we transitioned through, located in the next system. Approximately one full day at FTL." Allistor had felt like the trip to Rivian had taken a long time, but had mostly chalked that up to his anger and frustration causing time to drag.

"So if I were to place my second Eternity Gate here at Rivian, I'd have immediate access to opposite sides of the galaxy, and would have the only gate in this system."

"You would indeed." Harmon agreed. Longbeard was smiling, which Allistor took as a good sign.

"That'd be a smart choice, Allistor." He looked at Harmon. "How many inhabited worlds in this system?" Harmon zoomed in on Rivian's sun, then punched a few buttons. A total of six planets glowed green, indicating they were inhabited. Rivian was fourth among them, counting outward from the sun. "Five potential trade partners, easily reached at sub-light speeds."

"Or easily conquered!" Helen blurted out, then shrugged when she saw everyone staring at her. "What?"

Longbeard continued. "Controllin' two gates on opposite sides o' the galaxy be a difficult thing to achieve. Most factions would have to fight brutal, decades-long wars to secure planets so far apart, stopping to conquer other worlds to use as a supply chain along the way. Ye can skip all that bother and drop a gate here in one step. Yer allies would be pleased to have access to this region without payin' the hefty gate fees it would normally require. And those on this end would pay well for access to Orion's gate."

"Not to mention the enormous potential for new trade alliances." Harmon added. "Plus the value of property on Rivian, and the income my new luxury space station can generate, will soar."

Allistor thought about the image of the planet he'd seen on the viewscreen. "I don't know... Rivian is beautiful as it is. I don't want to turn it into an industrial wasteland."

"Then limit access, and permitted usage. Don't allow mining, or lumber harvesting. Restrict the size and population of settlements. You quite literally have absolute power over Rivian's future, Sire." L'olwyn actually smiled. "If you don't mind, I believe I myself would like to establish a residence here. The forest... speaks to me."

"Are you saying you want to be governor of the planet?" Allistor kept a poker face as he asked.

L'olwyn looked horrified. "Oh, no! Never that! I am quite content in my current position at your side. I would simply like to establish a... retreat."

"Fair enough. Pick yourself out a hunk of forest somewhere, and it's yours. The same goes for the rest of you. As my trusted friends and advisors, you are welcome to claim a parcel of land on any of our planets. Your presence, with my authority, can only be a good thing." He looked from the others back to L'olwyn. "The System granted each human survivor ten acres after Stabilization was over. What's an appropriate size for an elven minister's retreat? A hundred acres?"

Before the elf could answer, Longbeard cut in. "Ha! Dwarves need at least a thousand acres! We like our space." He tossed a wink at Allistor as the others laughed.

"A hundred acres is most generous, Allistor." L'olwyn cast a disparaging glance at the dwarf before gifting Allistor with a rare full smile.

"Alright, now that we've settled that, let's talk about this system. Before I place a gate here, I need to know something about the neighbors, and how likely it is I'll have to fight to defend Rivian and the gate. Also, we need to discuss fleet deployment. With another planet to protect, my existing fleet is getting stretched pretty thin." He stopped for a second, hearing his own words. "Damn, I never thought I'd say that."

"Ye can never have too many warships!" Longbeard thumped the table to emphasize his statement. "We can arrange to increase the size o' yer fleet easily enough. Do ye wish to purchase the ships, or trade fer 'em?"

"Trade, if possible." Allistor didn't even need to think about it. "The same as before. Land, tax discounts, access to the gates. Friendly factions only. I love the dwarven warships, but I wouldn't mind having a few more elven style ships as well. The Or'Dralon ships performed very well over Skapa Far."

"Do not forget that the remaining Al'drong ships on the surface are now yours. They are quite formidable as well. In addition to the five warships, there are half a dozen cargo ships, and the Patriarch's flagship, which is similar in function to the Phoenix."

"Oh, right!" Allistor beamed, his immediate problem temporarily solved. "Those five warships should be enough to guard Rivian until we can obtain more. We can leave just one of our ships to supervise them. Maybe we can even recruit the experienced ships' crews as citizens." Allistor needed to find someone he trusted to begin an academy of some sort for his... navy? He wasn't sure what to call it. He took out his paper pad and pencil to add that to his list. Tentatively he wrote "Gralen?" with a question mark next to it.

"We can use the cargo ships for relocating the Al'drong, then for local trade missions from here, and from Skapa Far." Allistor's mind was racing, his anger fading in the face of exciting new prospects. He glanced down at his hand-written list, and noticed a few tasks not yet accomplished. "Hey, do we know if there are any dungeons on this planet?"

*****

It was a full day and a half later when Phoenix, the five Al'drong warships full of nobles, and their escort arrived at Skapa Far. There had been a few delays in getting the family loaded and on their way.

First, Allistor had gone down to the planet and addressed the population that weren't part of the family. He informed them of what had happened on Skapa Far, the surrender of the now deposed Al'drong line, that they were all free, and any employment or indenture contracts were voided. Then he gave his standard recruitment speech, offering to let them all take the oath and become citizens. He outlined their options for them, and gave them a day to decide. Then he requested that all the ships' crews report to the main residence.

There he offered them significant salaries and signing bonuses on top of citizenship if they would swear an additional oath to defend Invictus. All but a few agreed, and were sworn in on the spot. More than enough to crew the ships needed to transport the Al'drong.

L'olwyn had been correct, there were nearly two thousand elves with Al'drong blood on the planet. E'bron reported that there were nearly a hundred more currently off-world on trade missions, along with three ships. He had sent a message recalling them, but was not confident they would return after the announcement of Al'drong's defeat.

Of the nearly two thousand, all but six agreed to swear the oath of service and relocate to Skapa Far. The six who refused, including E'bron's youngest brother, were executed in front of the gathered family members, ship's crews, and household staff. Allistor didn't make a big spectacle of it. He lined them up, and spoke to each one in turn.

"This is your last chance. Will you swear to serve the people your family has harmed? Refusal to do so means death under the terms agreed upon by your Patriarch."

As each one refused, he used *Unification*, the same sword he'd used to kill Loki, to take their head. Allistor had thought after the first death, the others would submit. But each one in line stubbornly refused, their pride preventing them from accepting servitude. Allistor grimly kept his word, taking head after head until it was done. He silently told himself that it was justice, and that the example would cause his potential adversaries to think twice about crossing him.

When they saw that Allistor was serious about removing their masters, most of the household staff and others present chose to swear the oath then and there. Helen administered it, as usual, and they began loading the Al'drongs onto the cargo ships.

Allistor was introduced to an elderly elf named Di'len, who had served as Steward of the family residence, and offered him a tour. The term *residence*, as it turned out, applied to a massive, sprawling compound with more than a hundred bedrooms, guest suites, servant's wings, several kitchens, extensive gardens, guard barracks, armory, and dozens of other ancillary buildings. Allistor gamely followed the old elf, who moved at a surprisingly brisk pace. Accompanying them were L'olwyn, Droban, and Helen.

Di'len pointed out the throne room, study, private dining room, and Patriarch's quarters in rapid succession, the areas he expected his new Emperor to care most about. Allistor made appropriate sounds of approval, and in a few cases, amazement. Especially when the old elf led them down to the family's prized wine cellar. Allistor stepped into a low-ceilinged underground room the size of a big box store on Earth. There were half a dozen round tables with comfortable chairs near the door, behind which were rows upon rows of wine racks. A closer inspection showed that the racks were carved directly from the stone as the room had been created. Connected at both floor and ceiling, there was zero danger that a misstep might cause one to knock over entire racks of wine.

As they walked toward the back of the cellar, the elf pulled a bottle here and there, initially presenting them to Allistor for inspection. When it became clear that he knew nothing about wine, L'olwyn took over. The elf was more than a little impressed with the collection, even going so far as to offer a joke. "Sire, those one hundred acres you mentioned...can one of them be down here?"

"Ha!" Allistor recovered from the surprise quickly enough. "You might have to battle Harmon for that. He does love his collection of wines and booze."

They reached the back of the cellar, and the old elf put his hand on a sturdy looking wooden door. "Emperor Allistor, this is the House vault. As the House assets have been legally ceded to you, I can authorize your access. If you'll just place your hand on the door?"

Allistor was raising his hand when L'olwyn cleared his throat. "Right. No touching anything. For now, L'olwyn is my designated vault access guy." Allistor immediately shook his head at the poor phrasing, but Di'len pretended not to notice. They quickly completed the process of authorizing L'olwyn, and removing all other authorizations except the old steward's. He explained that it took two authorized people to open the vault. Just to be safe, Allistor had him authorize Helen, Longbeard, and Droban as well.

When they finally opened the vault, Allistor wasn't impressed. The room was maybe thirty paces deep, and ten wide. Ornately carved wooden shelves line the walls, with more of the carved stone shelving in two rows down the center. Upon most of the shelves sat wooden chests. Some rather plain, others ornately carved. Nothing in the room sparkled or screamed *treasure* at him.

Di'len, noticing that Allistor was less than amazed, chuckled. "Each of these chests is a dimensional storage device. The combined space of every box in this room would be the equivalent of thirty cargo ships' holds."

That got Allistor's attention! As well as everyone else's. He gazed down the rows of shelves, counting sections. Then he counted the number of chests on the nearest section, and did some rough math. "There must be... close to three hundred chests in here."

"Three hundred and sixty, Sire." the old elf confirmed. He raised his arm and touched a device on his wrist. "If you like, I can transmit the inventory..."

"Yes, please. To all of us." Allistor confirmed before he realized that while his advisors all had the devices, he and Helen did not. "Well, all of them." Another thing he needed to address. His people weren't yet using the devices, which Harmon had explained were a biotech item, grown from an implant in the wrist.

Longbeard's whistle brought him out of his contemplation. "This be a lot o' items." Allistor could see his finger moving up and down, scrolling through the list.

Di'len nodded. "Most of them are of little value outside the family. Items of note crafted by family members, from their first attempt to their first master-crafted piece. A few items of historic value, such as weapons used in famous battles, or exceptionally valuable items claimed as loot. A few are quite... gruesome." The elf made a face that suggested he detected a foul odor. He pointed to a box one section down from the door. "One of those contains several preserved heads of vanquished enemies."

L'olwyn quickly explained. "As we have mentioned before, this was an old House. Elves were not always the civil, refined beings you see before you now. We evolved from more primal ancestors, just as any species must do. It was common, many eons ago, to display such trophies after a victory." He looked at the rows of chests, whispering, "I imagine there is a great deal of elven history in this room."

"Indeed there is." Di'len agreed. He walked partway down a row, looking for a particular box. When he spotted it, he opened it and retrieved an item. "My former master spent a good deal of time observing your rise to power, Emperor Allistor. Which meant I also observed you. When Master Daigath agreed to stay with you for a time, we were all greatly impressed. Because of your friendship with him, I thought you might appreciate this." He returned holding an item wrapped in cloth. Rather than handing it directly to Allistor, he placed it in L'olwyn's hands. The younger elf turned to Longbeard, who carefully unwrapped the item as L'olwyn supported it. The cloth fell away to reveal a beautiful sword crafted of gleaming ebony wood.

"Master Daigath spent some time on Rivian several thousand years ago. Some of our master crafters studied under him. He presented this to our then Matriarch as a gift before he left." The old elf blushed slightly as he continued. "They were rumored to be quite... fond of each other."

"That old devil!' Longbeard slapped his thigh and let out a boisterous laugh.

"Yes, well. I thought you might wish to own it yourself. Or perhaps return it to the Ancient One?"

"Oh, please... let me be the one to return it." Longbeard grinned shamelessly, waggling his bushy eyebrows.

Allistor looked at L'olwyn, who nodded his head slightly. Reaching down, he carefully lifted the sword in both hands. It was heavier than he expected, and its surface was well oiled. A quick test of the blade drew blood from a deep cut across his thumb. He absently cast a heal on himself as he admired the blade. "It's... beautiful. Beyond beautiful. It almost seems to be alive still."

"Oh, it lives." Di'len confirmed. "This is a masterwork by perhaps the most accomplished master crafter alive today. It is a very old blade that has claimed many lives, and has grown to become nearly self-aware. Master Daigath not only preserved the life of the tree from which this ebonwood was harvested inside the blade, he gave it the ability to absorb part of the life essence of those it killed."

Allistor quickly looked down at his newly healed thumb in alarm.

"Do not worry, it only takes essence upon death." The steward assured him.

"Thank you for this, Steward Di'len. It is truly a wonderful thing." Allistor carefully took the cloth from L'olwyn and rewrapped the sword before placing it in his storage. "Can I ask... are you willing to remain in your position here? We need someone to oversee this place, and I'm sure there is no one more qualified than you."

The old elf bowed his head. "I would be honored. This has been my home for some three thousand years, now. We understand each other." He smiled and patted one of the walls.

Allistor returned the smile, and his eyes unfocused. "In that case…" A moment later he watched as the Steward stiffened slightly, reading a surprise notification. "Governor of Rivian, Sire?"

"I suspect you know this place, and its people, better than anyone who will be remaining here. Who better to represent me when dealing with the populace? If you're willing to take the position, you'll receive a significant salary, a parcel of land for yourself, and the authority to act on my behalf in day to day operations here." Allistor held up a hand before the elf could reply. "But be aware, I may be placing an Eternity Gate in orbit here. If that should happen, the position of Governor will become much more complicated."

Di'len thought for a moment before asking, "I'll have the ability to hire staff? I may need a great many people…"

"You will." Allistor agreed, then motioned at the shelves. "I assume there are funds somewhere in here?"

"There are. Though this has not been a wealthy House for many centuries now."

"Without the nobles draining the House funds for their fancy feasts and pet projects, you should have more than enough to hire the additional staff you need, as well as cover the current payroll." L'olwyn replied.

"And if you need additional resources, we will provide them." Allistor added.

"Then I accept, most humbly. And I thank you for the trust you have placed in me, Emperor Allistor." The elf bowed his head respectfully.

Allistor considered something Di'len had mentioned. "Those preserved heads in the box over there… would there be any befit to us if we offered to return them to their families or Houses? Maybe gain some goodwill for Invictus? Or ransom them back to those who don't like us, help pay for Di'len's new staff?"

Both elves' eyes widened in surprise as Longbeard chuckled.

*****

Now Allistor watched as the Al'drong ships set down near the tower where he'd first encountered Dre'nir. A hundred battle droids emerged from the tower in formation and marched toward the ships, which were already unloading nobles in long lines. The droids spread out and politely but firmly escorted the elves toward the teleport pad where Allistor stood.

Standing with him were the Administrators from each city. They glared at the approaching elves from the House responsible for so much death and destruction on their world. Allistor saw the looks, and spoke quietly.

"They are an asset, here to help you rebuild. They are not to be harmed. I want that made very clear to our people. You don't have to like them, or even accept their assistance. But none of them are to be harmed. They are going to hate every moment of living in servitude, at least initially. Let that be their punishment."

He met the gaze of each Administrator, holding it until he received a nod or word of acknowledgement. They couldn't help but agree, he was their Emperor, and they had sworn oaths to obey him.

When the nearly two thousand elves had been gathered, he addressed them one final time. "Welcome to Skapa Far. In a few minutes you'll bear witness to the damage and suffering your House inflicted on this world. You'll be spending the next years of your lives trying to atone for that suffering through service. Hold to your oaths, work hard. You may eventually find that you enjoy helping others." He waved a hand toward the administrators. "These Administrators will be conducting interviews, then providing you with your new assignments for housing, and jobs. Good luck."

He gave a quick wave to the crowd, then walked back toward the *Phoenix*. The former Al'drong ships, already lifting off, would be accompanying him back to Orion briefly. They would be given a day to travel to his various worlds and witness for themselves how his citizens lived, then they would return to guard Rivian and pass on word of what they'd seen.

Chapter Seventeen

Fear Itself

Allistor and the kids were visiting with Sam, Meg, and their adopted son Cody in the penthouse suite they had claimed for themselves in one of the high rises near the tower. Allistor had rarely seen Cody in the months since he had joined the family, but the girls had apparently babysat for him several times, and knew him well.

They'd enjoyed a wonderful dinner of chicken pot pie and fresh vegetables prepared by Meg, and were sitting around the family room talking about old times. Sam was threatening to break out a bottle of the spider spit booze and make Meg drink some, when Nigel's voice surprised everyone.

"Sire, there is an urgent message for you."

"Go ahead, Nigel."

"Boss, this is McCoy. We've discovered another dungeon inside the city. We thought maybe you'd want to come check it out."

"What kind of dungeon, and where is it?" He was already getting to his feet, along with everyone else.

"As for the where, it's in the ruins of what used to be Bellevue hospital, over near the river. Nigel can ping the location for you. But we can't tell what type of dungeon it is. When I try to *Examine* it, it just gives me question marks."

"Bellevue? As in the insane asylum?" Allistor was even more interested now. The famous hospital had been featured in many stories, horror movies, and holovid shows over the years. Usually it was where they locked up the criminally insane, who promptly escaped and rampaged through the city.

"That's the one. We've been clearing buildings for rehab out this way, and stumbled across it in the sub-basement."

"We're on our way." Allistor looked at his kids as he reached for the door. "You guys stay here with Cody. We'll be back."

Meg shook her head. "You kids go to the tower. It's safer there. Cody, Sam and I will pick you up as soon as we're done." Allistor still had trouble reconciling the fact that there were young children like Cody, William, and Chloe who were above level twenty. They could cast spells and take more damage than many of the full-grown humans he'd encountered on his recruiting trips across the globe. Fights that he'd barely survived during Stabilization, these kids wouldn't even consider a challenge. They were stronger, faster, and more durable than he had been as a mostly grown man on the day the void titan had destroyed his hometown.

The three of them jogged out of the apartment building and down the street. This was another big change. Meg and Sam had both been fit for senior citizens before the apocalypse. Now, with their vastly improved attributes, they could run like they were twenty five again. Nigel's pinpoint placed the hospital approximately four miles north of their building, and they could have jogged that far without issue. But to save time, Allistor led them back to the tower where they grabbed a juggernaut. He drove east until they hit the FDR, then followed it north to the hospital. They parked at the corner where they found McCoy waiting.

"It's inside there, boss." He pointed to the ruined building. Being that far north, and right on the river, it had taken a lot of the abuse from the bombs that had been detonated in the early fights for the city. Allistor didn't know how tall the old brick building had originally been, but now there was nothing standing taller than twenty feet. Most of it was just tall piles of rubble.

"You were going to rehab this?" Allistor questioned McCoy."

"Nah, we were just clearing it. We'd have used the material to build something else. Whole lot of usable brick in there. We found a basement entrance that led into what I think was a morgue, and went in that way. Found a few signs of some monsters, but nothing living. And a whole lot of messed up human craziness. Shit scratched into and written on the walls that gives me the weebies." The man shuddered to emphasize his point. "I know they kept crazy folks in here for like, two hundred years, or something, and you can definitely feel it down there in the dark."

Allistor was following McCoy as he led them around to the entrance he had mentioned. The other raiders, mostly a group of low levels that McCoy was training, were standing around outside, shuffling their feet. None seemed anxious to go back inside.

"We cleared everything we could get to, boss." McCoy motioned toward the door, but made no move to lead them in. "Lots of places are cut off by collapses. Nothing moving down there anywhere."

Allistor grinned at the spooked senior raider. "No sweat, I've got this. You just hang here and make sure no leprechauns or anything sneak in." He started toward the door, and Sam followed, equipping a heavy-looking longsword. Allistor smiled again when he noticed Meg shaking her head and taking a seat on a knee wall, clearly unwilling to join them. Sam snickered, then stepped inside ahead of Allistor.

When he stepped through the door himself, Allistor immediately understood what McCoy meant. The place just felt creepy. This lower level looked as if it had been cut directly into the bedrock of Manhattan island, then had plaster smoothed over the rough stone walls. The corridor ceiling was half covered in conduit, both electrical and plumbing, running across hanging supports that were bolted into the stone above.

The two men cast light globes in front of themselves and moved carefully but at a steady pace down the first hallway, then down another that branched off to the right. McCoy had used chalk to mark arrows on the walls, giving them a clear roadmap to the dungeon entrance. Two minutes after entering the building, they were standing in front of the swirling portal. Allistor used his *Examine* skill, as did Sam.

"I'm getting nothing, like McCoy said." Sam grumped. Allistor, on the other hand, was getting some information.

You have discovered: Phobia Dungeon!
Dungeon Level: Scalable
This is not an instanced dungeon.

He read the notification to Sam, who took a step back. "What the hell is phobia dungeon? And what does scalable mean?"

"I don't know about the phobia thing, but I'm guessing it's nothing good. As for scalable, from what Harmon told me when we were discussing the dungeon cores, scalable dungeons are rare. They basically set themselves at the average level of the group that steps inside. So if you and I were to walk in there right now, this would be a very high level dungeon."

"No way in hell you and I are walking in there, though. Right?" Sam took another step back, and Allistor followed. He'd never seen the old Marine scared of anything before, and Sam's behavior was amping up the discomfort Allistor was already feeling himself.

"Nope. We're gonna bravely run away, and maybe come back with a solid group." Seeing the look on Sam's face, he added, "Or maybe not."

"You can go in there if you want to, son. I'm gonna take my happy ass out of here and never look back. This whole place is damned creepy. Like a slasher movie, or some shit." Sam picked up the pace, reversing their path, following the chalk arrows. Allistor kept up with him, resisting the temptation to wonder aloud if ghosts might have erased and re-drawn the arrows. While he definitely felt the creep factor in the old asylum basement, at his level he had little fear of anything that might be wandering about down there.

Inside the dungeon though, that might be a completely different story.

When they emerged, Sam's half-panicked face caused the waiting raiders to chuckle. If the place got to the tough old Marine, they felt a little better about their own fear. Sam went straight to Meg, gathered her up in a hug, and whispered something in her ear.

Meg immediately stood up, brushed herself off, and loudly stated, "Well, time to go! I got dishes to clean up!" She started walking toward the juggernaut, Sam right beside her. He shot one last look over his shoulder at the dark entrance, and picked up his pace a bit.

Looking around and not seeing any intact buildings through which he could speak to Nigel, Allistor motioned for the raiders to follow him, and jogged after his elderly friends. As soon as he was within range of the vehicle, he called out. "Nigel, get me Bjurstrom please."

He stopped next to the vehicle, holding up a hand to keep Meg from driving away. McCoy and the others caught up in time to hear Bjurstrom answer. "What's up, boss."

"McCoy and his group found a new dungeon under what used to be Bellevue Hospital..." he filled the man in on the rest of the details, watching as the lower level raiders reacted to the news. "I need you to get a top team of raiders down here, and send someone in a ship to Wilderness to request that Master Daigath join us here. Please call Harmon as well. No, never mind, I'll do that. Get everyone here as quick as you can."

"Roger that, boss. We're on it." Bjurstrom sounded excited about the new dungeon.

"Nigel, please connect me with Harmon if he's available." Allistor smiled at Meg and Sam, silently asking them to be patient. Now that they were away from the creepy basement, they seemed content to stay put.

"Good evening, Allistor." the orcanin's deep voice rang out from the vehicle's speakers. "What can I do for you?"

"Some of my people have discovered a scalable dungeon here in the city, and I have some questions I'm hoping you can answer."

"Scalable? That is interesting. I have only ever seen one scalable dungeon. Where are you?" The orcanin paused, then continue. "Ah, I see. Nigel has kindly marked your location for me. I'll be there shortly."

Allistor noticed McCoy staring intently at him, and raised an eyebrow. "What?"

"You're thinking about going in there yourself." It was a statement, not a question.

"Don't you dare!" Meg wagged a finger at him from the driver's seat. Sam remained neutrally silent, which Allistor appreciated.

"I am… considering it." He replied. "How many dungeons are high enough level for me to run? None of the ones we control. I'm like a billion xp from reaching level one hundred, and I can't just go around conquering planets everywhere to level up."

"All evidence to the contrary." Meg snarked at him. "What's the name of that new elfy world again? Riverdance?" Sam snorted next to her, grinning widely at Allistor.

"Rivian." Allistor rolled his eyes. "And that was sort of an accident."

"Like inheriting two worlds from killing a Norse god." McCoy piled on. Now everybody but Allistor was grinning.

"Fine. You all have a point. But I have zero plans to be conquering any more worlds anytime soon. We still have a ton of work to do here on Earth, and on the other worlds we already control."

"I'll take Riverdance if you don't want it." Meg offered. "It sounds real nice. L'olwyn says the air smells like flowers and honey."

"I like honey." Sam offered helpfully, pushing out his belly in a decent Pooh impersonation.

"You know, technically you are sitting in MY juggernaut. I'm tempted to keep it here and make you two walk back." Allistor grumped at the couple who had become like mother and father to him.

Meg's face went solemn all of a sudden. "Seriously, boy. Don't go in there. You have no idea what you'll find inside, and we can't afford to lose you. What if that place makes you insane, or something?"

"I like honey." Sam tried to lighten the mood, squeezing Meg's leg when she threw him a dirty look. To both Allistor and Meg's surprise, Sam took his side. "You gotta let the boy make his own decisions. He knows the dangers as well as any of us. Hell, he's the one who taught us. And he's overcome long odds time and again, winning fights he should have lost. We'll make sure he has a real good healer if he goes inside."

McCoy cut in with, "You know if you go in with a group, you being level ninety nine, you're going to raise the average level a good bit. The rest of us, even Bjurstrom, are thirty plus levels behind you." McCoy was among the last of the surviving gamers Allistor had found at the Silo. He understood full well what the scalable dungeon mechanics meant. "Let's say a group of five, everyone but you at level sixty five. If the math is anything like the old games, your presence might raise the dungeon level from a mid-sixties to over seventy."

"And that might get people killed." Allistor knew where he was going. "I'm aware of how it probably works. That's why I've asked Daigath and Harmon to come here, so we can figure that out. But we have some folks, allies who are as high level as me, or higher. If we can get a high level first kill on this dungeon, it might mean some truly legendary loot."

McCoy looked like he wanted to argue, but held his tongue.

"Don't worry. If what I'm planning isn't feasible, I'll let you and Bjurstrom take a few others in there to get the first kill." Allistor winked at McCoy, who held up both hands.

"Oh, hell no. I'm not goin in there, even for that sweet, sweet loot. My momma didn't raise no dummy. That place just screams 'gateway to hell' or some shit. That's a big nope. I'll wait out here with bandaids and tasty adult beverages for the survivors."

"Amen to that." Sam agreed from the passenger seat.

One of the junior raiders, a young woman Allistor didn't know, stepped forward and sheepishly asked, "What will you do once you beat it?"

"What do mean?" Allistor asked.

"Well, I mean… this thing feels bad. Not just creepy, but dangerous. Maybe even evil. Is it maybe better to take the core and destroy the dungeon, move it far away?"

"Or just destroy the core altogether, if that's even possible." McCoy added.

Allistor nodded slowly as he considered her suggestion. "That might be a good idea. We'll see what we find in there. If it's as bad as you think, moving it might be for the best."

Just then Harmon came rolling up in one of the massive orcanin armored transports. He and three other orcanin, including his grandson, stepped out and joined Allistor.

"Thanks for coming so quickly." Allistor raised a hand in greeting. He pointed toward the ruined building. "It's in the basement over there. Have you ever heard of a phobia dungeon?"

Harmon scratched his chin for a moment. "I have not. But based on the name, I could make an educated guess as to what it might be. And you say it's scalable?"

"Yep. That's what the description tells me."

"If I had to guess, I'd say the dungeon will present you with monsters that are commonly feared by the masses. Like giant spiders, snakes, undead, and the sort. Or it will present challenges like jumping from great heights, or walking through fire."

"You just *had* to say spiders." Meg scowled at the orcanin, who smiled back at her.

"Apologies, Lady Meg. They are a commonly shared fear among many species. Not orcanin. We find them quite tasty."

"You also find goblins tasty, so clearly you're all insane." Meg grumped half-heartedly.

"I would like to take a look inside, if you don't mind? It may be that I can obtain more information than you have been able to."

Allistor nodded. "I sent someone to retrieve Master Daigath, so we have some time. It's a short walk to the dungeon portal." Allistor started walking back toward the basement entry, the orcanin following along. When they got inside, Allistor recast his light globe and pointed out the chalk arrows. As they walked through the halls, he pulled the ebonwood sword from his inventory and handed it to Harmon. "Check out what I found on Rivian."

He waited for Harmon to unwrap the sword, then chuckled as he stopped dead in his tracks, staring at the weapon in his hand. "This is… this was crafted by Master Daigath." He looked up at Allistor, eyes wide.

"It was." Allistor agreed. "Several thousand years ago, apparently. And the best part is…" He paused to build up some suspense as the other orcanin leaned in to admire the weapon. "He apparently made it for his girlfriend, who at the time was the Al'drong matriarch!"

"No!" Harmon gasped at the juicy bit of gossip, which Allistor had fully expected.

"The House steward pulled it out of their vault and told me the story. I'm planning to ask Master Daigath about it. When the time is right."

"Oh, *please* let me be there when you do!" The giant orcanin practically squealed with joy at the prospect of witnessing the ancient elf being put on the spot.

"Heh. Longbeard said almost exactly the same thing." The two shared a quiet chuckle, the humor of the situation easing the feeling of impending doom in the basement corridor.

Harmon wrapped the sword and handed it back to Allistor. "That is a true work of art."

"The steward said it has taken a lot of lives, and is nearly sentient. Or something like that. Self-aware, is the term I think he used."

"Then it is a dangerous weapon for the wielder as well as their foes." Harmon continued walking. "It takes a strong will to master such a weapon."

Allistor was about to ask for more details when they rounded the last corner and came within sight of the dungeon portal. He watched as Harmon stared at the dark swirling pattern for several seconds, then blinked rapidly.

Turning to Allistor, he spoke quietly as he reported. "It is indeed scalable, but with an upper limit of level one hundred and twenty. At least, until it gets stronger. That is all the additional information I was able to see."

Allistor, feeling a strong urge to either flee, or fling himself into the portal, motioned for them to return to the others. Even the fierce and fearless orcanin warriors who had accompanied them didn't argue, giving the portal an uneasy glance as they departed. Harmon's comment as they rounded the corner and moved out of sight of the portal summed it up well.

"There is something… off about this place."

Allistor suddenly realized that Harmon had no idea of the history of the hospital, so he explained as they walked out.

"This place has been a famous, or maybe infamous, hospital for something like two centuries. When it was first built, my people knew almost nothing about mental illness. Anyone who acted strangely, or even didn't conform to societal norms back then, might have been declared insane and committed to an asylum like this one. And in a place as large as this, you might have had sane people who only suffered from unexplainable physical tics, or simple mental retardation, imprisoned alongside full-blown psychopathic face-eating murderers. There was little in the way of actual treatment, but lots of brutal experimentation going on. Drugs, electroshock therapy, aversion therapy, lobotomies. People might scream themselves into a vegetative state, break their skulls against the walls, or chew off body parts." Allistor shuddered slightly. "For someone locked up in here back then, this would have seemed worse than hell. They would have been afraid, confused, angry, and hopeless."

Harmon was quiet as they emerged back into the fresh air. "That might explain the feelings we all experienced inside. If such strong emotions were concentrated here for centuries as you say, the massive infusion of mana that occurred after Induction might have coalesced with the emotional energy stored in the structure."

"Creating a natural dungeon." Daigath finished for him as he approached the group alone. "Lady Meg and the others filled me in just now."

"Would you like to look inside?" Allistor stopped, prepared to turn around and take his third trip in to see the portal.

"That won't be necessary. I can feel the emanations from here, and have no desire to get closer. Emotional imbalance is particularly... uncomfortable for elves."

"Have you heard of a phobia dungeon before?" Allistor was hopeful that the ancient elf who seemed to know at least something about everything would have answers.

"I have not. Though I have heard of a dungeon created under a similar circumstance. It formed beneath an ancient prison where criminals were often tortured or forced to fight each other to the death for the entertainment of others. Those who entered the dungeon were afflicted with unreasoning rage, and often turned on their comrades with little provocation. The monsters they faced attacked with abandon, making no attempt to defend or evade, using no strategy, just mindlessly seeking to kill and consume the delvers."

Allistor sighed, not liking the sound of that at all. "So along the same line of thought, a phobia dungeon might cause raiders, or delvers as you call them, to go insane?"

Daigath shook his head. "I do not think so. The name suggests that those who enter might face something they fear. Possibly the thing they fear most. Focusing on those unreasonable fears that can leave you trembling or screaming." He was quiet for a brief moment, as if making a decision. "I, for example, am a creature of lush forests and open sky. I greatly dislike being underground in tight spaces made of stone and void of life. I can not imagine a worse fate than being buried alive."

"Harmon speculated that it would be full of creatures that are commonly feared, or physical challenges based on fear of heights, or fire."

Daigath nodded. "That may indeed be the case. Though, I would venture that the challenges inside will be more… focused. As in, each party member may have to face their own worst fear. Or possibly, all of them at once."

"So a cave-in or stone trap for you, having to watch helplessly as all my teammates die for me, and… what? A twenty foot tall horny lady goblin for Harmon?" Allistor grinned at his friend, who acted horrified at the thought.

"For me it would be facing a murderous elf without the ability to defend myself." Harmon whispered a moment later, instantly silencing the laughter. Everyone there knew that for him, that was a very real everyday fear.

"So how do we handle this?" Allistor asked the question mostly to himself.

Daigath shook his head. "Like any other dungeon, you challenge it and face the risks involved, or you leave it alone and risk it growing out of control."

Chapter Eighteen

The Other Cheek

The five of them stood outside the building as the first of the twin suns crested the horizon. Allistor was fitted from head to toe in crimson drake skin armor, presented to him the night before by Lilly. She'd spent nearly a week crafting it, with the help of several of her fellow tailors and leatherworkers. It was by far the best armor Allistor had ever worn, with boosts of +10 each to *Strength* and *Agility*, +20 *Will Power*, and a set bonus that reduced physical damage taken by 20%.

It had taken them a week to find an appropriate party to take on the phobia dungeon. Of the humans, Allistor was the only one going, the others being too far below him in levels. He'd decided on that first day that it needed to be him, and not his raiders, that took on this rare and dangerous dungeon. The level cap of one hundred and twenty was actually a blessing, as it allowed higher leveled party members to accompany him without raising the difficulty level. They were going to max it out at one-twenty, but Allistor was confident his team could manage it. He was the lowest level on the team, after all.

The first volunteer had been Longbeard. The moment the dwarf heard about Allistor challenging the dungeon, he had demanded a chance to join him. "It be a rare thing to find a dungeon that can challenge me, Allistor." He had explained. "At least, one that don't cost a fortune to step inside."

Now that he was level ninety nine, Allistor could see that the dwarf was level one fifty. In his dwarven-crafted lightsteel chainmail, a tower shield on his back, and carrying a battle axe that audibly hummed when he swung it, the dwarf was an impressive sight.

Daigath's friend Netsirk the druidess had agreed to serve as their healer. She was level one hundred ten, and while less excited about entering the disturbing dungeon, was quite curious about what they'd find. She wore grey leather from head to toe, and held a gnarled wooden staff with one hand. A long wooden blade, another example of Daigath's craftmanship, hung at one hip, and a slender silvery bladed dagger on the other.

The Azure order had sent a level one hundred twenty mage at Daigath's request. Cserald, a member of a serpentine race sporting rainbow-hued scaled skin, was an Arcanist with a wide array of powerful offensive spells. Dressed in the azure blue robes of his order, his weapons of choice were short sword and wand. Cserald had disclosed that he was the proud winner of a hastily arranged tournament held among a hundred of his peers, all vying for the chance to enter this dungeon.

Harmon had wanted to be their fifth party member, but his grandson had loudly and violently argued against it until he relented. Instead he chose a level one hundred orcanin warrior to represent their people. The massive fighter, whose name was Targon, was a good foot taller and wider than Harmon himself, and covered in battle scars. One tusk was splintered about halfway down its length, the other coated in metal that was sharpened to a gleaming point. He carried a sword taller than Allistor on his back, as well as a wicked looking axe in each hand. The veteran of more than twenty campaigns, he was one of Harmon's most experienced and trusted warriors. Allistor didn't know it, but Targon had been instructed to protect him at all costs. "Pick him up and carry him out over your shoulder if you have to." Harmon had commanded.

So with a dwarven tank, orcanin melee, a druid for healing, Allistor and a mage for ranged damage, crowd control, and pretty much everything else, their party was well-rounded.

Allistor had purchased a dozen of the highest quality health, mana, and stamina potions for each of them, as well as ten generic poison cures. Now they stood in a line as Daigath cast a buff spell on the group that offered a twenty percent increase in resistance to mental attacks. Of his many available blessings, that was the one he deemed would be most useful based on the presumed nature of the dungeon.

Helen, who was standing next to Daigath and surveying the impressive group, suddenly snorted. "Hey, Allistor?" She waited as he and the others looked over at her. "I just noticed... you're the red-shirt in this group." She grinned widely, waiting for him to make the connection. When he did, and rolled his eyes at her, she couldn't hold in her laughter. It was a dark joke, considering the circumstances. But they had found over the last year that gallows humor was sometimes the only way to keep from buckling under the pressure.

Everyone took a moment to conduct last-minute gear checks and to speak quietly to friends. When they each confirmed they were good to go, Longbeard set off without ceremony, stomping toward the basement entrance. "Let's go. There be work to do!"

The group had spent a couple hours the evening before discussing and coordinating their abilities into a rough sort of teamwork. Targon followed the tank, weapons at the ready even though they were minutes away from the dungeon portal. Behind him walked Netsirk the healer, then Cserald, and Allistor brought up the rear. Less of a specialist than the others, he had a variety of ranged attacks, as well as the ability to place a magical barrier behind them if the group was attacked from two sides.

The trip through the basement corridors was uneventful, though the uneasy feeling was clearly affecting everyone, including Allistor. He'd been in this basement several times now, but it didn't seem any less creepy.

Longbeard stopped when they reached the dungeon portal, looking over his shoulder at the group. "Last chance to back out." he whispered as his shoulders slightly hunched. "And if ye choose to, I can't say I'd blame ye." When no one spoke up, he raised his shield higher and nodded with conviction. "Alright, here we go!" The group stepped through the portal one at a time.

Allistor was last to step through, blinking as he found himself in a damp cave lit by a single light globe from Cserald. There was a dull roar echoing off the stone walls, and Allistor ducked down, frantically searching for the monster causing it. A moment later he realized the others didn't seem concerned, and that the roar was constant, not that of a beast.

Straightening up, he cast his own light globe, and pushed it to the other side of the cave so he could get a better look. It wasn't a large space, maybe ten paces across from side to side. To his left it dead ended in a rough stone wall. To the right it curved around a massive boulder and disappeared.

Targon, grunted as Allistor's light neared the boulder. He stepped closer to it, then placed a hand on it, and began shaking his head. "No. This can not be."

Longbeard, who'd been advancing to peak around the boulder toward the only exit, stopped and turned to the orcanin. "What is it, lad?"

"I know this place." Targon removed his hand from the stone, revealing a much smaller handprint underneath. "I have been here."

The mage was the first to make a connection. "Did something happen here? Something bad?"

The orcanin simply nodded, staring at the handprint. After a moment, he pointed to it. "That is my handprint. I made it when I was a child of eight years." He looked up toward the exit. "This cave sits in the mountain where I was born. Just above my father's village. Come, I will show you."

The big warrior strode forward, his steps not nearly as certain as they had been back in Invictus City. The others followed in silence, assuming he'd fill them in on whatever had occurred in this place.

The moment they rounded the boulder, they could see daylight maybe fifty paces away. The roaring was also explained by a sheet of water falling past the cave entrance. Targon strode forward as if he were about to walk through the waterfall, but stopped at the last moment and side-stepped to his left. There was a narrow gap and ledge between the stone face of the mountain and the falling water, not wide enough to walk normally, especially for the orcanin with wide shoulders. The party followed, steadily pacing to the side until they emerged above a wide pool. There was a series of moss-covered stones from an ancient rockfall at the end of the ledge, and Targon leapt onto the first of them.

"Be careful. The moss is slick." He warned the others as he leapt onto another stone, then another, slowly working his way down to a thick forest below. Longbeard paused at the top, leaning his back hard against the wall as he looked down at the swirling pool of water and scattered rocks far below.

"Damn, this be… high." His voice was hoarse and he visibly gulped.

"Just take it slow, and watch your footing." Netsirk patted him on the shoulder, carefully stepping past him. "Just step where I step."

Longbeard nodded uncertainly, but took the first step, mumbling. "Dwarves do not like heights. This be why we build sturdy railings on our bridges…"

When they'd all reached the bottom, Targon set off without a word, following a narrow footpath worn into the brush not far from the bank of the stream fed by the waterfall. "We used to come up here as children, test our courage by leaping into the pond below the falls. After each jump, we would challenge each other to go higher." He stopped for a moment, gazing up at the waterfall. The cave entrance was not visible, but Allistor guessed at its location from the rockfall. It was now at least a hundred feet above them. He tried to imagine human eight year-olds leaping from heights like that.

"My father's village is just down here." He resumed his walk, moving more quickly now. The others hurried to keep up, Longbeard with his short legs forced to jog occasionally. They traveled nearly a mile down the trail before Targon halted again. He crouched down behind some scrub near the edge of a clearing, motioning for the others to do the same.

In the clearing ahead of them, a scene of chaos and horror was playing out inside a small village of stone huts with grass-covered roofs. Scattered among the twenty or so structures, orcanin lay dead or dying. More were being attacked by figures in head to toe black leather wearing masks painted with skull faces. The orcanin roared in anger and despair, but not one of them held a weapon, or threw a punch as they were slashed and stabbed, kicked and punched.

Allistor immediately knew why. "Those are elves in the black gear."

Targon nodded, but didn't speak. His gaze was fixed on the slaughter in the village.

Netsirk shook her head, then spat in disgust. "They called themselves Cleansers." She lowered her eyes, then turned her back on the scene and sat with her knees bunched up against her chest, her arms hugging them. "When the treaty with the orcanin took effect, there was still much animosity on both sides. It had been a long, brutal war, with both elven and orcanin populations being greatly reduced." She shuddered, remembering more than one battle. "Within a couple of generations, the orcanin population was exploding, each female bearing multiple children. While we elves rarely reproduce. Some saw the threat of the growing imbalance as an excuse to embrace old grudges, and began attacking small, isolated settlements like this village. They slaughtered orcanin by the hundreds, knowing that either they would not defend themselves because of the covenant, or they would break the covenant and allow the elves to once again wage open war upon orcanin everywhere."

"We held to the covenant." Targon growled. "Even as they slaughtered us, not one orcanin struck back." Tears rolled down his face as he watched his friends and family slaughtered for a second time. "I had been at the falls with three other children. We watched from right here…" His voice broke, and he lowered his head into his scarred hands.

After a few ragged breaths, he continued. "One of the littlest ones cried out, and one of the damned elves heard. They charged toward us." Targon's eyes unfocused as he relived the scene in his mind. "I told the others to run, to hide in the cave, and wait for me. When they'd gone, I rushed out and yelled at the elf. When it struck at me, I did my best to dodge. The covenant did not allow us to attack an elf, but it didn't demand that we stand still and die. The elf's blade tore open my shoulder, and I fled, leading it away from the others. I saw my father lose his head as I ran, standing tall and defiant, roaring at the elf who slew him. Distracted, I slowed down, and the elf stabbed me in the back. I fell, and it returned to the slaughter in the village, leaving me for dead. As soon as I could, I crept back into the forest and made my way to the cave. That was my blood you saw on the stone."

Longbeard growled in fury. "Well, lad. This be a dungeon. Those be dungeon monsters, not real elves. Now's yer chance to get some satisfaction!" Without even looking back at the others, the dwarf got to his feet and pushed through the brush, making a huge racket as he raced toward the village. The others followed, ready to wreak bloody vengeance on the murdering elves. Targon's eyes widened in horror.

"You must not! The covenant!" He called out, getting to his feet and chasing after the others. "You harm those elves, and all orcanin everywhere will suffer!"

Hearing this, Allistor slowed, even as Longbeard shouted a battle cry and slammed his shield into the first skull-faced elf. The surprised cleanser was outmatched, knocked from its feet. Behind him, Cserald cast a group of icicles that blasted into two more elves, tearing holes in their leather gear.

"These aren't elves." Allistor tried again to convince Targon. "We're inside a dungeon. A dungeon that is forcing you to face your fear!" He shouted at the orcanin, who stood with hands at his sides, breathing hard and shaking his head in denial.

"I can not. They're elves. I... can not." His gaze shifted to where an exceptionally large orcanin was standing with his hands bound, glaring at an elf that was slowly drawing the tip of a sword across his chest, leaving a bloody but shallow cut.

Allistor looked toward the scene and cursed. "Targon! Is that your father? You must save him! I think that's what we're here for. You must fight!" The elf stabbed Targon's father in the thigh, causing him to bellow in pain. His leg gave out, and he fell to his knees. Allistor stared at the elf long enough to get its stats.

Elven Cleanser
Level 115
Health: 100,000/100,000

When Targon just continued to shake his head, more tears streaming down his cheeks, Allistor took action. He cast *Mind Spike* on the elf, who dropped its sword and screamed, grabbing its head with both hands. Though the elf was a higher level than Allistor, *Mind Spike* was one of his most-used and highest leveled spells.

"Fight!" Allistor screamed at all the orcanin, many of whom looked in his direction. But not one took up arms or made a move to defend themselves. A few, seeing the dwarf and other non-orcanin attacking, did move to put the fighters between themselves and the elves. There was no rule about letting helpful strangers slaughter elves in their defense, after all.

Allistor tried again with Targon. "It's a dungeon! Wake up! These are not real elves! Defend your family!" He swung upward with his fist as hard as he could, bashing the massive orcanin in the chin.

The blow barely moved Targon's head, but he blinked a few times and looked down at Allistor. "What?"

"They're not real elves! They are dungeon monsters! Kill them!" Allistor practically screamed up at his face, then turned and recast *Mind Spike* on the same elf, causing it to fall to its knees.

"Not… elves." Targon repeated, blinking rapidly as if just waking. "We're in the fear dungeon!" He nodded. "I will fight!" He charged forward, roaring out his fear and rage as he raised his massive sword with both hands. When he reached the elf in front of his father, he swung hard enough to bisect the elf at the waist. Not even pausing to watch the two halves fall to the ground, he shifted his grip on the sword and hurled it forward like a spear, pinning a second elf to a door frame as it emerged from a hut with a bloody sword. Targon drew his two axes and, sobbing, ran toward the next elf he saw.

Allistor wasted no time, targeting an elf that was attempting to sneak up on Netsirk as she healed wounded orcanin villagers. He cast *Shatter* on the elf's sword as they were raising it overhead to strike. The blade exploded, taking the elf's sword hand with it, and peppering the back of its head and shoulders with shrapnel. Netsirk took some shrapnel damage too, but nothing serious. The mangled elf fell, not dead, but badly wounded. Seconds later Longbeard stomped past, crushing its skull with his steel boot as he shouted a taunting challenge at two more elves.

Seeing their salvation at hand, the surviving orcanin all moved toward Allistor's party, and the elves followed, cutting down victims as they ran. The party moved together, forming a rough line behind which the orcanin could gather. Allistor and Cserald picked off elves with ranged attacks, rarely killing them, just slowing them enough for their victims to get safely away. An arrow struck Allistor's upper left arm, the head punching all the way through and dropping his health bar by about five percent. Grunting in pain, he did his best to ignore it.

When the last of the visible orcanin had gathered, Allistor saw a dozen elves still standing, or getting back to their feet. About half were wounded in some way, but far from out of the fight.

Targon stood next to Longbeard, who was steadily calling out insults and using his taunt ability to draw the elves to him. Allistor almost laughed when the dwarf shouted, "Bring your lanky asses over here, ye cowards! Me angry friend here has a taste fer elf testicles, and I bet him that yer all a bunch o' nutless overgrown goblin spawn!" He slammed a short sword against his shield. "Let's see what ye got!"

Allistor cast *Erupt* in front of the first elf to step forward, a massive stone spike shooting up into its chest and exploding out its back. The elf struggled briefly, waving its sword for a moment before dropping it to use both hands to try to push itself off the spike.

Cserald sent a triple burst of fireballs into a trio of elves on their left flank, only hitting two as the third one threw itself to the ground. Netsirk paused her healing long enough to cast a spell that had vines emerging from the ground surrounding that elf, wrapping around it and pulling it down. It struggled mightily, but more and more vines emerged until the elf was no longer visible beneath them. The two elves that had taken hits from the fireballs were knocked backward off their feet, but not killed. Allistor cast *Levitate* on the nearest, then flung it upward as high as he could. Not bothering to watch the smoking elf land, he drew his sword and quickly parried a blow from a black-clad elf that had run up on his right side.

He managed to stop the sword short of slicing into his head, and pushed it away with all the strength he could manage. As the elf withdrew the blade and prepared for another strike, Cserald stabbed it in the back of the neck. The elf's body went limp, the light leaving its eyes as it fell. Allistor nodded at the mage. "Thanks!"

Cserald was already casting another spell. "Close your eyes!" he shouted at his teammates two seconds before a blindingly bright flash of white erupted in front of their line. Two of the remaining elves had been intelligent enough to listen and close their eyes, but the others hadn't. They stumbled, blinded, and began to blink rapidly. One frightened elf began swinging its sword wildly in front of it, hoping to drive back any attackers. Instead it managed to nearly sever the arm of a fellow elf that wandered too close.

Allistor blinked rapidly, seeing spots. Even through his closed eyelids the bright light had had an effect. Seeing an elf that hadn't been blinded, he cast *Dimensional Step* and put himself right behind them. The moment he appeared, wobbling slightly, he drove the point of his sword into the elf's back, aiming for the heart. One of the ribs deflected the blade enough to miss the heart, and the elf spun around, the motion ripping the blade from Allistor's hand even as the elf raised its own blade.

Allistor quickly cast *Lightning Strike* directly into its face, blasting the enemy backward with his sword still embedded in it. Now behind enemy lines, Allistor grabbed the first weapon from his inventory that came to mind.

The semi-aware wooden sword that Daigath had crafted.

The weapon felt almost weightless in his hands as he quickly unwrapped it and dropped the cloth. The other elf that had the sense to close its eyes was pounding on Longbeard's shield as the dwarf laughed aloud in its face. The elf that had nearly severed its comrade's arm was still swinging wildly, blinking its eyes and shaking its head as its vision began to recover. Allistor didn't wait, stepping up behind the elf and using the ebonwood sword to remove its head. The moment he did so, a small thrill ran through him, and the sword seemed to pulse with pleasure in his hand.

Allistor nearly dropped the weapon then and there, but the elf with the wounded arm bumped into him. It immediately spun in his direction, thrusting an elven blade at his gut. Allistor leapt to one side, the blade deflecting off his armor, then sliced downward at the elf's arm. The blade cut cleanly through flesh and bone, leaving the wrist and hand holding the sword to fall to the ground. A quick thrust up under the elf's chin ended its misery. Another pulse of pleasure from the sword washed through him.

Breathing hard, Allistor turned and looked for another enemy. There were none left standing. Two elves still thrashed on the ground, mortally wounded but taking their time to die. Targon, bellowing in anguish, stomped forward and hacked into each of their skulls with a hand axe, finishing them off with sickening crunches. He immediately turned toward his father, who was back on his feet but heavily favoring his wounded leg. Targon strode in that direction, but stopped dead when his father, the other orcanin, and the village itself faded from view.

"What's happening?" the warrior spun around, frantically searching what was now an empty stone chamber that surrounded them.

Longbeard set down his shield, and sheathed his sword, then stroked his beard with his free sword hand. "I be thinkin' ye defeated the challenge."

Cserald nodded. "I believe Master Longbeard is correct. The dungeon appears to have created a scenario that forced you to face your greatest fear, or regret. Once you'd successfully overcome it, and the monsters it created had been vanquished, it ended the scenario."

Targon stood silent and still, staring down at the axes in his hands, seeing the elven blood that should have been there, but had faded away with the bodies and the village. He was breathing hard, and his grip on the handles was so tight his knuckles creaked. The others remained quiet as well, giving him time to recover. Allistor took a moment to check his arm. The arrow had disappeared, but the hole remained. Before he could cast a heal on himself, he felt one from the druid wash over him. He turned to her and smiled his thanks.

When Targon finally spoke, his voice was barely above a whisper. "From birth we are taught one rule above all others. One absolute that can not be broken. We do not raise a hand to elves under any circumstance. Even at the cost of our own lives." He let out a ragged breath. "I watched my family, almost everyone I knew and loved, tortured and slaughtered like animals. I watched, and did not act. Not then, not anytime since."

"Ye did what ye could, lad." Longbeard's voice was sympathetic. "Ye nearly got yerself killed protectin' yer fellow lil ones, and ye did it without breakin' the covenant. Ye showed courage and honor."

Targon nodded. "That is what Harmon said when he found us. He took us in, raised us, trained us to be warriors as if we were his own blood. He often caught me hiding somewhere, lost in my memories of that day. He would remind me of how our people suffered under the elves, and how many had paid the price for our freedom in the rebellion. And that, had I fought for my family that day, violated the covenant as those elves clearly desired, how many more would have perished. He would tell me he was proud of me." Targon broke down and sobbed, dropping his weapons to cover his face with both hands as he turned his back on the group.

Netsirk spoke even as tears rolled down her face. "It is a horrible thing, what my people have done to yours. Many of us did not approve of slavery in the first place, and refused to fight when your people rose up. The terms of the covenant are onerous, and shameful. Most of us despise those elves that take advantage of it the way the cleansers have. If I could speak for all of elvenkind, I would apologize on their behalf."

The massive orcanin whirled around to face the elf, a snarl on his face. "You can take your apology and-" He stopped mid-sentence when he saw the honest grief on their healer's face. His hands twitched, as if unsure what to do when not holding a weapon. Allistor and Longbeard moved in closer in case they needed to intervene, but a moment later he drew a deep, ragged breath. "I accept your apology as it was meant, and apologize for my reaction. It has been a... difficult day."

"Let's take a few minutes to rest and recuperate." Allistor suggested, pulling a water bottle from his inventory. They were all more than a little shaken by what they'd witnessed, and the implications behind it.

"And loot." Cserald called out from the center of the chamber, where he was sitting atop a large chest that glowed faintly. "This thing appeared a minute ago, but I didn't want to interrupt."

Chapter Nineteen

Down, Down, Down

The group spent half an hour in the nearly empty chamber, gathering their strength, and their nerves, and going over the loot.

Cserald had opened the chest once the others had gathered around. Each party member was instantly awarded a thousand gold coins, the glittering pile inside the chest disappearing. In addition, there was a scroll that glowed purple, and a battle axe. The axe was clearly meant for Targon, who had been the one to face his worst nightmare. When he reached into the chest and removed it, the weapon quadrupled in size in his hand. Even he was surprised by how large it became, but reported that it weighed much less than expected.

Allistor cast *Examine* on the scroll, and shook his head. By the looks on the others' faces, they had done the same.

Scroll of Fear
This scroll teaches the user to cast the Fear spell, which causes enemies within a twenty foot radius to cower, or even flee, in terror. Effectiveness is based on caster's Will Power versus that of the target's. Spell effect duration: Ten seconds. Area of effect and duration will increase at higher levels.

"That'd be a right useful spell." Longbeard mused before shifting his gaze to stare longingly at Targon's new axe.

"It should, of course, go to Emperor Allistor." Cserald observed. "This is his dungeon, after all." The others nodded in agreement.

Allistor shook his head. "We're equals inside this dungeon, so call me Allistor. And we'll distribute the loot fairly when we've beaten this thing. I'll hold on to the scroll for now." When they all nodded their agreement, he looked around. "I only see one exit. The tunnel we came in through has closed behind us." He motioned back where the entrance had been. It was now a blank section of wall, much like the rest of the cavern. The only opening was a dark archway on the opposite side.

"Well, let us get on with it." Longbeard's tone was less enthusiastic than it had been before they entered. None of them had witnessed Targon's nightmare and emerged unscathed. The dwarf took the lead, the others easily keeping up behind him. Two light globes kept pace, one above Longbeard in the front, the other above Allistor in the back.

Allistor occasionally spun around as they walked, keeping one eye on the rear. He cast *Barrier* behind him, and extended out the invisible shield so that it was almost as wide as the tunnel they found on the other side of the archway.

After ten paces or so, they reached a stairway that led down to the next level. Forty steps later, they found a landing, and another dark archway. Nothing could be seen beyond, as if a curtain of darkness had been pulled across. Longbeard stood just inside the arch and extended his sword forward as if expecting to poke an actual curtain. When nothing happened, he shrugged. "Here we go."

He stepped through, quickly followed by the others. The darkness lasted only a fraction of a second for Allistor as he passed through, his pulse quickening.

The other side was uneventful. They found themselves in another corridor, this one of smooth stone so polished that it gleamed in the light of the globes. It was wide enough for three to walk abreast, but they kept their usual single file formation, just staggered themselves slightly to one side, then the other.

The corridor stretched on for some time, thousands of paces, and Allistor noticed that the temperature seemed to drop as they went. He wasn't the only one, as Cserald produced a coat from his inventory and donned it. Allistor hadn't considered it before, but it occurred to him now that the reptilian mage might be ectothermic, or cold-blooded. As he watched, the mage hugged himself and shivered.

They had walked what seemed like a mile before the corridor came to an end. By then, the walls and floor were covered in frost, and their boots were crunching with each step. The doorway at the end opened into a small round chamber with a low domed ceiling. There were no other visible exits, except for a round hole in the floor maybe ten paces across.

Cserald had begun channeling some sort of modified fire spell on himself, warming but not burning him, as they stood around the edge of the opening. Longbeard sent his light globe down into the hole, and they watched as it illuminated more smooth stone walls on its way down. When it reached the limit of the dwarf's casting, which was more than two hundred feet, it winked out without having reached the bottom.

Longbeard leaned back, looking slightly queasy. "That be a long way down."

"Let's see if we can figure out just how far." Allistor pulled a salvaged road flare from his inventory, lit it, then dropped it. He counted aloud as they all watched it fall, and fall, and fall. By the time it hit bottom, suddenly winking out, it had been falling for roughly nine seconds by Allistor's count. He quickly did the math aloud. "Nine seconds, maybe a little more..." He whistled when the enormity of the number struck him. "That's somewhere between nine hundred and a thousand feet."

Longbeard took two steps back, shaking his head as he stared at the hole. The rest of the party members looked around at each other, except Cserald, who had his head down, still hugging himself, and stomping his feet.

"Are you alright, Cserald?" Allistor asked, becoming concerned. The chamber was cold, obviously below freezing, but was only slightly uncomfortable for himself and the others. The mage seemed to truly be suffering.

"I… can channel the spell that warms me, but it isss draining my mana. I am attempting to preserve asss much asss I can." They all noticed the pronounced hiss that was beginning to accompany his soft s sounds. "I do not want to be ussselesss to the party without mana."

Allistor shook his head. "Warm yourself, use as much mana as you need to. You're no good to us half frozen, either." The others nodded in agreement, and Cserald let out a sigh of relief. He made a small motion with one hand, and within seconds his shivering had ceased.

"Thank you." He bowed toward the group. "That wasss… unpleasssant." He peered down the hole as if paying attention for the first time. "How do we get down? I can levitate myself, and possssibly one other, but not for long enough to reach bottom. And not while channeling thisss warming ssspell."

"Same here." Allistor agreed. I can levitate myself down there. But if I tried to lower one of you, the spell would wink out when you get out of range, like Longbeard's light."

Longbeard produced a coiled rope from his inventory. "I've got two hundred feet o' rope." The others quickly checked their inventories. Allistor and Targon both had rope, but only another three hundred feet between them. "Only enough to get us halfway." the dwarf observed. I could hammer some pitons into the stone and work me way down, but I've only enough for maybe another two hundred feet."

Targon cleared his throat before speaking. "Your fire stick extinguished when it reached the bottom. Could it be that there is water down there?"

"We could drop something else and find out." Allistor replied while shaking his head. "But it wouldn't matter. Hitting the water from nine hundred feet up, or even three hundred feet up if we used both the pitons and the rope before falling, would be the same as hitting stone. Broken legs, at the very least, and more likely internal bleeding, concussion, unconsciousness. If we survived the fall, assuming the water is even deep enough to cushion our fall, we'd likely drown."

"I'll be checkin' the walls." Longbeard stepped away from the hole and produced a small metal hammer. "There must be some other way o' getting out o' here." He reached the nearest wall and began tapping lightly at it. The others watched for a while, then began to quietly discuss their options.

"We could just go back to where it was warm, try to break our way out. Abandon this cursed dungeon." Cserald offered hopefully. Allistor noticed his speech had cleared up now that he was warmer.

Targon shook his head. "We are unlikely to be able to break out. Dungeon structures are not easily damaged, unless they are designed to be. Like hidden doors or walls concealing caches." He paused before adding, "And it is our mission to defeat this dungeon. I vote we destroy the core when we reach it. No one should have to suffer what this place holds."

Allistor sympathized with the orcanin, and tended to agree. But he wasn't yet ready to commit to destroying something as valuable as a dungeon core. "I agree we need to finish this dungeon, though I'll reserve my opinion on destruction until we get there."

"This could be just another test of fear." Netsirk murmured, mostly to herself. But the others heard it.

"Meaning what?" Targon raised an eyebrow at her.

"The last test, once you faced your fear, the elves and village disappeared. Maybe this is the same? We have to leap, because leaping down a deep hole terrifies us." She looked over at Longbeard. "Some of us more than others, but I think this qualifies as a serious fear for each of us."

Allistor saw where her train of thought was going, and began to nod along as she spoke. "But I see one issue. In Targon's test, we had to actually battle the elves. We received real wounds, and could have died in the battle. Which might mean that we could die on impact at the bottom."

They grew quiet again, the only sound coming from Longbeard's hammer striking the wall in a steady rhythm. Netsirk eventually broke the silence. "Assuming my theory is correct, and the test is for us to leap... maybe the leap is all that is required. Maybe we never strike bottom."

Surprising everyone, Cserald volunteered. "I'll do it. Anything to get out of this cold. If there's water at the bottom, it's at least slightly warmer than up here." The grin he gave the others revealed a single ridge of teeth that stretched from one side of his jaw to the other.

Allistor argued. "If anyone should go, it's me. I can levitate myself down there just like you can, but my mana isn't being drained by a warming spell." Cserald bowed his head in acknowledgement of the point even as Targon shook his.

"If the druid is correct, and leaping is the point, then levitation might mean you fail the test and can not proceed. And if one of you were to leap alone, the rest of us might fail for remaining behind to see the result." He took a deep breath, clearly not happy. "No, I think we must all leap together, not knowing whether or not we leap to our deaths."

"Are ye daft?" Longbeard came stomping over, hands clenched into fists, a look of fury on his face. "Ye want us to just jump into a damned pit o' doom?"

"I want no such thing. But I fear it may be necessary. Unless you wish to remain here until we starve. Or you have a better way down. I take it you found no other exit?"

Longbeard huffed, not ready to let go of his anger. Or fear, Allistor suspected. The dwarf clearly didn't like heights. "No, no other exit."

"Parachutes." Allistor nearly shouted the idea as it occurred to him. "We have some rope, if we have enough cloth, we can make some rough parachutes and float down."

The druid shook her head. "I can't explain why I feel it, but I believe we must take the leap. Using parachutes would be just another failing scenario. It seems to me the goal of this dungeon is not to just get to the physical end, or to fight a series of monsters. It wants to force us to face our fears. Those are the monsters we must slay."

Again, silence reigned in the chamber as they all considered her words. Longbeard shifted his weight from foot to foot, staring uncomfortably down into the pit. After a moment, he spoke. "I'm sure it be no secret to any of ye, I don't like heights. Or rather, I don't like the idea o' fallin from great heights. Just the thought o' jumpin in this hole makes me want to piss meself."

"You're not alone in that." Allistor assured him. The others nodded too. "So the question becomes, how much faith do we have? Faith in Netsirk's theory, faith that the leap is what's important, that overcoming our fear and jumping passes the test, and that we won't have to land."

Targon took a single step closer to the edge. "To die challenging a dungeon is an honorable death. On the other hand, foolishly leaping into a deep hole and dying is much less honorable. I am willing to risk my life, and my honor. I will jump."

Netsirk simply nodded once and stepped forward to the edge as well. Cserald followed their example a moment later, saying, "Anything to get out of this cold before my mana runs out."

Allistor looked at his advisor and friend, the dwarf's body visibly trembling. He could sympathize, as his own gut clenched and threatened to empty itself out of both ends at the thought of jumping. "Master Longbeard? I'll go if you will."

The dwarf shook his head, not speaking as he stared into the abyss. His breathing had become rapid, and he began to wring his hands together in front of him. Finally, his head shaking stopped, and turned into a single nod. "I took an oath to protect ye, lad. If ye jump, I must jump as well. We'll find out together what comes next." He inhaled deeply, then blew out the breath quickly. "If we're gonna do this, let's get on with it. And if we reach the bottom, and I need to change me shorts, I'll clobber the first one o' ye that laughs."

Without speaking, the druid held her hands out wide to either side, offering a hand to Allistor and Longbeard. They each took a hand, and reached out themselves for Targon and Cserald. When they all had a tight grip on someone, Allistor counted down. "On three. One… two… three!"

Allistor and the others stepped into the void, Longbeard hesitating slightly, but dragged forward by the others. He let out a shriek that followed them down as they plunged into the darkness.

Allistor felt his stomach rise into his throat and clenched his teeth, even as he squeezed his eyes tightly shut. He felt Targon's iron grip begin to crush his hand, but didn't care. Terror made his heart threaten to thump out of his chest, and he was beginning to feel lightheaded. He tried to count the seconds as they fell, but his brain just wasn't cooperating. It was focused on not puking, voiding his bladder and his bowels all at the same time.

He was pretty sure he'd blacked out when a moment later he heard a splash, and cold water surrounded him. His ears filled with the muted sounds of others struggling in the water near him even as he opened his eyes. Everything around him was darkness, and he couldn't tell up from down. He quickly realized his lungs held very little oxygen as his body screamed that it needed air. He'd probably been screaming on his way down without even knowing it.

He was still mindlessly thrashing around, panic setting in as he began to drown, fighting not to inhale the surrounding water, when a light globe appeared not far away. Netsirk had found the presence of mind to provide them some light. Allistor immediately felt a little better, being able to see his companions. Even better, the light revealed the water's surface just a few feet above him. He quickly oriented toward the surface, kicked with his feet and pulled with his hands, propelling himself upward.

Allistor gasped when he broke the surface, drawing in sweet, sweet air. He began to tread water as he watched the druid, then the mage break the surface as well. After ten seconds, he began to worry that Targon and Longbeard hadn't appeared. Sticking his head back underwater, he saw a sight that horrified him.

The orcanin was swimming downward! Allistor initially thought he'd been disoriented and moving away from the surface, until he looked past the warrior to see a steadily sinking dwarf that was just beginning to pass out of the range of the light globe. Longbeard didn't appear to be struggling at all, and Allistor feared the worst.

He frantically cast Levitate on Longbeard, but the dwarf had passed out of his range. Taking a deep breath, he did a duck dive and began to swim toward his companions. Right at that moment, Targon reached the dwarf and snagged ahold of his beard, which was floating above his head. He immediately reversed direction and began swimming upward, dragging the dwarf behind him. A few seconds later the warrior's strength began to flag as he too ran out of oxygen. Allistor pushed himself, straining against the water to reach them. As soon as he was in range, he cast *Levitate* on Targon, lifting the orcanin quickly through the water. He stopped swimming downward and simply let himself float up toward the surface as he used his magic to push his friends along.

When he broke the surface Targon was already gasping for air, doing his best to hold the heavy, fully armored dwarf above the surface. Allistor recast *Levitate* on the dwarf this time, lifting him up enough that his head and chest were clear of the water, allowing Targon a chance to recover. They all watched, concerned, waiting for Longbeard to take a breath. When he didn't do so for half a minute, even after the druid cast a heal on him, Allistor began to panic.

"We need to get out of this water!" He looked around, but the light globe that was still under the surface didn't reveal much. Netsirk obligingly raised her globe up into the air, where it was immediately joined by one cast by Cserald. Allistor couldn't release his levitation magic to cast one himself. The two globes began to spread out, and within a few seconds the mage's globe revealed a rocky shore to their left. All of them began to swim, with Allistor's magic pulling Longbeard along behind him. It only took a few seconds to reach the rocks and climb up to a flat area above them. Allistor immediately deposited the dwarf on the stone floor and began CPR. The others looked askance at him, not recognizing what he was doing. Targon grunted in surprise when Allistor put his mouth over the dwarf's and pushed air into him before resuming compressions. He had to repeat that process twice more before the dwarf coughed up a spray of water and began to thrash.

"Ach! What're ye doin, boy!?" He batted at Allistor, whose face had been close enough to his to be caught in the spray. "This ain't no time to be kissin' me goodbye!"

Allistor snorted, backing away from the dwarf. "It was CPR, you old perv." He grinned, happy to see the dwarf alive. "You drowned. I just saved your life." He moved back further as Longbeard sat up and looked around, eyeing the nearby water with significant suspicion.

Targon nodded. "It's true, you did drown. As I nearly did myself. Allistor saved us both."

Cserald shook his head. "Targon nearly drowned swimming down after you, Master Longbeard. Your armor was dragging you down."

The dwarf listened, eyes wide, his gaze moving from one speaker to the next. When he finally comprehended what they were telling him, he got up, then back down on one knee, bowing his head. "I remember naught but blackness after we jumped. Not the fallin', not the swimmin'. I owe ye both me life."

Allistor was about to contradict him, but he saw Targon give a subtle shake of his head. Instead, he stayed silent as the orcanin spoke. "We are bound to each other in this adventure, dwarf. You will save our lives as we save yours. That is a debt we all share here. I put my trust in you the moment we stepped through the portal, and you have more than earned that trust since."

"As have you." The dwarf agreed, raising his head to meet Targon's gaze. "I thank ye." He turned his head to include all of them.

"We're a team." Allistor followed the orcanin's lead. "We get through this together, or maybe not at all." He looked around the area where they found themselves. "And speaking of getting through, we should prepare to move on."

"There's no chest." Cserald observed. "Unless maybe it was down there?" He pointed into the water.

"What do you mean?" Allistor frowned down at the water, wondering how deep it was. If there was a chest down there, he wasn't sure it was worth going after.

"I mean I don't think what we just experienced was one of the main floor challenges, like Targon's. There was cold, which is deadly for me, but I wasn't in any real danger unless I ran out of mana and used up all the mana potions. There was the great leap, which was a fear for all of us, and especially for Master Longbeard, then the near-drowning. But none of those things triggered a reward chest."

"So you're saying the dungeon is messing with us? Providing more generalized or less serious challenges as we move between the major ones? Like a normal dungeon would throw trash mobs at us." Allistor was beginning to get it.

"Like the voices." Netsirk nodded her head. "Does it seem to the rest of you that they've grown louder since we fell?"

"Voices?" Longbeard cocked his head to one side, listening. "I hear no voices other than our own." Allistor, Targon, and Cserald all nodded in agreement with the dwarf.

"You don't hear them? They've been whispering at us since we entered this place. I can't understand what they're saying, but their tone is... sinister. Angry, fearful, and threatening all at once." The elf hugged herself, and the shiver that passed through her had nothing to do with being wet.

"Must be yer elven hearing, lass." Longbeard concluded. "Much better than mine, or the others here."

"Or it's another challenge, like the cold was for me." Cserald offered. He waved a hand at the druid, and steam began to rise from her. "This will warm and dry you." He quickly did the same for the others, then himself, before producing and drinking a mana potion.

"Thank you, Cserald." She smiled at him. "That does feel much better."

Allistor agreed wholeheartedly, and made a mental note to ask the mage about that spell. It was very handy. He looked toward the back side of the open area they stood in. That was the location of the only exit, unless they wanted to get back in the water and search for another. "If everyone is situated, shall we go this way?"

The others agreed, and once again Longbeard took the lead. There was a rough, natural-looking opening on the rear wall of the area, and he pushed a light globe forward ahead of him. There was no dark curtain this time, just a natural tunnel that passed beyond the opening. He stood at the exit for a moment, looking left and right. The others waited in silence as he listened for any sound of movement in either direction. Then he put his ear to the wall and tapped it a few times. Shrugging, he turned to face them.

"I see and hear nothin' in either direction."

"Can you tell if there's a slope?" Allistor asked. His natural inclination in a dungeon was to move downward, especially since this dungeon seemed to progress in that direction.

"Aye, this tunnel slopes down to the left. Though it be very gradual." The dwarf's natural and unerring sense of direction while underground instantly provided the answer.

"Then let's go left." Allistor commanded from the back of the line. The others didn't seem to have an opinion to the contrary, or at least didn't express one. Longbeard nodded and set off in that direction, his light globe floating directly over his head.

They followed him down the tunnel, which proceeded in a nearly straight line, having just a few gentle turns here and there. The group moved in silence, other than the occasional scuff of a boot or creak of armor. At least, until the druid stopped dead in her tracks. "Beware!" She called out. Everyone else froze, their gazes fixed on her.

"The voices. One of them just called out a single clear word, beware."

"Well, that's not encouraging." Cserald's gaze flicked up and down the tunnel.

"Can you still not hear them? They've grown much louder." All of her companions shook their heads to indicate they could not.

"Could they be warning of something specific? Or was that just a general warning to put you on edge?" Allistor mused.

"I don't know. When I heard the word I felt… panic. As if something were about to happen. But as you say, that could have been the voice's goal."

Longbeard, who also had been scanning the tunnel in both directions, started cursing. He took a couple steps forward, crouching down and closely examining the floor. "There be a trap! A pressure plate…" He turned his attention to the wall next to the plate, following something across the floor, then up the wall to the ceiling. "Get back, this be a-"

"Incoming!" Allistor interrupted the dwarf, pointing past him at a rapidly approaching creature. It looked to be made of stone, its body squat, low to the ground and wide, and seemed to glide across the stone floor rather than walk. Humanoid with two arms and legs, its eyes glowed a deep green, growing brighter as it raced toward their tank.

"Stone elemental!" Longbeard called out. "Get back! The trap… run!" He leapt forward over the pressure plate and slammed the base of his shield down into the floor, bracing it from behind with his shoulder even as he spread his feet wide, one forward behind the shield, the other behind him.

> **Stone Elemental**
> **Level 120**
> **Health: 180,000/180,000**

The others didn't listen, none of them willing to leave behind a comrade. Targon hurled the axe in his right hand at the oncoming elemental, striking its chest with enough force to cause a small spiderweb of cracks to form around the area of impact. Allistor cast *Lightning Strike*, hitting the monster in the same spot immediately after, scorching its chest and widening the cracks. The two rapid-fire impacts, and the stun effect from the lightning spell, were enough to slow the elemental slightly, but not stop it.

As Cserald hit it with a fireball, Allistor cast another spell, placing a *Barrier* right in front of it, channeling the spell to make it as thick and strong as possible. The charging force of nature struck the spell, slowing only slightly more before shattering the barrier and continuing on. Targon threw his second axe, doing more damage but barely slowing its progress.

The only other spell that Allistor thought might be effective against the stone monster was *Shatter*, but as close as the elemental was, casting that might cause shrapnel damage to the entire party. He was casting *Levitate*, hoping to lift the heavy-looking creature and break its momentum, when they ran out of time.

The creature barreled into Longbeard's shield, creating a deep dent in the metal, and a loud gong that echoed through the tunnel. The force knocked the powerful dwarf off his feet, sending him rolling backward across the pressure plate he'd been trying to defend. As if aware of the trap, the elemental continued forward just far enough to stand on the plate, its eyes flashing as the earth around the group began to rumble.

"Run!" Longbeard gasped, laying stunned on the tunnel floor, his shield arm clearly broken and the dented shield laying next to him. He was staring with frightened eyes up at the ceiling, struggling futilely to get to his feet. Allistor dashed toward him, meaning to grab the dwarf and pull him back. He'd only taken a single step forward when a long section of ceiling cracked and gave way above them.

The earth swallowed them up, falling boulders as big as Targon or larger, smaller stones, and cascades of loose dirt poured down upon the party, the deafening noise drowning out screams and cries of pain.

One of the larger boulders landed squarely on Longbeard's chest, breaking ribs as strong as iron, forcing the air from his lungs in a grunt. Another glanced off of Targon's shoulder, snapping bone and tearing muscle as the massive orcanin was knocked off his feet. Allistor frantically cast *Barrier* over his head, but even the improved spell had no chance against the sheer weight crashing down from above. The spell held for less than a second, pushing him downward before shattering, allowing the dirt and stone gathered above to crush him into the floor as he curled into a fetal position.

Ten seconds after the epic collision of stone elemental and dwarf, the tunnel went silent. Dust floated through the air as the earth settled. An entire thirty-foot section of the ceiling had come down atop the party, filling the space nearly to the top with debris.

Chapter Twenty

Dead And Buried

Cserald snapped awake, coughing out a mouthful of dirt as he frantically wiped at his face with his left hand. For some reason he couldn't move his right. He cleared dirt from his eyes with nimble fingers, then blinked rapidly. The tunnel was dark, and he could barely breathe. Partly from the dust, and partly because there was a tremendous weight on his chest.

His brain kicked into gear, and he remembered. "The cave-in!" His voice was hoarse and dry when he spoke aloud. With a thought he produced a flask from his inventory, using his free hand to raise it to his mouth. A strong alkaline-tasting liquid slid into his mouth and down his throat. He sighed with appreciation, closing his eyes for a moment to enjoy the burn. The drink was a favorite of his people, one that both restored health and cleared the mind.

Casting a light globe above himself, he revealed the grim picture of their situation. Cserald himself was mostly buried at the back edge of the rockfall, his right arm and his body from the chest down still covered in earth. After a brief struggle and some shoveling with his left hand, he managed to free his right arm. "Hello! Anybody!" He called out, hoping to hear from his party members. They had all been ahead of him as he backed away from the elemental, and were completely buried as far as he could tell.

"A couple more steps, and I'd have been clear." He mumbled to himself as he began pushing dirt and stones away from his torso, digging himself out. He cast *Levitate* on a larger stone that pinned his legs, his arms not strong enough to budge it. A minute or so later he was able to drag himself free and sit with his back against a tunnel wall. "Hello! Can you hear me?"

His pulse began to quicken as he checked himself over. The good news was that his light mage's armor had mostly protected him. A few scrapes, lots of bruises, but no serious injury. The bad news… "I'm alone down here." He looked toward the pile of rubble that rose about three quarters of the way to the top of the tunnel. "No way they survived that." He looked the other way down the tunnel, back the way they had come. "I could get back in the water, levitate myself up through the hole we jumped down… but I have no way to get out from there."

Now his heart was pounding in his ears. A feeling of dread, of hopelessness and despair was settling over him. "I'm going to die alone in this dungeon." He hung his head, placing it in his hands as he leaned forward. His race abhorred solitude. From birth they were part of a brood, usually ten to twelve siblings who all hatched within a few hours of each other. They grew quickly, reaching full maturity in three years, living within the family unit, where they often remained their entire lives. A single family grew into a small village within three or four generations, and grew to full clans in ten. Clans traded younglings to keep a healthy and varied mix of bloodlines, and to form alliances. Entire cities grew when allied clans came together in mixed settlements. In Cserald's case, even though he had left his homeworld to join the Azure Order, he'd gone from a large extended family to a large class of new recruits. He'd slept in a dormitory with two dozen other fledgling mages, and taken classes with even larger groups. Meals were taken together, and he found it wasn't all that different from home.

Now, though, he was alone in a dungeon that had already managed to kill party members who were all stronger than he was. He only survived out of dumb luck. And when the rations in his inventory ran out, he would die slowly, painfully, and completely alone. Tears cut trails through the dust that covered his face as he stared at the unmoving debris pile. His only hope was to dig his way through, somehow defeat the elemental on the other side, and hope there was an exit beyond.

He sobbed quietly as he cast *Levitate* on a nearby boulder, tossing it down the tunnel behind him, bouncing off a wall and rolling several feet before settling.

*****

On the far side of the pile, the stone elemental detected movement. Someone was shifting debris. Its eyes flashed brightly, and it reached forward with one stubby arm. The earth and stone ahead of it seemed to soften, almost liquify, as it moved forward, pushing a path ahead of itself. The elemental was a creature born of earth and stone, and the debris pile ahead offered no obstacle. It began to advance smoothly forward, like a fish through water. In seconds it was fully engulfed, the pile flowing around it, massive boulders shifting and settling in its wake.

*****

Allistor jerked awake as something struck his back. He gasped in pain, but rather than air, he gulped in a mouthful of dirt. Instinctively coughing it free, he tried again to pull in some air, this time with his teeth closed to prevent dirt from flooding in. What little air he managed to pull through gave him a few moments to think. His mind reeled, rewinding back to the fight with the elemental, and the cave in.

Buried! I'm buried alive! Allistor began to panic, his body trying to take another deep breath as he struggled to move his limbs. Dirt clogged the spaces between his teeth, preventing all but the tiniest amount of air from slipping through. He tried to move his hands up to clear a space around his face, but they were trapped. Allistor focused his mind, trying to calm himself. His heart was racing, chewing through what little oxygen remained in his blood. He concentrated on taking a slow, smooth breath, pulling in just a little more air. After holding that breath for several seconds to milk it of every bit of oxygen, he exhaled sharply to push away as much dirt as he could. Then he took another breath. Then another. When he had reassured himself that he wasn't about to suffocate, he set part of his mind to continue the steady inhalations, while the rest of it worked on a way to free himself.

His arms and legs were trapped. His left arm sent sharp pains lancing upward when he tried to move it, suggesting it was broken. A trickling feeling on his back made him think that he was bleeding. A quick check of his interface confirmed it, he was suffering a minor bleed debuff. He tried casting a heal on himself, and the pain lessened, but he still couldn't free the broken limb. He could move his other arm and legs slightly, but the movements packed the earth around them, limiting how far they'd shift.

I can't muscle my way out of this. His thoughts were steadying as he pushed against the urge to panic. *I don't know if the others survived, and even if they did, I don't know if there's enough air for me to wait to be dug out.* Allistor's heart thudded as he realized this might be his tomb. *The kids! They can't stand to lose another parent so soon after Amanda was taken from us.* He pictured Meg and Sam trying to comfort a crying William, Addy, and Sydney. *And my people! What will happen to all of them when I'm gone?*

He focused on breathing for a moment, exhaling to blow away more dirt with each breath. He managed to clear enough of his mouth to generate some saliva and spit.

Magic. Magic is my only way out. It's dangerous, and I don't even know if it'll work with me buried like this, but I have no choice.

Allistor turned his focus inward, trying to picture the tunnel as they'd walked through it. He had no idea how much of it collapsed, so he pictured the flat area where they'd crawled out of the water. He spent several seconds remembering as many details as he could. The wet stone floor, the shape of the nearby rocks, and the shape of the opening into the tunnel. He was taking a huge risk, but the alternative was to suffocate here under a pile of stone and dirt.

Taking the deepest breath he could manage, he took a moment to calm himself, to focus one last time on his destination, then cast *Dimensional Step*.

What little breath he held was torn from his lungs as he croaked with pain. His body was ripped from the debris pile and deposited right where he'd pictured it, splayed out across the still damp stone. He hauled in a deep breath, then sobbed, a combination of pain and relief washing through him.

Allistor cast a heal on himself, then cast light globe. As the area lit up, he took a moment to survey his body. His armor was torn along his left forearm, where something had crushed it and broken the bone. The bone was mending, as was the flesh around it.

The sound of an explosion and a cry of surprise echoed down the tunnel, and Allistor used his good arm to push himself to his feet. Someone in his party still lived, and he needed to get to them! Moving on unsteady legs, he stepped through the opening into the tunnel and pushed his light globe ahead of him. Turning left, he stumbled down the tunnel as fast as he could manage, retracing the party's earlier steps. He cast another heal on himself as he went, then drank a healing potion from his inventory.

Another shout echoed down the tunnel toward him, followed by the sound of running footsteps.

Just as he was reaching the final turn before the section where they'd found the trap, Cserald burst into view, running with a slight limp and looking over his shoulder.

"Cserald!" Allistor's gaze took in the battered and bleeding mage, then flicked toward the tunnel behind him. "What is it? Where are the others?"

The mage slid to a stop next to him, eyes wide with amazement. "Allistor? How did you…? Never mind! The stone elemental is right behind me!"

As if to prove his statement, he turned and fired a burst of ice missiles down the tunnel. They struck the elemental just as it appeared around the turn. The multiple impacts staggered it slightly, and Allistor could see that the network of cracks on its chest had grown both wider and deeper. A second later a fireball sped from Cserald's hand to impact the monster's chest. "I've been alternating fire and ice, hoping the rapid temperature changes would damage it!" the mage explained, backing away as he cast another frost spell.

Allistor gritted his teeth and cast *Lightning Strike*. The impact had more effect than it previously had, stopping the elemental in its tracks for a full second. "Run! Stop casting and just run as fast you can!" He ordered the mage, who complied without delay. Allistor cast *Barrier* in front of himself and took a half dozen jogging steps after the mage before turning around. The elemental was just beginning to pick up momentum again when Allistor cast *Shatter*, doing his best to focus the spell on the cracked chest.

He didn't wait to see what would happen, turning to run after Cserald at his best speed. Two steps later he heard a loud crack, then an explosion. His barrier disappeared in a cloud of shrapnel, which then pummeled Allistor's back. He was lifted from his feet and thrown forward to slide on his face and belly a good distance along the floor. His health bar dropped down to twenty percent, and the bleed debuff icon reappeared on his interface.

"Cserald!" He managed to grunt through the pain. Ahead of him the mage stopped running and turned back. Allistor struggled to cast a single heal on himself before passing out.

*****

"Wake up, Allistor!" Cserald shouted, shaking his shoulders and accidently knocking his head against the stone floor where he lay.

"Ow. Please stop that." Allistor groaned as he opened his eyes, blinking away the dust that seemed to fill the air in the tunnel.

"Sorry." Cserald sat back, crossing his arms to keep himself for repeating the shaking. "It's just that the others are still buried. We need to try to get to them. If you're still alive, maybe they are, too?"

Coughing, Allistor nodded and got to his feet. He blinked a few times upon seeing a significant pool of blood where'd he'd just been laying. When he looked up at Cserald, the mage nodded. "Your back and legs were ripped up pretty badly. The healing spell you cast kept you alive long enough for me to pour a healing potion down your throat. I had to cast three more heals on you to completely expel all the shrapnel and stop the bleeding. My healing spell is pretty low level." He paused, tapping his chin. "Actually, I'm not sure all the shrapnel is out. You may need to have someone look at that later." He got up and began walking back toward the cave-in.

Allistor followed, checking to confirm his health bar was back up to nearly full. "How long was I out?"

"Just a few minutes." Cserald replied over his shoulder, picking up speed. "How did you get out? And behind me?"

"A spell called *Dimensional Step.*" Allistor started to explain, but found it wasn't necessary.

"Ah, yes. Dimensional magic. I've never had a talent for it. Maybe I should spend more time trying to learn it, though. It likely just saved your life, and mine. That elemental would have finished me."

They reached the debris pile as he finished that statement, and Allistor shook his head at what he saw. The tunnel ceiling was maybe ten feet high where it was still intact. The pile in front of them was taller than him, seven or eight feet in places. Right down the center of it was an oddly smooth section.

Seeing where he was staring, Cserald nodded. "That's where the elemental passed through. It looks like it made itself some kind of tunnel, liquifying the stone as it moved through.

"Must be what hit me in the back." Allistor muttered. "It probably inadvertently saved me, letting some air in as it passed." He looked back at the mage. "Maybe that's our way to the others?"

He produced his mining pick from inventory and walked forward. Taking a moment to look at the smooth area, he stepped back and swung the pick. Where it impacted, the reformed liquified debris crumbled like it was made of plaster. Setting down the pick, he punched at the surface, then kicked it. Each blow sent a significant amount of the fill crumbling away.

"Stand back." Cserald waited for Allistor to step aside, then cast a spell. A lightning bolt slammed into the broken surface, pushing deep and blasting away chunks of debris. When the dust cleared, the spell had cleared three or four feet.

"Again!" Allistor stood next to the mage while they both cast lightning into the tight space, one after the other. After two casts each, they paused to let the air clear. The opening now penetrated deep into the pile.

"That's enough." Cserald suggested. "We don't want to collapse it. I'll go inside and look for the others."

Allistor shook his head. "No offense, but I think I've got more points in Strength than you do. I can move rocks by hand in there if necessary."

"You're also an Emperor whose people might suffer greatly if you die in here. Moving things around in there might cause another cave-in."

"Then I'll escape the same way I did before." Allistor started walking forward toward the makeshift tunnel within a tunnel. Having no valid argument against his point, Cserald followed behind.

"Be careful in there, but hurry. Our friends may be suffocating, if they're still alive. I'll levitate as many big stones as I can off the top, to help reduce the weight." Allistor nodded, ducking down and stepping into the narrow space. He tried to picture where everyone had been when the trap caused the cave-in. Cserald had been farthest back, obviously. The druid had been just a few paces ahead of him, between Cserald and himself.

"That would put her right about... here." He turned toward the side of the tunnel and began to dig with his hands. It took nearly a minute, but he uncovered her hand. The moment he took hold of it, the fingers twitched, then tightened around his hand. He quickly cleared away more of the debris, following the arm up until he had cleared the dirt from her head. She took a heaving breath, then coughed until specks of blood splattered Allistor. He cast a heal on her as he spoke, making a tough decision. "The others are buried in here as well. I'm going to leave you here for a few minutes while I search for them. Breathe deeply, and continue to heal yourself if you can. I'll be back as quickly as possible."

She nodded once, understanding. "Go." She croaked, waiving her free hand at him.

"Cserald! I found Netsirk! She's alive and breathing. Going after the others." Allistor called down the tunnel as he continued on.

His next indicator of a survivor was five or six feet further down, when the dirt on one side shifted slightly, as if something were burrowing through it. Allistor clawed at the spot with both hands, ripping away fingernails in his haste. A moment later he found the toe of a boot. Clearing away more debris, he discovered the foot was much too large to be Longbeard's, so it had to be Targon. The foot twitched weakly.

"I don't have time to try to dig you out, big guy." Allistor muttered. He turned and shouted, "Cserald, move against one of the walls, I'm going to teleport Targon out!"

After giving the mage a few seconds to clear the area, Allistor stared down the short tunnel at a spot in the larger tunnel that was relatively clear of debris. Holding on to the orcanin's leg just above the top of the boot, he cast *Dimensional Step* on him.

Two things happened then. Targon appeared at the spot Allistor had chosen, coughing out dirt before roaring in pain, which Allistor took as a good sign. But he was immediately distracted as the void created by the warrior's sudden absence began to cave in. Allistor turned toward the still blocked end of the tunnel and rushed toward it, casting Lightning Strike one more time. The last couple feet of the elemental's wake blasted apart, and fresh air pushed past him. Allistor moved out from under the debris, immediately turned back to look for signs of Longbeard. The dwarf had been very close to the trap's pressure plate when the ceiling fell on them.

Not seeing any sign of the dwarf, Allistor began to dig by hand. He moved great scoops of dirt and small stones, lifted beachball-sized boulders and tossed them over his shoulder, using every bit of his improved strength. After about a minute, Targon joined him. The huge orcanin used sharp fingernails to dig great gouges into the debris, shoveling it past him in a shower of dirt, like a dog digging a hole. Allistor didn't waste any time talking, putting all his effort into digging.

"Here!" Targon grunted, uncovering a dwarven knee, then the entire leg. Allistor shifted closer to him, and they both dug even more frantically around Longbeard's body. When they reached his chest and encountered the large boulder, they couldn't shift it. Besides its own weight, there was tons of debris still pushing down on it from several directions.

Allistor took a step back, shaking his head. "It'll take too long to dig away all of this. I'm going to teleport him like I did for you."

Targon shook his head. "There is no need, my friend. He is gone."

Allistor looked more closely at the dwarf. His chest was pinned under the massive boulder, his armor dented inward. There was no movement, no indication that he was breathing. Allistor grabbed Longbeard's wrist and removed his gauntlet, feeling for a pulse. When he didn't find one, his head fell and his shoulders slumped.

"He died bravely." Targon began. "Trying to hold back the enemy and save us. Had we listened when he told us to run…"

"We might have been able to dig him out faster." Allistor growled, frustrated with himself for all the time he wasted.

"It likely would not have mattered." Targon shook his head, staring at their deceased friend. "The boulder strike likely stopped his heart."

Allistor blinked. "What did you say?" When Targon opened his mouth to repeat himself, Allistor held up a hand. "Never mind! Back up!" He grabbed hold of Longbeard's hand again and cast *Dimensional Step* on him, sending his body just a few feet back into the clear area of the tunnel beyond the trap.

Allistor immediately cast a heal on him, on the off-chance that there was even a spark of life left in the dwarf. Then he dashed over even as the boulder that had been crushing the dwarf fell into the now empty space below it. Targon shuffled quickly away, standing next to Allistor, who dropped to kneel next to the dwarf. "Get down here! When I tell you to, I need you to breathe into his mouth. Hold his nose shut first, like this." Allistor demonstrated, earning a look from the warrior that suggested he was insane.

"Just do it!" Allistor growled as he raised the dwarf's arms above his head, then pulled the chainmail up and off of him. Targon dropped to his knees and assisted, speeding the process up considerably. Allistor took a moment to channel *Mend* directly at the dwarf's chest, channeling the spell for several seconds. He thought he felt it working, but couldn't be sure. Gently pressing against the edges of the caved-in chest, he felt for broken ribs.

"I'm not sure I can do this without injuring him further." Allistor mumbled, hesitating, dearly wishing Amanda was there with him.

"He is dead, Allistor." Targon's tone was gentle and patient, as if speaking to a confused child.

"Good point. It's this, or nothing. Get ready." Allistor placed both his hands, one atop the other, over Longbeard's sternum. Leaning so that his weight was above his head, he pressed down five times in rapid succession. "Breathe!" he ordered Targon, who did as Allistor had shown him, pinching off the dwarf's nose and blowing a massive breath down his throat. Allistor saw the chest rise slightly, and nodded. "Perfect." He resumed compressions, ordering Targon to breathe into the dwarf after each set. While the orcanin was breathing, Allistor cast a healing spell.

After several rounds, when Longbeard hadn't responded, Allistor looked up at Targon. The expression on the warrior's face made it clear he thought they were wasting their time. He shook his head slightly, and let go of Longbeard's nose.

Allistor, not willing to give up yet, had one last thing to try. "Back away from him."

When Targon stood and took a couple steps back, Allistor placed both hands on the dwarf's chest. He tried to recall the proper placement, but wasn't sure he had it right. Closing his eyes, he pictured what it was he wanted, then cast *Lightning Strike*, focusing on a mental image of the dwarf's heart.

He felt the spell kick in, the magic flowing down his arms and through his hands. Longbeard's body arched upward, muscles seizing as the current passed through him. Allistor could clearly sense that the electrical charge had dispersed through the dwarf's body rather than focus on the heart the way he'd wanted. Taking a deep breath, he changed the placement of his hands, putting them under Longbeard's arms on either side of his chest. He then closed his eyes again and pictured the lightning bolt passing between his hands. He cast the spell again, demanding that it target the heart with all the will power he could muster.

This time he felt the charge pass down just his right arm, through his hand into Longbeard's chest. A moment later he felt a shock to his left hand and arm, and was knocked back on his butt, his own muscles seizing up.

He groaned in pain, shaking his head to clear it. "That was a bad idea." He muttered as he rolled up onto his knees. A wet cough brought his gaze snapping up to

Longbeard. There was a spray of blood droplets around his mouth, soaking into the dust. A moment later, the dwarf twitched and coughed again. Allistor cast heal after heal, shouting, "Come on, you tough old dwarf! Fight!" even as he cried, tears and snot dripping from his nose.

"By all the gods, how?" Targon dropped to one knee, placing a hand gently on the dwarf's shoulder. "Fight, my friend. Do as your Emperor commands. Live!"

Longbeard coughed once more, then sucked in a deep, ragged breath. He blinked several times, his eyes watering as they filled with dirt and dust. Targon obligingly produced a clean cloth and a water bottle, pouring water over the dwarf's eyes and wiping them clean.

"Thank ye." Longbeard rasped, opening his eyes to look up at the two of them. "What happened? I thought I were dead." He tried to sit up, groaned in pain, and gave up.

"You did die." Targon shook his head, gazing down at the dwarf, a look of wonder still on his face. "Allistor somehow managed to resurrect you."

"That don't be possible." The dwarf's eyes shifted to Allistor. "Ye ain't got the necessary trainin'."

Allistor grinned at the pair, wiping his nose on his shredded sleeve. "It wasn't a resurrection like that. I mean, I used magic, but it was mostly science." A movement to his left caused him to shift his gaze. Netsirk was emerging from the tunnel, supported by Cserald, who had apparently finished digging her out.

"How did ye do it?" The dwarf wasn't ready to accept the limited explanation. "It weren't none o' that foul necromancy? Ye wouldn't do that to me, would ye?" A look of panic crossed his face, and Targon leaned back, suddenly suspicious. Orcanin wholeheartedly and vehemently disapproved of necromancy.

"No. I don't even know any necromancy." Allistor started. He took a deep breath, then began to explain. "You all know my world didn't have magic before Loki triggered the apocalypse. We depended on science for all of our healing magic. Machines, and drugs mostly. Like healing potions, but with a wide variety that were each targeted toward a specific ailment. Antibiotics to fight infections, surgeries to repair damaged organs and muscles, including the heart. We had machines that could help people breathe, pump blood through their veins. We used radiation and controlled poisons to kill cancer cells." He watched all their faces as he spoke.

"And we had a process that sometimes helped revive people whose hearts had stopped, or who had drowned and stopped breathing."

"The pushing on the chest." Targon made the connection.

"Yes. It's called CPR. You compress the chest to put pressure on the heart, forcing it to pump blood. You breathe air into them, pushing it into their lungs to oxygenate the blood that the heart is pumping. That is often enough to keep their brains and body alive long enough for doctors to take more extensive and effective measures.

"But the pushing and the breathing did not work."

"Not by themselves, no. I think they just fooled Longbeard's body into believing it was alive enough for my healing spells to help with repairs. Then I shocked him." Allistor shook his head. "Part of the process involved using a machine called a defibrillator. It sends an electric pulse through the heart, shocking it into beating again. The heart is basically one big muscle, and using electricity to make it seize up and release sometimes starts it back up."

Netsirk shook her head. "I have never in all my years heard of such a thing."

Allistor smiled up at her. "You have always lived in a universe where your magic was the go-to tool for healing. We didn't have that, so we figured out other ways. It didn't always work, but I had to try something."

"And ye brought me back from the dead." Longbeard coughed again, both the druid and Allistor instantly casting more heals on him. Allistor cast *Mend* into his chest again, hoping to properly reform his ribs.

"He saved all of us." Cserald gently lowered the druid to a sitting position, then joined her. "The elemental was chasing me until Allistor destroyed it. Then he dug his way in to find each one of you. I tried to stop him…" The reptilian mage lowered his head as if ashamed.

"That were the right thing to do." Longbeard's voice was getting stronger. "He be an Emperor, and had no business diggin' thru all that," he waved at the tunnel through the debris. "to come after the likes o' me or him." He jerked a thumb at Targon.

"The danger to me wasn't as great as it seems. I teleported myself out the same way I did for the two of you. Had there been another cave-in, I would have done it again. The first one caught me by surprise, and I didn't think of it quickly enough."

The others had no immediate response to that, so Allistor continued. "I think we could all use some rest. Let's take an hour or two, maybe even sleep a bit. Do we want to stay here, or go back to the spot by the water?"

"Here should be fine." Longbeard looked down the tunnel. "I'll keep watch. Had more than enough of a nap already." He looked back at the debris pile and shuddered.

The druid cleared her throat to get Allistor's attention. "While we rest, if you have an alternate set of armor, I suggest you put it on. This one is pretty well shredded, and most of your cute little rear end is exposed." She winked at a now blushing Allistor.

Chapter Twenty One

Just Mostly Dead

The group needed a rest. All of them were tired, and shaken. Longbeard was more than a little out of sorts, sitting with his back against a wall, hands shaking. Looking down and seeing this, he clasped them together and squeezed tightly enough that his knuckles turned white.

"Are you alright?" Allistor took a seat next to him.

Longbeard looked down at his hands and shook his head gently. "No, lad. I died."

Allistor nodded his understanding, instinctively remaining quiet, waiting for the dwarf to say more if he was so inclined. It was a long minute before that happened.

"This dungeon be... evil. I know no better way to describe it. It pulls yer fears from yer mind, and uses 'em to attack yer soul. The fight against the elves were hard on the big fella over there." He nodded toward Targon, who was off by himself, quietly poking around the debris pile. "The long fall that came after, the drownin' then failin' to see and disarm the trap which nearly got ye all killed, then bein' crushed and buried alive... all deep fears o' mine. It ain't been a good day, lad."

Allistor took a deep breath. "Most of those are fears we all share with you. I was terrified to jump down that hole, and being buried truly sucked. Also, you weren't truly dead, just mostly dead." he offered, thinking of a favorite line from a classic late twentieth century adventure film. "If that makes you feel any better."

"No, it does not." The dwarf managed a small smile as he shook his head again. "But I thank ye fer tryin'. And fer bringin' me back."

"I found your shield." Targon called out, pulling the badly dented metal from the debris where Longbeard had fallen and holding it up. "I have found one of my axes as well. The other should be somewhere nearby…" He set down the shield and turned back to his digging without waiting for a response.

"He's havin' a tough time as well." The dwarf nodded toward Targon. "How bout you, lad?"

Allistor shrugged. "I agree that this place is horrible. The challenges have been harsh, even cruel. And having our druid peeking at my exposed ass wasn't my favorite thing, either." This time he got a chuckle out of the dwarf, and the elf, who was sitting against the opposite wall. "I'm not sure it qualifies as evil. Then again, I'm not even sure I know how to define evil."

Netsirk exhaled loudly, stirring up a small cloud of dust. "I concur. This place is awful. Elves love nature, forests, open spaces and wide skies. Being buried alive down here in the dead stone was… not something I ever wish to experience again. It is not just a personal nightmare of mine, but I imagine it's a deep fear of every elf. And very few who might enter this dungeon would be able to extricate themselves the way you did. Without your ability, I fear we would all have perished."

413

"It's not over yet." Allistor warned. "Who knows how many more levels, how many more challenges or nightmares we have to face before we reach the end?"

The others remained silent after that, each of them lost in their own thoughts. That is, until Cserald's voice came echoing down the tunnel. "I found another chest!" The group didn't react other than a slight headshake from Netsirk, and an eye-roll by the dwarf. A minute or so later their mage came staggering through the debris pile tunnel carrying another softly glowing loot chest. "It was back there where you killed the elemental." He set it down with a grunt, the item obviously heavier than it looked. "I brought it here, figuring you weren't anxious to pass back through the pile."

"You got that right." Allistor agreed. There was no guarantee that the pile wouldn't collapse again. And while he'd been willing to risk it to save his friends, he had zero interest in pushing his luck. "Go ahead and open it."

The mage happily did so, lifting the lid with eyes wide in anticipation. Immediately each of them received another stack of gold coins, and Allistor's notification included some diamonds and emeralds. Looking down into the chest, Cserald said, "I believe this one is for you, Master Longbeard." He pushed the chest across the floor toward the dwarf, who reached inside. When he withdrew his hand, it held a miniature tower shield. The moment it cleared the chest, it grew as tall and wide as Longbeard himself. Allistor cast *Examine* on it, as did the others.

Stalwart Shield

Item Quality: Unique
Attributes: Strength +20; Constitution +20;
Enchantment: Solid as Stone

> *This shield reflects its bearer's stout heart and determination. When activated, the Solid as Stone enchantment will bind shield and bearer to the earth below, making them utterly immovable and immune to physical damage for ten seconds.*

"This be... almost worth the dyin'." Longbeard ran a hand across the shield, the face of which featured a detailed image of the stone elemental they'd defeated.

"There's more." Cserald reached into the chest again and withdrew a scroll. "This one must be for the druid."

> ### Scroll of Stone Vines
> *Item Quality: Unique*
> *Attributes: Use of this scroll will permanently increase the user's Intelligence by +10. User will learn the spell Stone Vines, which will allow them to raise lifelike vines from the surrounding stone and control their movement.*

"It's just like the spell you used to trap that elf." Cserald observed as he handed over the scroll, a tinge of jealousy in his voice. The druid only nodded, a curious look on her face. She opened the scroll and began to read, a flash of silver light causing the others to blink before the scroll disappeared. She blinked a few times herself, obviously adjusting to the new knowledge in her head, then held a hand out to one side, palm facing the floor. A small tendril of stone rose up to meet her hand, then grew long enough to gently wrap around it. She tugged against it a bit, then again with a bit more force. Seeming satisfied, she nodded once and the tendril slipped back down into the floor.

"This will be useful down here." She commented, looking at Longbeard, who grunted his agreement.

Targon returned to the group, now holding an axe in each hand. "Is anyone missing any other equipment?" When the others all shook their heads, he grunted. "Good. We are ready to proceed."

Allistor shook his head again. "Have a seat, Targon. We all need a bit more rest. An hour more or less won't kill us."

The warrior raised one eyebrow, growling, "I would not be so sure."

"We'll keep an eye out." Longbeard reassured the big orcanin. "If ye see anything at all, call it out." He reached out a hand and accepted his dented shield from Targon, slipping it into his inventory after a brief examination and a shake of his head. "Crafted that shield meself. I'd have sworn nothin' short o' cannon fire could dent it."

"That was a level 120 stone elemental." Cserald observed. "You're lucky it didn't crush you."

"Bah! We dwarves, our bones be half metal, half stone!" the tank gave him a half-hearted grin. Allistor was glad to see he was making an attempt to shake off the recent traumas.

He relaxed a bit, leaning back against the wall and closing his eyes. "Someone please wake me in half an hour? I'll take over watch then."

*****

Nothing bothered the party as they took turns sleeping and guarding. At the end of the hour, they all looked more refreshed. The short naps had helped a little, but having time to sit quietly and process their experiences inside the dungeon had been key.

They proceeded down the corridor, the cave-in at their backs. It stretched another several hundred paces before making a sharp turn to the right. Longbeard crept up on the corner, shield ready, and gave a quick peek around. When nothing jumped out at them, he took a longer, more careful look. With a sigh of relief, he stepped out into the center of the tunnel intersection and faced the new direction. Holding up one hand, he knelt and put that hand on the stone floor, closing his eyes and tilting his head as if listening.

"No traps nearby." He reported. "Nor any movement that I can detect."

"I hear nothing moving." Netsirk confirmed, her elven hearing far superior to that of the others. "Though, I do smell something... familiar."

The group advanced down the new tunnel, Longbeard stopping every hundred paces or so to check again for traps. The dwarf was not about to let down his party a second time under any circumstance. He still viewed his failure to find and disarm the trap before it could be triggered as a personal debt to be repaid.

Ten minutes later the tunnel ended in another dark archway. One of those with the curtain of blackness blocking their view to the other side. Longbeard stopped in front of it, shaking his head, his shoulders slumping. "This'll be another test. Another nightmare." His voice was soft, and Allistor thought he heard a hint of fear.

None of the others replied, or made a move to advance. It was clear that no one was enthusiastic about stepping through.

"We don't have a way to get back." Allistor covered ground they'd already discussed, but he felt he needed to. "The only way out is through. Master Longbeard, if you prefer, I'll take the lead. You can cover our backs." He immediately felt bad for saying it.

The dwarf snorted, his back straightening, his chest puffing out as he raised his new shield. "That'll be the day, lad. Follow me." He took one last deep breath, and stepped forward to disappear through the inky blackness. Targon followed immediately, axes in his hands, and the others were right behind him.

When Allistor's vision cleared, his eyes quickly scanned the room. It was a small stone chamber with rounded walls that rose up into a dome maybe twenty feet high. His ears registered confused cursing from Longbeard as his gaze focused on the room's only occupant. At which time his jaw dropped, and he shared Longbeard's amazement.

"M-master Daigath?"

The ancient elf sat in the center of the chamber, not thirty paces away. His seat was a simple wooden crate, likely pulled from his inventory. As Allistor spoke, the elf got to his feet.

"Allistor. I'm glad you're finally here. I've been waiting anxiously for you all to arrive." He paused, looking at each of them. "I'm happy to see that you've all survived, though you look as if you've had a rough time."

Allistor opened his mouth to reply, but the elf cut him off. "I have come to prevent you from rushing to the surface. Nothing but death awaits you there." Daigath's face adopted a grim look.

"What?" Allistor was more than a little confused. "Death on the surface?"

Daigath tilted his head for a moment. "Did you not receive the notifications about the attack?" When Allistor and the others just blinked in confusion, he nodded. "I suspected as much. The dungeon has prevented you from receiving them." He took a deep breath. "Invictus City was attacked, Allistor. A massive armada dropped out of

FTL very near the planet. More than a hundred ships. They destroyed the defense satellites within reach, then the space station. All of your ships, as well as the Or'Dralon and Stardrifter ships that tried to assist, were destroyed or disabled in minutes. Then they began to bombard the city."

"The shields?" Allistor croaked, a sinking feeling in his gut.

"The shields lasted only slightly longer than your ships, I'm afraid. Your city was being systematically destroyed. It was decided I should come down here and warn you, as I was the only one nearby who could survive the dungeon to reach you."

"What about my Emperor?" Targon stepped forward.

"Harmon was forced to flee with your fellow warriors. The attacking ships are elven, and he could not do otherwise." Daigath bowed his head as he spoke the words. "He asked me to apologize on his behalf, Allistor."

Targon spat on the floor in disgust as Allistor made polite noises, his mind racing. "My people?"

"Most of them have moved underground, into the subway stations and tunnels. But the bombardment is... effective. I fear that by now not many will have survived. We sent a call for help, but by the time they arrive, the damage will have been done. I'm sorry, Allistor."

"We need to get out of here! Get up there and help my people!" Allistor started frantically looking for an exit.

"You cannot help them, Allistor. What will you do? Block projectiles the size of your juggernauts with your barrier spell? What is important is that you survive. As long as you live, your empire lives. The enemy has no way to know that you're in this dungeon, or even that this dungeon exists. You are safe in here until reinforcements arrive."

"No!" Allistor wanted to vomit. His people were dying! His heartrate skyrocketed. "My kids! My family! I must try to save as many as I can. I can't hide in here and-"

The druid cut him off, placing a hand on his shoulder and spinning him around. "This is not Daigath. It's another test, another challenge. The dungeon is preying on your fears."

Allistor didn't hear her at first, turning back to beg Daigath to show them the way out. "How do we get out of here, Master Daigath? Show us!"

The elf ignored him, staring at Netsirk for a moment. When he spoke, his voice was cold. "You are not to leave here, Allistor. I will do what is necessary to ensure that you remain until it is safe for you to leave." He took a step back, and all of a sudden his right hand held a wooden blade.

"The druid is correct." Targon snarled at Daigath. "This is not Master Daigath. It is another foul deception created by this cursed dungeon." He tightened his grip on his axes and spread his feet apart, ready to attack.

421

"Hold, orcanin." Daigath's voice grew louder, somehow stronger. "Think on what you are about to do. If you so much as raise a weapon against me, all of elvenkind and our allies will hunt your people to extinction!" He looked back at Netsirk. "I do not wish to kill you, my dear friend. Simply stand aside, do not participate, and you will not be harmed."

"Aye, they're right. Daigath would never make such a threat. This is another creature o' the dungeon's design. Let's get this done." Longbeard raised his new shield, glancing briefly over his shoulder as he moved between the ancient elf and Allistor. "Wake up, lad!"

Allistor blinked several times, trying to reconcile what he was hearing to what he was seeing. "But Master Daigath is many times our level. He could just wipe us out without even trying."

"This is not Daigath, Allistor." The druid shook her head. "I have known him for a thousand years or more. This is not my friend. We must kill him."

"He be limited by the dungeon's level, lad. Just like the others." Longbeard slammed a sword against his new shield. "Come on, elf! I'll hang yer pointy ears and yer shriveled nuts above me hearth!"

Allistor blinked again as the elf snarled and charged. He saw Longbeard crouch slightly, slamming his shield down and leaning into it. Behind him, Targon was moving to attack. A fireball sped past Allistor, Cserald getting into the fight. The spell was too slow, though, as

Daigath activated some ability that granted him great speed.

The elf sped forward almost faster than Allistor could follow, slamming into Longbeard's shield as the fireball passed harmlessly behind him. But the dwarf had activated the new shield's enchantment, and the elf bounced on impact, momentarily stunned. Longbeard stabbed forward with his sword, the first few inches of the blade penetrating the elf's thigh. A moment later Targon was there, his right axe swinging for Daigath's head, looking to end the fight right there.

Daigath recovered quickly, raising his blade to deflect the axe, striking the handle and managing to sever a couple of Targon's fingers in the process. The druid immediately began healing as the orcanin roared out his pain and anger, never losing his grip on the weapon.

Allistor saw the blood spray from Targon's hand, and that more than anything snapped him out of his confused paralysis. He cast *Lightning Strike* at the elf, followed immediately by *Mind Spike*. The latter had no discernable effect, but the lightning bolt staggered the elf for a moment, causing him to miss a follow-up strike aimed at Targon's belly.

Right then Longbeard dashed forward and slammed his shield into Daigath, briefly pinning his sword hand against his body. Targon flung the axe from his wounded hand from three steps away, burying the blade in the elf's shoulder.

"Allistor! You must listen! I am doing this for your own good!" Daigath shouted, pulling the axe free and casting a heal on himself. "Stop this nonsense before I am forced to kill your companions! Do you want their needless deaths on your conscience?"

Despite himself, Allistor hesitated for a second. This fake Daigath seemed incredibly real. The elf took advantage of that hesitation, bashing his shoulder into Longbeard and knocking him back a step, freeing his sword hand. A lightning-fast slash opened a deep wound across Targon's chest.

The orcanin shrugged it off, stepping forward to swing his remaining axe at the elf's head. Daigath ducked and kicked him in the knee, shattering the joint and sending the warrior falling backward. Before the elf could step in and finish him, a cluster of small fireballs sped his way. He managed to dodge most of them, but four impacted his torso, one striking him in the face.

As the druid grabbed hold of Targon and pulled him back, Longbeard charged in again. The elf didn't see him coming, and his shield slammed into Daigath's knee, doing similar damage to what the elf had just done to Targon. Not done yet, Longbeard jammed his sword upward, driving it into the elf's groin. The wound spurted blood, and the elf staggered.

Allistor raised the ebonwood sword that had been crafted by the real Daigath. Holding it at the ready, he cast *Dimensional Step*, placing himself right behind the elf. As he turned to face Daigath's back, he swung the sword down from overhead.

Even disabled, the elf was much faster than Allistor. Not bothering to turn around, he altered his grip and thrust the blade of his sword backward past his hip, driving it deep into Allistor's belly. Allistor's downward stroke faltered, but gravity and momentum kept it moving with enough force to chop into the same shoulder Targon had wounded. The partially healed wound reopened, and blood spurted. Despite the pain of his belly wound, Allistor felt his sword's desire for more blood.

The pain only increased when the staggering Daigath yanked his sword free of Allistor's belly, causing blood and other things Allistor didn't even want to think about to spray outward. He coughed involuntarily, and his health bar dropped below fifty percent.

A lightning bolt from Cserald slammed into the elf, who was bent with one hand on a knee, breathing heavily as he cast another heal on himself. Both his inner thigh and his shoulder were bleeding profusely, though the flow was already beginning to slow. The lightning stunned him, his muscles seizing for a moment.

Allistor and Longbeard both struck at the elf, one from behind, the other in front. Longbeard's short sword buried itself in his chest up to the hilt, the point emerging from his back even as Allistor used his remaining strength to strike at Daigath's neck, cleanly decapitating him. The sword sang with pleasure, mostly ignored by Allistor who was falling to his knees and trying to hold his gut wound closed with his free hand.

A sobbing Netsirk was there in seconds, placing a glowing golden hand over his wound. Allistor felt the warmth of the healing spell, and gasped. The feeling of his innards knitting themselves back together was unpleasant, to say the least. When his health was back above sixty percent, the druid removed her hand and cast a standard healing spell on him.

"Thank you." Allistor managed as he sat back on his butt. "That sucked." He looked over her shoulder at the orcanin. "How's Targon?"

"Already itching for the next fight." She smiled sadly down at Allistor, tears visibly flowing across her cheeks. "It will take some time for his fingers to regrow. A few hours."

"It wasn't him. It took me a while to accept it, but you were right. It really wasn't him."

She nodded, wiping the tears from her face. "I know. Still, it was… difficult." Allistor just nodded, understanding completely.

"Another chest. This one's bigger, and it's glittering like it's made of diamond." Cserald stood over the spot where the imposter had fallen, pointing at a chest that was nearly waist-high to him.

Allistor blew out a heavy breath, trembling slightly after the troubling and brutal fight. "Go ahead, open it." He pushed himself to his feet, his mostly healed stomach complaining about the effort. Sheathing the wooden blade, he walked with his tank and healer over to the chest. Targon joined them a moment later, and all four watched the mage lift the lid. A bright, clean light shone on all their faces.

This time the first notification said that they'd each received platinum coins. The next one told Allistor that he'd received a surprisingly high number of experience points. As he blinked them away, Cserald reached into the chest. When he withdrew his hand, he was holding a staff as tall as he was, made of polished wood, with a diamond the size of an apple mounted at the top.

Staff of Insight
Item Quality: Unique
Attributes: Intelligence +20; Wisdom +10;
Enchantment: Insight

The wielder of this staff has a 50% chance of seeing through illusions and
other deceptive magic, as well as a 50% chance to detect lies.

"This must be for me." The mage hugged the staff to his chest, petting it like a favored puppy. After a moment he leaned forward to peer into the chest, his eyes growing wide. "There is more, and I'm quite sure this next piece is for you, Allistor."

Allistor stepped forward and leaned over to peer inside. What he saw made his heart race. "The dungeon core?" he whispered, reaching down with both hands to lift the softly glowing orb that swirled with a riot of colors that matched the chaos of the dungeon's nature.

"Yesss!" Cserald clapped his hands together. "We've beaten this place! Destroy that core and let's get out of here."

Longbeard and Targon both nodded their agreement, while their healer just stared at Allistor, her face neutral.

Allistor stood there, staring into the chaotic swirl of color, feeling the urge to smash the orb into a million pieces. His anger at all the horrible things the dungeon had done to them made him tighten his grip on it. But a more rational part of his mind held him back. The core was valuable, whether as a training tool to toughen up his people, or as an asset to be sold.

Sliding the orb into his inventory, he turned to the others. "I'll make that decision later. For now, let's get the hell out of here." He looked around the chamber, and found an archway that hadn't been there before. Beyond it was a stairway leading upward. Without hesitation Allistor ran toward the stairs, the others right behind him. He jogged upward at the best pace he could manage, and the stairs seemed to go on forever. Allistor's strength flagged, and he tried to remember just how far they had fallen into the water, and calculate how many steps that would be. The answer had him flagging even more.

Taking deep breaths, he continued upward, walking now instead of jogging, conserving his energy. The others kept pace with him, none of them speaking as they climbed.

After what seemed like an eternity, a landing appeared above them. A landing with a swirling multicolored portal.

"This is it!" Allistor gasped as he pushed himself to finish the climb. He was slightly dizzy from blood loss, but his goal was in sight. When they reached the top, Longbeard moved in front of him. Targon took hold of Allistor's bicep, supporting some of his weight.

"Take a moment and catch your breath, Allistor." Netsirk encouraged him. "You must look the part of a victorious Emperor when you emerge." She cast one last heal on him, then cast a cleansing spell on each of them, removing the blood and grime from their skin and gear.

Allistor nodded and collected himself, breathing deeply several times. He took out a health potion and drank it down, hoping it would replace some of his missing fluids. After half a minute, he nodded at Longbeard, who saluted before stepping through the portal. Targon was next, followed by Netsirk, Cserald, and finally Allistor.

The moment he stepped out of the portal, Allistor was overwhelmed with notifications. The others were crying out in dismay as he read the one that stood out, being in bright red bold letters that screamed for attention.

Attention!

Invictus City is under attack by an unknown force! Defend your city and its people!

The ground shook as Allistor stared past the notifications at the basement corridor outside the portal.

Dust filled the air, falling from the ceiling as Allistor reached out to brace himself against a wall. Maybe twenty paces ahead of him, a gaping hole in the ceiling exposed the ruined building and open sky above.

A sky filled with burning projectiles falling on his city like a meteor shower. He watched as several more struck tall buildings, blasting them apart and causing the ground to shake with each impact.

"Oh, no." Was all Allistor could think to say. The implications of what he was seeing struck him like a physical blow. "My city. My people!" He closed his eyes and held them shut for a moment, hoping it was all an illusion. Then a new thought caused them to open wide in horror. "That was the real Daigath. The attack is real. He really was trying to protect me. And we killed him!"

Out of the dust-filled gloom ahead, two figures stumbled across the quaking floor toward them. Allistor barely registered their presence as horror overtook him. "What have I done?"

"Allistor!" Helen's voice echoed through the corridor. The roar from the explosion of a nearby impact drowned out the rest of what she said. Allistor focused, staring at the approaching figures, which soon enough he was able to recognize as Helen and Bjurstrom.

"Helen! What's happening?" Allistor stumbled forward to meet her, reaching her as they both stood directly under the opening in the ceiling. Now Allistor could see even more of the rounds falling from orbit, more of the devastation.

Helen put her face inches from his, shouting to be heard. "What are you doing out here! Daigath was supposed to keep you inside!" She motioned toward the portal. "Did he not find you?"

Allistor shook his head, his mouth dry. "He found us. We... we thought he was a dungeon construct. We killed him." Behind him, Netsirk sobbed.

"You fool!" Helen shouted, shoving him toward the portal. "Get back inside! They're going to flatten the city trying to kill you!"

Allistor stumbled, then righted himself. "Who are they? Why did they attack?"

"Does it matter?" Bjurstrom shouted at him, a scowl on his face. "You've pissed off the wrong people, Allistor! Now we're all paying the price."

Allistor straightened, stunned as if the man had punched him in the face. Something clicked in his mind, and he closed his eyes. He pulled up his recent notifications and scrolled through them as Helen began yelling for him to return to the dungeon. He felt hands on his arms, but ignored them.

When he finished scrolling, he opened his eyes. Drawing his sword, he stabbed Bjurstrom through the chest, then slashed at Helen. Looking at Longbeard, he shouted, "We're still in the dungeon! None of this is real!"

That was all the dwarf needed to hear. He slammed his shield into Helen's back, knocking her facedown onto the ground. He was raising his sword to finish her when Targon simply stomped on her neck, killing her instantly.

"Are ye sure, lad?" The dwarf eyed Allistor's dead friends, then looked up at him.

"If that was the real Daigath, we never would have beaten him." Allistor replied. "And there was no first kill notification. If we beat the dungeon and took the core, there would have been one." He shook his head, then looked up. "This, all of this, is just the dungeon continuing to screw with us. My worst fear, exposed for all of you to see. Losing my people, failing to protect them. The destruction of everything I've built."

"And the horror of thinking we'd actually killed the real Daigath." Targon added, nodding. "It makes sense."

"But how do we defeat this challenge?" Cserald asked. "We can not fight ships in orbit."

Allistor considered it for a moment, then withdrew the dungeon core from his inventory. Dropping it to the ground, he looked at the dwarf. "Master Longbeard, would you please smash that thing for me?"

The dwarf grinned, producing a massive war hammer from his inventory. Without hesitation he swung it overhead, then down onto the core with every ounce of strength he had. The swirling mass of colors exploded in a shower of glittering particles that pulsed outward in waves like ripples on a pond.

Immediately the ground ceased shaking, and the scene overhead faded from view. Allistor released the breath he'd been holding, and his pounding heartbeat began to slow a tiny bit. In seconds the party was standing back in the same chamber where they'd fought Master Daigath. The same glittering chest was there, standing open.

Sitting inside was the same swirling multicolored dungeon core.

"Well, shit." Allistor cursed as he looked down at it.

Chapter Twenty Two

Not So Fast...

Allistor stood with the others, looking down into the loot chest. The only thing visible inside was the same swirling dungeon core that had appeared before. He made no move to retrieve it, still trying to wrap his mind around recent developments. This dungeon was not only ruthless, it was vindictive. It took shots at their psyches that would mess with their heads long after they defeated it and exited its confines. This was the weightiest reason to lean toward destroying the core. Surviving the dungeon didn't necessarily mean beating it.

"Is it just messing with us again?" Allistor looked at his companions one by one to gauge their reactions. None of them seemed to have a strong opinion either way. They were tired, stressed, and just wanted the dungeon to be over with. Allistor didn't blame them one bit.

Reaching down with both hands, he lifted the core out of the box. The moment he did, the group was showered with experience and notifications. Allistor took a deep breath and scanned his own, looking for one specific... THERE!

Congratulations!

Achievement Earned: First Kill!
You are the first group to defeat the Phobia Dungeon!

For being the first, all loot received will be upgraded by two quality levels.
Experience earned is doubled! Each group member receives a permanent +40% resistance to mental attacks.

You have received: Phobia Dungeon Core. You may assume ownership if this dungeon core, discard it, or destroy it.

"Uh, guys? I need some advice. It's giving me the option to take ownership of the core, discard it, or destroy it. If I take ownership, does that mean I take the core with me? Carry it around like I have been the others?"

"If you declare ownership, you may remove the core, or leave it here." Cserald answered, then anticipated Allistor's next question. "And should you choose to change its status at a later date, you need only step into the portal to the first safe zone, not conquer the dungeon all over again."

"I still vote to destroy it." Targon grumbled, scanning the chamber as if expecting to be attacked again. Longbeard grunted his agreement, staring at the orb with a look of pure disgust. Netsirk remained neutral, while Cserald cleared his throat.

"If I may be so bold, I believe the Azure Order would compensate you handsomely were you to cede ownership of the core to us." When the others all turned in unison to stare at him, he shrugged. "What? It is a valuable and challenging dungeon. The order does not share Allistor's concerns about the safety of those who might enter to test themselves against it. Ours is a... competitive society"

"Cutthroat be more like it." Longbeard chuckled, then looked up at Allistor. "Do what ye like with it, lad. Just know I'll no' be settin' foot inside here again, ever."

"Nor I." Targon agreed.

Allistor didn't know what to do with the core. What he did know was that he was in no mental state to be making serious and consequential decisions. "I'll take ownership, and leave it here for now. I need to get my head straight before I deal with this."

He made the appropriate mental selections, and more notifications appeared. He ignored those, his attention grabbed immediately by a portal that appeared behind the loot chest.

"Why is the chest still here?" He looked down inside it, but saw nothing. He cast *Examine* on it, and did not like what he read.

> ### Pandora's Box
> ### Item Quality: Unique
> *This box now contains the fear, anger, despair, and other strong emotions bled into the core from the surrounding area. Should you decide to transfer the core, do so inside the box. Failure to transfer the box with the core will greatly reduce the dungeon's power and effectiveness.*

Feeling more than a little creeped out, Allistor closed the box and placed it in his inventory. "I'll explain later." He told the others, then turned toward the portal. "Weapons ready, just in case this is another trick." He drew his ebonwood blade and stepped toward the swirling portal. Once again Longbeard took the lead, physically shoving Allistor aside this time as he moved to take the front position. A moment later he disappeared through the event horizon, followed quickly by Targon and the others.

*****

The first thing Allistor did when he emerged from the portal was to look up. The ceiling of the dark hospital basement corridor was intact. The ground wasn't trembling from impacts, and everything was pretty much as it had been before they entered the dungeon. No new notifications of any invasion popped up, and he released a long-held breath in relief.

"Aye, lad." Longbeard was grinning at him. "I think we be truly done with the dungeon this time. Let us leave this place and never look back."

Allistor motioned for him to proceed, and noticed that the group's pace was quicker than normal as Longbeard led them out of the basement. He was surprised to find the sun shining when they emerged. A moment later as they rounded the ruins, he was equally surprised to find that Helen and the others were still waiting near the juggernaut.

437

Helen seemed surprised to see him, as were the others. Bjurstrom called out, "Hiya boss. Was it too tough for you?"

"What do you mean?"

"You've only been gone about forty minutes. We were just discussing where to get some lunch."

"Time dilation too." Cserald muttered. "This dungeon is worth more than I thought."

Allistor shook his head, continuing to approach his people. "It was a hell of a lot longer for us. We beat the dungeon, but it beat back." He paused and scooped Helen up in a bear hug, lifting her off the ground and spinning around before setting her back down. "I'm glad to see you. All of you." He patted Bjurstrom on the shoulder, resisting the urge to hug him, too.

"Was it that bad in there?" Helen had been studying his face, and she looked worried.

"Worse." Allistor looked down at his feet for a moment. "I'm not sure I could even explain how bad."

Targon took a shot at it. "The dungeon seeks out your nightmares, your worst fears, and forces you to face them."

Longbeard chimed in as well. "Imagine a nightmare, the kind that makes ye wake screamin. Then imagine it's real, it's tryin to kill ye, and it won't stop. That uneasy feelin ye all got when ye were close to the portal? It be ten times worse inside."

"Did you get good loot, at least?" Someone among the raiders asked.

"Aye, but it ain't worth goin' in to get it." The dwarf shook his head. "First time I ever said that." The others in the party nodded their heads in agreement, and the crowd began to murmur.

"We can talk about all this later. We're exhausted, and I think we each need a little quiet alone time to deal with what happened in there." He climbed into the juggernaut, the others quickly joining him. He allowed Helen and Bjurstrom to join them, the raid leader taking the driver's seat, but the others were dispersed to other vehicles, or opted to walk back.

Once on the road, Allistor looked at the others. "I want to thank you for joining me in there. And to apologize for the way it turned out. If I had known…"

"We all volunteered." the druid spoke softly, but firmly. "We all received great benefit from our time in there, and I believe we'll recover soon enough."

"Aye, lad. No need to apologize. There be no knowin' what's in a brand new dungeon, and we all made the decision to find out." He held up his shield for a moment, as if he'd forgotten it was still on his arm." Me clan'll be right jealous o' this shield. Don't think I'll tell 'em what it took to get it." He stowed the shield in his inventory and sat back in his seat.

"I shall inform Emperor Harmon, but will recommend he not share the information with our people.

Foolish warriors will see it as a worthy challenge and rush to enter the dungeon. I fear many would not return."

"And those that do…" Cserald didn't finish his thought. He didn't have to.

Allistor hadn't thought about what to tell people about the dungeon. He thought Targon was probably right. "Nigel, ask Prime to station a dozen droids to guard the entrance to that dungeon. No one enters without my express permission. Bjurstrom, no raid groups are to be organized for that one. I'll explain why later. For now, keep what you've heard to yourself, and ask the others to do the same when you see them. It's not top secret, or anything, just… let's not encourage too much interest."

"Roger that, boss. Almost home. I'll run interference for you, let everyone know you're tired and want some alone time. No interruptions short of an attack on the city."

Allistor and the others cringed at those words, but let them pass.

*****

The suns were rising as Allistor and his kids ate breakfast up on the tower roof. Fuzzy was there, as were the drakelings. The cute little baby drakes weren't so cute anymore, having grown to triple the size they were as hatchlings. They ate a lot more as well, evidenced by the pile of raw meat on a cart that the kitchen had sent up along with the human breakfasts.

440

The kids were training the drakelings, offering fist-sized bits of meat as rewards when their pets followed commands like sit, lay down, and play dead. William had wanted to teach his to roll over, a trick his long-lost puppy had learned, but Allistor convinced him that rolling probably wasn't good for their wings.

Daigath had told them that the type of simple commands didn't matter at this stage, what was important was that the little drakes learn to obey their companions without question. Only that level of training would be able to overcome their base instincts to feed or fight, allowing them to live among humans without presenting a danger. They were still cute and cuddly, but soon they'd be large enough to bite a human in half, something Allistor was all too aware of. Somewhere he still had armor made from the skin of a drake who had killed friends of his.

So he smiled and did his best to relax as the kids ran their drakes through various commands over and over again. He nibbled on a tasty apple turnover and drank a frozen hazelnut coffee, enjoying a few of the little luxuries that had returned to their lives. As an Emperor of several planets, he had the wealth and connections to dine on only the most exquisite foods at every meal. But he preferred the simpler things. And Meg's pastry chef had raised his skill enough that the turnover provided a plus five to stamina regeneration for six hours.

Many of the foods the tower cafeteria served these days provided significant buffs, in addition to tasting wonderful. Meg was a force of nature, and a gifted chef, and she pushed her people to improve their skills

441

constantly. Combined with the improved ingredients they were getting from Nancy's druids and botanists, the buffs were getting impressive. Even the beef they ate came from cows that fed on magically enhanced grass and grains. Cows that lived on a mana-dense world, and grew much larger than they would have just a few years earlier.

Allistor had even heard a report that one of the bison had defended his herd against a roaming pack of canids, killing several of them and leveling up. He'd also eaten chunks out of one of them, becoming the first known carnivore or omnivore bison. His cowboys weren't sure what to do with it now. It showed no aggression toward them, but its teeth had grown sharp, its horns longer, and it was a third bigger than it had been before the attack. General consensus was to just leave it alone, let it breed, and see if they got more carnivore bison.

Fuzzy nudged his leg, the bear having stretched out on his back, paws in the air while Allistor scratched his belly absently with one foot. The bear cub was jealous of the meat the drakelings were receiving. Allistor grinned down at the bear, deciding to mess with him a little. He looked at the meat cart, choosing a large chunk and casting *Levitate* on it. With a flick of his hand, he sent it gliding over to Fuzzy's open maw, the bear not even bothering to lift his head.

"Lazy fuzzball." Allistor scolded, halting the meat in mid-air a foot or so above Fuzzy's head. The bear eyed him for a moment, looking from him to the meat and back, then gave a soft growl of impatience. "Nope, you want the meat, get up and grab it." Allistor shook his head, suppressing a smile. By this time the drakelings had been distracted by the hovering meat, which had caused the kids to watch the interaction as they restrained their beasts.

Fuzzy's growl turned into a plaintive whine, and he flashed Allistor his best puppydog eyes. A look that nearly always worked on Amanda and Helen both. He pressed one paw against Allistor's knee, and sent a mental image of the meat gliding gently into his open mouth.

Allistor couldn't help but laugh. "Nice try, buddy. Come on, up you go. The tasty steak is right there, just waiting for you." He lifted his foot off the bear's belly, not wanting to give him an excuse not to get up. When Fuzzy still didn't move, he upped the ante. "Okay, if you're not hungry, I'm sure one of the little ones…" He started to move the meat in the direction of the drakelings, much to their excitement. Fuzzy was up in a flash, his bulk moving the sofa Allistor was sitting on as he spun to his feet and lunged at the meat. It was gone in a single bite, and the bear eyed the drakelings with a gloating look as he licked his snout clean. With the meat gone, the drakelings ignored him, their attention back on the smaller humans who still held treats.

Allistor closed his eyes for a moment, breathing slowly. It had been a couple days since he cleared the phobia dungeon. His people had been very understanding, allowing him as much undisturbed time as possible. He hadn't taken any meetings, and only answered a few inquiries through Nigel. Now he was expecting Master Daigath, who had requested a meeting. Allistor was feeling a little uncomfortable about seeing the ancient elf, whose facsimile they had to kill inside the dungeon. It promised to be an awkward meeting. But Allistor had made a plan to help offset that.

As if summoned, Master Daigath stepped off the elevator onto the roof. The elf preferred early morning meetings and open spaces, which is why the family was taking breakfast on the roof. The elf took some time to watch the kids and their drakes, then walked over to take a chair near Allistor. Fuzzy immediately stuck his nose in the elf's chest, begging for ear scratchings. The elf knew exactly where all the best spots were, and he happily obliged the bear cub.

"Good morning, Master Daigath." Allistor smiled at his mentor.

"Allistor, children, various ferocious beasts." Daigath greeted them all, giving Fuzzy's head a rough but affectionate shake. The bear's nub of a tail wagged like a dog's.

Allistor motioned toward the loaded breakfast cart? "Can I get you something to eat? Some juice?"

"I'll help myself, you stay where you are." Daigath pushed Fuzzy's head aside and got to his feet, walking to the cart. "I hear you're still recuperating."

Allistor snorted. "I'll be fine. That dungeon was just a little…" Allistor stopped himself, not wanting to discuss it in front of the kids. They'd experienced more than enough trauma in their young lives already. And he didn't want them to see their father and protector shaken.

"Yes, so I have heard. Netsirk gave me a complete recounting of your adventure." Daigath gave him a look that said he knew exactly how traumatic it had been.

With a sigh, Allistor resigned himself to discussing it with his mentor. "Kids, how bout you take your training down to the courtyard? I'm sure the other kids would enjoy watching. Take the meat with you."

The kids didn't argue, sensing that the grown-ups wanted to have a serious discussion. They began pushing the meat cart toward the elevator, their drakelings hopping along after. Fuzzy took about half a second to decide to follow the meat, abandoning Allistor without a backward glance, earning a smile from both him and Daigath.

When they were gone, Allistor called out, "Nigel, please have the others join us."

Daigath raised an eyebrow at that, but didn't ask. Instead, he said, "Netsirk will need some time to recover. I am helping her, but she is still hearing an echo of the voices in her head. And she has apologized at least half a dozen times for killing me." He grinned at Allistor.

"Yeah, that was tough. I was frozen at first, didn't know what to do. Having you seemingly betray us, then having to fight and kill you, on top of the trauma of thinking the city was being wiped out…" Allistor paused. "But definitely killing you was the worst." He gave the elf a small smile.

"I imagine I did not enjoy it either." The elf returned the smile. "The dungeon has been rough on

Netsirk, who has led a reasonably serene life for the last several decades. You, on the other hand, have been dealt trauma after trauma since Earth was Initialized. I came to see how you are holding up."

Allistor considered it for a moment before answering. "It did mess with my head quite a bit. But I think maybe the fact that I *have* been facing so many battles is actually helping me deal with it. Like, this is just another shot to the body. Or the mind, in this case. I just keep telling myself that none of it was real."

"That is a mistake, Allistor. It was all more than real enough to kill you. From what I've been told, you all would have died in the cave-in, or shortly after in Cserald's case, had it not been for your dimensional ability. You need to keep that in mind."

Allistor was confused for a moment, until he realized what Daigath meant. "You mean as I decide whether or not to keep the dungeon."

"Just so. It is fine to pretend it was all imaginary for your own mental health, but do not allow that thought to lessen in your mind the danger that dungeon represents to anyone who enters. I know you want training tools for your people. And a scalable dungeon would remain useful to them for a very long time. But consider the cost, the consequences to them. How would you gauge how mentally damaged a group of your raiders are when they emerge?"

Allistor nodded. "You're saying I could have people come out of there insane, and not know it until they snapped out here in the real world."

Daigath just nodded.

"So you think I should destroy the core?"

This time the elf shook his head. "I think it has its uses. But that only a select few should be allowed to make use of it, and those should be carefully monitored afterward." He took a breath and leaned forward, placing his hands on his knees. "I got permission from Netsirk to tell you this. She was imprisoned underground for several years as a small child, her village having been raided by slavers. During that time, her mother went insane. She was locked in a dark cell with a mother who never ceased rocking back and forth, whispering to herself. Every night, every day for years. When she entered that dungeon, she began to hear whispers again. Though she told herself it was the dungeon playing on her fears, it reached deep into her psyche and prodded at that frightened little girl." Daigath actually shuddered, and Allistor got goosebumps.

"I will assist her to the best of my ability, and she will recover in time." He looked into Allistor's eyes. "Harmon tells me that Targon was similarly shaken after having to face a traumatic childhood memory." Allistor saw where the elf was going.

"I had a great childhood. Almost no trauma in my life until the world ended. Beyond the usual, the death of our dog, a girl breaking my heart. Nothing like what they experienced."

Daigath nodded. "Then you see my point. You seem to be adjusting better than those who had more... deeply buried traumas that made them vulnerable. I believe in the future, those with similar deep-seated issues should avoid that dungeon. Others like yourself will fare much better, both inside the dungeon, and afterward."

"That sounds like very good advice, Master Daigath. Thank you."

The elf smiled at him, his mood instantly seeming to lighten. "Now, I'm told that Longbeard screamed like a little girl when you all jumped into the hole. Is this true?"

"It were a savage battle cry!" Longbeard huffed as he and Harmon stepped off the elevator. "Though, I regret lettin' out so much air right before hittin' the water."

Harmon snorted as he patted the dwarf's shoulder, while Allistor and Daigath grinned at the response.

"And don't ye be spreadin' no rumors, either!" Longbeard glared at Daigath, who held up his hands in mock surrender.

"Your brave leap will be a topic of legend, while your savage battle cry will remain a secret known only to we few." Harmon assured the dwarf.

"Indeed, your vocal foible does not in any way lessen the courage you displayed." Daigath agreed, solemnly holding a hand to his heart. "I only wished to confirm both with one who witnessed it." He did his best to keep from smiling.

"Bah! We all have things we would rather not be known. Right, Allistor?" The dwarf gave his emperor a significant look.

"Yes, that is true. For instance..." Allistor withdrew a bundle from his inventory that made both the dwarf and the orcanin smile. "I was given this by the Al'drong House Steward when we took the planet. He told me quite a story about its history..." He held the bundle out toward Daigath with both hands.

The elf took the bundle and deftly unwrapped it, eyes widening as he recognized the blade. Looking up at Allistor, he asked, "What exactly did this Steward tell you?"

"That ye made it fer yer girlfriend!" Longbeard cut in, a wide grin spread across his entire face. "And that she were the matron o' the House at the time." This time he made a smoochy face with kissy noises at the elf, causing Harmon to laugh. Allistor was able to maintain at least a semblance of a poker face.

Daigath blushed.

"HA!" Longbeard pointed and did a brief jig. "That right there be what I was hopin' for!" He looked up at Harmon, whose eyes were watering from laughter, both at the elf and the dwarf. "I thank ye, Allistor, for lettin' me be here today."

"I thought it might ease the tension after the dungeon run." Allistor smiled at him. "Now, take a seat, both of you. I believe Master Daigath has a distracting and fascinating tale to tell us."

The old elf sighed, then nodded. Allistor knew if he framed it as a form of mental therapy for himself and Longbeard, his mentor wouldn't refuse to tell the story. As Daigath began to tell them how he came to be on Rivian, Allistor realized he'd forgotten to include Helen in this little group, and she'd missed Daigath's reaction.

She's going to make me pay for that. He thought to himself before focusing on the story.

*****

A week later, Allistor was having a wonderful time. He was seated on a throne taken from the palace at Rivian, a temporary substitute for one that Daigath was crafting for him. The throne was placed at the top of the stairs in front of the old capital building at the Bastian. The same spot where he'd taken Loki's life. Below were gathered more than a hundred thousand of his citizens, representatives from every world he controlled, as well as from allied Factions and Houses. Humans from settlements they'd encountered all over Earth had been invited as well.

Allistor had thrown a party for the occasion, and everyone had embraced the idea. Hundreds of tables full of food and drink were lined up down below, foods from every nation, from multiple planets. His people had been eating, drinking, and mingling since noon that day under a beautiful clear blue sky. There was a soft breeze, just enough to keep the air cool and flutter the multiple banners that lined the walls around them. Allistor had mingled with his people, embracing old friends and meeting new citizens. Fuzzy and Fiona had worn themselves out playing with human, beastkin, dwarf, elf, gnome, and even a few xylon children. They had romped through the grass and around the trees, stalking the children or being stalked themselves. There had been mock cavalry battles with three or four children riding each bear as they charged each other. The spectacle had drawn a crowd of thousands who cheered and placed good-natured bets.

All in all it had been a wonderful day for Allistor. Even better, he hadn't told most of his honored guests what the occasion was. Those who'd bothered to ask all got the same reply. "I'm the emperor, do I need a reason to have a party?"

Now, as the afternoon began to turn to evening, Allistor was ready to reveal his nefarious purpose for bringing them all together. Standing in his formal outfit, dark grey pants, shirt, and boots with a black cape, all highlighted with gold and silver embroidery, he looked every bit the leader of an empire. He made a mental note to reward Lilly for her efforts as he raised his hands in the air to motion for quiet.

"Citizens of Invictus and honored guests! Please grant me your attention!" He called out, Nigel amplifying his voice to be heard by everyone below, at the same time transmitting it to everyone he could on all of Allistor's planets, space stations, and ships, who were all encouraged to hold smaller celebrations of their own. When the crowd grew mostly quiet, he continued.

"We've had far too few celebrations in the last couple years, and that's partly my fault. I should have taken more time to celebrate our victories, our good fortune, at least as often as we have come together to mourn our losses. Today I start to make up for that!" The crowd cheered their approval, many of them holding up drinks or plates of food.

"Those of us who were born on this formerly insignificant little backwater planet, far out on one of the spiral arms, have survived the near extinction of our race. We hunkered down, gritted our teeth, and fought for our lives, our families, our world. We came together, and Earth is once again ours!" He raised the sword Unification, and the crowd roared up at him.

"But we didn't do it alone. We owe much of our success to our non-human allies! They have joined us as friends, protectors, allies, and in some cases, family! Without them we might still be scratching in the earth, hiding in our individual Strongholds, filled with fear and anger. Instead, we welcome them among us and celebrate their contributions to our success!" The cheers weren't quiet as enthusiastic, but still loud and friendly. Allistor smiled to see humans embracing beastkin and fist-bumping orcanin in the crowd below.

"Now, the reason I have gathered you all here today, beyond just a general celebration of our new lives together, is that several of you have gone above and beyond in your efforts on our behalf. And while I have done my best to reward those who've earned it as we've overcome the many challenges we've faced, I have been remiss in that effort. So today we're going to remedy that!"

"First, a few general announcements. I have made arrangements to more than double our space fleet. We've a lot of planets and millions of people to protect, and I'm taking that responsibility very seriously. Which means we have about ten thousand new crew positions to fill! If you have any interest in serving in our space force, let Nigel know. You'll get training, room and board, and a good salary. This applies to every citizen of Invictus on every world." There were some scattered cheers among the polite applause from the crowd.

"Next, our small army of class trainers is being overwhelmed! They're making a valiant effort, but there are just too many citizens now. So I've asked my advisors to find and hire a thousand more. In addition, we've picked up a significant number of new citizens who are master crafters, merchants, and tradespeople of a hundred different professions. I'm going to ask them to take on apprentices who are interested in learning their trades. Those who agree will be compensated for their efforts." The cheers were a bit louder that time, especially amongst the non-humans who were more familiar with the value of an apprenticeship.

"Now, it's time to embarrass a few of my friends!" Allistor's smile was both wide and wicked. "Starting with Helen, who got me into this entire mess in the first place! Helen, where are you? Get up here!" He found her in the crowd and waved her forward. "Nigel, please have the other special guests come up as well. As much as I'd like to watch each of them walk up individually, we'd be here all night!" he laughed with the crowd as Helen was followed by dozens of confused and suddenly wary comrades.

"For those that don't know, Helen was a park ranger before the world ended. I found her in a dark hole in the ground out in a forest. To show her gratitude, she cursed me with a title and set me on this path, granting me ownership of all the national parks and making me a noble. She claimed at the time it was an accident, but I don't believe her!" Helen blushed as she moved to stand next to him. "She is devious and cruel, and I can not imagine what my life might have been like without her by my side. She has been my sister, my partner in crime, and a very good friend." He stopped to give her a hug, getting some whistles and catcalls from below.

"She's already one of my Ministers, a small form of retribution on my part." The crowd chuckled at this. "But I'm officially getting my full vengeance by granting her enough land to make her a Baroness!" He quickly opened his interface and selected the proper tab, awarding her a property that had caught her eye when they were discussing possible targets for acquisition. As he completed the action, and the System-generated lights began to swirl around her, he shouted, "I give you Baroness Helen of Dunvegan Castle in Scotland!"

Helen flashed him a dirty looked, blushing furiously as the crowd cheered her good fortune. Then they both laughed as someone in the crowd shouted, "Marry me, Helen!"

"Next we have Sam and Meg, who have been with me since the day our little town was crushed by a void titan. They adopted me, and have watched over me every day since. They don't hesitate to call me on my bad decisions, and have saved my life more than once." The two of them moved to stand next to him, holding hands as he spoke. "They are my family and I love them, even if Meg won't let me hug her!" She shot him a dirty look and stuck out her tongue as Sam and everyone else laughed. "To them I grant... a lifetime supply of toilet paper!"

Meg sputtered indignantly as Sam roared with laughter. Those in the crowd who got the joke joined the laughter, while the rest just looked confused.

"Just kidding! Well, I suppose you can have the toilet paper if you want it. But the two of you are now Baron and Baroness! I'll leave it to you to choose what land you want. You can choose one big chunk somewhere, like your own tropical island, or scatter your holdings around wherever you like." Allistor shook Sam's hand, then pretended to hesitate as he moved to hug Meg. She smacked his arm and grabbed hold of him, hugging him fiercely.

"Thank you, you little shit." She whispered before letting go and leading Sam back into the crowd behind Allistor.

"Lady Melise of House Or'Dralon, please step forward." Allistor waited as the stunningly beautiful elfess

455

stepped forward, and bowed to him. She was wearing a simple gown of emerald silk that somehow looked more elegant than if it had been a formal ballgown. He returned the bow with a nod of his head, conscious of their relative stations during an event such as this. "Lady Melise, you have been a faithful friend to us, coming to our aid in a time of need, providing light mages that saved the lives of many of my people." He paused, then added with an awkward smile. "And have been very understanding regarding... other matters." He blushed slightly himself. "You are already a noble in your own House, and not one of my citizens, so I cannot bestow a title upon you. But I can reward you with land of your own! Again, I'll allow you to choose the location at your leisure. Thank you, from the bottom of my heart." Allistor didn't hug her, as that would have been scandalous. Instead he favored her with his brightest smile and a wink, to which she curtsied in reply.

Allistor continued to call forward friends and allies. Bjurstrom, McCoy, Chris, Dean, Andrea, Kira and Gene were all promoted and awarded lands. Allistor expanded the holdings of Lars and all the Stronghold leaders who'd joined him in the early days, plus a few of those who'd joined more recently. Commander Enalion of the Or'Dralon was gifted a fighter jet that Gene and his engineers had refitted with hydrogen engines, as a reward for not killing Allistor when they first met.

All of Allistor's first group of analysts were given titles and land as well. L'olwyn took his land on Rivian, as expected. Harmon was officially awarded the rights to place space stations above Rivian and Skapa Far, as well as a permanent waiver of taxes. The latter seemed to make the merchant happier than the former.

Gralen was given ownership of *Opportunity*, as well as a formal commission in the space force, and command of five more warships. Allistor left it up to him to promote his own captains. Cogwalker was promoted as well, and asked for a cargo ship rather than a warship, which Allistor happily granted.

Since his becoming Emperor of the planet had rendered the former governments mostly moot, Allistor declared Secretary Marschner a Baroness as well, permanently ceding to her all the property she controlled in and around DC and elsewhere. He also invited her to become one of his formal advisors, and gifted her a residence in Invictus City near the tower. This neatly folded the remnants of the government and its military into Invictus.

Andersson and Allistor had previously met with the other Stronghold leaders in his region, and they had agreed to his promotion. So Allistor called Andersson up. "I am creating a new title here, so that I can formally declare you Jarl Andersson of Norway!" His fellow Norwegians raised drinks and roared their approval of Andersson, quickly joined by the crowd, who by this time were beginning to get inebriated, even with their improved stats.

It took more than an hour to work through all those rewards and others. When he was done, Allistor made a few more general announcements. "For all of my newer citizens who haven't yet done so, don't forget to claim your ten acres of land. It doesn't have to be on your homeworld, you can choose from any of Invictus' planets. As our population grows, this benefit may no longer be possible in the future, so please take advantage while you can. Simply speak to Nigel, and he will organize the rest." Allistor had planned to announce that he was placing his second gate at Rivian, but held off. He didn't want a mad rush for property on that world until after his people had claimed theirs. Depending on how many settled there, he might rethink the gate placement. He was in no rush.

"It is my hope that, going forward, Invictus will remain at peace. That all of my citizens, all of *you* will prosper and live long, happy lives. But I must plan otherwise, for we have enemies, both known and unknown, out there in the universe. The most vital part of my plan involves making you as strong as possible. I won't force you to take advantage of what I'm offering you, but I hope that you will. Choose a class and visit a trainer. Sign up for some dungeon runs. Ask your regional leaders for quests to help you level up. Learn a trade and build your fortunes!" He paused to breathe as the crowd cheered. He hoped other crowds across his worlds were cheering as well. "Your success is my success! We work together, lift each other up, and make each other stronger!" He pumped a fist into the air, roaring out a battle cry as he found Longbeard and gave him a wink. The good-humored dwarf shot him a bird, but winked back.

"Now, wherever you are, if you can hear my voice, let's celebrate! Relax, eat and drink your fill. Tomorrow everyone has a day off to recover!"

Chapter Twenty Three

Haggling for Dummies

Cserald sat across from Allistor in the rooftop lounge area, a wide smile on his reptilian face. "I passed on your warnings, along with several of my own. Still, my foolish colleagues wish to proceed with the proposed arrangement. After I expressed your concerns, they even offered me a significant bonus if I can convince to you agree."

"Did you tell them I was considering destroying the core?"

"Oh, yes. Grandmaster Omidia was horrified, though you did not hear that from me. It was her that offered me the incentive to win you over."

"Heh. Alright, well I'm always happy to help my friends cash in." Allistor smiled at the mage. Just so we're clear, the dungeon stays where it is. The Azure Order will set up a small Outpost nearby, and provide full time guards to organize and restrict access. You will send a group through to clear the dungeon at least once per month to keep the dungeon from overflowing and releasing nightmares into my city."

"In return, each member of each group to enter will pay five hundred gold for the privilege, and Invictus will be paid ten percent of the value of any loot they receive in the dungeon." Cserald nodded his head as he spoke. "Our estimates are that the Order's use of the dungeon, assuming one team of five per day, will earn Invictus approximately one hundred thousand gold per month. Your own people can, of course, enter the dungeon at no charge, but will need to schedule the runs with our staff at least a week in advance."

Allistor shook his head. "I doubt many of my people will want to risk it. Most of my raiders don't even want to get near it. I know I'm never going back in there." He met the mage's eyes, and they shared a knowing look.

"I feel the same. Once was more than enough. But my colleagues are already lining up to make the attempt. The Order is instituting special procedures, like in-depth interviews to determine participants' worst fears in hopes of predicting what challenges the dungeon might throw at them. This will, in theory, allow them to structure teams and skills to successfully overcome those challenges. I'm betting a good number of them will still die in there, but that is their choice."

Allistor shook his head at their foolishness. "The gold they contribute will go into a fund that will support a wide variety of programs. Some of it will go toward the salaries of Ramon's inscription teams, who are still scrambling to create just the basic scrolls for all of our people. Our exponential growth has far outpaced their production capacity. Some of the gold will go to the families of those who perish defending Invictus. The rest will go toward hiring more trainers."

Cserald shook his head. "You are the only Emperor I know of that offers his people such access to class

461

training and dungeons. You could charge double the rate your citizens currently pay for training, and it would still be a small fraction of what others charge. They fill their coffers with millions that you just leave on the table. You even send your trainers out to make... what is it you called them? House calls? Instead of requiring people to travel to the trainers."

Allistor chuckled. "That's only on a limited basis. I send trainers out with the recruiting teams to help entice folks to join us. Most people will have to make appointments and travel to the trainer compounds for anything beyond their initial class training session."

"Still, were I not already a loyal member of the Azure Order, I would be tempted to pledge myself to Invictus and become a citizen."

"You and your family are always welcome here, Cserald." Allistor reflexively started to slip into recruitment mode, but held himself back, and left it at that.

"I am honored, Emperor Allistor." The reptilian mage bowed his head. "Now, I must return to the Grandmaster, let her know that we have an accord, and collect my bonus!" He stood, offering another bow. "Whom should we contact to execute the formal agreement?"

"L'olwyn loves that sort of thing. He'll be our representative for this." Allistor resisted the urge to shake the mage's hand before he departed. "Travel safely, my friend."

As Cserald stepped onto the elevator, Nigel's voice echoed around Allistor. *"Sire, you wished me to remind you when your departure time approaches. Lady Kira has asked me to let you know she will pick you up here on the roof in fifteen minutes."*

"Thank you, Nigel. I had forgotten." Allistor had scheduled a trip to the last of the properties he'd inherited after killing Loki. This one was a space station formerly owned by Hel. No one that he'd asked knew anything about it. Hel had been both devious and secretive by nature, and much like her moon that had been destroyed upon Loki's death, visitors had not been welcome on the space station that orbited it.

It had been more than a month since Allistor was awarded the station, along with the other properties, and it was past time that he visited it. Allistor paced slowly around a sofa as he thought back on recent accomplishments. His biggest challenge had been housing, feeding, and finding work for the millions of former slaves on Skapa Far. The city administrators had stepped up, executing his orders and organizing the massive undertaking. Allistor hadn't even really needed to commit much in the way of resources other than what was already on the planet. Loki's hoarding, or lack of attention, had provided most of what was needed.

There were still a large number of former slave owners who'd been unwilling to accept the new reality on Skapa Far, and were awaiting transport off-world. Some more patiently than others. There had been some friction, even a few scuffles. A dozen crafters and two farmers had been executed for attacking former slaves, their assets seized and their families promptly banished. The executions had been very public, and were transmitted live throughout Invictus as an example for those who might misbehave.

Thanks to the ancient Steward on Rivian, things there had gone much more smoothly. All but the nobles who'd been sent to labor on Skapa Far had sworn the oath and become productive citizens. Ships had been sent to neighboring worlds within the system to make introductions and attempt to secure trade agreements. So far none had been finalized, but all of the worlds' leaders had been willing to talk, at least.

Allistor's inner core of analysts had hired a small army of additional analysts, researchers, and operatives to assist with the requirements of his rapidly expanding empire. It was becoming more and more rare for Allistor to recognize the people he encountered inside the tower day to day. He was doing his best to remember the faces and names of key individuals, but it was an uphill battle. Luckily, Nigel had volunteered a solution. He had the ability to transmit text notifications to Allistor, and began discretely sending him names and brief summaries of the folks Allistor focused on or spoke to. It was a huge help, and yet another way Nigel had begun anticipating his needs rather than just responding to requests.

Things were also going well on Aegrin. Several of Allistor's raid groups had traveled to the planet to run the dungeon there, mingling with the xylon while they visited. A contingent of humans, beastkin, and former slaves of multiple races from Skapa Far had elected to take up residence on that planet. Most of the slaves had worked as farm labor, and were happy to claim ten acres on Aegrin to farm for themselves. They chose to stick together, claiming adjacent tracts of land. As a result there was a bustling new farm community forming on the surface.

A similar occurrence was happening on Orion. Land was being settled by citizens from multiple worlds. A few of the cowboys from Cheyenne had bribed Cogwalker into transporting a small herd of cattle and six breeding pairs of bison to Orion. Allistor granted them a large tract of land to use for a breeding program. Since there were no predators anywhere on the planet, the livestock were free to roam and breed in peace. The cowboys were already talking about making a second trip.

Allistor's musings were interrupted as *Phoenix* rose up alongside the tower and hovered so that the cargo ramp was just a foot off the roof's knee wall. Allistor hopped up onto the ramp, which began to close behind him as the ship gained altitude. He waved at the twenty raiders who were gathered in the mess hall as he passed on his way to the bridge.

"Good morning, Kira. How are things on this fine day?" He smiled at his ship's captain and her bridge crew.

"Just peachy." Kira returned the smile. "We have our course. We'll hit the Orion gate, travel to one about midway down this arm." She pulled up her navigation holo display and pointed to a spot on the same spiral arm that Earth was now located. "From there it's about six hours by

FTL. We've got Cogwalker and Gralen on their ships as our escort."

"Excellent!" Allistor looked around the bridge again, seeing fewer bodies than he expected. "Did Harmon not join us? It's not like him to pass up a chance to poke his nose around a space station."

"He and Longbeard and the others are in the owner's mess, waiting to speak with you." Kira informed him. "Said you would need some privacy." She flashed a meaningful look at the many adolescent ears at various bridge stations. The kids may have leveled up as much as many of the adult citizens had, but they weren't emotionally any older than their chronological age, and couldn't be depended upon to keep juicy secrets.

Allistor nodded in understanding. "Thanks everyone, for all your hard work." He waved at the crew, who all waved back with serious faces. Allistor stepped through the hatch into the corridor, then on a whim stuck his head back in. "Hey, Kira… are we there yet?!" he watched her stick out her tongue as some of the kids laughed.

"Don't make me pull over and come back there!" She teased back, leaning forward like she might get out of her captain's chair. Allistor pretended to be afraid and dashed away down the corridor to the elevator. He went up one level and found the others in the smaller, more luxurious dining area meant to serve the ship's owner and important passengers. Harmon, Helen, Longbeard, and

William were sitting at a round table, laughing about something when he entered.

"I hear there's top secret discussions going on in here, but it doesn't sound very serious." He raised an eyebrow at William, who was looking slightly guilty.

Harmon raised a hand in greeting. "Young William was just sharing an amusing story about trying to bash your brains in while you worked at your forge."

Allistor winked at his squire to let him know it was okay. "Good training, that was. For both of us!" He took a seat at the table with the others. "So, what's up?"

Harmon gave a quick glance at William before speaking, and Allistor took the hint. "William, how would you like to spend a little time training on the ship's weapons station?"

The boy was on his feet and rushing toward the door before Allistor had time to take a breath. Allistor chuckled, "Let's hope he doesn't accidentally target any elven ships."

Longbeard absently nodded in agreement. The dwarf had been much less jovial than normal since their time in the phobia dungeon. Allistor understood completely, and was determined to give his advisor as much time as he needed to recover. "We be needin' to discuss this station o' yours."

"Okay, have you learned some more about it?"

The dwarf shook his head. "Not a thing. We sent two emissaries to have a look around, but both were threatened as they approached. We know nothin' more than we did two weeks ago."

"Except that we can be reasonably sure that it will be dangerous." Harmon added. "Any station owned by Hel is sure to have hidden traps, as well as potential assassins and spies aboard. The question is, are they still there, or did they perish when she did, due to life bonds?"

"So you're saying this station might be like a dungeon, filled with traps and bad guys trying to kill us." Allistor looked at Harmon, then at Longbeard, concerned that the dwarf might not handle such a situation well.

"Aye, close enough!" Longbeard actually seemed pleased. "Be good to deal with straightforward physical or magical traps, and normal baddies!" he surprised Allistor with his enthusiasm. "Cogwalker brought a team o' snorgs in case there be changelings."

Allistor nodded. They never had figured out who sent the changeling that had set bombs on his new space station above Earth. That memory, combined with the talk of traps on the station they were about to explore, had him sitting in somber silence for a while. The others simply waited.

Finally, he shook himself out of it. "The last report I saw mentioned that there appeared to be exterior damage. Either from an attack, or from when the moon exploded?"

"Yes, it was stationed not far from the moon, next to a large asteroid that was being mined for materials to expand the station. It likely took some impact damage when the moon disintegrated." Harmon agreed.

"Will it even be safe to board, then?" Allistor didn't ever want to see anyone else sucked into space through a hole in a space station.

"It's quite a large structure, more than twice the size of your Earth station. And like all space structures, it will have been segmented so that any section that loses pressure can be sealed off. There should be at least some areas that are still secure. Cogwalker's engineers are prepared to perform inspections and repairs."

"Give 'em something to do besides constantly fiddlin' with that ship o' theirs." Longbeard chuckled. Cogwalker's engineers had been rather famously improving their ship's systems during their down time. Which was most of their time since their last fight at Skapa Far.

There was a delay once they reached Orion, as Allistor received a message that several representatives of powerful factions had arrived at Harmon's station and wished to speak with him. An Emperor would not be expected to travel from his home world to meet with such people, and normally they would just meet with one of his advisors if they weren't willing to travel to Earth to request an audience. But since Allistor had traveled to Orion on his own, he didn't want to refuse to meet with them and risk alienating potential allies or trade partners.

So the *Phoenix* docked in the VIP landing bay and Harmon led them to his deluxe suite, which took up an entire floor near the top of the central hub. He offered Allistor the choice of a meeting room with a conference table, or a more casual lounge area in which to host the representatives.

Allistor chose the meeting room, the more formal setting. He was already caught off balance by the impromptu requests, and he just felt more in charge sitting at the head of a long table. Harmon took a seat to his right after Allistor asked him to remain and advise him, with William to his left, and Helen next to him. Longbeard took the seat next to Helen, placing himself between her and any potential threat from the visitors. Harmon's staff quickly filled a side table with a selection of food and drinks.

The first of the visitors was shown in a few minutes later. It was a tall, dark-skinned elf adorned in black silk from shoulders to knees, with black sueded leather boots that made no sound as he entered. He paused at the door to bow deeply to Harmon, whom he immediately recognized, then offer Allistor a much less respectful bow, barely bending at the waist. "Emperor Harmon, Emperor Allistor, it was most gracious of you both to alter your plans and make time for this meeting." He placed one hand on his chest as he spoke. "I am Be'linor of House Ci'Lantro. Myself, and several other representatives, were about to board a ship bound for your Earth when we heard that you were already on your way here."

"Then our timing was fortunate." Allistor kept a neutral look on his face. "Please have a seat, and share with us what you wish to discuss." He glanced at Harmon as the elf focused for a second on moving to the opposite head of the table and pulling out a chair. The big orcanin turned his head slightly away from the elf and winked at Allistor. "Would you like some refreshment before we continue?"

The elf paused midway between standing and sitting, caught off guard by the timing of the offer. Proceeding to sit, he bowed his head. "Some water would be most kind."

Without needing to be told, William got to his feet and moved to the side table, pouring a glass of iced water from a pitcher and delivering it to the elf with a polite bow of his head. Seemingly aware of William's title and position within Allistor's household, the elf nodded back and smiled. "Thank you, Squire William." He took a polite sip of the water, then carefully set down the glass. "I will come straight to the point, as I am aware your time is valuable, and there are several others waiting for an audience."

"Your directness is appreciated." Allistor leaned back in his chair and relaxed, trying to project an air of indifference despite his curiosity.

"My father, the Patriarch of House Ci'Lantro, has been following your progress over recent months. Ever since you became the first on your world to earn a Title, in fact. We had just decided to establish a settlement on Earth when you were awarded the remainder of the unclaimed territory. Congratulations, by the way." He paused briefly for a reply, then continued when Allistor simply nodded his head.

"We would like to discuss purchasing a significant section of land on Earth, and on Orion as well, if you are willing. I assure you we would make good neighbors and trade partners. I am sure House Ci'Lantro's reputation speaks for itself."

Now Allistor was stuck. This was precisely the type of situation he preferred to avoid. Taking a deep breath, he leaned forward and placed both hands palms down on the table. "I do not wish to offend you, or your house, Be'linor. But as I'm sure you are aware, I am quite new to the Collective, and have been very busy fighting to survive and build my empire since I earned that first title. I regret that I have not had the time to learn the names or reputations of even a fraction of the Houses, Empires, or Factions."

The elf's eyes widened briefly, the only indication of a reaction, and he was opening his mouth to respond when Longbeard cleared his throat. Allistor looked to him as he offered, "If I may, Sire?" When Allistor nodded, he continued. "I know of House Ci'Lantro. They are an ancient House, one of the original Hundred that established the first ruling council of elves. Their origins were in agriculture and alchemy, and the House was famous for its trade in high quality potions and ingredients." The elf smiled slightly and nodded as the dwarf spoke. "In recent centuries they have established new settlements on every newly stabilized or colonized world, where they have attempted to monopolize mercantile interests. Due to those

472

efforts, their reputation has become somewhat… diverse. There are those who greatly admire Ci'Lantro, and those who feel quite the opposite."

"Much like your own reputation, Emperor Allistor." The elf actually smiled for the first time. "Especially since your execution of Loki."

Allistor leaned back again, taking a few heartbeats to absorb what Longbeard had said, looking for any hidden meaning in his words. The dwarf was usually extremely forthright, but in this situation…

"I assume that in mercantile situations, there will always be those who feel they've been taken advantage of. Especially if agreements were reached using unfair or deceitful practices, wouldn't you agree?" Allistor raised one eyebrow as he asked the question.

"Indeed. Though House Ci'Lantro abhors such tactics. We prefer to achieve our goals through well-timed expenditures of immense resources, granting us a certain level of control over the markets we participate in."

"We called that monopolizing on my world. Lots of the biggest corporations did it. It wasn't illegal, or where it was, they found ways around the laws." Allistor watched the elf's face for any sort of reaction, but got none. "I suppose as Emperor I could make monopolies illegal on my planets…" This time there was slight raising of the eyebrows. "But I suspect it won't be a problem. As long as your practices don't cross the line into intimidation, extortion, or the like." Harmon actually chuckled as the elf's face went back to neutral.

"I can assure you we have no such intentions, Emperor Allistor."

"What type of property did you want to purchase, and how much of it?"

"We would wish to grow our own crops for ingredients, so a significant acreage would be required. Ideally something close to a natural water source. Say ten thousand acres?"

This time Harmon's eyebrows went up. "That is a significant investment."

The elf gave a slow nod of respect and agreement. "Indeed. House Ci'Lantro sees this solar system as an emerging market, and we wish to invest in it early. My Patriarch has great faith in you, Emperor Allistor."

Allistor thought about it for a moment, leaving the room silent except for William fidgeting in his seat.

"I am going to assume that the other representatives waiting outside have similar requests. So I'm not just considering your potential impact on the future of Invictus, but all of theirs as well. After all, I can't really show favoritism, being a fledgling Emperor, can I?" He waited for the elf to reply, but only got another nod of agreement.

"Earth's economy is fragile, and humanity is still recovering from being nearly wiped out. While we are making great strides in rebuilding, I'm not sure we're ready for a massive influx of competitors for the fledgling industries we're establishing." He tapped his chin, thinking. "Orion is also just beginning to rebuild, but is nearly uninhabited. And most of the inhabitants on the planet or this station are lifelong members of the Collective, with the knowledge and history that come with that. So I see no harm in allowing… enthusiastic investment." He smiled at the elf, who gave a half smile in return.

"I'll sell you your ten thousand acres on Orion, assuming our factors can agree on terms. You can establish your operation and try to corner your markets while I continue to stabilize Earth. After I've had a chance to observe your practices for a while, we'll revisit your potential presence on Earth."

"That is most gracious of you, Emperor Allistor. Thank you." The elf rose to his feet, bowed once to both of the emperors in the room, and favored William with a smile as he left.

"That were well done, Allistor." Longbeard grinned at him. "Ye made a dark elf raise his eyebrows."

"Ha!" Harmon joined in. "I could barely keep from laughing myself. That was indeed well played, my friend. You gave them enough to avoid offending an old and influential house, provided a perfectly plausible reason not to allow them to operate on Earth, and offered hope that they may yet get what they want if they behave themselves here on Orion!"

"Which I'm hoping you and your people here on the station will help me with." Allistor looked to Harmon. "I'm sure they have all kinds of tricks that I and my people have never even imagined."

475

"Indeed. But you're learning quickly." Harmon gave him his new favorite sign of approval, the double thumbs-up.

Longbeard looked at his wrist display for a moment. "There be six others out there, and as ye guessed, they all likely want the same. If ye offer them all space here on Orion, it'll be fun to watch em' try to eat each other over the coming years."

Allistor grinned at his advisor. "Then I'll put you in charge of negotiating the agreements and selecting the locations. Make sure and charge them as much as possible for the land, and they get nothing without entering into the same mutual defense agreement that the Or'Dralon, Azure Order, and the dwarven clans signed."

The dwarf gave a dramatic eye-roll at being handed the job, then chuckled. "It'd be me pleasure."

Harmon used his wrist unit to signal his staff to send in the next representative. Two hours later they had made tentative agreements with two more elven Houses, the same mining clan of Dwarves who had abandoned Orion previously, a prosperous Beastkin merchant who wanted to establish a modest trading house near the gate, a representative of an auction house that competed directly with Grandmaster Igglesprite's Ethereal Auction, and an ambassador from a species of aquatic mammals called dolphidions, whose faction wished to purchase the rights to establish a kelp farm at the bottom of a large freshwater lake. He looked very much like an earth dolphin, but his tail fin had evolved into feet, and his pectoral fins into arms with three-fingered hands.

Allistor was actually intrigued by the possibility of dolphidions settling on Earth and establishing relations with the dolphins there, and extended an invitation. The ambassador wasn't authorized to accept such an offer on behalf of his faction, but assured Allistor that if his superiors weren't interested, his own family would be. After he left, it occurred to Allistor that he hadn't actually seen any dolphins since the apocalypse, and didn't know if any had survived. He made a mental note to check on that immediately.

With their meetings concluded, and a significant influx of potential income arranged for Invictus, Allistor and company boarded Phoenix and resumed their journey to the new space station.

Chapter Twenty Four

Shotgun Diplomacy

"Approaching ships, this is space station Charon. Do not approach. I repeat, do not approach or you will be fired upon. Leave our space immediately."

Kira looked up at Allistor, who was standing at her left shoulder, staring along with the rest of the folks on the bridge at the space station ahead of them. It had been growing larger as they traveled closer for the last several minutes, but now the Phoenix was halted, floating stationary in space. "How do you want to respond?"

"Please open a channel so I can speak to them." Allistor's eyes didn't leave the station on the screen. It was obviously damaged, several sections of the exterior dented and even holed, probably by debris from the now nonexistent moon. They had passed through some of its debris as they entered the local region of space.

When Kira nodded at him, he spoke loudly and clearly. "This is Emperor Allistor of Invictus, new owner of your space station. I have come to inspect the station and meet its inhabitants."

There was a long moment of silence, then a terse response. "We don't care who you are. This station is ours. Leave now, or we will fire upon you."

Harmon cleared his throat, causing Allistor to look over at him. He was studying a hologram and some scripted information being displayed from the sensors station on the bridge. He met Allistor's gaze and shook his head. "May I?"

"Of course." Allistor motioned toward the screen, inviting his friend to speak.

"Space station Charon, this is Emperor Harmon of the Orcanin. I am looking at sensor readings of your station. All but three of your weapons turrets are damaged and non-operational. The three that can fire aren't nearly enough to even damage the shields of the three ships that currently surround your station."

There was only silence from the belligerent station occupants, so Allistor took up the baton. "Space station Charon, I mean you no harm. I simply wish to visit the station and discuss your potential future with you. Stand down and let us dock. If you continue to refuse to allow me access to my own property, I will take it from you. It is unlikely you will survive such an action."

"So you're here to murder us!" the same voice screamed through the coms at him.

"No, I'm here to *talk* to you, as I have said twice now. But I *will kill you* if you fire upon any of my ships, or refuse to allow me access. You have one minute to comply before my ship advances."

The voice began screaming nearly incoherent obscenities at him, and he motioned for the transmission to be cut off.

"Harmon, I need to know two things. Can we disable the remaining guns without destroying the station? And if we're forced to attack, how do we kill those inside without completely destroying the station?"

The big orcanin chuckled. "If you'll allow me to take control of the weapons station, yes I can disable the remaining guns with little difficulty or collateral damage. As for killing the occupants… it would be difficult to do with this ship's weapons, which are not designed for the type of surgical strikes that would be required. You could have Cogwalker launch several drone fighters. With their smaller weapons and ability to move in close, they could puncture each section of the station's hull, venting all of them. There is always the risk of explosive decompression, or that a strike to the hull might penetrate more deeply and damage a critical system. The only other way would be to board the station and use troops to clear it."

Allistor didn't like the idea of risking lives by taking the station via face to face combat. But he didn't want to risk a wild shot destroying the whole thing, either.

"What are the odds that if we board the station, they have some sort of fail-safe self-destruct device in there?" He was afraid he already knew the answer, but asked anyway.

"Being that it was Hel's station? Assume there's at least one, if not several backups as well. And I'd bet there are interior automated defenses, and no shortage of lethal traps."

"And if Phoenix were docked in the station when it exploded, would her shields protect her?"

Harmon just shook his head.

Allistor sighed. His minute was running out quickly, and he now regretted starting that clock before he'd thought out all his options. "Nigel, can you hack the station's AI and take control?"

"As you have been declared owner of the station by the System, there is no need to hack. The station AI will grant me access. Though it objects quite strenuously to being erased in favor of my taking control. As I'm sure you are about to inquire, the station AI is a higher level than I am currently, and capable of defending itself."

Harmon nodded. "It's an old station that has had plenty of time to level up, and Hel obviously would have had access to the most advanced tech. Nigel would lose that fight, and would be at risk of deletion himself."

"Nigel, will the AI obey my commands, as long as I leave it in place?"

"It would, Sire. Charon has confirmed your right to ownership." Allistor immediately received a notification asking if he wished to take ownership of the station. He selected *Yes* before answering the AI.

Allistor was sure the minute clock had run out some time ago. "Kira, move us toward the docking bay." Kira nodded and made some quick adjustments to the helm controls. As the ship began to move forward again, Harmon poked at his hologram, and a section of the station

481

lit up on her display, showing her where to go. "Coms, tell Gralen and Cogwalker not to fire unless fired upon. And to only target weapons systems if they do fire."

Allistor took one step forward, placing his hands on a rail that ran in front of Kira's chair. "Let's see if they fire on us. Nigel, please introduce to me to Charon."

A moment later a new voice echoed through the bridge. It was deep, gravelly, and monotone. *"Greetings, Emperor Allistor. I am Charon. How may I serve you?"*

"Greetings, Charon. I'd like some information to start with. How many beings are currently aboard your station?"

"There are six thousand, eight hundred and thirty two current occupants. More than twice that number perished at the same instant that the nearby moon was destroyed. Another one thousand one hundred and seven perished when the station was damaged by debris, or during subsequent fires and system failures resulting from that damage."

"That was a very thorough answer, Charon. Thank you." Allistor smiled at the image of the station on the screen. "Now, if I were to order it, could you deactivate whatever self-destruct mechanisms are installed on the station?"

"I have that capability, yes . There are three such systems on board the station. None of the remaining occupants have a sufficiently high security clearance to override a shutdown. Though there is a possibility that a

*manual override could be accomplished. Two of the
occupants would need to reach the power core and institute
a feedback loop that would overload the core and cause it
to detonate. This process would require three minutes from
the time they trigger the loop until detonation."*

"Can you also seal all the doors within the station?"

*"I can close and secure all operational doorways. I
have complete control of most systems within the station,
including power, defense, and life support."*

Kira gasped. "Did that AI just hint that you should
suffocate the people over there?"

Charon, assuming Kira wanted an answer, provided
one. *"That protocol has been instituted a total of three
times by Hel's personal command since this station's
construction."*

"Wow." Kira leaned back in her chair and hugged
herself. "That's brutal. Kind of glad she's dead."

Harmon nodded. "She would have considered it an
efficient way to deal with any potential traitors, thieves,
assassins, or moles working for Loki."

"And all the people who died before the moon bits
hit would have been the ones bonded to her, the ones she
trusted to run the place." Allistor nodded. "So the people
who are left were… the worker bees?"

"And either still loyal to her, or greedy enough to
want to try and seize the station for themselves." Helen
added.

They had closed nearly half the distance to the station at this point, and still had not been fired upon. Allistor decided to take that as a good sign. "Charon Station this is Emperor Allistor. Please open the docking bay doors."

No sooner had he finished speaking than the two nearest operational gun turrets turned and pointed at *Phoenix*. A second later, they each fired a small plasma round at the ship. The third turret, which was too far around the station to target *Phoenix*, fired at *Opportunity*. None of the blasts did anything more than make the ships' shields flare slightly. Harmon began to walk toward the weapons station to take control, but he only made it two steps before Gralen and Cogwalker's ships fired on the two guns that had fired on *Phoenix*, destroying them both. A moment later Cogwalker took out the third.

"Dammit!" Allistor slammed a fist on the rail. "Charon, please deactivate all the self-destruct and defensive systems, exterior and interior. Seal all the interior doors. Can you tell me how many people are currently in the station's bridge? Or control room? Whatever you call it? And please transmit what I'm about to say throughout the station.

"As you command, Emperor Allistor. There are currently nine life forms in the station's main control room. Proceed when you are ready."

"Occupants of Charon station, this is Emperor Allistor, the new owner of this station. I am approaching your station as I speak, and have been fired upon by

484

whomever is in charge of your control room. I came here in peace, but they have now put all of your lives at risk. I am in control of the station, and have sealed all the doors. You will remain where you are until I say otherwise." He paused, thinking quickly. "To those who are in the control room. I am going to give you the benefit of the doubt, and allow you to save yourselves. Kill the raving lunatic that was speaking to me before, and the one that gave the order to fire on my ship, if they're not the same person. I give you two minutes to accomplish this and respond."

Allistor began to pace back and forth in front of Kira's chair, only able to take three steps before having to turn around and pace the other direction. Now he was thinking that he'd allowed too much time on the deadline clock. Shaking his head, he looked again at the screen. The destruction of the guns had caused some debris, and two bodies, to float away from the station. He hoped those bodies were gunners, and not innocents who happened to be walking by when the turrets were destroyed.

"If there is such a thing as innocents on that station." He mumbled under his breath, looking down and kicking one of the rail supports.

Kira, who was looking at a watch on her wrist, called out "Thirty seconds left."

Allistor looked up at the screen again, about to order Charon to shut off life support to the control room, when a new voice came across coms. "Emperor Allistor, this is Charon station. I am Communications Technician Broogian. Engineer third class Evani, the individual to whom you spoke, is dead. He was also the one who ordered us to fire upon you. An action which I did not agree with, and deeply regret."

"Communications Technician Broogian, are you in charge of the station now? Are there others with you who oppose your actions?"

"There are none living, your Majesty. Evani had two supporters who also perished."

Charon's voice rang out. *"I can confirm that there are now only six living occupants in the control room. In addition, two of those appear to be seriously injured."*

Broogian's voice replied, "Aye, Evani put up a fight, and managed a couple lucky shots, Majesty."

"Do you have access to health potions there?" Allistor asked, concerned.

"There is a supply in the meeting room next door, but the door is sealed."

"Charon, please unseal that door." Allistor ordered. A moment later Broogian spoke again.

"Thank you, Emperor Allistor. We've got the potions, and everyone is being healed up just fine."

Phoenix was now moving into the docking bay, the door having been opened by Charon without Allistor even asking the AI directly. It seemed Nigel wasn't the only AI capable of anticipating. Cogwalker and Gralen held their positions not far from the station, turning their ships outward to defend if necessary.

"Broogian, I'm on the station now. Before I exit my ship, tell me what has happened there since Hel's death." He could hear the communications officer take a deep breath before speaking.

"A lot of things happened all at once. The moon exploded, many of the senior staff and crew on board the station just dropped dead, and we all received a notification that Hel had died, and that our contracts were voided. None of us even had time to read that notification before debris began to strike the station. A lot more of us died before we managed to get the damage under control." There was a hitch in his voice as he spoke that last sentence, and a long pause.

"Take your time Broogian."

"Many of the station's systems were compromised, and the most senior people were dead. We've been organizing and making repairs the best we can, but resources are limited, and being rapidly depleted. Our focus has been on restoring the station, and not our directive."

"What was your directive?" Allistor looked to Longbeard and Harmon, who both just shrugged.

"We have been mining the nearby asteroid for rare metals. We harvest the asteroid, bring the ores back here to the station to be refined, then load them onto cargo ships that take them wherever Hel instructed. I heard rumors of a manufacturing plant on the moon, but that's obviously gone now."

"What metals were you harvesting?" Longbeard was suddenly interested.

"There was a wide range brought in. But the ones Hel was focused on were platinum, rhodium, iridium, osmium, and gold." Broogian paused. "We also pulled a stockpile of gems, but Hel was much less interested in those. We use them as unofficial currency here on the station."

"And why'd ye stop harvesting? Them metals be among the rarest anywhere, and would buy ye plenty o' food and supplies if ye traded."

"The ships we used to bring the materials from the asteroid were all destroyed, except for one that was docked there, still loading. No one has replied to our messages, we assume the entire crew died like so many of the others. We continued to refine what had already been offloaded before the explosions, once we secured all the compromised sections of the station and got life support back online. I suppose all those refined metals are yours now, Emperor Allistor."

Longbeard didn't say anything, but the wide smile half hidden under his moustache suggested the stockpile might be of value.

"We can talk about that later. For now, I'm going to bring a party to meet you on the bridge. Try to relax, I mean you no harm. We'll see you shortly."

"Emperor, I should warn you there are more on this station that feel as Evani did. They were loyal to Hel, even if she did treat us little better than slaves."

"Thanks for the heads up." Allistor was already leaving the bridge, Harmon, Helen, and Longbeard behind him. William remained on the bridge with Kira, knowing better than to ask Allistor if he could tag along.

"Charon, please upload a station schematic to the *Phoenix*, and to Harmon and Longbeard. We'll need to know the shortest path to the control room from this docking bay. Also, as we proceed, please open the doors as we approach, and seal them behind us."

"Schematics uploaded. I have indicated the shortest route through the remaining intact sections. I estimate twenty minutes to reach the control room." Charon responded.

Allistor reached the cargo bay and found both raiding parties geared up and ready to go. Bjurstrom and McCoy were both leading dungeon runs back on Earth, so these groups were only partially familiar to Allistor. On average they were between level fifty and sixty, and were all experienced raiders. The group leaders were Theado and Anderson, both level sixty.

Allistor stood in the center of the cargo bay and motioned for the raid leaders to join him. The others all gathered around and listened as he spoke. "Alright, we're about to walk into potentially hostile territory. Charon, the AI that controls the station, says he's turned off all the automated defenses. I don't know that I trust that to be true. And we've been warned that there will be hostile crew. So treat this like a real raid. I want tanks front and back, healers in the center, you know the drill. Not all of the crew are hostile, so don't attack unless I do. Do not trust anyone. These people worked for Hel, who was basically the first or second most devious entity in the galaxy. We'll keep folks sealed up where they are until we can administer oaths or move them off the station in some manner."

The group of twenty raiders, plus Allistor, Helen, Harmon, and Longbeard exited the ship down the cargo ramp. Two tanks took the lead, shields up and ready, with Longbeard right behind them, his wrist device showing a hologram of the station with a blue line running from the docking bay to the control center, which was near the top of the station's hub. Allistor and the melee fighters came next, followed by the healers and casters. Harmon brought up the rear with the remaining two tanks.

They crossed the bay floor without incident, though Allistor kept a sharp eye on two pairs of gun turrets set high on the walls on either side of them. When the tanks reached the wide double doors in the back wall, they opened with barely a whisper. Beyond the doors was a wide corridor, meant to accommodate large amounts of cargo and equipment. Allistor figured it was at least wide enough for two pickup trucks to pass by each other. Longbeard turned left and followed his map.

The group made no effort to be silent. They'd already announced their presence, and didn't see any point to it. Metal boots clomped on the metal floor of the corridor, and the raiders spoke quietly amongst themselves as they walked. Just a hundred feet or so down the corridor, someone began pounding on a door as they passed by. "Open up! Let us out!"

Longbeard looked back at Allistor, who stepped forward near the door. "Who are you?"

"I'm Spindlesprocket! Who are you?!" the voice was high pitched, muffled by the sturdy door, but had a clearly hostile tone.

"I'm the guy that decides whether you get out or not. Who else is in there with you?" Allistor growled loud enough for them to hear through the door.

"There's a dozen of us trapped in here! Some fool had all the doors sealed. Let us out before we suffocate!"

A light bulb went off in Allistor's brain. "Charon, is life support still operational everywhere there are people trapped?"

"*It is. Both air and temperature control. There is no danger of suffocation.*"

"And… could you, I don't know, reduce the air flow enough to render everyone unconscious while we secure the station?"

Allistor saw both Harmon and Longbeard shaking their heads, already knowing the answer that Charon offered. "*I can reduce oxygen levels, however some of the species aboard the station are hardier than others. Reducing the oxygen enough to render them unconscious*" *for an extended period of time would result in the deaths of those with weaker constitutions."*

"Can't do that, then." Allistor shrugged. "Charon, what is the average level of the station's remaining crew? And who is the highest level?"

"The average level of the surviving crew is twenty seven. The highest level individual is the one you are currently communicating with. Weapons Engineer Spindlesprocket is a level forty two gnome."

"Gnomes rule!" The voice shouted through the door right before a loud thunk suggested he kicked it from inside. "Let us out!"

"What will you do if I let you out?" Allistor stalled for time, trying to decide how to proceed. If they stopped to clear every room along the way, it would take forever to reach the control room.

"I'll do my damned job! We were grabbing parts to repair the gun turrets when we got sealed in this storage bay! Now let us out! If I have to say it again, I'll bust your damned kneecaps, then work my way up to your ugly mug!"

"Don't listen to him, you're not ugly." Helen winked at Allistor, who rolled his eyes.

"What makes you think I'm ugly?" Allistor was just trolling the annoying gnome at this point, still undecided whether to let him out or let him stew in his storage bay.

"Ya sound tall. Which means you're no gnome. Which makes you ugly!"

"Shaddup ya big eared, flat footed, unholy get of a goblin and a fairy!" Longbeard growled through the door. "Ye be speaking to Emperor Allistor! Show the proper respect!"

"Is that a dwarf? You sound like a dwarf! Open this door and I'll shove my flat foot right up your polluted-"

"HEY!" Allistor roared at the door, drowning out what the gnome was saying. "You've made my decision easy. You'll stay in there until further notice. I'll send someone by with food and water in a day or two."

"Wait! I'm sorry ugly… errr… Emperor Allistor. Please don't leave us in here." The voice had gone soft and pleading, with none of the spirit from just seconds before.

Allistor was silent for a while. On the one hand he was curious to meet this gnome. On the other hand, he wanted to get to the control room. Finally, he nodded. "Charon, please open this door." He motioned for one of the tanks to move in front of him, and cast *Barrier* in front of the doorway, just in case.

The moment the door slid to the side, the tank raised his shield and stepped into the doorway. He grunted, then cried out in pain as a dozen plasma bolts struck his shield from different directions. A few of the bolts hit his legs, not penetrating his armor, but heating it to a painful level. Allistor and the others immediately started casting spells as the other lead tank crowded in to offer support to his partner. Melee fighters dashed to the left and right of the tanks, swords, spears, and axes flashing as they attacked.

Allistor cast *Mind Spike* on three of the attackers in rapid succession, then cast *Lightning Bolt* on another. That put a third of the attackers on the ground, out of the fight. There were cries of pain as attackers were hacked down and raiders were hit with plasma rifle fire. He saw one of his casters struck by a stray bolt that burned through a raised arm, nearly severing it.

The fight lasted less than half a minute. His people were efficient and brutal, killing all but three of the station crew in the room. Those three were all wounded, and included the one Allistor had hit with lightning, Spindlesprocket, and one other gnome who had not been armed and had raised her hands in surrender as soon as the door opened.

Allistor checked to make sure his people were all right. Most had minor burns, except for the mage with the injured arm, who was being helped by two healers. Once he was sure everyone would be okay, he turned to the gnome.

"Spindlesprocket, you have tried to kill the owner of this station, who also happens to be an Emperor. Before I have my friend the dwarf stomp your face into the floor, tell me why you attacked."

"You killed our mistress! Murdering scum!" the gnome, who was laying on the floor and cradling a badly slashed arm, spat at him."

"That is true. Though it was unintentional. I executed Loki, and that somehow triggered an explosion on the moon here. I had no idea that would happen."

"Doesn't matter if it was unintentional! She's dead, and you're to blame! Give me my blaster back, and I'll unintentionally melt your face!"

Allistor considered trying to plead his case, to reason with the angry gnome. But not only did he think it would be a waste of time, but he couldn't be seen as weak for letting someone attack him and live. "Master Longbeard, please dispose of this gnome."

"No!" Spindlesprocket used his stubby legs to push himself away from Allistor and an advancing Longbeard. "Not the beard-tugger! If you're going to kill me, do it yourself."

"Yer not worth me Emperor's time." Longbeard growled as he grabbed the gnome by the throat and lifted him up. "Ye tried to lure him in here and ambush him like a coward!" He shook his arm, throttling the gnome whose eyes were bulging, his mouth moving but making nothing more than an "erp" sound.

The gnome did manage a single violent contortion that allowed him to kick the dwarf in the face, smashing a steel-toed boot into his nose. Longbeard roared and spun around, launching the feisty gnome into a nearby wall head first. There was a crack as Spindlesprocket's neck snapped, and he fell limply to the floor where he lay unmoving.

A whimper from the back of the room brought everyone's attention to the female gnome who hadn't fought. She was slumped into a corner, curled up and doing her best to make herself small, both hands covering her face. Allistor stepped toward her as Theado casually stepped on the neck of the other remaining gnome, crushing it.

"You can relax, the fight is over." Allistor spoke softly to the gnomess. "What is your name?"

She peeked between her tiny fingers for a moment, her eyes taking in Allistor and all the raiders in the room, as well as her dead crewmates. With a sniff and a hiccup, she lowered her hands. "I'm... I'm Bellatrix Spindlesprocket. Cook's assistant." She stared at the dead gnome at the base of the wall. "That was my father."

"I'm sorry for your loss, Bellatrix. But he tried to kill us."

The little gnome sniffed again, nodding her head. "I know. I begged him not to. He was just so... angry."

"Come with us to the control room, and you can rest there. I'm going to have to seal this room again, and you shouldn't be left alone in here." Allistor held out a hand to help her up, forgetting all of L'olwyn's many recriminations on touching people.

Bellatrix nodded slightly, her oversized eyes brimming with tears. She reached up with her left hand and took hold of Allistor's, allowing him to pull her to her feet.

"Thank you, she mumbled. Allistor opened his mouth to reply, but never got the words out. She tightened her grip on his hand, yanking it toward her with surprising strength for such a small creature. At the same time she launched herself upward, using his hand to pull herself close to his face, snarling. A dagger flashed in her free hand, the blade slamming into Allistor's throat. "For Hel!"

Chapter Twenty Five

Side Quests Suck

"Healers!" Longbeard roared toward the doorway where most of the raid group had exited back into the corridor once the fight looked to be over. Immediately three healers pushed through and started casting their biggest heals on Allistor, who was laying on his back with a small dagger handle sticking out of his throat.

The moment Longbeard saw that the healing was taking effect, he bent and gripped the dagger handle, ruthlessly yanking it free of Allistor's flesh. He watched, anxious, as blood spouted from the wound. A few seconds later, the gushing flow turned into a trickle, then slowed to a stop. He still held his breath as the skin began to knit itself back together, not releasing it until Allistor took a gasping breath of his own.

Allistor coughed up blood, spraying it all over Longbeard and the healers. He instinctively rolled over onto his side to cough up the rest, taking ragged breaths and coughing out the blood that had leaked down his throat and into his lungs. When he finally opened his eyes, he recoiled. Staring at him from inches away was Bellatrix's severed head.

"Did I do that? I don't remember doing that." Allistor croaked, rolling onto his back and staring up at the multiple concerned faces staring back at him from above.

"No, that was me. But I used your sword." Helen held the bloody blade up where he could see it. "You weren't using it at the time. You were busy falling down, all "ack, gag, glurg." She grabbed her throat with her free hand and bugged her eyes, sticking her tongue out to one side.

"Ha, ha, ha." Allistor checked that his health bar was back to full, then sat up. Longbeard offered a hand and helped him to his feet.

Helen continued. "It wasn't easy. Taking her head, I mean. She climbed right up you like a little monkey, stabbed you, and looked like she was ready to chew your nose off. I hit her with a *Mind Spike*, and she just shrugged it off, riding your body down to the floor, growling the whole time. It wasn't till after you landed and she sat up that I had a clean shot without cutting you, too. It didn't help that you were thrashing around like a mechanical bull underneath her."

Allistor gave her a soft smile and took his sword from her hand. After wiping the blood from it using Bellatrix's clothing and sheathing it, he stepped closer and pulled her in for a hug, holding her tightly. He could feel her body convulse as she broke down into a sob, grabbing hold of him just as tightly.

"Stupid jerk. Nearly got yourself killed." She mumbled into his shoulder. He nodded for everyone else to leave the room and just held onto his best friend for a few minutes. When she managed to collect herself, she let go and took a half step back. "I mean... I do want to be

Empress and everything, but like, I wanna earn it. Stab you in the throat myself when I decide it's time." She offered a weak grin.

"Heh. I love you too." He reached out and ruffled her hair, earning him a scowl.

Allistor looked down at the beheaded gnome. "She really surprised me. Looked so innocent, and then so… and she was *fast*." He rubbed the front of his throat where the blade had been pushed in.

"She really was." Helen agreed, then snorted. "Big level ninety nine tough guy, got your ass kicked by a three foot tall girl."

"Sssshhh! Don't tell anybody." He grinned and shot a meaningful look at the doorway and the couple dozen people beyond, making her snort again. "We okay?"

She took a deep breath and held it for a few seconds before exhaling. "Yeah, let's go. But uh… maybe not hit all the rooms on the way?"

"Good plan. Glad I thought of it!" He gave her butt an attaboy smack as he stepped past her. "All right everybody, show's over. Let's head to the control room. No more side quests. They suck." Several of the raiders chuckled as they formed back up, reassured that their beloved bossman was okay.

They didn't follow the straightest path to the control room, as several of the outer sections of the station had been compromised. They had to make several detours, even going down one level and across a glass tube bridge before ascending back to the level they'd started at, and continuing farther up. It was more like half an hour before they reached the control room, the delay mostly due to Allistor almost dying.

When they reached the door, all four tanks moved to the front, Charon closing the bulkhead thirty feet behind them. The tanks formed up, locked their shields together, and braced themselves. Behind them, casters and archers had attacks ready. "Please open the door, Charon." Allistor drew in a deep breath, prepared for another ambush.

This door was an iris design rather than the straight sliding doors they'd encountered elsewhere in the station. It spiraled open like a blooming flower to reveal six crewmembers of various races standing with empty hands out to their sides. The tanks moved three steps into the room and planted their shields, the others flowing in behind them and moving to either side, except for the healers who remained behind the tanks. Allistor surveyed the room, spotting blood trails leading to three bodies that had been piled to one side against a wall.

As one, all of the crew bowed deeply at the waist. A recognizable voice came from the nearest crewman, who looked to be a mixture of elf and dwarf. He was five feet tall, with pointed ears, red hair and beard. Though the beard was little more than peach fuzz.

"Welcome, Emperor Allistor. I am Broogian, your humble servant. My apologies once more for my former superior's behavior upon your arrival." He bowed again, and the others followed his lead. When he finally raised his head and noticed the quantity of blood covering Allistor, his eyes widened, and a sick look crept across his face. He visibly gulped and began to wring his hands together in front of his belly. "Your... Majesty?"

Allistor looked down at the blood and chuckled. "You were correct about some of your crew not embracing the change of ownership."

Broogian looked unsteady, like he needed to sit down. Allistor imagined that if something similar had happened to Hel while she was on the station, Charon would have gotten his fourth purge order. Clearly the crew were expecting a similar reaction from him.

"Relax, all of you. Those who attacked us are dead. Some more dead than others." He shot a look at Helen, who smirked back at him. "I don't hold you responsible. While I certainly don't trust any of you yet, I'm not going to punish those who may be innocent just to satisfy some urge for vengeance."

All of the crew visibly relaxed. Broogian bowed again, causing all of them to do the same. It was becoming comical at that point. "Please, no more bowing. You'll pull a muscle or something." Allistor moved to take a seat in what would have been the captain's chair if this were a ship's bridge. The raiders behind him relaxed, leaning against the wall or sitting and zoning out to check their notifications. A few pulled out snacks.

"Broogian, do you or these others here know the crew well enough to know who's likely to oppose me?"

"I know some…" He responded, then looked around the room at the other five, who either nodded or shrugged, all of their eyes flicking nervously to Allistor and back. "But I doubt we could point out all of them. We were not encouraged to socialize when Hel was our mistress. Since her passing we've had to work together more than usual in order to survive, but even now I couldn't say I know a tenth of the crew very well."

"Alright, we'll do this another way." Allistor leaned forward in the chair. "Charon, please transmit my voice through the entire station." He waited a moment, then began.

"Crew of Charon station, this is Emperor Allistor again. I'm speaking to you from the control room. I've got a few things to tell you, so make yourselves comfortable." He paused for ten heartbeats before continuing. "First, two Spindlesprockets and their friends died trying to take my head a little while ago. They set an ambush, and paid the price. Any of you with similar thoughts, we'll be visiting you shortly, and you can take your shot."

Hearing himself growl as he spoke, he softened his tone. "But we didn't come here to fight. I inherited this station upon Hel's death, which I was indirectly responsible for. I have already claimed the station, and plan to continue its operation. Ideally with an experienced crew who understands its systems and processes." He let that sink in for a breath or two.

"I don't know how much information you've seen or heard about me, but I do my best to improve the lives of my citizens. No one is forced to work for me, except for a few nobles of a house that attacked one of my worlds. They are laboring for the families of those they killed as punishment for their misdeeds. Everyone else is free to live their lives as they see fit, with as much encouragement and assistance as I can provide. I'm told that all of your contracts with Hel expired upon her death. So you're all free to join me as citizens of Invictus, or to leave this station, as you choose. Before you decide, let me tell you a little about what it means to be a citizen of Invictus..."

He spent the next five minutes giving a slightly modified version of his usual recruitment speech, focusing on comparing their lives under Hel's rule to what they might be like under his. When he was done, he made the offer.

"So, any of you who wish to become citizens of Invictus, and either remain here and work on the station, or relocate to one of my worlds, all you have to do is take the oath now. Just repeat after Helen." He leaned back in the chair and waited as Helen recited the oath one line at a time. All of the crew in front of him happily repeated the oath, and he watched as the swirling lights indicated the System's acceptance of it.

"Charon, how many of the station's occupants are now citizens?"

"*Six thousand three hundred twenty three.*" the AI answered. A holographic three dimensional map of the station appeared in the air in front of him. Spread throughout the station were clusters of green and red dots, the green vastly outnumbering the red.

"Just under five hundred holdouts." Helen did the math quickly.

Allistor nodded. "I'm going to assume that some of you are declining my offer out of loyalty to Hel, or some sort of greed, maybe hoping to claim the station for yourselves. That's not going to happen." He took a deep breath and continued. "Some of you may have doubts about my sincerity. Or questions. If you have questions, call out Charon's name, then state your question, and he'll relay it to me."

The first question rang out about ten seconds later, in the voice of the one asking. Charon had recorded and replayed it. "How do we know you won't just kill us if we surrender?"

"I could have killed everyone on this station with a single command to cut off life support, without even stepping aboard. I could still do so right now. But I'd much rather have you as productive and loyal citizens of Invictus than corpses I have to dispose of."

The next question came the moment Allistor stopped speaking. "You killed our mistress! Why should we trust you?"

"I did not intend to kill Hel. I executed Loki for his crimes against my people. There were billions of humans on Earth before he triggered the apocalypse at a time when he knew it would cause the most deaths. He wiped out nearly our entire species, killing more than a million people for every one of you on this station. It seems that Loki's death triggered some kind of failsafe to ensure that his daughter, his nemesis, would not outlive him." Allistor would not have hesitated to kill Loki even if he knew that Hel would die as well. Though the collateral deaths involved would have given him pause. He didn't feel the need to explain any of that to these people.

The next question was more hostile. "Why don't you come here and kill us yourself, instead of having Charon do it. Coward!"

"Tell me where you are, and I'll do just that." Allistor growled. "I'll not leave any hostile crewmembers on this station. You can join me, you can leave, or you can die. It's that simple."

"How do we leave? There are no ships." A new voice inquired.

Allistor had to think about that one for a moment. He motioned for Charon to stop transmitting and turned to the crew in the room with him. "How large is the transport ship that's still at the asteroid? Would it hold several hundred people and enough supplies to get them to a planet?"

"Easily. Those ships were built to move massive amounts of cargo. If you empty the ore, there's plenty of room for all those who have not sworn." Broogian shook his head. "But that is a valuable asset. And the only ship left to use for transporting ore if you wish us to continue operations of this station. Assuming the ship is still operational."

"Ye could send one o' the goblin ships, Allistor." Longbeard offered. "They be large enough fer the job, and less valuable than the one yer thinkin' o givin' these mongrels."

"Why give them a ship at all?" Helen asked. "Have one of our crews take them somewhere and dump them. Use battle droids for guards to make sure they behave."

Allistor nodded, then asked Charon to transmit again. "Alright, here's your answer. I'll have a colony ship here in a few days. It will transport those of you who refuse to join us to the nearest inhabited planet. From there, you're on your own."

There was a long silence during which no more questions were posed. Allistor was about to order the non-citizens to surrender and gather somewhere, when a final question made him smile. "Could you repeat that oath? A few of us would like to swear..."

Helen didn't wait for him to ask. She began reciting the oath again, and when she was through, two hundred more citizens joined Invictus.

"Welcome to all you newcomers!" Allistor grinned up at the holo display that showed so many new green dots. "For those of you who wish to leave, stay where you are. We'll figure out a place to hold you until your transport gets here, then move you from whatever areas you're in now. Any attempt to damage or sabotage the station will result in the deaths of everyone in your area. So if you see someone about to do something stupid, I suggest you stop them." He looked at the holographic image of the station. "Those of you who are now citizens, you'll be released as quickly as we can get to you. Some of you are mixed in with folks who refused to swear the oath, and we'll have to come separate them out. Charon, please unseal only those areas where everyone is now a citizen."

He watched as the green dots began to leave their sections and filter throughout the open areas of the station. The red dots seemed to be concentrated mainly on a lower level of the station, with large clusters of them in three areas. There were other small groups and scattered single red dots on most levels, but Allistor decided to start with the bigger groups.

"Where's a good place to keep three hundred prisoners?"

Broogian considered it for a moment. "One of the smaller loading docks? That way if they try something, you can just open the outer door and vent the atmosphere."

"Good call. I probably wouldn't flush them all out into space, but they don't know that. Should keep them honest." He looked at the largest cluster, which was roughly fifty red dots. They probably wouldn't be a match for his twenty raiders, even if they were armed and intent on resisting. But he might take casualties, which he wasn't willing to risk. "Theado, contact Cogwalker and Gralen. Tell them I want twenty more bodies to help round up the holdouts. And bring the battle droids off of *Phoenix*. They can act as guards."

"I'll act as a guide, to show your people where the loading dock is." Broogian offered. Allistor nodded, and the crewman led the raiders out of the control room toward the lower decks. Allistor remained in his chair, studying the station holo. After just a moment, one of the sections started flashing red.

"Coolant distribution line has been damaged on deck nine, subsection C7." Charon reported.

Allistor motioned at the hologram, zooming it in on the flashing area. It was a section of corridor with only one inhabitant. A red dot.

He looked at Helen. "Let's go deal with this." She nodded and produced her bow as they both headed for the door. Their target was only a few levels down and a quarter of the way around that level from their location. Charon obligingly had an elevator waiting for them. When they stepped off on the correct level and turned toward their destination, they found several citizens already moving in that direction. The moment they spotted Allistor, they all dropped to their knees and bowed their heads.

"Please, get up. No need for that." Allistor spoke as he moved between them. "Where are you all headed?"

The citizen nearest him got to her feet. She looked to be another half-breed, at least part orcanin, though Allistor couldn't tell what her other ancestry might be.

"We saw the damage alert, and were on the way there to deal with the bastard doing the damage."

"I appreciate that." Allistor smiled at all of them. "I'll deal with them myself. But if any of you here are qualified to repair whatever the damage is, your assistance would be appreciated." He didn't wait to see if there were any volunteers. Turning back toward his destination, he broke into a jog. Helen fell into step right behind him, and he could hear what sounded like a whole crowd following. Shaking his head, he kept going.

In less than a minute they reached the bulkhead door that sealed off the section of the corridor containing the saboteur. "Charon, please open it." Allistor cast *Barrier* in front of himself as the door separated in half and pulled back to either side. The section was filled with a cold mist, likely from the damaged coolant line. Allistor could only see a few feet past the doors. He drew his sword and was about to step forward when a metal wrench flew out of the cold fog toward his face. It bounced off his barrier, then clanked on the floor beside him. A moment later the lone occupant of that section emerged.

Allistor would have said he was a goblin, but he was at least twice the size of any goblin he'd ever seen. He took a moment to stare at the angry creature.

> *Derglig*
> *Hobgoblin Engineer*
> *Level 31*
> *Health: 34,000/34,000*

"Murderer!" the hobgoblin shouted, pulling a plasma cutting torch from his inventory as he ran at Allistor, raising the torch like a club with blue flame at the end.

Allistor heard an arrow whistle past his shoulder, and a fraction of a second later the shaft was poking out of the crazed engineer's chest. The impact didn't knock him down, but it cut his momentum a good deal. Two steps later he slammed into Allistor's barrier, pushing the arrow deeper into him and smashing his face flat. This time he was knocked back off his feet to sprawl on the floor.

Bodies rushed past Allistor, and before he could do anything other than blink, there was a small mob of stomping, kicking citizens. They snarled and cursed at the hobgoblin, even spit on him as they beat the life out of him.

"Apparently Derglig wasn't a popular guy." Helen observed once the crowd backed away from the corpse. Allistor had noticed that several of them leveled up from the kill.

The female half-orcanin wiped some brain matter stuck to the sole of her boot on the hobgoblin's pants, then turned to Allistor, bowing just her head this time. "Thank you for the opportunity to end that scum."

"Um, sure?" Allistor hadn't exactly offered them the opportunity. He just hadn't killed the creature fast enough to beat them to it. "Was he a bully?"

"Worse. He was an informer. He would lure people into illegal trades, or convince them to steal from the mistress, then turn them in to the overseers to collect a reward, including the experience from their deaths. The traitor was only level twenty five when I got here." She hung her head as she continued.

"He made advances toward my younger sister last year, and when she rejected him, he reported her for inciting insurrection. She was no insurrectionist, and he offered no proof. But it didn't matter. They stripped her naked, publicly whipped her with a pain flail to make an example, then flushed her out the airlock the next day." She took a ragged breath, clearly emotional. "It felt good to crush his skull and avenge her." Several citizens who had gathered behind her nodded their heads in agreement.

"Happy to oblige, and I'm sorry for your loss." Allistor offered. "He's yours to loot, assuming he was carrying anything valuable."

One of the crowd stepped forward holding a heavy looking pouch. "He only had a few klax, and this bag of gems." They looked and sounded disappointed.

Allistor remembered hearing that the crew used the gems as currency on the station. "What's wrong with the gems?"

"Nothing wrong with them, they're just not worth much to us. We use them for stakes in our poker games here on the station. Or in the rare event we were able to travel to the mistress's moon, we could trade them for goods in the market. Extra rations, basic tools, a bottle of brandy…" The loot holder explained. "But now the moon is gone."

"We could also manage the occasional bribe of senior officers for days off, better quarters, or a trip to the moon. But they're all gone, too."

Allistor shook his head and held out his hand. "Can I see them?" When the bag was placed in his palm, he opened it and poured out part of the contents. There were diamonds, sapphires, emeralds, and others. "First, you are now citizens of Invictus. You are free to travel where you like, no bribes necessary. Second, I think these might be more valuable than you've been led to believe." He poured the loose gems back into the bag, then hefted it in his palm. "I can't claim to know their exact value, but I'll offer you five hundred gold coins for the bagful. I can use them to help me level up my enchanting. Or you can divide the gems up amongst yourselves and hold on to them until you reach a more… honest marketplace than it sounds like the one on Hel's moon might have been."

The half-orcanin didn't hesitate. "We'll accept your gold." The others behind her murmured agreement. "But first, I am honor bound to confess to you that I was among those ready to fight you and your people when you arrived. Had you not sealed us in where we were, I'd have been among those who planned to attack you in the landing bay." She bowed her head as if ready to accept punishment. The others all took a couple steps back and to either side, not wanting to get caught in whatever blast of magic they expected Allistor to unleash.

"What changed your mind?" Allistor was curious.

"You did. I listened to your first speech, and frankly thought you were just another smooth-talking tyrant planning to trick us into swearing an oath rather than having to fight us. Then the questions began, and you pointed out that you could have killed us without effort, and that got me thinking. I asked Charon what level you were, and when he told us, I knew that you could single-handedly kill us all one at a time without much effort if you chose to. But what finally convinced me was when you offered to transport those of us who hadn't sworn your oath to an inhabited planet. Not just habitable, where we might be marooned, but inhabited. The fact that you cared enough about people who rejected you to make sure that they would have a chance to survive... that convinced me. I was among the second group to take the oath."

"As was I." The looter spoke up. "Most of us here had no hope of a life outside of this station. We are... *were* mostly indentured. Sold by our families to absolve their own debts. I was a mercenary, captured in battle and sold to slavers who had contracts with the mistress. I was assigned a level of debt that would have taken me two lifetimes to repay. The fact that you were willing to release and relocate us after we refused to comply with your wishes, even though we are completely at your mercy, convinced me that the rest of your promises might be truthful."

"Well I thank you, all of you, for coming to my rescue just now." He winked at them, eliciting a few chuckles. Putting the bag of gems into his inventory, he quickly counted ten citizens gathered around and produced ten stacks of fifty gold, handing a stack to each of them. "I assume that you each have your own bags of *currency* as well. I'll set up a system where you can sell them to me at their true market value, or as I said before, you can take them with you should you choose to leave the station. And while I'd appreciate you staying to help run this place, I won't demand it. Or even ask it of you. You're absolutely free to go where you want and be whatever you want from this point forward."

*****

Over the next few hours Allistor's people cleared the station of red dots. They began with the largest cluster, entering the hostile area as a single large group. There was minor resistance, a few of the station crewmembers perished, the rest got rounded up, and Allistor's people received only minor injuries. When the large clusters were dealt with, the raiders broke into smaller groups and quickly spread out through the station to gather up the smaller clusters and individual red dots. Only a few resisted, and by the time they were all herded into one of the loading bays, only a dozen had been killed. Those that were injured had been healed by Allistor's people, then restrained. The group was given food and water, and warned against misbehaving, lest the bay door be opened and they all get flushed into space.

Cogwalker sent a shuttle to the asteroid to fetch the cargo transport and assess the mining operation. Then he flooded the station with his clan, all of them itching to work on station repairs. Each of his engineers was assigned a team of several new citizens to assist in the work. With a workforce of six thousand crew and a couple hundred dwarven engineers, repairs went quickly. By the time the goblin colony ship arrived two days later to transport the prisoners, the station was back to eighty percent functionality. Cogwalker made good use of the refined metals stored on the station, and even sacrificed a few components from his ship when necessary. Allistor promised to compensate him for whatever he needed to use.

Broogian had guessed correctly, the transport ship's crew had died when Hel did. Their ship had been on the lee side of the asteroid when the moon exploded, and other than some strain to the docking clamps, had suffered no damage. Cogwalker's crew finished loading the ship and brought it back so that the station crew could resume refining operations.

Helen, Anderson, and Theado set up several long tables in the landing bay next to *Phoenix*, and along with ten other raiders who volunteered to help, they met with each of the new citizens to find out what skills they had and what they wanted to do. It took nearly a week to organize and speak with them all, during which time Allistor explored the station, then the asteroid, and spent some time in one of the engineering sections crafting. Much to the amusement of those working around him.

From the first day, Helen reported an unfortunate trend. More than half of the crewmembers they spoke to that day wanted to leave the station. Each subsequent day was roughly the same. At that rate, they would not have enough bodies remaining to operate the station. No way was Allistor going to go back on his word and require any of them to stay. So he called together his advisors, as well as Gralen and Cogwalker.

"I've been questioning Broogian and a few others. It sounds like we'd need at least five thousand minimum crew to keep this place running. Optimally more like eight thousand when you figure in support and security personnel."

Longbeard and Cogwalker both nodded. Harmon spoke up. "My own station above Orion requires seven thousand staff, and we're not doing any mining or refining."

"Which has me thinking." Allistor nodded as he spoke. "How hard would it be to move this station? And the asteroid we're mining?"

Cogwalker laughed, giving Longbeard a wink. "We been wonderin' how long it would take ye ta ask." He stroked his beard as he grinned at Allistor. "We've already sent fer the ship we'll be needin to tow the station. I'll use me own ship to tow the asteroid. It'll take a week ta get em both to Orion, if that's where ye want em."

Longbeard added. "I took a shuttle out past that asteroid to the next nearest. It be not as large, but has most o' the same mineral content. If I were you, oh wise and beneficent Emperor, I would claim this system and all the asteroids in it, if ye can. At least, claim the nearby planet and a couple o' the asteroids, and tow them home. There be great wealth here. When Hel were alive, none would dare to try and claim it. But when word gets out…"

"There will likely be a gold rush, so to speak. Meaning that this station wouldn't be safe here either unless I left a fleet of warships to protect it."

"Maybe not even then." Harmon offered.

"Alright, we move the station. Which apparently is no surprise to anyone but me." He mock scowled at the two dwarves. "Now, how do I go about finding out details on this system, whether any of the worlds are occupied, and how I might go about claiming it all?"

Helen snort-laughed at the casual manner in which he talked about taking ownership of an entire star system. "Emperor Fancypants. Who would have thought the nervous boy who found me in that cellar would turn out to be the ruler of a galaxy?"

"Shut up, this is mostly your fault." He glared at her. "Besides, I'm nowhere near the ruler of a galaxy."

She poked him in the belly and gave him a sideways look. "Not yet, you're not."

Chapter Twenty Six

The Thing About Griblins

It turned out that there were three inhabited worlds out of the seven situated within the same system as Hel's moon and Charon station. All three were already inducted into the Collective. The first was the planet that Hel's moon base had previously orbited. As it turned out, this was also where the station crew holdouts had been dropped off. The other two were both closer to the sun.

As his people worked to settle the station's crews, Allistor learned what his advisors could gather for him about all three worlds. All had been owned by Hel, and were now in upheaval as those in power on each world, who'd survived her death, fought over the right to rule in her place. As it was on the station, the most powerful and influential had been bonded to Hel, and their deaths left a tremendous power vacuum.

The nearest world was sparsely populated, and Hel had used it to provide food and other resources for the inhabitants of her moon and station. Three major cities had grown on its surface, along with thousands of small farming towns.

L'olwyn and Selby had come to the station along with the goblin ship, and they took the lead in contacting the inhabitants of the three worlds. In each case there was no longer a single recognized governmental entity, so the process took two full days of reaching out to the leaders of the most powerful factions. For the first world, which was named Triendal, each of the cities had a ruling faction that was trying to conquer the others. Allistor invited them all to the station, but none were willing to place themselves in his hands. Eventually they were convinced to meet in neutral territory on the planet's surface, each of them bringing a contingent of security personnel.

The meeting was set at a spaceport Hel used to supply her people. It was a wide open space with a single colossal building. From the roof of that structure one could see for miles in every direction. As Kira lowered Phoenix to hover a foot or so above the roof, Allistor observed the three factions. They were spaced far apart, each of them consisting of twenty heavily armed guards and between one and three representatives.

He stepped off the cargo ramp with Harmon at his side, Longbeard, L'olwyn, and Selby right behind them, and ten battle droids formed up in a half circle around them, shields and plasma weapons at the ready. Doing his best to look both serene and friendly, Allistor marched forward to the center of the triangle formed by the three factions. The representatives also stepped forward, leaving their details in place by previous agreement. This whole meeting had been strictly choreographed by L'olwyn ahead of time.

The representatives halted twenty paces from Allistor and bowed at the waist. None of them spoke, waiting for him to begin the proceedings. Instead of greeting them right away, he motioned to his advisors. They moved in front of him and began producing chairs they'd grabbed from the station, one for each representative. The chairs were placed in an arc in front of Allistor, who produced his own, much fancier chair that he'd stolen from Hel's private quarters on the station. Harmon planted a much larger chair next to his. He and the big merchant took their seats, then Allistor motioned for the others to do the same.

"Please, take a seat. We have much to discuss." He kept his tone neutral. Reports were that the fighting between the three factions had been brutal, and that thousands of civilians had been killed, both in the cities and in the smaller farming towns that happened to be in the way.

The representatives all bowed again before sitting. There were a total of six of them, three from one city, two from another, and just one from the third city. Allistor took a moment to catch each of their eyes before continuing. "I appreciate your willingness to meet with me. It is my understanding that you've all been involved in a brutal conflict since shortly after Hel's demise. I'm hoping to put an end to that conflict." He leaned back in his chair, carefully placing his hands on the arms of the chair, resisting the urge to squeeze them.

"Before I offer you my proposal, I want to be sure that you know your current situation. For some five thousand years I'm told Hel has held this system in an iron grip. Your people have both suffered, and thrived, under her protection." He waited for them to react. A few nodded their heads, the single representative, a humanoid with golden hair and mottled black and silver skin, just smirked.

"That protection is now gone. Across the galaxy wars have broken out much like the one you're fighting now. But these wars are a hundred, a thousand times larger. They span whole star systems, and in a few cases multiple systems. Worlds are being destroyed, entire civilizations wiped out. The only reason you haven't witnessed this for yourselves is that those who might come for you are busy attacking or defending more valuable assets elsewhere. Make no mistake, it won't be long before they settle things closer to the core and turn their gazes your direction, and come to take what's yours."

The representatives all looked uncomfortable now, likely imagining themselves losing everything they'd gained.

"Now, what I'm offering is this. As Emperor of Invictus, I already own several planets, and have been fortunate in earning several powerful allies. I had planned to simply claim the station above that the System awarded to me. Circumstances have changed since I arrived, and I have altered my plans to compensate. What I propose is that you recognize my authority as Emperor of Triendal. You will each maintain control of your individual cities and some portion of the surrounding lands. I will take ownership of the rest, minus the properties already owned and being farmed in the outlying towns, which I will grant to their current occupants. You will do the same within your cities, keeping the properties you currently own, allowing the citizens who already own property to retain theirs. That, and the complete abolition of slavery, are my two absolute requirements. In return, I will bring some of my own people, and those of my allies, to your world. We will enter into mutual protection agreements, and ensure that other, much harsher masters do not take your world, and your lives." Again he paused to watch their reactions, this time waiting a full thirty seconds. The two larger delegations leaned in and muttered amongst themselves, while the lone representative just smirked again.

"I will give you one day to consider my offer, discuss it with whomever you need to. During that time I'll be making the same offer to the other two inhabited worlds in this system."

The lone smirker called out. "Might we ask a few questions, Emperor Allistor?"

"Certainly. Ask away." Allistor leaned forward slightly.

"What will you do if we refuse?" The smirk widened into a full sneer, and Allistor began to dislike him.

"Well, that depends on what the other worlds choose to do. If all of you reject my offer, I may just take my station, a few of the nearby asteroids, and leave you to your fate. If you refuse, and the others accept, then I may move my station into orbit near them, drag some of the asteroids into orbit, and consolidate my interests there, leaving you alone to suffer whatever invaders eventually arrive. It may be that they'll wipe you out and then seek an alliance with me."

The sneer faded from his face. He'd clearly expected Allistor to threaten invasion, and had planned to use that as leverage to frighten the others into joining him. Instead, Allistor had done the very same thing, using an unknown outside threat, making himself seem the safer, wiser option.

One of the paired representatives asked, "Who are the powerful allies you speak of?"

Allistor was actually a little surprised that they didn't already know, he was so used to the aliens he encountered having been watching him and aware of his situation. He blinked once, then answered. "My closest ally is Emperor Harmon of the Orcanin Empire, whom I also consider a close friend." He bowed his head to Harmon, who returned the gesture before flashing a tusk-filled grin at the representatives. "I also count as friends and allies House Or'Dralon, the Lighthammer and Stardrifter clans, and the Azure Order, all of whom have established settlements on my various planets. Other factions have expressed interest in joining, and I expect many more will follow in the coming days."

The leader of the third city's representatives asked, "Why would such powerful factions wish to ally themselves with a youngling such as yourself? Our informants tell us your world was just inducted less than two years ago." The tone of the question was, if not outright hostile, at least condescending.

"Well, it's more like they've allowed me to ally myself with them. But to answer your question, it is because I control a newly stabilized world with a very high mana density after Loki caused the deaths of several billion of my people. And because I own two eternity gates, one of which I placed in orbit around Orion, a world I seized from some goblins who made the mistake of attacking my homeworld. Lastly, it is because I have given them generous chunks of my various worlds and assets, making it in their best interests to help me defend them."

The representatives eyes widened at the mention of the gates, and he simply nodded his head in acknowledgement.

The smirker, sensing another opportunity, asked, "Will you be placing your remaining gate here in our system?" The greed in his eyes was plain to see. Behind Allistor, Selby snorted.

"That is a possibility." Allistor replied, then shook his head. "But for purposes of your current decision making, assume that I will not be placing a gate here."

Foiled again, the smirker frowned and crossed his arms.

Silence reigned for nearly a minute as Allistor allowed them to whisper amongst themselves a bit more. When no new questions arose, he thumped his hands on the arms of his chair, getting their attention. "Hearing no other questions, I'll leave you now. I've got two other worlds to visit today." He stood unexpectedly, forcing the others to stand as well so as not to offend. They quickly offered deeper bows than previously, and waited for him to acknowledge them. "I'll return at the same time tomorrow to hear your decisions."

Not waiting to see their reaction, he stored his chair back in his inventory, turned and walked with Harmon and the others to the *Phoenix*. They left the chairs for the representatives behind.

*****

The conversations on the other two worlds went much the same, though on the last planet, the meeting took an unexpected turn. Vinarin was the closest planet to the system's sun, and the six representatives that showed up for the meeting were all griblins. Allistor made his speech for the third time that day, and the diminutive beings listened politely. Their faces remained mostly neutral, with just the occasional head bob giving him the only indication that they were actually listening.

L'olwyn had insisted they bring several of Cogwalker's Stardrifter griblins along for the meeting. They had stood patiently behind Allistor as he spoke, and though he couldn't see it, they gave occasional smiles and quick waves to the planet's representatives as he spoke. When it came time for him to ask for questions, the lead Vinarin griblin motioned toward those behind him. "We wish to speak with our cousins."

This development not being unexpected, Allistor nodded. "Of course." He waved them forward, and the discussion quickly became much livelier. There were smiles and hugs exchanged between the griblins, then a group discussion during which they all seemed to speak at the same time, yet understand each other just fine. The exchange lasted about ten minutes, during most of which the Stardrifter griblins seemed to be telling an animated tale. When it was over, they all turned toward Allistor. There was much head-nodding amongst them before they all took a knee and bowed their head.

They hadn't said anything more to him, so it was a surprise when he received three notifications.

System Alert!

Emperor Allistor of Invictus has been acknowledged as Emperor of the planet Vinarin!
May he rule long and wisely!

Congratulations! The inhabitants of Planet Vinarin have elected you their Emperor!
> *For acts of kindness and understanding, the respect you showed the griblins you have encountered, and your impressive achievements as Emperor of Invictus, the griblins of Vinarin have elected you their Emperor.*

Level up! You are now Level One Hundred! You have earned ten attribute points.

The surprise was quickly replaced by lightheadedness as the effects of reaching the milestone level of one hundred flooded his system. Had he been standing, his legs would have given out, and his first act as planetary emperor would have been to fall on his butt in front of his new subjects. The rush that normally accompanied a level increase was multiplied tenfold upon reaching level one hundred. And instead of the usual two free attribute points, he'd been awarded ten.

When he finally came down from the short-lived high, he saw everyone staring at him expectantly, the griblins still on one knee. Taking a deep breath, he carefully pushed himself to his feet. Favoring the griblins with his warmest smile, he dipped his head slightly. "I am honored that you have chosen me as your Emperor, and I pledge to do my utmost to protect you, to help you grow stronger, and happier."

There was an enthusiastic cheer as the griblins jumped to their feet, waving hands in the air and clapping each other on the back. There were hugs all around, and a few of the little guys even mobbed L'olwyn in a group hug, which he tolerated with a hint of a smile. None dared to approach Harmon or Allistor for hugs, but Allistor didn't mind. Helen gave him a sympathetic pat on the back after she'd been practically buried in griblins herself, then set free. She didn't even complain about the several gropings she'd felt.

The parties were invited into a nearby town square, where an impromptu feast was quickly arranged. Not having any particular plans until morning, Allistor gladly stayed to enjoy the friendly hospitality, even calling Kira, William, and the *Phoenix* crew out to join the celebration. Before the food was served, all of the ten thousand plus griblins in the town took a knee and swore the oath Helen recited for them. The lead representative, whom Allistor learned was named Beedalin, promised that runners would be sent to every settlement on the planet, and all its inhabitants would swear the oath within a week.

The celebration extended well into the night. Food was eaten, spirits consumed. L'olwyn insisted on tasting any food offered to Allistor before he ate it, and Longbeard did the same with the drinks. The dwarves both got roaring drunk, singing and dancing with the griblins along with Selby, who at one point danced atop a table, garnering thunderous cheers and applause from the griblins. Along with several dozen marriage proposals, and others that were less committed.

Allistor and company slept aboard the *Phoenix* that night, and enjoyed a hearty breakfast with the griblins just after sunrise. Longbeard and Cogwalker supported each other as they stumbled down the cargo ramp, suffering epic hangovers. After a good meal and a couple of snorts of brandy, they were both feeling much better. Selby slept right through breakfast, but L'olwyn considerately saved her a heaping plate.

They spent the balance of the morning on Vinarin while L'olwyn worked out some logistical details with the griblins, and Harmon negotiated a trade agreement. Hel had claimed the planet in a brutal fashion, killing more than half of its population in the process. The griblins that remained had served her for hundreds of generations, living at just above subsistence level while she took the fruits of their labor. They were ranchers, for the most part, raising and breeding several species of livestock. There were also limited mining operations – spice, not metal, large fishing fleets harbored on the coasts of the planet's three oceans, and a significant leather products trade fed by the hides of the butchered livestock.

Without Hel confiscating most of their products, the griblins were already living better than they had in millennia. They were in the midst of establishing a more robust barter economy amongst themselves, and were thrilled to hear that they could now sell or trade their excess through off-world markets to obtain better tools, clothes, and even luxury items.

By the time Allistor left their planet, the little griblins had warmed his heart, and reduced his anxiety considerably. At least for a little while. It was time to return to the first planet, Triendal, and deal with the smirker and his cohorts. Allistor wasn't looking forward to the encounter, but was hopeful that the threat of invasion from harsher factions would convince them to cooperate.

Phoenix had just entered the atmosphere and was coming out of the heat bubble that surrounded her upon entry, when alarms began to blare on the bridge. "Incoming missiles!" Brooke reported from the sensors station. The main screen, which had just been showing heat distortion during entry, cleared up in time to show several dozen projectiles headed their way at great speed.

"Weapons! Defensive systems!" Kira barked, the weapons officer already way ahead of her. Defensive turrets across the hull were already sending a storm of anti-missile fire in a wave ahead of *Phoenix*. "Shields at maximum! Sensors, find out where they came from!"

Allistor braced himself against a rail as the missiles raced toward them. The first several intersected with the defensive fire and disappeared in clouds of fire and shrapnel, some of which helped to destroy or disable other missiles coming in behind them.

Kira executed a steep dive, hoping the missiles would simply pass on by, but had no such luck. The missiles were intelligent enough to alter their course to match hers. Cursing loudly, she turned *Phoenix* into a sharp one hundred eighty degree turn and pushed the throttle to maximum, hoping to outrun the weapons. The defensive fire never ceased, and nearly half of the missiles had been destroyed before reaching *Phoenix*. But there were still at least two dozen in the air, closing quickly.

Harmon growled. "Treacherous dogs! They timed the strike so that our sensors would be blinded by re-entry. A smart move, but one that will cost them dearly when it fails."

Kira shouted at her daughter. "Coms! Alert the other ships! We're going to need backup!"

Hillary turned in her seat, her eyes wide as they shifted from her mother back to the viewscreen. "Already done, Captain! ETA eight minutes for *Opportunity*, fifteen for Cogwalker's ship. His people were mostly on the station." Cogwalker cursed loudly at that, causing the girl to shoot him a nervous look.

"Sorry, young lass. I be angry with meself, not with you. Ye tell me ship I said to launch now, do not wait for the full crew. If there be a pilot and a gunner, that be enough!"

Hillary nodded once and dutifully relayed the message, giving him a thumbs-up when the ship replied. "ETA for your ship now eight minutes."

The ship rocked as a missile penetrated the defensive fire and exploded against the shield. Another explosion immediately followed, and the shield visibly flashed a dark red. There was a brief reprieve when the defensive systems managed to hold back the next wave, but it was short-lived. Three more missiles got through and struck nearly simultaneously. The shield flared again, then disappeared.

"Shields are down!" Kira shouted unnecessarily. "Six more missiles incoming!"

Allistor and everyone else on the bridge held their breath as first one, then another missile exploded out in front of them. A single missile got through, wobbling slightly as its navigation controls were damaged by antiballistic rounds, but still managing to impact the underside of Phoenix's hull. The ship rocked with the impact, more alarms blaring over the screech of bending metal. Nigel's voice rang out.

"Hull breach. Aft engineering section and cargo hold. Repair bots dispatched."

Cogwalker and Longbeard rushed off the bridge, intending to serve as damage control. After a brief hesitation, Helen ran after them to lend whatever help she could. Down in the cargo bay, half a dozen battle droids activated and made their way toward engineering.

Kira growled as she banked the ship hard to the left to avoid another missile that made it through. The projectile adjusted, but was already too close to achieve a proper angle of impact. It's nose skidded off the top of Phoenix's hull then angled away a second before exploding. The force of the blast still rocked the ship, but wasn't strong enough to do more than scorch the hull.

The very last remaining missile made it through when two of the defensive turrets paused for the two seconds it took to reload. The missile grew larger on the viewscreen so rapidly that several of the bridge crew leaned back in fear or ducked down and covered their heads. The impact struck the nose of the ship, causing her to shudder. Fire washed across her hull and over the cameras that fed the viewscreen. For a moment, all the crew could see was fire. Brooke whimpered at her station, terrified. Hillary abandoned her post to grab hold of her sister and comfort her.

There was a crackling sound, and the weapons station lit up with a surge of power. The missile strike had caused some kind of power feedback, which fried the unfortunate young man whose hands were laid upon it. He seized up, his hair crisping on his head, a strangled scream cut off as his insides cooked. A moment later he slumped in his chair. Allistor had already cast one heal on him, and instantly tried another, as did Kira and several of the crew members. None of the spells registered.

Allistor gagged as the smell of cooking meat filled the bridge. A few of the traumatized crew members vomited up their breakfasts as Brooke wailed into Hillary's shoulder. Kira had tears rolling down her cheeks as she fought to keep the ship under control.

"I'm landing her right here, right now! We can't leave with open hull breaches." She called out to Allistor. "Hillary, back in your chair! Everyone buckle up! Allistor…" She stopped and gulped once, looking at the weapons station, then at William standing next to her, unable to finish vocalizing her order. Understanding, he grabbed the boy and moved to the weapons station. As gently as he could, he pried the corpse loose from the chair and set it off to one side, then sat William in the seat. Seeing that the harness was mostly melted, he produced a rope from his inventory and quickly wrapped it several times around a complaining William and the chair, securing the boy against a rough landing.

The viewscreen cleared up, though the image was not as sharp as usual due to the camera lenses taking some heat damage. Allistor saw that the ship was descending rapidly before shifting his gaze from the approaching ground to the sky ahead of them, searching for more missiles.

"Nigel, our weapons station is down. If there are more incoming threats, we need you to take control of weapons!" he called out.

"Of course, Sire. I will exhaust every resource to protect you. I request that you allow me to harvest some of

the metal resources in engineering to manufacture more antiballistic rounds."

"Do whatever you need to do. Authorized." Allistor replied, placing a hand on William's shoulder. The boy was creeped out over being in the chair where a friend had just died. His gaze kept falling to the burnt corpse on the floor not far away, and he hugged himself tightly, tucking his hands up into his armpits so as not to touch the console.

Allistor couldn't help but look at the young man's corpse as well. He was the same kid that had nearly started a war with the Or'Dralon on their first trip into space. Allistor had spent some time with the kid since then, and often teased him. Now he was gone, like so many others, in a pointless attack launched by greedy, small-minded... "They're gonna pay for this." Allistor growled loud enough that the crew heard him. Harmon grunted and nodded his agreement, as did Kira and a few of the crew.

"Shields recharged and active." The crewman on shields reported.

"Great, thank you." Kira barely acknowledged them as she focused on landing the ship. Her gaze flicked back and forth between the viewscreen and the navigation hologram in front of her chair. As she scanned the horizon, she saw what she was looking for. "There!" Allistor watched as she touched a point on the hologram, and the viewscreen altered its focus. He saw a strip of forest that nearly butted up against a steep cliff that rose maybe thirty feet above the treetops. "That'll offer us some protection if they launch more missiles."

535

Allistor bit his lip as Kira expertly maneuvered the ship into the gap between the cliff and the thick cluster of trees, then set her down. The landing was rougher than usual, but Allistor didn't complain even a little bit. "Great flying, Kira." He smiled at her, surprised to see her flash with a golden glow as she leveled up.

"I got a quest from the System to land the ship without killing you. Leveled up, and bumped my piloting skill up two points." She explained.

Allistor just nodded, unwrapping William so he could get out of the chair. The boy immediately ran toward their quarters to change his clothes, hiding the tears on his face as best he could. Allistor produced a blanket and wrapped the burned crewman in it. Looking up to Kira, who had been watching him even as her two girls piled into her lap and held her tightly, he asked, "Do you want to evacuate the ship? Or stay here?"

Kira shook her head, stroking her girls' hair before gently pushing them to stand upright. "We stay here. Shields are back up, and the defense system will get some help from the terrain. This is the safest place we can be. Reinforcements will arrive in a couple minutes." She gave Hillary and Brooke a gentle nudge. "Back to your stations."

Harmon added, "I doubt they have many more missiles to launch, or they would have sent them with the first attack. Likely they were a stolen cache waiting to be shipped to one of Hel's facilities or ships. She would not have left a significant arsenal on a planet that might rebel."

"Or that's how many they've managed to manufacture since she died." Allistor offered. Either way, he agreed with Kira's judgement in staying on the ship. "Brooke, I mean... sensors, have you been able to determine where the missiles were launched from?"

The girl turned toward him, a look of shame on her tear-stained face. She shook her head, and replied in a meek, shaken voice. "I... I got the data, but I can't re... remember how to..." She hung her head in defeat.

"Not to worry, little one." Harmon moved to her station and scooped her up with one hand. He sat down in her seat, looking like a linebacker visiting a kindergarten classroom and sitting in the little chairs. Lifting her up and setting her on his shoulder, he quickly manipulated the sensor console as she watched. The little girl looked like a small show monkey sitting on an organ-grinder's shoulder. "Here we go." Harmon sent a command and Kira's hologram shifted to a view of the planet from above. Allistor could see all three major cities, and after a few seconds, missiles rose up from each of them, coming together in the air where *Phoenix* had been.

"So they cooperated in attacking us." Kira stated the obvious.

L'olwyn and Shelby entered the bridge just then, in time to see the holographic missile launch replay. "Oh, my." The elf shook his head, then noticed the wrapped body on the deck. "On, no."

Selby was much more forceful in her reaction, cussing loudly and stomping closer to the hologram to get a better look. Her face was growing red with anger. "They nearly killed us all. They did kill one of us. I say we glass this planet and start again!"

Allistor had a similar inclination. "Coms, instruct Gralen to take up station above us while we make repairs. Cogwalker's ship is to stop here and pick him up, then proceed to the nearest city. I have a message for them."

Chapter Twenty Seven

Vengeance For The Lost

Allistor paced back and forth in the cargo bay as people worked around him. His two other ships had arrived, and both offloaded some people to help with repairs to the *Phoenix*. They had inspected the three areas that got hit, and put together a plan to speed up repairs. The ship's bots, controlled by Nigel, were hard at work even before she landed. But the dwarven engineers who'd been able to make it onto Cogwalker's ship before it departed were much faster.

Cogwalker himself stayed to help with repairs, leaving his first mate to undertake the mission Allistor gave them. Before taking up position above the *Phoenix*, Gralen and his beastkin gently removed the weapons officer's body and stored him in one of the ship's void cabinets to be returned to Earth. Nigel had informed them that the kid had both a father and mother back at Cheyenne. Allistor was not looking forward to telling them that their son had survived the apocalypse and all the battles that came after, just to be killed by some backwater planet alien assholes.

While repairs were underway, the dwarven ship traveled to each of the cities, a small swarm of drones deployed around it in case of more missile launches. The ship was directed to hover above each city, and transmit a message on all channels, as well as via loudspeaker. The dwarves turned up the volume loud enough to shake the buildings below when they played Allistor's recorded message.

"People of Triendal, this is Emperor Allistor of Invictus. Yesterday I met with the leaders of your three major cities. I offered them an opportunity to become a part of my empire, a peaceful alliance. A chance for all of you to be free, to thrive, rather than fall victim to the coming wars for territory and resources. I made the same offer to the other two inhabited worlds in this system as well. As you may have seen, one of those worlds has already accepted my offer. I came back here today, in good faith and in peace, to meet with your representatives and hear their answer." Allistor's voice switched to a growl as the message continued.

"Their answer was a cowardly sneak attack on my ship as we were blinded by entry into your atmosphere. I'm sure most of you noticed the missiles launching from your cities, since they came from all three. That attack killed a young member of my crew, and nearly killed the rest of us aboard my ship. This was an overt act of war. As of that moment, your world, specifically your three cities and all the occupants within, are at war with Invictus!" He paused to let that news sink in for a moment.

"I'm going to kill those responsible for the attack. The ship hovering above you right now has the capability to flatten your entire city in a matter of moments. You citizens of the cities have two choices. You can round up those responsible for attacking me, bring them to the place where we met yesterday for execution, and we can discuss options for peace when they're dead. Their dead bodies are just as good, as long as they're identifiable. Or you can try to flee your cities before I flatten them. You have one hour."

After playing the message over each city the ship moved on to the next, covering all three in about twenty minutes. It then moved to hover over the meeting location to monitor any activity there. Drones were spread out miles in every direction to detect any hostile activity, movement of weapons, or evidence that the people were complying with Allistor's ultimatum.

All three ships were monitoring communications between the cities. Immediately after the first message was delivered, the three representatives from that city began calling the smirker in the third city, filling him in on Allistor's message. They berated him for the attack's failure, accused him of convincing them to start a war based on false assumptions, and threatened to take his head if they survived the day. The smirker scoffed at them, called them cowards and weaklings. Their transmissions were cut off abruptly mid-threat, and Allistor hoped it was because the citizens rose up and took them. Allistor had expected at least one group to contact him and plead innocence, claim that a few unauthorized rebels launched the missiles without them even knowing. But none of the groups bothered.

To Allistor's great surprise, shortly after the message was played above the third city, the smirker sent a transmission directly to him. "Emperor Allistor, I'll be there at the appointed time. My people had nothing to do with the attack, and I won't allow you to kill innocents because of my failure. Please do not hold them responsible. Please do not destroy my city."

If Allistor didn't already know that he was the driving force behind the attack, he might have respected the smirker for taking responsibility and willingly showing up for his execution.

Before the hour was half gone, drone feeds began showing people streaming out of the cities. A small convoy of ground vehicles exiting the first city was attacked, resulting in a running battle between the six vehicles in the convoy and a dozen others that rushed to surround them. Allistor and his advisors watched the transmitted live feed. Eventually the convoy was halted, the vehicles disabled. Its occupants were dragged from the vehicles after a staggering number of losses for the attackers. More than half of those who went to capture the convoy were killed.

The second city, the smallest of the three, showed no signs of evacuating. Instead a series of shield domes went up one by one, followed by a single massive dome that covered the entire city. Gun turrets could be seen appearing atop taller buildings. "Someone must have seized control of the city and begun building defenses." Allistor shook his head. They were putting him in a tough situation, which he supposed was the point. They were calling his bluff, forcing him to let them be, or kill many thousands of civilians in an attack.

With *Phoenix* still being repaired, Allistor and his advisors boarded *Opportunity* and hitched a ride to the meeting place. The ship hovered over the same spot as the previous day, with Cogwalker's crew higher up on overwatch, monitoring their fleet of drones. It was only a minute or so before a large group of locals dragged a half dozen others into view, dropping them a dozen or so paces in front of where Allistor had resumed his seat. One of the armed crowd motioned toward the group on the floor. "These are the ones who attacked you."

Allistor looked at each of them in turn, recognizing three of them as the representatives he'd met the day before. "I know these three. Who are the others?"

The new representative pointed to the three one at a time. "This one is their security chief. This one the tech who actually fired the weapons, which that one transported into the city overnight." He spat on the ground near the prisoners. "We did not know they would attack you, Emperor Allistor. We thought they would accept your offer until the missiles launched." Allistor stared at the speaker, but saw no indication that they were lying. Of course his entire experience with this species consisted of a single short meeting the day before.

"They speak the truth, as far as I know." The smirker walked toward them, alone and seemingly relaxed. "It took me half of the night to convince the others to attack you, and the rest of the night to organize the distribution of the missiles. I made the others promise to keep it all a secret, in case you already had spies in our midst."

"You don't seem to regret your actions." Allistor observed.

The smirker bowed his head slightly, mockingly. "I do not. I saw an opportunity to gain power and wealth quickly, and I took it. I had a solid plan, or so I thought. My plan failed, and I pay for it with my life. You cannot win big without great risk."

Allistor agreed, to a point. Looking at the others, still sitting on the ground, he asked, "Can you confirm that these six were involved as the others have reported?"

"I can, and do. Along with another half dozen in the other city. Which I understand has decided to fight you. This makes me sad. Many innocents will perish for the pride and obstinacy of a few."

"That is the way of war." Harmon replied, his voice calm, his tone sorrowful.

"Will you spare my people?" The smirker asked, then glanced at the other group. "Our people? Our two cities have met your demands, after all."

"I will give them all the opportunity to swear the oath we spoke about, to become citizens of Invictus. Those who refuse, or resist... I am not sure yet what I'll do with them."

The leader of the mob from the first city stepped forward. "Our society is not genetically diverse. Too many generations of population restrictions and forced isolation between cities. The loss of even a fifth of our population, roughly the number in the other city, would be devastating to us, to our species reproductive capabilities."

"That is something your leadership should have considered before declaring war. I offered all of you a good life, with little oversight and meager responsibilities. You could have intermixed with other cities, other worlds if you chose to do so."

The smirker took a step forward. "Look at things from our... from their perspective. After untold generations of oppression under the mistress's thumb, we are finally free. Just as we are beginning to come together and organize our future, a new master shows up and demands our loyalty. A new oppressor who killed our old oppressor. Would you not resist under such a circumstance?"

"I would. I have resisted and fought against the injustice of the genocide of my own people. Fought to take vengeance on the ancient ones who caused my world to be all but destroyed. I fought for my friends and loved ones initially, as well as for my own survival. Then I fought for all humankind. Which eventually led me to Loki's execution, and by extension, Hel's. However I don't believe your resistance, or theirs," He motioned toward the six prisoners. "had anything to do with bettering anyone's circumstances other than your own."

"True enough." The smirker acknowledged without hesitation. "I only wish to help those who will survive your wrath to present their case."

Allistor nodded at the mob. "I saw the sacrifices you made to capture these six. Some of your people that charged the convoy toward the end had no weapons. They drew fire and sacrificed themselves so that others could reach the vehicles. I recognize and honor their sacrifices." Next to him, Harmon grunted in approval.

Allistor spoke to the leader. "If you haven't already, invite the rest of your group to join a party. I require the deaths of those who attacked my people, but I don't need to take their lives myself. Those of you who fought for it should receive the experience."

The leader nodded, and Allistor watched her people zone out briefly as they accepted party invites. He crossed his arms and leaned back in his chair. "No big speeches. These few are guilty of starting a war the rest of you may have to suffer for. Take their lives and benefit from their deaths."

The mob lined up behind the smirker and the others. Those on the ground begged and struggled weakly, to no avail. The smirker stood tall and simply closed his eyes as a knife blade slid into his neck at the base of his skull. He immediately went limp, and some of the crowd leveled up. The others died more messily, struggling and crying, but it was all done in less than a minute.

"Return to your city. You'll be given more information, and the opportunity to accept the offer these fools rejected, once I've dealt with the remaining holdout city." Allistor motioned for the mob to depart, which they did without delay, dragging the bodies with them. When he was sure they were out of earshot, Allistor looked at Harmon. "I don't want to kill a whole city's worth of people. It would make me the ruthless tyrant those assholes tried to paint me as. On the other hand, I can't be seen to be weak in the face of an attack. The same old problem, again." He sighed as Harmon placed a hand on his shoulder in silent support. "I have a plan, but it'll take some resources."

The orcanin chuckled. "Luckily, resources happen to be something you *don't* have to be concerned about. How can I help you, my friend? I smell a sale approaching!"

*****

Allistor took the time to meet with the representatives of the middle planet, though he was a few hours late for their scheduled meeting. L'olwyn had contacted them and explained about the attack, the damage to Allistor's ship, and the ongoing situation on Triendal. They agreed to reschedule for later in the day. Allistor left instructions with Cogwalker, then hitched a ride on *Opportunity*.

The middle planet was named Galdan, and its inhabitants were a mix of several races. Some that Allistor recognized, like elves, dwarves, and even xylon, which Hel had brought to the planet to act as a security force. It was the most technologically advanced of the three worlds, with its focus being research, development, and manufacturing.

The representatives here came from a dozen different regions, each of them pretty much self-sustaining. There were heavily populated cities where the work that was important to Hel took place. Each city was supported by surrounding agriculture. There were wind farms that provided power for irrigation pumps on an enormous scale. Mines provided needed ores and minerals for tech manufacturing as well as construction within the cities. Factories pumped out everything from basic farming tools to the very same missiles that had been launched at Allistor.

The representatives of Galdan hadn't displayed any hostility, or even seemed to be nervous about Allistor's presence on the first day. They hosted him in an open air amphitheater, which was good because each of the dozen regions sent six to eight representatives to the meeting. They'd listened, asked a few questions, and retired to discuss Allistor's offer amongst themselves.

Allistor had to fight the urge to apologize for being late. His upbringing practically demanded it, but L'olwyn had been fighting to drill it into his head that emperors don't apologize to commoners. Instead he compromised with himself. "Thank you for adjusting your schedules to accommodate the… unexpected events of the day. I'll get right to business so as not to keep you here longer than necessary. Have you reached a decision?"

"We had not, as of this morning. However, we have received reports from our people on Triendal regarding the attack on your ship, and your reaction. Had Hel, or even one of her upper level functionaries, been attacked in such a manner, she would have laid waste to any and all cities involved. Rather than react in a similar manner, you responded in a reasoned, merciful way. Even when the central city refused to surrender, your dealings with them have been measured."

Allistor smiled. "So far. Do not give me too much credit yet, as I may be forced to attack the city. Only time will tell."

"We understand that may be a necessary outcome. Those of us who were resistant to your offer as of this morning were swayed by your actions on Triendal. We have voted unanimously to accept your offer, and wish to become citizens of Invictus."

Ignoring the system notification that popped up announcing his taking of another planet, Allistor replied, "I am very pleased to hear that." Allistor's smile was open and honest. "If this group would like to swear the oath, we'll get started working on the logistics of welcoming everyone on your world into Invictus, and finding out how best we can help each other."

The representatives all took a knee before Helen even had time to step forward. She recited the oath, which they repeated, and Allistor had nearly a hundred new citizens, with a few million more to come. He invited any who wanted to make the journey to visit Earth and the other worlds accessible via teleport or gate travel. A few dozen accepted, and arrangements were made for them to be picked up for the return trip when Allistor was finished resolving the issue on Triendal.

On the short trip back to that world, L'olwyn and Selby burned up the coms lines, assigning some of their newly hired analysts and researchers, as well as a couple of ships and a small army of support staff, to travel to the system. They would take up residence on a colony ship and work with the inhabitants of all three planets to get them situated.

Allistor half listened to their conversations, his own mind turning over and over a single topic. He was considering placing the second eternity gate here, instead of at Rivian. While he liked that planet, and the potential for trade alliances with neighboring worlds, he now owned, or would shortly own, this entire system. Placing the gate here would accomplish two very important things. First, it would allow him to more effectively defend against the incursions he'd just warned these people were coming. As things were now, he'd need to station a significant portion of his available ships here to defend his assets, and probably ask his allies to do the same. With a gate, he could have most of his ships, wherever they were stationed, in this system within a few hours, rather than a day or more. Second, much like with Orion, placing a gate here would make these worlds into valuable assets, trade centers. And he wouldn't need to move the space station, or any of the asteroids.

He tabled his internal discussion as *Opportunity* landed near *Phoenix*. Longbeard had reported that repairs were complete, and that the dwarves couldn't resist upgrading a few systems while they were there. Most notably the shield generators had been improved, strengthening the shield by more than twenty percent. Allistor inspected the hull, praising the crews for their good work. If he didn't know where she'd been hit by the missiles, he wouldn't have been able to point out the repaired sections.

Boarding *Phoenix*, he gave her bulkhead an affectionate pat as he climbed the ramp. "Good to have you back in one piece. What's the term the navy used to use? Ship-shape?" He smiled to himself as he made his way to the bridge. Kira had already taken off by the time he arrived, and they were just a few minutes' flight from the shielded and hostile city.

Allistor could just make out the speck that was Cogwalker's ship hovering above the city, out of range of the rooftop turrets. The drones had not detected any attempts to leave the city, and the streets had been quiet since the shields were activated.

Kira moved Phoenix over top of the city, and Cogwalker moved away, flanking the city along with Gralen's ship. Once they were in position, Allistor began transmitting, his voice booming down via loudspeaker as well.

"This is Emperor Allistor. Your city has chosen to support those who attacked my ship and killed one of my people. That is a death sentence. Since you've chosen to remain, that is exactly what you'll do. Your city is now quarantined. Anyone attempting to leave will be killed. Anyone attempting to enter will be killed. No supplies will be delivered. Whatever food and water you have inside your walls is all you will ever get." He let that sink in for a moment before continuing.

"The other two cities chose wisely, and brought me the leaders responsible for the attacks. They've been executed, and the cities are free. The other two planets in this system have already joined my empire, willingly and happily. I expect the rest of this planet will do so as well. That leaves you completely alone, with no allies, no help coming. If you don't die of thirst, you'll get hungry. You'll begin to kill each other for food. But I'm betting whomever has taken charge of your city won't have that problem. My guess is that they have a stockpile, knowing this conflict was coming. So you'll starve to death while they sit comfortably somewhere. And they'll let you starve, because for them surrender means death."

Allistor looked around the bridge. The young crew were staring at him, wide-eyed in surprise over the way he was talking. He winked at Hillary, trying to convey that it was all a ruse. From the looks on their faces, he should probably have invested more points into Charisma.

"You have a way out. Bring me the people responsible for attacking my ship. Bring those murderers to justice, and I'll release your city. Refuse, and a month from now, or a year, I'll send in teams to collect your bodies and clean the stench from your homes, your streets. We'll burn what's left of you in great pyres outside the city. Your friends and families in the other cities will suffer for the loss of you, your gene pool being so drastically reduced. I sympathize with them, but that's not my problem. I've offered you peace, twice now. Suffer the consequences of your choices."

A lone missile rose up from the city, speeding toward Phoenix, whose defensive weapons swatted it out of the sky. "Target the structure that missile came from. All ships, break that shield and destroy that building!" Allistor shouted the command. Immediately all the weapons on all three ships targeted a six story structure with a gun turret and missile launcher on its roof. Plasma cannons fired fiery rounds that splashed against the shields, while kinetic rounds from railguns thumped into it, causing the shields to ring with deep notes, the way Allistor imagined the bells of hell would sound.

Allistor flashed back to when Gralen and his beastkin mercenary crew attacked the Bastion from aboard *Opportunity*. They'd used some kind of bomb to break the shield dome he'd put up. Allistor hadn't thought to bring any bombs on what he'd hoped would be a simple trip to claim his station. But maybe Gene had left a couple in the ship's storage? He was about to ask Kira, when the shields below faltered. The combined firepower of the three powerful ships was too much for the single dome that stretched over the whole city. It reddened first, the color spreading out from the points of impact above the target building. The gong of a final kinetic round fired by Cogwalker spelled its doom, the now deep crimson colored dome blinking out of existence.

Next came the smaller shield that covered the building and a small region around it. This one actually held up better, its structure and power not stretched as thin as its larger cousin. The booming notes as the railgun rounds struck were higher pitched as well, sounding more like the church bell in his now destroyed hometown.

The turrets on the roof fired up at the three ships, but at that range were ineffective. Gravity was on

Allistor's side. His ships could hover high above the city and rain down punishment.

When the smaller shield began to turn orange, Theado approached Allistor. "You want our people to be ready to clear the building? We can work it from the roof down."

Allistor shook his head. "Nope. We're gonna knock it down from up here. Then we're gonna pulverize what's left until it's nothing but dust and rocks the size of golf balls. Anybody in there is about to be very, very dead."

"Right on." Theado chuckled, appreciating his emperor's gesture. He was about to tell the two raid groups to stand down, when Allistor had an idea.

"Hang on. We need to make sure they don't escape. I'll have Kira lower you down behind a building a block away. Can you form a workable perimeter at a distance that's safe when the building falls?"

Theado looked down at the building and streets around it. "Sure thing, boss. Twenty of us should be fine. Even better if we can borrow the droids."

"They're all yours." Allistor nodded. "All ships, we're going to insert a team around the building. Be careful not to hit them. Kira, bring us..." He looked down at the street himself. "Bring us south one block, then down behind that neighboring building. Shields on max, we're gonna be in range of those turrets for a bit."

"Aye, shifting now." Kira's voice was calm. Harmon had already assured them that *Phoenix*'s shields would hold up to more than those roof-mounted turrets had to offer.

Less than a minute later the two raid groups hopped the last ten feet from the cargo ramp to the street. They split up, Theado's team going left, Anderson's team going right. Kira lifted Phoenix back into the air, the turret fire splashing on her shield as she cleared the roof of the adjacent building and rose rapidly out of range.

Even without the firepower *Phoenix* contributed, the other two ships managed to break the smaller shield before Kira had them back into position. Allistor watched with a satisfied grin as chunks began to be carved from the upper floor. A kinetic round fired almost directly down at the roof penetrated deep, causing windows to explode outward all the way down to the second floor.

Allistor called for Nigel to activate loudspeaker and transmit on the local channels. "For those still living inside the building, I'll give you one last chance to surrender."

Five seconds later Nigel relayed a transmission from inside the building. "Suck my snardlebun! If we surrender you'll just kill us anyway! Death to the evil emperor!" A moment later the building collapsed under the punishing fire from above.

"What's a snardlebun?" Helen asked, her head tilted to one side.

"Don't know, don't think I want to." Allistor shrugged. "Continue firing until that building is a smoking pile of gravel." He commanded all three ships.

"Boss, we got a dozen or so that tried to escape. Some of them are banged up pretty bad." Anderson reported.

"Got nine on our sides." Theado added. "And based on what's left of the building, I don't think anybody else will be coming out."

"Hold your positions, just in case." Allistor ordered. "If any of the wounded are likely to die, throw enough heals on them to keep them alive."

"Shit! We're taking fire from down the street! Northeast side!" Anderson called out. "Shifting tanks and returning fire!"

Allistor was about to command Kira to circle in that direction and fire on whomever was attacking his people, but he remembered that her weapons officer was dead. William had reluctantly taken over the position, but he wasn't experienced enough to pick off single targets from such a distance.

"Gralen. Take overwatch. Circle the block and take out anyone firing on our people."

"Happy to oblige." The beastkin growled through coms. *Opportunity* kept firing on the collapsing building as it lowered down to a few hundred feet and began to fire down the street in question, its cannons providing support to the raiders. The building was now little more than a two-story pile of rubble, Cogwalker and Kira still pounding at it. As Allistor watched, there was an explosion on either the ground level, or an underground level, that sent a plume of debris skyward like a small volcano.

"Raiders, take cover! Falling debris!" Allistor shouted, his voice instantly relayed to everyone below.

Theado responded a few seconds later. "We're all good, boss. Saw it happen and took cover. One of the prisoners was a little slow to move, and a piece of flying metal took off a leg. We're keeping him alive." There was a short pause, and then, "Uhhh... boss? I think you're gonna wanna see this. Something came tumbling out of that explosion. It looks like... a vault? Big cube of burned up, scratched up metal. Looks mostly intact, still."

Allistor looked at the viewscreen showing the feed from a camera under the ship's belly. There was indeed a large metal structure of some kind that was laying half a block down the street from the former building's location. He noted that the building itself was now just a wide, smoking hole in the ground, three or four stories deep.

"Cogwalker, cease fire. Kira, same for you, and take us down. Gralen, maintain overwatch and blast anyone who fires at our people. Theado, Anderson, have five of your people round up the prisoners and bring them to me. The rest of you, check out the ruins. I want to know if there were any tunnels down there they could have used to escape."

Allistor and Helen made their way down to the cargo bay as Kira descended once again. She landed on a rubble-strewn street right in front of where the building had been. A couple of the tanks and a few melee raiders helped her out by tossing or simply kicking a few of the larger pieces out of the way so that the landing gear could set down safely.   Then they approached the pit that had been a building, took a moment to look around, and leaped down inside.

Chapter Twenty Eight

Mindless Aggression

It turned out that the metal vault was actually a safe room. When they rolled it over and found the door, the raiders had several of the droids use plasma cutting tools to try and open it. While the metal did not cut, it did heat up significantly. After about ten minutes, those inside started shouting for them to stop. A few minutes later when the metal had cooled off, they opened it and emerged. The four sweating people inside were herded along with the rest of the prisoners to stand on the street before Allistor.

"Well, I recognize a couple of you." Allistor spoke to the two prisoners who had been the representatives for the city at their previous meeting. They'd been among those inside the safe room. "Just out of curiosity, what made you decide to attack us? You had to know you couldn't win."

"We didn't expect to win." The nearest of them sneered. "We just wanted to show everyone else what a tyrant you are. The rest of my people here in this city, the other cities, and across the Collective."

Allistor knew he shouldn't ask, shouldn't give them the opportunity to keep talking, but he found that he couldn't resist. "How does responding to a cowardly missile attack that killed a young member of my crew make me a tyrant?"

"Taking our planet makes you a tyrant!" The other one responded this time, spitting on the ground at Allistor's feet. "You came here and bullied us into joining you, threatening us with some mysterious and probably non-existent '*other factions*' that would come here and enslave us if we didn't accept your offer!"

Allistor shook his head. "Those other factions are out there. I'm going to guess that you've led very sheltered lives under Hel's rule, with no one daring to attack, or even defy her in her own territory. She was among the most powerful individuals remaining in the Collective, or so I'm told. So it may be that you were innocent enough to believe that you'd be safe out here without her."

"We were safe enough before you came along!" The first one shouted, his face turning a deep purple in his anger. "If you had only left us alone, my family would still be alive!"

"If you hadn't attacked me, your family would still be alive!" Allistor roared at him, stepping forward to place his face less than a foot from the belligerent being's purple one. "Did I ever threaten to harm you myself, before you attacked? Or did I tell you that you'd be left on your own if you refused to join me?"

The two representatives opened their mouths to reply, then closed them. Allistor could see the realization cross their faces as they thought back to the initial meeting with Allistor.

"Let me refresh your memories for the benefit of these others standing here, these people that you've convinced to doom themselves. I offered you the chance to join me, to become citizens of Invictus, where you would be free to live your lives as long as you held to a simple oath to not harm any other citizens, and to support your community in some way. The alternative that I gave you, in case you elected not to join us, was that you'd be on your own. No direct support from me, financial, defense, or otherwise. But that you'd be free to trade with your neighboring cities." He paused for a moment, thinking. With a brief nod, he added, "I swear by the System that what I've just said is true." He waited as the others watched a golden light flow around him, the System's confirmation of his statement.

The other survivors turned incredulous and angry faces toward the two representatives. There were murmurs of recrimination, and a few threats voiced. One of them stepped forward. "Emperor Allistor, we were misled about you, about our situation. I realize that this will not stay your hand, but I ask that you allow us to deal with these traitors before you take our lives."

Allistor considered it for a few seconds, then shook his head. "They committed an act of war against me. It is my right to end them as I see fit. And while I understand your anger, and share it myself, I don't feel that I owe you any favors, since you participated in the attack."

A small voice near the back of the crowd spoke up. "I did not participate. I was a servant to this man." She nodded toward the one-legged man being supported by two others just in front of her. I had nothing to do with attacking you." There were tears in her eyes, and she sniffed loudly, wiping her nose. "I don't want to die because of them."

Allistor paused. He'd assumed there might be some civilians in the building, and that a few of them might even be innocent. But he'd tried to put that thought out of his mind, to focus on the bigger picture. A swift and brutal response to be seen as an example to others who might attack. He'd learned the hard way that the Collective in general valued life very little. At least, the lives of those they considered beneath them. If Allistor showed that he'd be merciless in his retribution against those responsible for attacks against his people, regardless of the collateral damage...

His stomach lurched and he felt the urge to vomit as the realization hit him. He was acting just the same as those he despised. Willing to sacrifice an acceptable number of innocents just to make a point. His hands began to shake as a wave of self-loathing washed over him. Sensing something was wrong, Helen placed a hand on his shoulder.

He took comfort in the gesture, and did his best to collect himself. Clearing his throat and hoping that the tears he felt forming in his eyes weren't obvious, he motioned with one hand as he spoke. "Please come forward."

The crowd parted as a small female of their species stepped forward. If Allistor were to guess, he'd say she was the equivalent of a human in their late teens or early twenties. His age. When she stopped in the front row of the crowd, hands clasped in front of her, eyes on the ground, Allistor asked. "How many of you claim to have taken no part in the attack on my ship?"

Six hands went up in the air as their owners shuffled feet or mumbled quietly.

"All of you step forward. I'm going to give you an opportunity to save your lives. Swear by the System, as I just did, that you took no part in attacking me or my people, and I'll allow you to live. You'll be given the same choice I gave them, to swear the oath and become citizens of Invictus, or to remain separate and on your own."

Of the six who'd raised their hands, two looked suddenly fearful and lowered their hands, trying to disappear behind others. The four with their hands still up stepped forward to stand next to the female. One by one they swore that they had nothing to do with the attacks, starting with her. Allistor was glad to see the System confirm her statement with the flash of golden light. The fourth to swear had apparently been lying, and attempted to defy the System. He paid the price with a black shroud that momentarily surrounded him, followed by a wave of pain so intense that he fell unconscious, slamming his head on the street.

The others, including Allistor, stood in shock for a moment. It was the first time Allistor remembered seeing the System act directly against someone since it had killed a kid who'd violated his oath as a citizen. In that case, it had caused the kid to take a fatal fall from a Stronghold wall, and at the time Allistor hadn't been positive that the System was responsible. This time, there was no doubt.

He looked at the remaining prisoner, who hesitated for a moment, wide-eyed with fear. Swallowing audibly, he swore on the system, and sagged with relief when it confirmed his honesty. Allistor noted that he was the one who'd asked to kill the other two before being executed himself.

Looking at the man, he drew his sword. "Since you weren't involved with these others, I've decided to grant your request. Take this sword, and take their heads." He pointed to the two representatives, who'd been sullenly silent since being proved wrong about Allistor's so-called threats. He held out his sword, and the man took hold of the hilt. Two of the others who'd just passed the honesty test quickly grabbed the two representatives, pushing them forward, then knocking them down. They roughly yanked them back up on to their knees, growling quiet commands, or threats. Allistor couldn't tell.

The sword bearer wasted no time, using the extremely sharp blade to remove their heads one at a time, after which he leveled up. When he was finished, he wiped the blade on his own sleeve, then returned the sword to Allistor. "Thank you, Emperor Allistor. You have allowed me to remove some of the stain of my dishonor."

Allistor nodded in acknowledgement as he sheathed the blade. Looking at the rest of the prisoners, he called out. "Last chance. If any of you were not involved, speak up now, and be given the chance to save your life. I'm not interested in taking innocent lives."

One of those who'd passed the System's test snorted, then spat. "You took plenty already. There were at least twenty others inside the building like us, who had nothing to do with the attacks, but who weren't allowed to leave."

The accusation hit Allistor like a kick in the gut. Still, he did his best to maintain his posture and neutral expression. "I regret their deaths, and as a human being, I shall bear that burden for as long as I live. But as an emperor, I did what was necessary." His voice was rough as he spoke, and none of those present doubted that he meant every word. "If they had families, we will find a way to provide some restitution for their loss."

Needing a moment to better collect himself, he gazed out over the crowd of prisoners, waiting for any of them to speak up and claim to be innocent. He gave himself, and them, a full minute before speaking again. "Since none of the rest of you have come forward, I'm going to assume that you're all guilty in some way. The only sentence for killing a citizen of Invictus is death."

None of the prisoners spoke a word, or reacted in any way. Allistor was turning to instruct his raiders to carry out the sentence when one of the prisoners rushed forward. Allistor had only seen the motion out of the corner of his eye, and already had his back to the group. He spun around while unsheathing his sword and casting *Barrier* without even thinking about it.

The prisoner charging him began to scream something unintelligible as he opened his arms wide. Allistor managed to bring his sword around to drive the point into the attacker's chest. At the same moment, the prisoner exploded in a flash of blinding light. The explosion popped Allistor's barrier like a soap bubble before scorching him even as the force of it knocked him backwards. He vaguely registered screams, some of them quickly cut off, as he impacted a nearby building, his health bar dropping to less than ten percent.

Allistor was blind from the flash, and could hear nothing but a ringing in his ears. He lay there against the wall, shaking his head. He tried to put a finger in his right ear, but his arm wouldn't move. Grunting from the pain of trying, he managed to cast a heal on himself.

While it didn't fix his broken arm, it did eliminate the blindness and ringing. Now the screams returned, along with shouts, and crying. Allistor felt another heal wash over him, raising his health back to about fifteen percent, and he managed to sit up enough to lean his back against the wall.

What he saw when he took in the scene made him lean over to one side and empty his stomach.

Nearest the center of the explosion, where he and the prisoner had been standing, was a scorched area littered with burnt body parts. The suicide bomber's, and those of the prisoners who'd been standing nearest to them. Farther out in an arc were the mangled, burnt, yet somehow still bleeding bodies of several more.

There were wounded laying in the street, crying out for help, or just screaming in pain. As far as Allistor could tell, only a couple of them were his people. "Helen!" He began to frantically search the area for her. He remembered she'd been standing just behind him. Looking to his left, then his right, he found her sprawled on the ground near the same wall he'd hit. He immediately cast a heal on her, sobbing as he crawled in her direction, afraid that she'd been killed.

He nearly collapsed in relief when she groaned and rolled over. After receiving another heal, she croaked, "What the hell happened?"

"A bomb. Hold still." Allistor reached her, sitting once again with his back against the wall and gathering her into his lap. With his improved strength, and the adrenaline pumping through his veins, she seemed to weight nothing at all. He hugged her to his chest, not caring about the tears that streamed down his face.

After several seconds, she patted him on the chest and mumbled, "Love you too, but I can't breathe." He quickly let her go, an apology on his lips, when he saw her grin up at him. She wrapped her arms around him and hugged back.

Theado came walking up, looking uncomfortable as he cleared his throat to get their attention. "Sorry to interrupt, boss." He cast a heal on each of them before speaking again. "Glad to see they didn't take you out. We lost one of ours in the blast, and almost all of them. We're healing the survivors, and everyone still breathing should make it."

"Who did we lose?" Allistor gently set Helen aside and got to his feet, then helped her up. He grimaced when he saw the entire left side of her torso covered in blood. After taking a moment to make sure she wasn't still bleeding, he looked up at Theado.

"Ari, one of the dps mages." Theado bowed his head for a second. "He just didn't have enough armor or health to withstand the blast."

Allistor nodded, casting another heal on Helen, then himself. His health bar crept up a bit more. At level one hundred, his limited healing spells didn't do much for him. "Thanks for letting me know. We'll take him home for a funeral." The raid leader nodded and turned away, looking over his shoulder once as he walked back toward the wounded, checking to make sure Allistor was still okay.

"That sucked." Helen let out a pained breath, holding one arm against her wounded side. "I'm going to stop hanging out with you if you keep almost getting me killed." She tried to lighten his mood, poking him gently in the belly as she spoke.

Allistor just shook his head. The emotions of the past several minutes were overwhelming him. He needed to put up a brave front for his people, and for anyone who might be watching, but he wanted to just sit down right where he was, put his head in his hands, and rest.

Once again Helen put a hand on his shoulder. "You can deal with all this when we're alone on the ship. Hang tough for a little while longer. I know you've got it in you."

Allistor nodded, straightening his back and raising his head, taking a few deep breaths to center himself. "All part of the new job, right?" He mumbled mostly to himself.

Helen heard it though, and nudged him with her shoulder. "It's why they pay you the big bucks."

The raiders who'd been down in the hole came rushing back out, having heard the explosion. When they took in the scene, most of them immediately started helping with the wounded. Anderson located Allistor, and with a look of concern on his face, trotted over.

"You alright boss?"

Allistor nodded. "I'll live. It was close, though. They very nearly took both of us out. Ari didn't make it."

Anderson quickly looked around, spotting the body of their comrade, giving a sad nod of recognition, unsure of what to say.

"Tell me what you found down there." Allistor changed the subject.

"We didn't look for long, because we heard the explosion. But the only tunnel we saw down there was some kind of utility run. Probably too small for anyone to use, unless they crawled." He paused and looked over at the hole. "We can go back down and take another look…"

Allistor shook his head. "Don't bother. We caught the ones responsible. The leaders, and a bunch more." He looked over at the bodies sprawled out around the epicenter. "Pretty sure they're all dead now. And so are a few innocents who were standing too close."

Helen looked at the raider. "How did this happen? Did you guys not search them?"

Anderson's face paled. "We did. We searched them for weapons. But if they had something in a storage device…" He shook his head. "I'm not sure I could even identify Earth explosives unless it looked like a stick of dynamite, or had C4 stamped on it."

Allistor held up a hand to stop him talking. "This is not on you. Not even a little bit. We're still like infants, stumbling around in a universe we don't begin to understand." He paused, staring at the crushed man in front of him. "Let me say it again. This was not your fault." He caught Anderson's gaze and held it for a moment before the man nodded.

Allistor sighed, feeling both physically and mentally exhausted. The adrenaline was wearing off as well, the come-down taking its toll on top of everything else.

"Help take care of the wounded, then get everybody back on the ship." Allistor saw that all of his people were now back on their feet, and two of the locals as well. He was glad to see that one of them was the young woman who'd spoken up. He initially thought the other survivor was the one who'd borrowed his sword, but a moment later he spotted him laying nearby with one arm missing and most of his face burned away.

Allistor and Helen left the scene, walking back to Phoenix. The moment he was close enough, he called out. "Nigel, loudspeaker please. From all three ships. And transmit on all channels." He waited a few seconds, then spoke in the steadiest voice he could manage.

"This is Emperor Allistor. Those responsible for attacking my people are dead. Too many innocents died with them. I'd rather not destroy your entire city because of the actions of a few, so I'll make you this offer. You have one day to choose new leaders to represent you. I'll return to this location, and we can once again discuss the future of your city. Let me be clear. Any further hostile action by any of you will have devastating consequences for all of you."

He took a seat on a crate and watched his people gather up the two surviving locals. Over to one side, half a dozen droids were carrying the safe room toward the cargo bay, one of the roguish raiders in charge of looting walking behind them. When they all reached the ship, he motioned them over. "I'll give you a choice. You can come with us back to the station and rest, after you swear our oath. Or you can remain here and tell your people what happened. It'll be up to you whether you tell them the truth, or not."

They both elected to stay, and Allistor let them go. Already locals were streaming out of nearby buildings and moving tentatively toward the crater where the building had stood. As soon as the last of the raiders and droids were aboard, Kira lifted off, and all three ships returned to Charon station.

*****

Allistor woke early the following morning. He'd gone to bed after checking on William and the rest of the crew, and spending a little time in the mess hall with the raiders, drinking a toast to their lost comrade. It was all he could do to hold himself together until he got to his quarters. Helen had offered to sit with him a while, but he'd declined and sent her to her own rest.

After breakfast he'd called together his advisors to get their opinions on whether to place the second gate at Rivian, or in his newly acquired system. Opinions were mixed, and a few of them actually changed their minds after hearing each other's reasoning. In the end, the vote was nearly even, but Allistor had been given a lot of new information to consider. He thanked them all and released them to whatever they'd been planning for the day.

He spent some time in engineering, crafting a set of daggers while William pounded against his barrier. The boy was much stronger now, and initially overpowered the spell much more quickly than Allistor had expected. As a result, his squire scored a solid hit against Allistor's back before he could react. It was several minutes of victory dancing and gloating before he managed to get back to work, smiling with pride as the boy resumed pounding with his staff. Pulling heated metal from the forge, he made a silent promise to himself to spend more quality time with

572

William and the girls. As well as Meg, Sam, Ramon, Nancy, and the rest of his inner circle, who were now his adopted family. They were always there when he needed them, and it occurred to him that they rarely came to him asking for anything.

The meeting with the last city's new representatives didn't take long. When Kira landed in the street, there were twenty people standing there waiting for him, with several thousand gathered behind them.

Allistor kept his distance after the previous day's attempt, and rather than his simple Barrier, he used his newly acquired *Battle Dome* spell to cast a protective dome over himself and his people. For just a moment he kicked himself for not thinking of it during the attack, but he simply hadn't had time to think. He'd cast *Barrier* at the last second more out of reflex than anything else. Behind his little group, Allistor's raiders were spread out, ready to attack if necessary.

Allistor spent a few minutes detailing his offer, running through his modified recruitment speech yet again. He half-shouted as he spoke, making sure the crowd gathered behind their new leaders could hear him.

The group's spokesman stepped forward then, and bowed at the waist. "Emperor Allistor, we sincerely regret the events of the past few days, and offer our humblest apologies. We've been informed of what happened yesterday, of the additional attempt on your life, and of the mercy you showed both before and after." There were nods from the other chosen representatives. "We appreciate the opportunity you have offered us, and we surrender the city to you. And while we cannot speak for all of our people, those of us who've been chosen to lead all wish to become citizens of Invictus." He bowed again, along with all nineteen of the leadership group, and most of the crowd behind them.

Allistor didn't answer, he simply waved Helen forward. She recited the oath, and most of those present repeated it back to her.

"For those of you who've chosen to join us, welcome to Invictus!" Allistor raised a hand and gave them a half smile. "For the rest of you, and for those who are not in attendance, I hope you'll choose to join us as well. I think you'll find that there are a great many benefits to being a citizen, and few drawbacks." He paused to look over the crowd, a few of whom were shaking their heads or scowling at him. "For those who wish to leave, let your new leaders know, and we'll arrange transport in the coming days. For you twenty..." He motioned them forward. "We have some logistics to discuss. Please step aboard my ship and L'olwyn here will get things started."

There was no celebration, and Allistor was glad. He was still reeling from the accusations thrown at him, and his insight into just how accurate they appeared to be. His inner turmoil followed him back onto the ship, where he hid in his quarters while his advisors dealt with their new citizens.

Eventually Harmon knocked on his door and was invited in. He took a seat on a sofa across from Allistor.

574

"Discussions are wrapping up down there. I've been in communications with the others. Or'Dralon and Lighthammer ships are on their way here, along with representatives who will want to discuss their potential interests in this system. I have six of my own warships, along with two colony ships, already on the way here as well." He grinned at Allistor.

Allistor smiled despite his ugly mood. "You and your people are always welcome on any of my worlds. All I ask is that you meet with the locals on the planet and agree on locations before you move in. If they resist, then I'll get involved."

"Are you going to let me sell more defense satellites for each of the worlds?" The orcanin emperor merchant showed his tusks in his version of a wide smile.

"I suppose I should do that." Allistor nodded. "Even with your ships and those of our allies, I don't know if we can defend this system. Or how soon we might have to defend it. This place might have been ignored up till now, but after the Systemwide announcements, I'm sure some factions are turning their sights this direction."

"Indeed. That is the best argument I can think of for placing your second gate here. Beyond the obvious wealth being gathered and processed at the station, there will be those among Hel and Loki's former allies, as well as other ambitious factions, who are motivated to attempt to take this system just because they don't like you."

"But if I put the gate here, then enough other powerful factions will come and invest here that those

575

attackers might think twice." Allistor concluded. "But what's to stop them from attacking Rivian instead?"

"That system is much older and more settled, with powerful factions occupying the neighboring worlds. Several of whom you now have trade agreements with. Not to mention the alliances you have with several other powerful factions. While some might risk alienating all of us to seize an entire system, it is unlikely they would do so for a single planet like Rivian."

Allistor scratched his head as he thought. Not yet fully decided, he was leaning toward installing the gate here. Harmon distracted him with another bit of news.

"I would like to remind you that my wares include many millions of items other than weapons and defense systems. For instance, I happen to have available a glorious selection of attire appropriate to one of your station, and easily altered to fit you."

When Allistor just blinked at him, confused, Harmon chuckled. "It is my understanding that Lady Melise will be leading the approaching Or'Dralon delegation. And not to criticize, but you have been burning through your current wardrobe at a rapid pace. We can't have our handsome young emperor wearing patched and stained clothing in public, now can we?"

Allistor sighed. He didn't have time to return to Earth and let Lilly whip him up new clothes. "Fine. As long as the clothes don't cost as much as the satellites." He grumped at his gigantic friend.

Chapter Twenty Nine

Baldur walked into Odin's audience chamber to find six more of his people present. The mists that filled the room transmitted his surprise at finding them there. This wasn't just unusual, but unheard of in recent centuries. The few of his kind who hadn't ascended lived solitary lives, spread across the galaxy, pursuing their own interests and rarely interacting even remotely with each other. Now, with his presence added, there were eight of them in one place.

He recognized each of them, of course. In an epoch past they had all coexisted within the same system, then the same small cluster of systems. There stood Vidarr and his broodmate (or brother, in human terms) Vali, Magni and Modi who were broodmates of a younger generation, Hodr who was broodmate to Baldur himself, and Idunn who was amongst the most beloved of all his people, second only to Baldur himself. Next to Odin sat Frigg, Baldur's broodmother, whom he thought had ascended long ago. He tilted his head and extended his tentacles outward in a sign of deference to his parents.

"Father, I have answered your summons. Frigg, I am pleased to see you." He exuded warmth and happiness through the mists. "I was not aware we still shared this plane of existence."

"It does my heart good to see you as well, child. My long absence was not intentional. I was exploring the limits of meditation, and pushed myself into a state of being that more resembled hibernation. The passage of time became a vague and meaningless concept."

Odin waved one tentacle to silence them. "I gathered you here to celebrate the return of my mate, and to let you know that I have decided to ascend." The mists relayed a variety of reactions from the gathered Aesir, from shock to sadness. "I have long been weary of this existence, but have remained out of a sense of duty to those we watch over. Recent events, the genocide of the humans, the realization of the scope and horror of Loki's innumerable crimes, the deaths of both Loki and Hel, and the overwhelming chaos of war and murder throughout the Collective that has followed…" Odin's tentacles all went limp at his sides, and his head drooped. An intense wave of deep shame and sorrow reached all of them through the mists. "I am… disheartened."

One of Frigg's tentacles reached over and gently rested upon Odin's. "As always, beloved, I will remain at your side. When you ascend, I will follow."

"When will you go?" Idunn asked.

"Soon. There are some things I hope to accomplish first. Baldur and I will continue to strive to settle the chaos that fills the vacuum left by Loki and Hel. I would ask that each of you do what you can to assist in those efforts. Though I am anxious to go, I could not leave the galaxy in such a state and ascend with a clear conscience."

Each of the others moved their tentacles in a pattern that indicated both obeisance and agreement. A warmth of pride and gratitude spread from Odin throughout the chamber. "We accepted the role of guardians from our predecessors so long ago that I can barely remember their passing. Most of you were not yet born, and of those who were at my side, only Frigg remains. Among my greatest regrets is the irredeemable wrong committed by one of our own against the humans. Genocide has been common enough within the Collective, but never against an uninitiated world. Worse, Loki found a way to trick the System into committing this heinous act for him. The burden of that must be borne by all Aesir."

Odin raised his head to gaze upon the others. "I summoned you here because you are all that remain of our people who have had interactions with them, spent time among them in the past. I would ask each of you to do what you can, within the limits imposed by the System, to help them recover. The most successful of them, Allistor, has reached great heights in a short period of time. He is an example of their potential. If allowed to grow, they could be a great force within the Collective, and at the moment I am uncertain whether they will be a positive or negative influence. They have legitimate cause for their anger and mistrust. Let us work to assuage that anger, encourage them toward a more enlightened path."

*****

Allistor ducked behind a tree as a spell aimed at him streaked past, striking another tree with an explosion of blue sparks. "Ha! Missed me!" he called out as he ducked down and moved behind a nearby bush. Another missile

580

struck the foliage, this time exploding into pink glitter that rained down over him. A wicked grin on his face, he popped his head up and fired off a spell of his own, hitting Sydney as she prepared another pink missile.

"Ow!" She complained, lowering her hands to see them covered in red goop.

"Oh, it didn't hurt. Stop complaining!" William called out, laughing as he launched a second blue missile at his adopted father, who had kept his head up too long while he watched Sydney pout. Allistor barely ducked in time to avoid being hit.

Addy had come across a scroll during a low level dungeon run that taught her a spell meant for kids, or possibly illusionists. It allowed the caster to send a fast-moving bolt of magic at a target, and upon impact release an explosion of harmless magic. The caster could modify the color, form, and consistency of the spell's explosion. She had immediately taken the scroll to Ramon and begged him to make copies for everyone in the family right away. The next day she dragged them all out to the woods near Daigath's clearing, and they were playing a magical version of laser tag combined with paintball.

Helen was there, along with Fuzzy and Fiona. And while the bears couldn't cast the spell, they took great enjoyment from romping through the brush and surprising one of the players, tackling them and licking their faces as their form of attack. Both bears sported a veritable rainbow of hit indicators across their bodies, but refused to quit playing and 'die' according to the rules. Not that anybody minded.

Allistor laughed aloud as he half-crawled into a low spot on the ground, listening for any nearby movement. He couldn't remember when he'd had so much innocent fun! He fully intended to crush his competition without mercy, and didn't feel even a little bit guilty about it.

"You should know you can't hide from a ranger." Helen's voice behind him caused him to spin around just in time to take a green bolt to the face. The explosion covered his entire head and shoulders in green slime. He sputtered, sitting up and wiping his face to clear his eyes. The moment he sat up, blue and yellow bolts struck his back.

"We've done it! We've defeated the mighty Emperor! Now, who will take his place?" Addy eyed William for a moment, then blasted him in the ear with a yellow bolt that tinkled like a thousand tiny bells when it exploded. "Not you!" She gloated, then began to giggle. A moment later that giggle turned into a cough as green slime enveloped her head as well.

"Victory!" Helen thrust both arms into the air. "I have vanquished all of the contenders for the throne, and declare myself the new Empress!"

The others laughed as they took a knee and bowed their heads in mock reverence. A moment later the multicolored magical effects faded away. Fiona emerged from the bushes behind Helen, casually swatting her legs out from under her, causing the new empress to land ungracefully on her butt. The bear grinned at her

582

companion, licked her face, then stood up on her hind legs and raise her forepaws up into the air in a mockery of Helen's victory gesture.

"Ha! Fiona says she's the empress now!" William stood and gave the bear a courtly bow worthy of a medieval squire. "Well played, M'lady!"

Taking a break for a picnic lunch, the group sat in Daigath's clearing around a blanket filled with food Meg had personally prepared for the outing. Allistor leaned back on his hands and looked up at the clouds drifting overhead, taking a deep breath and letting it out slowly.

"This has been a perfect day." He whispered to himself. "Not so long ago, I was sure none of us would ever see another day like this."

"You've earned it." Helen bumped him with her shoulder. "Nobody has worked harder for this than you have."

Allistor watched as Addy teased Fuzzy with a cupcake, holding it out for him, then pulling it back and hiding it behind her back. Fuzzy, not to be denied, simply nosed her chest hard enough to bowl her over backward, then claimed the crushed treat from her hand with a deft flick of his tongue. "Hey! Cheater." Addy complained as she righted herself, earning a cupcake flavored lick to the face. "Ew!"

Chuckling, Allistor lay back in the grass and placed his hands on his chest, fingers laced together as he sighed with contentment.

It had been a month since he returned from claiming his new solar system. In that time he'd focused on keeping his promise to himself, spending as much time with his loved ones as possible. He'd taken the kids with him nearly everywhere he went, laughing and joking together, but also having some heart to heart discussions, the kind that Amanda had been sharing with them. He'd learned a lot about his adopted children, who were much wiser and more mature than he'd expected them to be. His smile faded slightly as he thought about all the trauma that had forced them to grow up far too quickly.

His thoughts were interrupted when Fuzzy plopped his massive body down next to him, rolled over until he nearly crushed Allistor, then waved his paws lazily in the air. His way of demanding belly scratches. Sitting up on his knees, Allistor obliged even as he scolded his bear. "You smell like you've been rolling in murder chicken poop. How does a civilized bear like yourself, who lives in a city, manage to get himself so stinky?"

Fuzzy ignored the jibe, rolling slightly to give Allistor a better angle as he closed his eyes and let his tongue loll out one side of his snout. William approached to help with the scratchings, and Allistor warned him. "Don't get too close to his butt. That's the dangerous end." Fuzzy opened one eye to glare at Allistor, causing them all to laugh.

Allistor looked around the clearing. Daigath was away on Rivian, having traveled there to reacquaint himself with the forests he'd spent time in long ago. Netsirk had accompanied him, the druid still not fully recovered from their time in the phobia dungeon. Without the presence of the two elves, the forest seemed less welcoming.

A bee landed on Fuzzy's nose, causing him to snort. The presence of the bee reminded the bear that the druid had established a honeybee colony just outside the clearing. Allistor could read the bear's mind as he rolled up onto his feet and headed in that direction.

"Oh no you don't. Get back here, fuzzball. No raiding the hive when the druid's not here to protect it!" Allistor called his companion back. Fuzzy grumbled, but complied. Mostly because he knew that if he stole honey now, she might cut him off in the future.

Looking up at the sun, Allistor decided it was time to head back. "Let's get packed up and start for home." He motioned toward the blanket covered in food. The kids tossed both bears a few last pieces of roasted chicken before scooping everything else up in their storage rings. The mutant chickens that Chloe had created were five or six times the size of a natural chicken, each drumstick large enough to constitute a meal for a human. Bears, on the other hand, felt they needed several each before they were full.

With everything packed, they set out on the trail that would take them back to Wilderness Stronghold and the teleport back to Invictus. Meg and Sam would be celebrating their fiftieth wedding anniversary that night, and a tremendous party had been planned in their honor.

They were nearly back to the Stronghold when both bears stopped in their tracks. Fuzzy lowered his head and growled, while Fiona's ears and tail went down and she lowered her belly to the ground, whimpering. Allistor followed the gaze of both bears, drawing his sword. Behind him, Helen produced her bow from inventory and nocked an arrow, and the kids each produced weapons of their own. "Get in close behind me." Allistor whispered. When they complied, he cast his *Battle Dome* over top of them all.

The brush rustled ahead of them, and out stepped a creature that had haunted Allistor's nightmares.

Fomorian Matron
Level 110
Health: 150,000/150,000

She stood eight feet tall with emaciated but muscular limbs that ended in long, sharp claws. Her snow white hair extended most of the way down her back, and was tangled with leaves and twigs. Her leather armor was stained and ripped in several places. Glowing green eyes blazed with hatred as she glared at Allistor.

"You." She spoke one word as she stepped free of the brush and onto the trail ahead of them. "You slaughtered my clan. My mate, my scion. You stole our orb." Her voice was flat, nearly monotone, but the hatred behind it was clear.

Allistor fought the fear that caused his gut to roil. When he'd defeated the fomorians he'd been a much lower level, and had no hope of defending himself against the powerful Matron. Now, he was close to her level, and had at least a decent chance. Behind him, the girls began to sing a song that gave everyone in their party a significant boost to *Wisdom* and *Intelligence*. They'd already decided that with the bears on hand to provide brute strength, this fight was going to be about magic. Allistor nodded his approval.

"I did kill your mate, and your scion, but only after your clan attacked my people. And I do not have your orb. It is long gone."

The matron tilted her head to one side as she listened, her clawed hands tightening into fists. "Where? Where did you hide the orb?" Her voice became rough, nearly a growl. "Tell me, and I will kill your family quickly. *You* will die slowly, either way."

Allistor didn't see any reason why he couldn't be honest with her. He doubted the Arkhons had anything to fear if she showed up looking to claim her orb. In fact they might appreciate the opportunity to kill her. "I sold it to the Arkhons months ago."

"The Hated Ones have my orb?!" She screamed at them, causing even Fuzzy to flinch. "No! They will destroy it! They will enslave the souls of my ancestors!" She waved a hand and everything around the protective dome went black. Allistor had forgotten about the fomorians' darkness spell, and its appearance sent a chill down his spine.

A moment later the Matron's claws impacted the dome, causing it to shudder and glow a bright orange. Helen let loose her arrow, firing past the visible hands into the darkness, then releasing a second arrow immediately after. Allistor cast *Mind Spike*, which had worked well on the scion, but didn't appear to have any effect on his much higher level mother. The claws smashed into the barrier again, making it glow a bright crimson this time. Allistor knew another hit would defeat the spell and allow the darkness to engulf them.

He cast Lightning Bolt into the space between the hands, knocking back the Matron and apparently stunning her, since she didn't immediately attack. He took the opportunity to recast *Battle Dome*, renewing the strength of the barrier. A scream of rage preceded another pair of blows against the dome, and Helen fired more arrows as rapidly as she could.

Allistor cast *Erupt* on the ground just outside the barrier, causing a huge stone spike to rise up in the location he thought she'd be standing, allowing for her long arms. Another scream suggested he'd been at least partially accurate. The hands pulled back, but Helen and Allistor both oriented on the sound, her sending another arrow, him casting a second *Lightning Bolt*. William contributed a bolt of his own, the much lower level spell likely not doing any damage, but giving the frightened boy a boost of confidence.

Seconds later the Matron screamed again, her entire body slamming into the barrier shoulder first. It flared, then disappeared with an audible pop, allowing her to stumble through, the magical darkness cascading in around them. The girls cried out in fear, ceasing their song even as Fuzzy gave a defiant roar. Unlike the humans, his nose told him exactly where the Matron was, and he charged. Allistor shouted, "Move! Run forward! Get out of the spell radius!"

There was the sound of impact as bear met fomorian, and a grunt of pain. Allistor heard bone crunch a moment later. Though he couldn't see it, Fuzzy's jaws had clamped down on one of her legs and broken a bone. Then Fuzzy whined in pain as she ripped at his hide with powerful clawed hands. Allistor hesitated for a second, unwilling to leave his bear cub in the monster's grip, but unable to see any way to help. He dashed forward, tripping over brush and bouncing blindly off a tree before he exited the darkness spell's influence. He immediately spotted Helen with a grip on Fiona's fur, and the girls who were standing with swords at the ready, but not William.

"Run to me! Follow my voice!" He called out to both his squire and his bear. The others gathered up behind him and the girls began to sing again as Allistor recast his dome. This time he attempted to modify the spell, channeling more mana into it, hoping to give it more strength. There was no sound from inside the darkness, from the Matron, Fuzzy, or William. The eerie silence scared him more than any scream might. He quickly sent party invitations to everyone, and was relieved to see William accept it a moment later.

That relief was short lived. Another whine from Fuzzy was followed by a scream from William that was abruptly cut off. The Matron's voice drifted to them out of the darkness. "I have your scion, thief. Murderer! You shall suffer as I have!" William screamed again, long and loud as she did something to hurt him.

Next to him Helen sobbed in frustration, unable to fire without risking hitting William or Fuzzy. William whimpered, then began to beg the Matron not to hurt him again, the sounds both breaking Allistor's heart and sending him into a rage.

"Damn you!" He roared at the Matron, who chuckled at the pain and frustration in his voice. Allistor looked around, memorizing the ground at his feet. "Move back a step. Close to the back edge of the dome." He instructed everyone. They did as he said, clearing the center of the space. "Be ready."

Without another word Allistor activated his *Quicken* skill and charged forward, leaving the dome in place and entering the darkness again. He spread both arms out wide, covering as much ground as he could as he blindly ran toward the sound of William whimpering. When the sound grew closer he picked up speed and lowered his center of gravity. A moment later he impacted what he hoped was the Matron, driving into her body and lifting with his legs. His hopes were confirmed when her claws dug into his back, at least one of them scraping against his ribs. Lifting her higher, he roared as he pushed her through the darkness and out the other side.

Blinking at the suddenly bright sunlight, he could see that her hands were free, that she no longer held his son. Less than a second later she recast the darkness spell, still ripping into him with her claws. He cast a heal on himself, then closed his eyes and focused. A moment later *Dimensional Step* took them both back into his protective dome. Surprised, the Matron released her hold on him and he slammed her into the ground. Helen fired an arrow directly into her throat from point blank range, then another into one eye as the monster struggled beneath Allistor. As strong as he was, she was stronger. Within seconds she managed to fling him off of her. Despite her wounds, she started to rise, but was inhibited by the arrow that pinned her throat to the ground.

Going berserk, she ripped the arrow free of her throat and sat up, casting a heal on herself. Allistor had gained his feet by then, and drew his sword. The girls charged forward with their own swords swinging as Helen put an arrow into the back of the Matron's neck, scoring a critical hit. Not wanting to risk injuring the girls, Allistor halted his swing and converted it into a thrust. His blade plunged into the Matron's chest and out her back. Addy screamed in rage as she took a mighty swing, cutting deeply into one shoulder. Sydney followed Allistor's example and thrust her blade forward, using her momentum. The point skittered across the matron's face, failing to penetrate the skull underneath, but tearing a wicked and jagged wound that bisected her nose and struck the shaft of the arrow still embedded in her eye.

The matron shuddered from the combination of blows, one hand reaching out to grab hold of Allistor's leg. Her claws penetrated deeply into his calf as she fell backward, yanking him off balance. As he fell, Helen switched her bow out for a woodsman's axe she kept for

591

camping trips, and began to smash at the fomorian Matron's skull.

On his back now, Allistor twisted around, ignoring the pain in his leg as he swung his sword. The blade severed the Matron's forearm, releasing him. He cast a heal on himself, then scrambled back to his feet. Helen and the girls were recklessly hacking at their prone enemy, and even a terrified Fiona got into the fight, grabbing hold of the leg that Fuzzy had broken and shaking her head as she bit down.

Allistor was about to strike again when another blow from Helen's axe crushed through the incredibly strong skull and into the brain. The Matron went limp, the darkness disappeared, and all of them except Allistor leveled up.

Allistor turned and rushed toward William, who was laying limp on the ground not far from Fuzzy. The boy was breathing, but unconscious. Allistor cast a heal on him as he ran, the others immediately doing the same. He watched William's health bar fill as he slid the last several feet on his knees and scooped the boy into his arms. A quick glance to his left showed a badly injured Fuzzy trying to get to his feet, horrendous gashes crossing his hide and bleeding profusely. Allistor cast a heal on him as well, then another. Helen took over healing the bear once she confirmed that William was recovering.

Allistor rocked back and forth, squeezing William to his chest as the girls piled on, hugging them both and crying. William's muffled voice said, "Dad? Dad? I'm okay." It took Allistor a moment to register what the boy had said, but when he did he relaxed his grip enough for William to take a deep breath and smile up at him. "That hurt, really a lot." His eyes scanned the ground around them. "Is she gone?"

"She's gone. Dead." Sydney kissed the boy's forehead a few times, then wiped her tears off his face. "You were very brave."

Addy shook her head, wiping the tears from her own face. "No you weren't. You screamed like a little girl. We all heard it."

Allistor was about to scold her when William groaned. "You'd scream too if a giant mean lady pushed her claws into your guts!"

Addy winked at him. "Okay, maybe I would." She leaned in again and practically grabbed the boy out of Allistor's arms, hugging him tight.

"Hey, I leveled up." William squeaked as he was being squeezed. "Like, a bunch of times!" Despite the recent scare, his eyes immediately unfocused as he read his notifications. When they refocused, he looked up at Allistor. "Totally worth it."

Allistor just mutely shook his head, trying his best not to break down now that the threat was eliminated. He'd very nearly lost William, a loss he was sure would have broken him. He clamped down on his emotions as he clamped his jaw shut, denying the sob that threatened to erupt from him. He couldn't prevent the tears that rolled down his cheeks, but Addy noticed them and wiped at them with her sleeve before they dripped off his chin and onto William.

The boy squirmed a bit, wanting to be let go. Allistor obliged, lifting him up and setting him on his feet. He remained on his knees, not trusting himself to stand just then.

Helen and Fuzzy approached, the bear giving William a good sniff before headbutting Allistor's chest, a demand to have his ears scratched. Allistor did as his bear cub ordered, grateful for the momentary distraction. "You're the very bestest, bravest bear cub EVER, buddy. You probably saved us all." He stopped scratching long enough to hug the bear's neck, his arms barely able to encircle the thick mass of muscle. "All the steaks you want when we get home!"

Fuzzy licked his face, his breath smelling like fomorian flesh, but Allistor didn't mind. A moment later he was distracted by a sharp pain in his leg. Looking down, he saw that Fiona had grabbed hold of the Matron's severed forearm. The claws were still embedded in his calf, and the bear's attempt to pull it free had reopened the wound. Helen immediately dropped down and gently took the limb from her bear, speaking softly to her. Then she carefully pulled each clawed finger free of Allistor's flesh one at a time. As soon as they were free, everyone cast a heal on Allistor, and Helen handed the prize to her bear. Fiona raised her head proudly as if to claim a solo victory over the enemy, then trotted off with her stubby tail wagging. Fuzzy followed, his eyes laser focused on the prize.

Allistor had his family all sit on a clean patch of grass and cast his *Battle Dome* over top of them again. He was pretty sure, based on what Daigath had told him of fomorians, that the Matron had come alone. But after coming so close to losing his son, he wasn't taking any chances.

William appeared to shake it off much more quickly than either Allistor or Helen. With the typical resiliency of a kid, he chatted about where he was assigning his attribute points, and how much it hurt when the Matron sunk her claws into him. Allistor suspected the boy was just putting on a brave show for his sisters, but he didn't try to interfere. He'd sit with William later, when they were home and had some privacy. Though, by the looks of things, the girls weren't letting him out of their sight anytime soon. They sat on either side of him, harmonizing as they hummed a healing tune, each of them scanning the surrounding brush for any danger. Both still held their weapons in their hands, ready for a fight.

Fuzzy and Fiona were likewise on alert, though in a more relaxed manner. They sat shoulder to shoulder behind William, allowing the kids to lean against their backs as they sniffed the wind for any hint of intruders.

Helen sat next to Allistor, the two of them on the opposite side of the dome from the kids, watching carefully. After a long silence, she asked, "How does it feel?"

"How does what feel?"

"Having that weight off your shoulders." She paused and looked over at him. "Now there's no more wondering if she lived, and if she's coming for revenge. No more fear. She finally came after you, and you killed her."

"I think you actually killed her. Going all psycho axe murderer on her head."

"Well, you can thank me by giving me… Ireland, I think. Yes, I think I'd enjoy owning all of Ireland. At least until you go and get yourself killed and I become Empress Helen."

"It does feel better, I think." Allistor ignored her ramblings. "At least, I think it will, when I quit shaking over seeing William laying there all bloody."

"Yeah." She just nodded once, going silent. She loved those kids every bit as much as Allistor did, as Amanda had. William's terrified screams had been the trigger that sent her into a blind axe-wielding rage.

"I'm thinking it's time to head back. Don't think I'm going to relax until we're back in the tower with about ten thousand people with sharp weapons surrounding us." She scanned the brush as she spoke.

"I agree. He's not going to like it, but I think the boy and I are going to be hanging around the tower working on our crafting for the foreseeable future. I know it's being overprotective, but right now I'm feeling like I haven't been protective enough lately."

"Don't even think that." Helen scowled at him. "Those kids have never been safer, since the world ended, at least, than they are when they're with you."

"William got shot out into space, was aboard *Phoenix* when it was nearly destroyed, and just now had his guts shredded by that bitch." He gestured toward the Matron with his head. Her body still lay where it had fallen, just outside the current dome. None of them had bothered to loot her yet.

"And before you found him, he'd seen his family and friends mutilated by monsters, an earthquake knocked buildings down around his head, and he nearly starved to death while hiding in an airport." Helen reminded him. "William is one tough little dude. In a few years this will just be a cool story he'll tell a bunch of aliens in a bar on a space station somewhere."

Allistor shook his head. "I hope you're right." Getting to his feet, he called to the kids. "Let's loot her body, and get moving."

The kids needed no encouragement, though William was hesitant to approach the corpse to loot it until his sisters each took a hand and walked with him.

The loot was mostly unimpressive. They each received some platinum coins, a couple of claws, and Allistor received her damaged heart, which he'd driven his sword through. Still, it was a purple item, indicating it had value. By far the most interesting thing was the scroll that they received.

Scroll of Darkness
Item Quality: Epic
This scroll teaches the user to cast the dark magic spell commonly used by fomorian mages. At level one, the spell creates an area of complete darkness in a ten foot radius around the caster. Caster will be able to see through the darkness. Spell effect duration, five minutes, or until cancelled. Spell cost: 200mp.

Allistor tucked the scroll away, intending to give it to Ramon for duplication. It had been effective against him and his people, forcing them to use the droids to counteract it. Only Fuzzy's nose and a little luck had allowed him to overcome it and defeat the Matron. He spent half of the hike back to Wilderness imagining ways the spell might be useful in combat.

Chapter Thirty

Thar Be Monsters

Allistor stood on the deck of the former fishing trawler, turned research vessel, turned back to fishing trawler, that they had first used to catch a giant shark and a sea monster. The crew had renamed the ship the *Sea Monster* and painted a scary face with sharp teeth on her bow.

"Yesterday, when I called you and told you William wanted to take a family fishing trip, I was thinking a pontoon boat on a lake, not offering up my entire family as kraken food." He grunted at Andrea.

She favored him with a smile that made it clear she regretted nothing. "Trust me, this is going to be a blast!"

The word blast had Allistor cringing. The way they'd killed the sea monster last time was to detonate a goblin wearing an explosive vest that had been eaten by a shark that was in turn eaten by the sea monster. Apparently the crew had refined their methods in the intervening months. Instead of a goblin in a vest, they had packed a giant tuna with explosives and a remote detonator. They planned to drag it behind the boat on a steel line specially forged by the Lighthammer dwarves to be lightweight and flexible, yet strong. The way Allistor understood it, they had tried this method several times before, to varying degrees of success.

"The monster we killed last time was bigger than this boat." Allistor reminded Andrea and everyone else standing around on the aft deck, where the crew were grilling pork ribs from the island's feral hogs, and mixing boat drinks. "If they've been eating each other down there in all the time since then, we could run across one big enough to *eat this boat*."

"Cool!" William pumped a fist in the air, excited by the prospect. It had been a week since their fight with the Matron, and he was mostly back to his normal self. Allistor had heard the boy cry out while having a nightmare two nights ago, which was the reason he'd planned a fishing trip. Or rather, allowed Andrea to plan a fishing trip. He was starting to regret not asking Helen to do it.

"I'm having Kira stay nearby in case this boat gets bitten in half." Allistor shot Andrea a look that got her chuckling again.

"Ready to cast the bait!" one of the crewmen shouted from his position near the crane at the stern. The giant tuna, at least ten feet long, was hanging from a giant hook at the end of the crane's cable. The so-called casting was accomplished by swinging the fish out over the stern rail and releasing the crane's line to spool out.

"Cast away!" the captain shouted from the bridge. William clapped his hands and bounced up and down in anticipation, while Helen and the girls sat in the shade and sipped cool beverages, occasionally glancing at the waves port and starboard in search of giant fins or tentacles breeching the surface.

Allistor bit his bottom lip as he stood well behind the crane arm with one hand on William's shoulder, gently restraining the boy to keep him from running to the stern rail. He kept his other hand tightly gripping a metal support post for the deck above. Big monsters made big splashes and big waves that could wash little boys overboard. Their fathers, too. He glanced nervously at Helen and the girls, but they were strapped into chairs that were in turn bolted to the deck. The crew apparently did a lot of sport fishing using rods and reels, fighting fish that were several times their size and weight. So they had secured a dozen of these chairs to assist their efforts.

They watched as the steel line played out, the weight of the fish being dragged through water pulling at the line. When it was about three hundred feet behind the boat, the crewman manning the crane flipped a lever, and the line stopped unspooling. The bait rose to the surface and began to skip along in the water.

"This is where it got bad last time." Allistor mumbled, tightening his grip on the life vest William wore, against his will. Feeling tense, he looked over at a wildly grinning Andrea and mouthed the words *I am NOT having fun*! Her enthusiasm faded, but only for a moment. The ship's intercom relayed Kira's voice from the *Phoenix*, which was hovering a few thousand feet above them.

"Uh... boss? There's something big down there. We can see it on sensors. It's down deep, about a thousand feet below you, and rising rapidly."

Allistor growled, "How big, Kira?"

"We can't get an accurate measurement because it's vertical and directly beneath both us and you. But it's... forty feet wide left to right. And... oh, shit! It just angled off! I can see it on the viewer now, like a shadow in the water. Boss, you're gonna need a bigger boat!"

Allistor blinked a few times at the iconic old movie reference from the previous century. A moment later he gritted his teeth. "Dammit, Kira! That wasn't funny. Nearly gave me a heart attack. Keep your eyes peeled for an actual monster."

"No joke, boss!" Kira sounded scared. "That thing is twice the size of your ship! I don't think it could swallow you whole, but it could take a friggin big bite! Recommend you cut loose your bait and run as fast as you can while it snacks!"

Allistor was about to ask again if she was messing with him when the water in their wake exploded upward. A massive head and body rose up from the surface. Its jaws were long and squared off at the end, almost like a crocodile's. A line of finlets rose up from its forehead and along its spine to a massive dorsal fin the size of a racing yacht spinnaker. That was as much of the body as Allistor saw before it plunged back into the water.

The crane squealed with strain and the ship's stern dipped low in the water for a second before the crewman released the lock and allowed the line to spool out. Which it did so quickly it let out a high-pitched metallic scream. A water pump on the crane began pouring water on the spool to cool it down.

The captain's voice rang out over the speaker system. "Hit the button! Hit the button!"

Andrea had been given the detonator, and she let out an excited "Yeeehaw!" as she flicked the safety switch off and pressed the button."

There was a brief delay, then another explosion of water, this one more resembling a giant bubble bursting violently up from the depths. A pink, frothy, bloody bubble that erupted just off the starboard rail. The monster had apparently snagged the bait and dove, then moved toward the ship. The entire deck, along with Allistor and family, were soaked in bloody, chunky spray.

"Cutting the engines!" the captain called out again. The crane operator began to reel in the line while others moved to the rail to see what they could. Allistor held William back with him. Less than a minute later a carcass broke the surface. It floated belly up, a huge hole blasted out from its gilled throat. It's body was at least half again as long as the ship, and Allistor took a moment to *Examine* it.

Adolescent male kraken
Level 120
Health: 0/350,000

Allistor gulped upon reading the health pool information. The thing was just twenty levels higher than him, but its health pool was roughly triple his own. And it was only an adolescent? How big were the full grown adults? He really wanted to get out of the deep water and off this ship. William's timid voice drifted up over the excited shouts of the crew. "Dad? I think I might have peed myself a little.

Allistor patted his shoulder reassuringly. "Don't worry son, so did I."

The crew fired several harpoons into the kraken's body using a harpoon gun, then secured the lines to heavy bollards that had been welded to the deck. Once the catch was secured, the captain put the ship into gear and aimed her for home. The crew cheered and broke out a bottle of rum, which they passed around. All of them except Allistor had leveled up, a circumstance he was getting used to. Though he did receive a large amount of experience, it was nothing close to the nearly one billion points he needed for the next level. In addition to the levels, the crew were already spending what they expected to be huge bonuses for the catch. It seemed kraken meat was considered a delicacy on many worlds across the Collective, and they planned to sell it by the pound through the kiosks. And the other parts, the scales, teeth, claws, even the brain were valuable crafting components. They'd risked their lives, and they had at least a day of nasty, smelly harvesting ahead of them, but were expecting a big payoff.

Allistor looked down at William, who was subdued and looking down at his feet. The girls where quiet as well, watching the crew celebrate. He shook his head, whispering to himself. "We can't seem to just have a peaceful day of relaxation. When we get back, we're going to need a vacation from our little family vacations."

*****

Allistor sat with his inner circle of analysts and several of his advisors around the big conference table in the tower. Each seat at the table was filled, as were a dozen or so chairs along the walls behind them. Sandwiches had just been delivered and passed around, along with drinks.

"How's young William doing?" Harmon quietly asked before Allistor called the meeting to order. He was sitting on Allistor's left, directly across from Helen.

"We talked a bit last night. He was pretty shaken up, as was I." Allistor replied quietly.

"Understandable. In the same situation I might have voided my bladder." The big orcanin grinned. "I predict he will recover quickly. Your squire is a child of formidable will."

"I agree, and I hope we're both right." Allistor nodded. Seeing that everyone was seated and ready, he began the meeting.

"As always, thank you all for coming. I know you've all become very busy as we've grown our holdings and brought in so many new people. And speaking of new people, Bjurstrom?"

The raid leader nodded. "Our senior raiders have been running our mid-level people through dungeons at least once a week. They have in turn been taking groups of lower levels through dungeons at least twice a week. So nearly everyone on Earth who has requested it has been through at least one of the new dungeons. They're gaining levels quickly, and putting some loot in their pockets. This is mostly the new recruits from the past couple months, the ones spread across the planet. And speaking of recruiting…" He made a hand motion and a holographic globe appeared above the table. It was dotted with a series of multicolored symbols, most of which were green.

"We've had a hundred mixed recruiting groups of raiders, trainers, and crafters flying all over the world this past month. That's double the number of groups we had last month. In the last sixty days we've brought in just over a million new human citizens. A thousand here, five thousand there, some groups were as small as a few hundred. The ones marked in green are all ours." Allistor watched as the globe spun slowly, showing green dots on every continent except Antarctica. "The red dots are folks who responded with hostility. Blue triangles are allied settlements, human or otherwise. We still have more than a thousand sites identified by the satellite surveys to visit." He paused to check his notes. "Oh, and the yellow ones are folks who are citizens from other worlds like Skapa Far, who've created settlements here. We made them yellow because we thought you'd like to see how many of them there are."

Allistor studied the globe again, quickly estimating how many yellow marks there were. By the time it had done a full rotation, he guessed there were close to a hundred. "Very cool." He smiled at Bjurstrom.

"Lastly, the purple squares are non-human settlements we've come across. Those that landed here between the end of Stabilization and when you took control of the planet. We've only approached a few, and those are either red dots or blue, depending on how they reacted. The purple are ones we haven't had meaningful contact with yet."

"Those can wait, as long as they're not bothering anybody. Our number one goal right now is consolidation. Gathering up as many of the human settlements as possible, making sure they're doing okay, and recruiting them if you can. Up the ante if you have to. If you think they're on the brink of accepting but not quite there, offer them some extra free gear. Or better quality free gear. We have a whole planet of crafters we can draw from now. It doesn't take a fancy cost-benefit analysis to know that a few bits of inexpensive gear are nothing compared to thousands of new citizens."

Droban cleared his throat, and Allistor nodded in his direction. "I feel it should be pointed out that you are now the sole and ultimate authority here on Earth. You could save time by simply informing everyone on the planet that they are now subject to your rule."

"I don't want to be that guy." Allistor shook his head. "I know it's costing us valuable time and resources, but I want them to come to me of their own free will." He shifted his gaze to Bjurstrom. "You're doing great, just keep it up."

When Bjurstrom simply nodded to indicate agreement, Allistor moved on to the next in line. "McCoy?"

McCoy left the globe display up, spinning it slightly to poke a location. "We've found another wild dungeon!" Allistor nodded as the raid leader zoomed in on a location in Australia. He'd seen the notification when they claimed it on his behalf, but had elected to stay home and spend time with the kids. "As your high and mighty Emperorness decreed, the team that found it got the first run. They were on a recruiting visit, and the locals requested help dealing with a wave of critters that had attacked their Stronghold. The team tracked them back and found the dungeon. The outside was guarded by all kinds of nasty mutated local fauna. Dingos, kangaroos, scorpions as big as great danes, and flying bugs as big as my head. The locals joined them in clearing the area outside the dungeon, then the raid group went it." He bowed his head and his voice softened.

"They failed to clear it. Lost one of their tanks to a scorpion floor boss, and decided to pull back." He looked up at Allistor, slightly uncomfortable. "I told them they could have another shot at the first kill once they replaced him."

"I'm sorry to hear that." Allistor hadn't been told about the loss, though it had happened a few days ago. "And yes to them getting another chance. But make sure they're prepared. Properly geared, and with potions and such. Give them the best shot possible."

Ramon was next to report. "We're cranking out nearly two thousand scrolls per day at this point. Obviously, that's a small drop in the bucket of what we need, but it's the best we can currently do. We've been researching whether there is a way to mass produce the simpler scrolls, but with no success so far. The good news is there is an inscriptionist's guild on Skapa Far. We've reached out to them to see how many members they have, and what their skill levels are. If we can recruit them into our operation, or even hire them on a contract basis, we could greatly increase our production." He flipped a scroll to Allistor. "Here's the first copy of that *Darkness* spell you took off the Matron. I made it myself, and I gotta tell you…" He stopped and took a drink of water. "I don't want to make a whole lot of these. Making that one gave me the weebies, and I nearly lost my breakfast. It's the first dark magic scroll I've made. Might be easier for someone who specializes in dark magic, but I don't have any of those on my staff."

Allistor held up the scroll. "Thanks for this. I'm afraid I have to ask you to make a few more. Maybe… a dozen? To be distributed amongst the top raid groups." Ramon looked queasy at the idea, but nodded.

Nancy was sitting right beside Ramon, as always. "We've been building greenhouses at as many of the new settlements as possible. Current count is… two hundred thirty. Plus we've planted scores of orchards as well. I have eleven hundred new recruits who've chosen either the Druid class or a new one that popped up called Horticulturist. That's aside from the huge number of farmers we now have. We're bringing a hundred of the first two classes at a time to our island for training, cycling through a group each week. I'm afraid I've pretty much monopolized the three druid trainers we currently have." Allistor just smiled at her. He trusted her to manage their resources in the best way possible. "The Revivification Tree has already produced fruit!" She beamed at this. "We've had a waiting list of ladies who want to try it, and we're distributing portions of the fruits as we harvest them. Daigath was there for the initial harvest and advised us on which ones to pick, and how to portion out the individual fruits. We've been having the ladies check in every week after eating the fruit, and so far there have been no negative side effects or worrying symptoms. Two of them are already pregnant." Her smile was much wider this time. "I've had a request from several beastkin and other non-human ladies..."

Allistor didn't even have to think about it. "Sign them up. First come, first served. Assuming of course there's no biological reason the fruit might not help them, or might harm them."

Nancy blew him a kiss, causing the others around the table to chuckle. "We'll check into that very carefully." She set down her list and her expression became guarded. "This last thing... I'm a little hesitant."

"What is it? There's nothing you can't tell me. Is Ramon eating too many cucumbers again? If so, I fully support you making him sleep on the sofa. I've been stuck in a room with him when he gets the farts." He tried to lighten the mood, but only got a half-smile from Nancy, and a middle finger from Ramon.

"The thing is, I had a visitor early this morning. I was out checking on the bees around sunrise, and a woman approached me. Only she wasn't a woman, I don't think."

Now Allistor, along with everyone in the room, was leaning forward, curious. Even Ramon, who apparently hadn't heard about this visit either. "What do you mean?"

"She was big, tall, with golden hair and glowing eyes. The moment she appeared I could feel her... aura, I guess? She said her name was Idunn, which is a name I recognize."

Allistor sat back in his chair, his pulse rate spiking. He recognized the name too, as did most of the non-humans in the room. Allistor already knew what Nancy was going to say next.

"I think she was one of the Ancient Ones, like Baldur and Odin." She looked sheepish as she purposely avoided mentioning Loki. "I know you hate them... but I couldn't bring myself to attack her."

Allistor shot forward in his seat, alarmed. "No! Nancy I would never ever expect you to attack one of them. Don't even think about it! They're so much more powerful than we are, you'd be throwing your life away for nothing." He looked around at the others. "That goes for everybody. If you encounter one of them, don't piss them off. Get away if you can without risking your lives. As far as I know none of them are hostile towards us." He looked at Harmon, who shook his head.

Ramon pulled Nancy in for a brief hug, then asked, "What did she want."

"She gave me a gift." Nancy reached into her pocket and pulled out a golden apple. "This is what she's famous for in our mythology. Her apples. They're supposed to be the food of the gods. When I tried to refuse it, she laughed. Not in a mean way. She said that the myths were an overstatement. The apples do promote healing, and offer significant temporary buffs. Ten percent faster mana regeneration, ten percent boost to your constitution for twenty four hours. They also grow twice as fast as our Earth apples. Idunn explained that the myth was based on the fact that she denied them to humans when she visited Earth. She did so because Earth hadn't been inducted yet, and the amount of mana in the apples would have killed them."

Allistor nodded. "Makes sense, knowing what we know now." He was conflicted. A part of him still craved vengeance against the entire race that had nearly killed humanity. But his logical mind knew that all of them couldn't be held responsible for Loki's actions any more than every human could have been held responsible for Hitler's or Mao's or Stalin's. He'd spent the entire first year after the apocalypse hating and vowing vengeance against those responsible. And he'd had his vengeance in the form of Loki's death. Which came with the horrible and unintended consequence of causing millions more to die, and starting wars in which many more millions might be killed.

No, he was not anxious to take on any of the Ancient Ones anytime soon. His conscience couldn't handle the likely fallout.

Allistor realized everyone in the room was staring at him. "I would say hold onto the apple until you can speak with Daigath about it. But let's assume it was a gift offered in good faith. Please give her my thanks if you see her again."

The sound of held breaths being released around the table could have been heard down the hall. "Were you all afraid I'd lose my shit and start to rant about killing her?" He eyed each one of them in turn. Many of them smiled or nodded their heads in confirmation.

"Yeah, I suppose I've done my share of that already. I'm trying to be a new, smarter Allistor who doesn't do stupid shit without thinking and get his people killed."

Sam started to golf clap, grinning down the table at Allistor. Meg joined him, then the rest of the humans in the room. Not understanding the significance, but seeing that it was well-intended, the non-humans joined in. Allistor stood and took a mock bow, then stuck his tongue out at Meg and Sam as he sat back down.

"Alright Sam, mister smarty pants, what do you have for me?"

"Food supply's good." Sam thumped a hand on the table, then leaned back in his chair and folded his hands over his belly, clearly thinking his report was complete.

"Care to elaborate?" Allistor wasn't letting him off that easy.

"Sure. Nancy's people are fast-growing fruits and vegetables by the acre. They're not just growing faster, their yield has increased. Same with the livestock. The cattle are already growing half again as large as they used to be, as are the bison. The wild critters that the hunters are bringing in are bigger too. I saw a deer brought in the other day that must have weighed seven hundred pounds. Not to mention the fishing fleets bringing in mackerel the size of dolphins and tuna that have to be dragged home in giant nets because they're too big to lift onto the boats. With all the additional farmers we've got, and the extra planets full of land and resources you brought in, we can feed everybody, no problem."

"I'm very glad to hear that. Thank you, old man." Allistor moved on before Sam could respond. "L'olwyn?"

The hologram changed from a depiction of Earth to a map of the new solar system. "Charon station is now fully operational with a crew of nearly nine thousand. The partially mined asteroid, along with two others of similar size and composition, have been towed into a synchronous orbit near the station. All three planets in the system have satellite defenses operational, and a force of six warships, including one carrier, are currently deployed in the system, along with two cargo ships and two colony ships who are making regular trade runs between the three planets. Current estimates are ninety percent of the inhabitants of all three planets are now citizens of Invictus. Efforts are being made to reach the more rural and isolated inhabitants. Those who have declined have been informed that they will be moved, but as they are doing no harm where they are, those operations are a low priority."

The hologram shifted to a view of Rivian and its system. "Master Daigath has reported that things are running smoothly on Rivian. The former House servitors have proved to be loyal and productive citizens. Trade agreements with the neighboring worlds are in place, and already proving beneficial. Three of our ships are deployed there, and ships from the new trade partners have already made several visits to purchase and sell goods."

Once again he waved a hand and the hologram showed Skapa Far. "All former slaves have been processed, provided with proper housing, and are being fed. Seventy percent have found gainful employment or started business enterprises of their own. The regional administrators for all ten cities have been hard at work, and expect that number to approach one hundred percent within the next month. Those who wished to decline citizenship and depart are being provided transport, as a medium priority. They have caused a few incidents, and those responsible were dealt with harshly."

Lastly, an image of Orion with the gate and Harmon's station in orbit appeared. "Business on Orion is booming. More than two hundred Houses and Factions have purchased property on the surface, at exorbitant rates,

I might add, and the list of applicants is growing. The gate operations are still only at about twenty percent of max capability, but we expect that usage will grow steadily over the coming years. Already the gate fees collected have reached a substantial sum." The elf bowed his head to indicate that he was done.

Chris spoke up next, unbidden. "Since finances were mentioned, let me just say that you are one really, insanely, offensively super wealthy dude. The likely annual Orion gate fees that L'olwyn mentioned alone are mind-boggling. When you add the amounts collected from land buyers, the taxes projected from your various planets, and potential fees from a second gate… I don't even know what to call a number with that many digits. I can give you a written breakdown if you like. But unless you do something stupid like purchase another solar system or an eternity gate or something, you won't run short of pizza money in the next million years."

"Can we do that? Can we purchase another gate?"

Harmon and several of the others nodded. Harmon smiled at him. "You can. But despite this young man's optimistic and entertaining report of your substantial assets, you are not yet quite that wealthy."

"Good, keep him from getting a swelled head." Helen snarked from across the table. "Well, any more swelled than it already is."

"My head is the perfect size. As Emperor and ultimate authority and all that, I declare it so." He winked at her as she rolled her eyes.

"Longbeard?" Allistor turned to the dwarf, who was in slightly better spirits these days.

"Yer new ships be under construction. The twenty from last month's order have been delivered. We be trainin' crews as fast as we can fer yer new 'Space Force'." The dwarf paused and stroked his beard. "Still think ye need a better name." Allistor grinned. He agreed, but annoying the dwarf with the stupid name was too much fun to give up on. "There be eleven thousand cadets currently enrolled in the academy ye established. Another class will be startin' in a week, and we should have enough bodies ta fill the new ships when they be delivered." He let out a long sigh. "But they'll be inexperienced and stupid, to start."

"You still recommend we hire some mercenaries to help crew the ships and train the newbies."

"I do." Longbeard thumped the table for emphasis.

"Gralen?" Allistor looked to his most senior beastkin advisor. "Your opinion on that?"

"My old guild could provide a thousand or so experienced ship's crew that could supervise and train your inexperienced cadets. It would be expensive, and might prevent them from taking more lucrative contracts during that period." He smiled, revealing extremely sharp teeth. "But as you know, they owe you a debt."

Allistor smiled back at him. "Any chance you still have contacts within the guild that could help ensure that most of that thousand were old, injured, approaching the

617

ends of their contracts, and might be open to recruitment, along with their families?"

Gralen's smile grew wider. "That is a possibility."

"I'll leave that in your capable hands, then." He looked around the table. "I think you all know this already, but I'm not just recruiting humans. Spread the word among your families, former clans, your people. Invictus needs good people who are willing to contribute in order to reap the benefits of citizenship. Trainers, crafters, farmers, ship's crew, even unskilled people who are simply willing to work hard. We have the room, and the will to grow. Right now I'm focused on consolidating the assets we already have, smoothing out the rough edges, and ensuring we're operating as one entity to the benefit of us all. But once we're fully established and stable, it'll be time to start expanding again."

There was a short silence then, as everyone considered the future for a moment. The silence was broken by Selby, who stood up in her chair about halfway down the table. "The big question is…" She stepped onto the table and began to walk toward Allistor, her head passing cleanly under the holographic display of Orion that was still up. When she got to the end of the table, she leaned in so that her face was less than a foot from Allistor's. "Where are you going to put the second gate? Rivian? Or the new system? And by the way, what are you going to name the system?"

Allistor avoided the first question. "I was considering calling it Selby system. After a certain rambunctious gnome whose breath smells like she's been sampling some of Harmon's spider brandy."

"Eep! Busted!" She giggled and turned away from Allistor, belatedly covering her mouth. She ran back down the table rather faster than Allistor thought was safe, and dove back into her chair. Her voice echoed from below the tabletop. "Selby system is a great name!"

"You could call it Invictus system." Helen pointed out the obvious.

"Or Charon system." Sam offered. "It's a cool name, and a little bit scary."

"Selby!" the voice under the table shouted again. "Gnomes rule!" that statement was followed by a muffled hiccup.

"I vote for Unity system." Lilly spoke up from one of the chairs along the wall. "Or Harmony."

That one struck a chord with Allistor. He remembered something from college, a Latin class he'd mostly slept through because it was an early morning class. "Concordia."

"What?" Helen asked.

"Harmony in Latin is *Concordia*. I always thought it was a cool word.

"Concordia systems sounds nice." Droban mused.

"Sounds like something ya play polka music on." Meg muttered.

"That's an accordion, my love. And you *like* polka music." Sam nudged her gently with his elbow. "I think Concordia sounds good. It has strength, and class." Others around the table nodded their head as the sound of Selby snoring drifted up from under the table.

Allistor chuckled. Selby was going to hear no end of teasing later. "I think Concordia is our winner. Assuming there's not already a system with that name." Allistor watched as both Harmon and L'olwyn did quick searches on their wrist units. When both shook their heads, it became official.

"To answer Selby's very important question… I am going to place the second eternity gate in the Concordia system. For several reasons. L'olwyn, please notify the Arkhons of our chosen location and arrange delivery. They don't need to rush, I'd like to have the rest of my warships delivered first, to guard the gate." A second thought struck him. "Oh, and let them know that the fomorian Matron showed up and is dead, in case they were concerned."

"I doubt that they were, but I shall pass on the information."

Allistor nodded, then a wicked grin spread across his face. "Also let them know that I have her heart, and would be happy to trade it, plus one hung over gnome, for another gate…" This earned him laughs from around the table, and even the normally stoic elf smiled.

Allistor sat back and relaxed, trying to clear his mind. He knew there were other things they needed to discuss, but couldn't recall what they were. The others waited patiently while he tried to remember. Helen interrupted his thoughts.

"Just so everyone knows…" She looked at Allistor. "When I inevitably take over as Empress, I'm totally renaming it Selby system."

*****

Allistor and company stepped off a teleport pad they hadn't used in some time. The group was quiet, the mood somber, though there wasn't any obvious cause. Fuzzy walked next to him, followed by Helen, Fiona, and the kids. Behind them in a loose group were Sam, Meg, Ramon, Nancy, Chloe, and Lilly.

"It looks so small." Chloe remarked as they passed through the gate. Inside, things were quiet. Several of the current residents waved or called out greetings, and the group waved back.

"I think it's been a year since I was last here." Ramon looked around. "And Chloe's right. Compared to Invictus City or our Citadel, this place is tiny."

Allistor turned and glared at them with mock indignation. "Hey, it was the best I could do at the time!" They all grinned at him, then the grins faded as they all remembered.

It had been just a few days after the apocalypse when a void titan wandered into their small town and stomped it into ruins, killing most of the residents who hadn't already left town or been eaten by spawning canids and octopoids. That included Allistor's parents.

Allistor and a small group of survivors had fled into the forest, then returned to take shelter in what was left of the City Hall building. He'd accidentally stumbled upon the ability to create a Stronghold, the very one they stood in now, which Chloe had named The Warren.

Of all those who'd started that fateful day in their town, this group were all that remained. They'd lost some quickly, others had lasted longer, becoming family, making their eventual losses hurt even more.

"This is where it all began. Where we stopped just surviving and started to live." Allistor whispered. The group's obviously somber mood had created concern among the residents, many of whom had gathered around, and so were able to hear his words.

"This is where you learned how to save the rest of us." Lilly stepped forward and put an arm around him. "You created a safe place where we could sleep in peace. Where we could bring others." She motioned at the growing crowd.

"Where Chloe could play with her mutant bunnies." Ramon chuckled, tousling the girl's hair. For once she didn't object.

One of the crowd stepped forward, a familiar face, but one Allistor couldn't put a name to. "You took in my kids and I without hesitation. We were starving, running and hiding from the spawns, scavenging junk food here and there. When your hunters found us, we wouldn't have lasted another week."

622

Allistor shook his head. "It wasn't me. We all helped each other back then. It's what kept us alive."

"But you started it, boy." Sam put a hand on his shoulder. "You gave us rest, and hope, and your anger motivated us. This scrawny little gamer kid, a college puke, angry at the universe and determined to get revenge on whoever was responsible."

"And look at you now." Meg put an arm around Sam. "Emperor of the Earth and... how many other planets? You've helped to save millions of us. Despite all the setbacks, all the monsters the universe threw at us, and all the friends and loved ones we lost along the way, you never let it beat you."

Allistor was getting emotional, and could feel tears forming, until Helen broke the somber mood. In a vapid voice, with her eyelids fluttering, she gasped, "You're our hero! I wanna be just like you when I grow up!"

The crowd laughed, including Allistor who quickly wiped at his eyes, hoping no one noticed. "We should put some kind of plaque here, to commemorate what this place has meant to us."

"Or a statue! A great big statue of Allistor holding his spear and fighting the super smelly void titan!" Chloe clapped her hands in excitement.

The current leader of the Warren, a man named Chupp, stepped through the crowd. Allistor remembered him mostly because the man had somehow obtained a pet alligator that was bonded much like Fuzzy. He was also a sniper, and had defended more than one wall alongside Allistor. "Good to see you back here, boss."

"Just a little walk down memory lane. I take it things are going well here?"

"No complaints. Plenty of food, lots to do, gathering resources. I'm almost ready to expand this place." He paused, sensing the mood amongst the others. "That is, if you don't mind."

"Of course not. No sense in keeping this place as some kind of shrine. This was, and always will be a place for people to live and grow. If that means you need more space, then it's a good thing!" Allistor looked around. "What were you thinking?"

As Chupp began to describe his plans, Chloe instantly got bored. Looking at William and the girls, who had never been to the Warren, she said, "Come on, I'll show you where we used to live, and the bunny hutch!" and dashed off without waiting for a reply. The kids followed, as did the bears, and soon disappeared in the underground space.

Allistor and the others listened to, and approved of, Chupp's plans for expansion. Looking around, Allistor got a smile on his face. "Would you... mind if I did the expansion?"

"Be my guest! It would be an honor. I may run this place, but it'll always be yours. Literally and figuratively." Chupp winked at him. "You do own the whole planet, yaknow."

Allistor pulled up his interface and the Stronghold tab, momentarily concerned that Chupp and his people hadn't gathered sufficient resources for the planned expansion. That was always a concern in the early days, and being where he was, he naturally fell back into that mindset. He nearly smacked his forehead when he remembered that he was emperor, with enough resources to build anything he wanted.

Resisting the urge to giggle like a twelve year old, he opened the tab for the Warren and began to add in the items Chupp had described, placing them where the man had indicated. Then he added more. He expanded the walls, added a stronger shield and several more defensive turrets, and a lookout tower. He added a barracks and armory off to one side, and a small area behind it with a sturdy gate. When he was through, he upgraded the Stronghold to a Citadel, complying with the System prompt to assign sufficient resources for the upgrade. He chose gold, as it was easiest to quantify.

"Here we go!" he confirmed his selections, and watched the faces of the crowd as the lights and fanfare started and the Warren transformed. There was clapping and cheering, and Allistor's group gladly joined in. When it was over, Chupp noticed the additional structures and the upgrade immediately. He raised a questioning eyebrow at Allistor.

"Well, I figured if you want to grow this place, we might as well go all out. You're going to need the extra space, because you're going to be getting a lot of visitors." He pulled out the insect dungeon core and showed it to everyone. "If you like, I'll plant this here. You guys can use it to level up your own people, and you'll get regular visits from our other raiders who want to level in the dungeon. Not to mention crafters who'll be after the insect parts."

The crowd began to celebrate, shouting out claims for dibs on the first run, which Allistor took as a yes. He walked through the new gate into the small area he'd created for this purpose, and set down the orb. As it sank into the earth, he reached out a hand for Chupp to shake. "May it bring you good luck and prosperity."

"Thank you, Allistor. Like the System says every time it makes an announcement about you doing something cool... May you rule long and wisely."

End Book Six, and the Shadow Sun series.

Acknowledgements

It has been a long journey since I first imagined Allistor and his town being stomped by the stinky void titan. The story grew much larger than I expected, and while there's more room for Allistor and company to expand into the universe, I felt it was time to wrap up their adventure. At least, for now, and let them live their lives in peace.

Thanks as always to my family for their love and support. They are my alphas, my sounding board, and the ones who aren't afraid to tell me when something sucks!

For semi-regular updates on books, art, and just stuff going on, check out my Greystone Guild fb https://www.facebook.com/greystone.guild.7 or my website www.davewillmarth.com where you can subscribe for an eventual newsletter. Or you can follow me on that friggin Instagram thing at www.instagram.com/davewillmarth. For lots of LitRPG info, and to chat with other authors, join my new LitRPG and GameLit Readers Facebook group https://www.facebook.com/groups/940262549853662/

And don't forget to follow my author page on Amazon! **That way you'll get a nice friendly email when new books are released**. You can also find links to my Greystone Chronicles, Shadow Sun, and Dark Elf books there! https://www.amazon.com/Dave-Willmarth/e/B076G12KCL

PLEASE TAKE A MOMENT TO LEAVE A REVIEW!

Reviews on Amazon and Goodreads are vitally important to indie authors like me. Amazon won't help market the books until they reach a certain level of reviews. So please, take a few seconds, click on that (fifth!) star and type a few words about how much you liked the book! I would appreciate it very much. I do read the reviews, and a few of my favorites have led to friendships and even character cameos! There were several in this book.

You can find information on lots of LitRPG/GameLit books on Ramon Mejia's LitRPG Podcast here https://www.facebook.com/litrpgpodcast/. You can find his books here. https://www.amazon.com/R.A.-Mejia/e/B01MRTVW3O

Here are my other favorite LitRPG/GameLit community facebook groups. (If you have cookies, as always, keep them away from Daniel Schinhofen).

https://www.facebook.com/groups/LitRPG.books/

https://www.facebook.com/groups/541733016223492/

Made in the USA
Las Vegas, NV
13 July 2022

515111 16R00344